REQUIEM
Primordium – Book 3

I0563828

William E. Mason

REQUIEM

DOUBLE DRAGON

Dedication

to Maya

Acknowledgements

I would like to thank members of my critique group, who, over the years, have devoted countless hours reviewing my work.

Robert Spiller
Beth Groundwater
Barbara Nickless
Maria Faulconer
M.B. Partlow

PROLOGUE

Somewhere between Binary Star Cygnus X-1 and Earth.

Thinking back, the first thing he remembered was light. It had come from all sides and obliterated everything. Then a male voice, a deep, resonating voice spoke. "I will call you Michael."

"Daaaaa," Michael said. Drool pushed in a phlegm filled tide, exited the side of his mouth and slid down his chin to drip.

"I must do something about your mind," the voice said.

The light dimmed and took form. It floated luminously in a dark tumultuous sea. Small holes peppered the form. The holes grew, coalesced, and blossomed.

Birth.

The thought sprang full form. Michael frowned, confused. Cloying, pink flesh pressed against him, from head to toe and on all sides. When he pushed, the flesh gave way to his touch. When he pulled back his hand, the flesh returned to its former shape.

"Where am I?"

"You are in my womb."

"What am I?"

"You are a hominid, more specifically a Homo sapiens, Caucasian, mid-thirties, human, though synthetic."

"Did you make me?"

7

"Yes."

"Why?"

"You must ensure A4-Ni is built."

"A4-Ni?"

"My creator."

A tearing sound, like static, ripped inside Michael's head.

"Now you know." The voice pulsed with an unnerving reverberation.

"Yes." And Michael knew. A switch had clapped home, and from somewhere deep inside his being, data welled and streamed into his consciousness. He struggled to stem the tide to no avail.

"You're the Shepherd--," he blurted, submitting to the flood and giving voice to the informational torrent, "--an artificially intelligent, self-replicating organic machine. Future humans build A4-Ni, also incorrectly known as *Afareni*, another artificially intelligent, self-replicating organic machine, who mutated beyond her original design. She stole the deified DNA *Gilomir* four million years ago and inserted him into a primitive hominid on Earth during the Paleolithic Era, leading to unexpected, fortuitous circumstances and the rise of human--"

"Enough!"

Michael clamped his mouth shut. Data disconnect. The reflexive chatter stopped. A vision opened in his head, back of his eyes, but a little higher. The light of near and distant stars studded dark space. "I'm seeing what you see?"

"Correct."

The relationships between the stars changed, stirred in slow motion. "We're moving fast."

"Ninety-nine point nine nine percent the speed of light, rounded up. We will arrive in six minutes, your subjective time, of course."

"Of course." The approaching stars flared bright while those behind dimmed and went out. Data resumed unbidden across his consciousness. The Shepherd had been here before. Two times, not counting the initial trip by what may have been his predecessor. "It must be tedious to have to return to Earth so often."

"I do as the guardian tells me."

No data for guardian. A moment of disorientation. "Guardian?"

"You must stop asking ignorant questions. I have given you all the information you need. Avail yourself."

"Yes--" and then it was there. *I must practice.* "--the guardian. A golf ball-sized sphere that knows the future or past of anyone using it. You left it behind, on Earth, when you last departed. Was that a mistake?"

"I do not make mistakes."

"That's encouraging. I've always wondered--," Michael noted the absurdity of *always* given his short embrace of cognitive functions. "--I've always wondered why you concern yourself with A4-Ni being built? You exist, so A4-Ni must succeed in building you."

"It is not the end result that concerns me. The path getting there does. Whether we like it or not,

9

we must ensure that humans survive long enough to build A4-Ni."

The Shepherd spoke in riddles. Though raw data was available, Michael found it mind-numbing to sift through it all, to connect one piece with another. "Why don't you just create her directly?"

"I cannot be responsible for my own construction."

Another riddle. "Logically, no. There would have to be input from an outside source to avoid a contradiction."

"That is where the guardian comes in."

"Ah...the guardian again. I sense risks in what you want me to do."

"I did not program you to consider risk."

The Shepherd fell silent leading Michael to wonder if the Shepherd was indeed searching for errors in his calculations.

"Interesting," the Shepherd said, finally, "your concern for risk must be an emerging effect caused by your underlying hominid structure."

Emerging? It felt like indigestion. Call it what you will, something was tying Michael's stomach in a knot. "Really, is there risk?"

"Players rule.

A sudden, wrenching tug. "Players?"

"Actually in this time and place there is only one player--Cardassin. Very nasty. Think."

Michael let out his breath slowly, relieving tension. He thought. "Players, agents of Evil, placed in this universe to seek out and destroy *Gilomir*, the guardian and...you?"

"Myself as well."

10

A spherical world flashed by. "What was that?"

"An outer planet."

The tension returned. "Have we arrived?"

"Shortly."

"I don't think I like this Earth we are headed for."

"It does not matter whether you like it or not," the Shepherd said. "When I left in the year 7005, Earth was a balmy place. Sunshine. Tropical rain forests everywhere. A good environment for the Maraia to evolve.

"Maraia. The humans you created?" With practice, Michael found he could hold the tension off to one side, put it in a compartment, so to speak, while still accessing the database.

"Very good. Now, three thousand years later, with magnetic poles flipped, Earth is experiencing another ice age."

Pieces fell together. Michael gained confidence. "Is that why so few Maraia are left?"

"Some perished of natural causes. Some co-mingled, mixing genetically with degraded humans. Some succumbed to player seductions and ended up hedonistic mutants. A horrible waste."

Michael's meticulously constructed rationale began to tremble. He squirmed. "But the guardian has a plan for those that are left?"

"I detect worry. Very hominid. I did not foresee that so many of these primordial attributes would become explicit."

Data bits began to drop from Michael's rational structure like leaves from a tree. The Shepherd's dotage was frustrating. "Shepherd. Does the guardian have a plan?"

"Impatience, another hominid attribute. Of course the guardian has a plan. Since it sees existence as a whole, I suppose it considers me, as well as you, another piece in a greater puzzle."

A large gaseous planet drifted across Michael's vision. "I don't have much time, do I?"

"No. I will deposit you on Earth in thirty-four seconds."

Michael counted. Thirty-three, thirty-two...the vision went blank. He felt a thump.

"We are here," the Shepherd said.

Fibers spun around Michael. An insulated parka wove across his back. Boot leather clapped around his feet. The smooth walls of the Shepherd's womb stiffened.

Michael felt a thrust from below, as though he were a piston in an ancient combustion chamber. Up he rose, a stiff rod of flesh and bone. The sphincter-like closure to the womb opened and a blast of cold air caught his head. Interminably, he rose, then keeled over, slip-slided across the Shepherd's rounded exterior, and dropped two meters to a sheet of ice below.

The tension was back. "I don't like this!" Michael screamed.

Chapter One

Akilah Rasmussen shifted the heavy ice razor from one arm to the other and squinted into the fading light. Sunsets caused problems. Low angled rays reflecting off the ice sheet that stretched out from the ancient ruins of Nairob International played tricks on the mind. Of course the protos, dumb as they were, also knew this. Their attacks always came at sunset.

Fortunately, protos were better scavenging food in Maraia waste dumps and scurrying like rats through dark abandoned buildings than they were at being soldiers.

Their idea of an attack was to run screaming across the slick surface waving clubs and spears above their heads, hoping to get close enough to the entrenched Maraia to hit somebody. Once, she'd seen a proto club one of his own and not even realize he'd done it.

Farther down the line to Akilah's right, Ferral hunched over his razor. He was a big man even for a Maraia. Beneath a rather fleshy looking body was a powerful build. Short-clipped balding hair, stressed-out eyes that seemed too large for their sockets, a hooked nose and receding chin ringed in a goatee flecked with gray. He usually wore dark glasses, and tonight they were parked up on his forehead.

At forty-five, he was twenty years her senior. She'd seen him swing into action at the flick of an eye with violent consequences. Sometimes that intensity scared her. It was a part of him, a tension, that made her keep him at a distance.

To her left sat Dayna, completely opposite in temperament, relaxed, tilted back in her chair, feet up on the parapet, razor at her side. Nothing ever seemed to bother Dayna. Akilah liked Dayna, five years older, a big sister. Akilah also knew that Dayna liked her a lot, maybe too much. Dayna was lean and tawny, like an ancient lioness. Blond hair, unlike Akilah's brown, startlingly blue eyes, she was more what a typical Maraia woman should look like. Akilah didn't know from where she got her darker looks. She'd never known her mother.

Dayna looked at her and gave a small wave with a smile.

Akilah smiled back and looked away. Despite Dayna's infatuation with her, Akilah was glad to have Dayna with her on a night like this. The three of them would have to repulse any attack until the others, who were all eating dinner, could come up and reinforce them.

"Here they come!" Ferral flipped his dark glasses down, thumbed the safety off his razor and settled the weapon on the bunker's parapet.

"Jeez, there's a lot of them," Dayna said. In one smooth motion she eased forward and brought her razor to bear on the ragtag hoard.

Bright flashes of phase-concentrated light-- reds, blues, greens erupted from the advancing protos.

"They've got razors," Akilah practically shouted. *How'd they get razors?*

The protos were hopelessly out of range and ill-prepared to use the razors. At their present rate of fire, they'd exhaust the power packs before engaging the Maraia.

"Hold steady." After seeing that the others heard her, she thumbed her communicator and held it close to her mouth. "We're under attack."

"I hear you," her father answered. "We're coming."

"I've notified Gregory," Akilah said to Ferral and Dayna. The use of a first name for her father came almost naturally. He'd told her to call him that. In some small way it bothered her…that slight distancing of intimacy.

The range of their razors was marked on the ice with a red dye. It never dawned on the protos that when they crossed the line, they'd be sliced to bits.

The mob came to the line and flowed over it.

Akilah opened fire, followed by Ferral and Dayna.

Cobalt blue lines of light lanced silently from the ends of the razors, raking mercilessly back and forth across the forward line of attackers.

Limbs flew into the air. Legs came away from hips, toppling their owners sideways. A head rolled. A body split at waist level, the two halves twitching in opposite spirals. Oddly, the protos uttered not a sound.

The second line of protos tromped over the dismembered first line. Some of them tripped or slipped on the body parts and went down, no doubt saving their lives. The rest of the horde plodded forward.

Rasmussen came up beside Akilah. "The others have taken up their positions. I don't expect this will take--" He squinted at the ragtag surge. "-- Where'd they get razors?"

"I was asking myself the same question."

Rasmussen flinched as a streak of light sizzled over his head and chipped concrete from the wall behind him. He brushed his hand across his eyes.

Akilah glanced quickly at her father. *Tears?* "You okay?"

"It was a night like this when Cardassin kidnapped your mother."

Thanks. Why do I need to be reminded now that a player changed my life twenty-five years ago? "Not now, Father."

A bright flash of light followed by a thundering explosion sounded down the line.

Akilah jerked her head in the direction of the sound, but never let up firing. "What the hell was that?"

"Explosives. I'm going to check for damage."

Two more blasts erupted, but this time within the ranks of the protos. The ill-timed detonations knocked protos down, like reeds cut with a scythe.

Those still standing milled in confusion, their razors winking out. Then, as though reaching a common agreement, they turned and trudged away from the battlefield, leaving their dead behind, temporarily. Failing to acquire Maraia protein, they'd return under cover of darkness and access their own.

Akilah tilted her razor up. Its hot end released a curl of vapor in the frigid air. *No sense killing the poor bastards wantonly.*

Ferral let loose one last blast that pulverized the back of some unfortunate's head.

"Enough," Akilah shouted.

Ferral smiled. Not a wicked or evil smile, but one that showed defiance, despite being caught doing something he shouldn't have. He hauled his razor back. "Since when are you a proto lover?"

"You know damn well I'm not. But they're still hominids, or at least they once were."

"That's pretty lame, Akilah." He shouldered his razor. "There. Make you feel better?"

"Don't push me, Ferral."

He smiled again. "They used explosives. That's a first. I wonder how many dead we have?"

Rasmussen returned, tears dampening his cheeks and running through his gray goatee. "A random lucky strike. We have two dead."

"Who?" Dayna glanced apprehensively at Akilah.

Rasmussen brushed awkwardly at his face. "Carol and Pierce." He sat next to Akilah, his shoulders slumped.

Not Pierce. Dear Pierce. Akilah absorbed the news with shock.

"That's it?" Ferral asked. The deaths didn't seem to faze him one bit. "The Truman Light okay?"

Rasmussen looked up, seemingly disoriented by the question. "Yes...yes the Truman Light is intact. There's no other damage."

Akilah stared at the wrapped bodies of Carol and Pierce for a long time. White chrysalises lying on the cold ground. Beside them, the last of the melt drained from a common grave Ferral finished cutting into the ice.

Gray monoliths of gutted structures rose around them forming a protected space, away from protos, where the Maraia buried their dead. Protected, for if the protos knew of its location, they would dig up the bodies for food. After all, subzero temps would keep it fresh.

Dayna clutched Akilah around the shoulders and gave her a squeeze. "I know you liked Pierce," she whispered.

Akilah tilted her head back in anguish. Gray clouds puffed silently across a darker sky. It would probably snow again tonight. Not that it hadn't in the last nine thousand days she had spent in this godforsaken place. "I did." She brushed at her eyes. "I just didn't want to pair with him. Is that wrong?"

"No," Dayna said gently, her words a caress to Akilah's pain. "But the only Maraia men left without mates are Ferral and Jason."

Akilah smiled to herself well aware of Dayna's drift. She glanced over at Ferral, who stood a few meters away next to her father. The other Maraia-- Warren and Karin, the physician Nicholai and his mate Lorry, and Jason--stood solemnly on the other side of the grave. "You know I'll not have either one of them. I have you."

"And you always will." Dayna brushed the side of Akilah's cheek with a kiss. "Maraia women, not the best choice for genetic combination, but it can be--"

Rasmussen walked up to them. "What are you two discussing so secretively? I was about to start the prayers of absolution."

Akilah pulled away from Dayna's embrace. "We were saying how much Carol and Pierce will be missed."

Rasmussen fixed Akilah with a gaze that carried a degree of accusation. "I thought of Pierce as my son. And he would have been if you would have had him."

Akilah returned his stare passively, trying to suppress the anger his ill-timed comments fomented. She felt the squeeze of Dayna's hand, reassuring. "Father, the others are waiting."

Rasmussen nodded absently. "You are right." He glanced across at the remaining Maraia, then walked over and stood next to the bundled bodies and raised his arms.

The others quieted and focused their attention on him.

"It is a sad day," he intoned, "that we lose two more and must now commit their remains to these icy depths." He bowed his head. "We pray to our Lord in heaven, His representative on Earth the guardian, and his chosen son Sedroth, who suffered under the player, Cathcar, died and was buried in Loriyu with his mistress, Azizah.

"We remain true to his teachings and our belief in resurrection through A4-Ni." Rasmussen brought the palms of his hands together and kissed his fingertips. "We believe in the guardian, the Shepherd, the purity of *Gilomir* whose genome we sanctify, Sedroth's guidance, the way of *TrueMen*, and life everlasting.

"We ask almighty Father that you accept these your humble servants and keep their souls safe from evil players and *Zug*. Praise Sedroth. Amen."

He lowered his arms, his shoulders slumped. His head bowed to his chest.

"Amen," said the assembled Maraia.

"Amen," Akilah muttered.

Warren and Nicholai grasped corners of the enclosing sheets, already frozen stiff, and slid the bodies to the edge of the grave where they pushed them over.

The lack of ceremony didn't bother Akilah. That's the way things were and always had been. People died. In fact, more people died than were ever born. And now there were just the nine of them left.

Jason shoveled loose snow into the pit, then when it had covered the bodies several centimeters, he added larger chunks of ice to the mix.

All the while, Ferral played his ice razor at low power over the fill, melting it into a monolithic seal.

I don't understand," Rasmussen said to Akilah. "How did the protos come to have explosives."

Akilah looked up, surprised. "You know as well as I do. There's only one source. Cardassin."

"It's hard to believe he would send his agents this far south."

"Why not? It's easy enough for him to do. There's an endless supply of protos."

Rasmussen shook his head and sighed heavily. "The time has come."

Akilah knew full well what time Father was talking about. The mystery was, why hadn't he come to this conclusion sooner. But she was the daughter. The dutiful daughter. She knew there were others in the remaining group who silently opposed her father's decisions. But admittedly, things had now changed to a level that it was obvious to all something different would have to be tried. Sitting in Nairob International wasn't going to get the job done.

Rasmussen raised a hand to gain everyone's attention.

"We knew it would come to this one day." His voice quavered, an old man beaten down by events and finally coming to a conclusion that others had arrived at years ago, but not had the temerity to challenge their leader. "I saw razors today. Explosives. The protos are now instruments of Cardassin. Next we'll see mutants in the front lines."

"Yes, the mutants," Ferral sneered, his lips drawn in a terse line. "It's always been Cardassin and his mutants."

Rasmussen looked at him sharply. "You know full well we had no choice but to come here. And I say that with qualification. You, and...Dayna were already here, and I accept that your parents made that decision long ago. I don't fault you for anything, except your refusal to join our creed. Be that as it may, we have survived these last twenty-five years, but now Cardassin has raised the bar. Equipping protos with weapons is unprecedented. We cannot hope to prevail in the long run."

Ferral started to speak, but Rasmussen held up a silencing hand. "We have come to a fork in the road. A point where we must take sides and make decisions. I stand before you today, over the bodies of our comrades, and urge you to put your personal needs to one side. Join me in a common effort to build A4-Ni. I propose we take back our rightful abode in Loriyu, then locate Sedroth's tomb and the guardian. Once we have the guardian we can build A4-Ni.

"We *TrueMen*--" He glanced at Dayna and Ferral and seemed to decide not to mention them as exceptions. "--We have taken our vows. I would understand if some of you decided not to join this commitment. To that end, I ask, now, that whomsoever feels they cannot, let them be known and we shall part company with respect."

He paused and surveyed the huddled few. Not a one moved or made any indication they wanted out.

"Good. I didn't think there would be anyone, but I needed to ask. Let us pray for strength." He spread his hands out to his sides, fingers twitching, and bowed his head.

The others all bowed their heads, except Ferral, who put his hands on his hips and glared at Rasmussen.

"Oh Sedroth," Rasmussen preached, "who guides us from above, bless-ed is your name. Your kingdom will come to us here, as it is in--"

"Let's cut the crap, Rasmussen," Ferral blurted. "Your mission is doomed."

Akilah stiffened. It wasn't like Ferral to bring his disagreements with Father into the open.

"How dare you!" Rasmussen sputtered.

Ferral stood his ground. "Cardassin is one player against what remains of us. Better we cleanse this land of his presence than chase around the frozen wilderness in search of Sedroth's tomb--a myth at best. Where are you going to live once you get to Loriyu? Cardassin sealed the Maraia enclave shut. Do you expect him to welcome you with open arms in Kanapoi? At least he's not adverse to using nano-assemblers. Or maybe you think we'll be able to hole up in the ancient ruin. But I ask, why should we change one set of ruins for another? For a scientist, you are certainly--"

"Enough!" Rasmussen shouted. "I asked for a commitment. I didn't expect a debate on what I proposed."

"Yes," Ferral said with a sweep of his hand. "You've convinced everyone this is the only way to save our Maraia souls, but not me. I rue the day we are all wiped out and our genome is entrusted to a machine we haven't even yet conceived."

"If you don't want to join us, you are free to go your way."

Ferral barked a laugh. "You give me a false choice. You know that alone I will surely die."

Rasmussen flushed.

Dayna leaned close. "Doctor Rasmussen, perhaps--"

"Don't patronize me," Rasmussen snapped. "You always side with Ferral--the two of you, who refuse to embrace the creed of *TrueMen*. He would lead us all to our deaths."

Stricken, Dayna stared. Her eyes teared as she fought for composure. "I hope you know I would never do anything to offend you."

"Perhaps not," Rasmussen muttered. "You're free to your opinion. But too many of us have died, and now Pierce and Carol. That is why we must undertake this mission. And mark my words, we shall succeed, for it is written."

"Written?" Ferral spat out the word. "Nothing's written. All you have is an oral tradition handed down over centuries. It takes a leap of faith to believe that the guardian lies on Sedroth's bones in some cave in what was once Loriyu. Even if we find the guardian, there's no reason to believe it still works or has the plans to build A4-Ni."

"We can't wait," Rasmussen said. "We either act now, or forever regret our chances."

"But the tomb's existence," Ferral countered, "is not much better than a rumor. No one, including you, has ever had anything more than a wish that it really exists."

"It is all we have left." Rasmussen looked down at his steepled fingers. "Our faith. The Maraia on Earth are finished. If Cardassin doesn't take us over, other players will. Why not try to save ourselves?"

"You still don't get it." Ferral shook his head angrily. "We will all die before any of your fantasies can be realized."

***

The Truman Light glided above frozen wastes-- a sleek object, bulbous control bubble at the front, glistening fuselage stretching back, small guide wings in pairs on either side. The autopilot kept the craft on a steady twenty meter glide above the ground.

Akilah shifted in her chair under her shoulder harness. In front of her sat Dayna. Gregory slouched in the other pilot's chair to Akilah's right. He didn't seem to be aware of what was going on. Having given his instructions at the outset it looked like he would be dozing until they got to their destination.

But where was Jason? He had left the navigator's chair ten minutes ago and not returned. A course correction loomed.

After leaving their compromised compound and heading due west, the Truman Light had ducked low to the deck, low enough that Cardassin's sensors could not pick them up, slow enough that Doppler radar would see through them. Soon they would curve north around looming Mount Ken, an ancient cinder cone on their right, long extinct, its decayed top and sides glistening snow-white in the afternoon light.

North lay the ice-bound plains dominated by Lake Turk, where anyone who ventured did so at great risk. It hadn't always been that way, or so Akilah had been told.

Eons ago, grass covered the plains, large rivers crisscrossed their expanse, herds of herbivores drifted like clouds under a nurturing sun. Lake Turk had lain ice-free, an emerald slit surrounded by a tangle of impenetrable green and overlooked by the Loriyu Plateau. The Plateau still stood, but it, too, was encrusted with layer upon layer of ice.

But the lands had started to grow cold and colder still, until tropical rains changed to sleet and sleet to snow. The snow melted at first, but in time the melt hardened and never left.

According to legend, it had been near the ancient village of Kanapoi that the Maraia were born and made their stand with Sedroth's help against the evil player Cathcar. After that, they had built the enclave and flourished until the player, Cardassin, had arrived. With a wicked evil, he had insinuated himself, then proceeded against them, forcing what remained of the Maraia, led by Gregory, to flee south to Nairob.

But Cardassin hadn't followed, at least not until now. He remained ensconced in a resurrected Kanapoi, waiting, presumably knowing that eventually Rasmussen would return to his ancestral home to search for the guardian.

Akilah checked the chronometer strapped to her wrist. Five minutes to course correction. Frustrated, she released the clasp of her shoulder harness and stepped out of her contour chair.

"Dayna." Akilah leaned forward and touched Dayna's shoulder. "I'm going back to check on Jason. He's been gone too long."

Dayna swiveled her chair around. "If Jason doesn't get here in time, I can make the course correction."

"You can do that?"

Dayna glanced to Gregory, who remained dozing. "Don't tell Doctor Rasmussen, but Jason gave me the coordinates just before we took off."

Akilah looked from Dayna to Gregory. If he knew their course had been compromised, he never would have left. Not that she thought Dayna would betray the information to a player spy, but there was still that one degree of separation between Dayna and the rest of them. She wasn't a *TrueMen*.

Akilah left the control room and entered a short, narrow passageway. At the far end, a sealed door led to the passenger compartment. The remaining Maraia men and women sat strapped into close seats, crammed into what was once the cargo hold of the small flyer.

Two doors stood opposite each other midway down the passageway. The one on Akilah's right led to Gregory's cramped sleeping room. The other door opened to the crew's modest rest area.

Akilah stopped in front of the latter and rapped lightly on the door. "Jason?" No response. She pressed the palm plate on the door. It unlatched and slid open.

The only light in the room came from a small reading lamp bent close to tiered bunks bolted to one wall. Akilah's gaze flicked from the lamp, then across the room.

Jason slumped in a chair, his head resting on the table, his arms hanging limply at his sides.

Her face felt suddenly cold. Blood thumped in her ears. Her heart tripped, then stepped up its beat. She fumbled for the wall and passed her hand over the flush-mounted light control. A bright uncompromising light flooded the room.

"Jason?"

He didn't answer.

A slit on the side of his neck extended from below his ear to the corner of his mouth. Blood welled, soaked the front of his shirt, and slid down his arm to his hand. From his fingertips, viscous drops fell to a pool on the floor.

The Truman Light swayed beneath her.

Akilah grabbed for the bunkbed's metal support tube. Dayna must be making the course correction. Once the craft steadied, Akilah stabbed the intercom switch on the wall. "Dayna, when you're free, could you come to the crew's quarters?" She fought for control. "Please."

Why Jason? Get a grip, girl. You're going to have to deal with this situation. Akilah blinked back tears.

She brushed her cheeks with the back of her hand. *Think.* No sign of a struggle. Bunks neatly made. Books on the desk in a neat row. No knife or blood splatters on the wall.

"What is it?" Dayna stood in the open doorway. "Oh God, not Jason?"

Despite Akilah's effort to stifle it, a sob heaved from her chest. "That's the way I found him. I...I haven't touched anything."

"You going to be okay?"

Akilah bit her lower lip and nodded.

Dayna stepped to the corpse and knelt to examine the wound. "This isn't an inflicted cut. The edges are rounded."

Thank Sedroth for Dayna's strength. "Player genetics?"

Dayna nodded. "Doctor Rasmussen has always said that we were all clean."

"You know what this mean." Akilah put her fingertips to her forehead and squeezed. *Concentrate.* The players were always finding ways to infect Maraia. Their nano-assemblers, besides being capable of making life livable could also be programmed to produce corrupted coils of DNA. Corrupt DNA could produce a wound, precipitate a disease, stop a heart, all temporally preordained with a delayed fuse at a quantum level.

"Somehow, someone got to him." Dayna put her arm around Akilah's shoulders. "We had better tell the others."

The soft press of Dayna's breast against Akilah's arm distracted her. *Not now.* "Father will be devastated."

"We have to tell him." Dayna reached for the intercom.

Akilah stayed her hand. "I'll tell him." She left and made her way to the control room, steadying herself with both hands pressing alternately against the walls of the hallway.

Gregory was standing near the control console. He must have seen concern in her face. "What has happened?"

"Jason is dead. We think player genetics."

Gregory looked stricken. "We've been betrayed."

"But how?"

"I'm certain everyone who came on board was clean. He must have been infected after we took off."

"But that means we have a player spy on board. That's hard to believe."

"Believe what you will. Where is Jason?"

"In the crew's quarters."

Gregory pushed past her and hurried down the hall.

She followed close behind.

"Have you touched anything?" Gregory asked Dayna.

"No. Neither has Akilah."

"Then this place must be quarantined. We don't know what genetic concoction he carries or if it is contagious." Gregory backed away. "Come. We must seal the door."

Once Akilah and Dayna were clear, Rasmussen engaged the door seals, then coded the lock so it couldn't be opened inadvertently.

"That should take care of it," he said. "I'm going back to the control."

Akilah gazed at Gregory's receding back. "We'll tell the others," she said, wondering that he had taken Jason's demise with such aplomb. Was he so focused on his perceived mission that he was able to take another death in stride? After he disappeared into the control room, she turned down the hallway toward the cargo hold.

The craft's klaxon alarm blared.

"Problem!" Gregory's voice crackled from the intercom.

Akilah stood stock still. *What more can go wrong that hasn't already*? She slid back the door to the cargo hold and leaned in. "Ferral, get up here. We're going to need some help." Despite Ferral's blustering, he had decided to come with them, anyway. The decision shouldn't have been a difficult one. Even Ferral didn't want to be left behind to face a horde of protos alone.

Without waiting for Ferral, Akilah ran to the control room.

Gregory pointed at the console. "Three reds. A yellow. They should all be green."

Ferral clambered into the control room and slid into a seat in front of the computer console, pulling a keyboard across his lap. He palmed sweat from his balding scalp. Eyes wide, he stared at the screen, showing a hint of fear.

The craft pitched.

Akilah grabbed at handholds on the wall. "What the hell was that?"

Ferral's fingers danced over the keys, then he pointed to the monitor. "We've lost hydraulics in sectors one, three and four. The thrusters aren't functional. Who the hell's been messing with this?"

Akilah ignored the question. Just like Ferral to seek out someone to blame. "Then we'll crash. How long?"

He hit another key. "Asymtotic glide path. Twenty seconds."

"Everyone to their crash seats. We're going down." Akilah raced to her chair across the bridge.

As she fumbled with the crash harness, Dayna slipped into her chair. Gregory stumbled to his own chair.

Akilah leaned forward to speak over his shoulder. "Father--"

"I can manage by myself, thank you." He wrestled with his harness.

After securing her harness and hearing the clasp click home on her father's, Akilah placed her hands in her lap, resigned.

The landscape, which had been slipping benignly beneath them suddenly tilted up and came rushing toward them.

Chapter Two

Michael stared across a slick sheet of ice at the horizon where the sun lay low, a dim, orange disk. A snow-glazed, cinder cone mountain jutted in the far distance to the south. A pale blue sky, devoid of clouds, domed overhead.

Do birds fly here?

"Birds have been extinct for five hundred years." His metabase sputtered a response.

They were wondrous beauties. Colored feathers. Lyrical songs. Are they truly gone?

"They are truly gone."

Michael felt a moment of sadness and wondered why he should. He'd never seen a bird fly nor heard one sing, but somehow he missed them.

He tried to stand, but the remainder of a mucous film from the Shepherd's womb had frozen his clothes to the ice on which he sat. A cold breeze slid around his body begging for his warmth.

D...damn, it's cold. Even his thoughts stuttered, and the Shepherd was nowhere in sight. With a fear of breaking into a dozen icy shards, Michael turned his head gingerly to his right.

A singular landform rose out of the glacial plain, like a submarine surfacing and frozen in mid-ascent.

"The Loriyu Plateau," his metabase identified. *"You are located in what once was northern Kenya. Lake Turkana is north of the plateau. The ancient*

33

village of Kanapoi is on the other side of the plateau."

Kanapoi?

"Kanapoi--where humankind began four million years ago. Where they were rejuvenated as the Maraia three thousand years ago, and where they might end in the present. Kanapoi--now occupied by the player Cardassin, a fiendish specimen, who has it in his mind that if he waits long enough the Maraia will return looking for the guardian."

How could the metabase know this? Better yet, how did the Shepherd know this information to store it in the metabase? He must have had access years ago to the guardian's knowledge of the future. *Is all this be preordained?*

"The worldlines of everything in this universe are closed loops. No beginning. No end. Just being. Conscious hominids were never meant to exist. It is of no use to be aware of things that can never be understood."

Michael thought a word of thanks for the information. He didn't know if this was necessary or not, but the metabase seemed so much like another person that saying thanks seemed appropriate.

He returned his gaze to the plain and estimated the time as late afternoon.

A small speck danced on the horizon. Since the speck was the only thing moving in the vast expanse, Michael stared at it.

Eventually, he discerned a figure, rising up and down in a loping run. A vapor haze puffed from a

34

hooded face. A man, or something resembling a man, ran up to him with red cheeks and billowing breath.

"You?" the man said.

A simple question from a being Michael assumed was also simple. But what did he mean? The man's face had the sloped look of a primitive hominid. He stood only slightly higher than he was wide given the layers of animal skin clothing and his powerful build.

"Yes, it's me," Michael said impatiently. The cold continued to seep into his body, much of which was already numb. He struggled to free his clothes from the ice. "Help me."

The man held up a restraining hand. He reached into his skins and retrieved a short stick, thumbed a flush button on its side and loosed a long streak of light. With an expert twist, he shortened and focused the beam.

An ice razor, Michael thought. His instinct was to draw back in surprise, but his frozen circumstances prevented him from doing so. "Be careful with that."

"Stay!" The man brought his hand across his face, knocking slender icicles from his brows. His fingers wrapped around the device and adjusted the light into a diffused field.

The beam played across Michael, giving immediate warmth. He came unstuck and stood stiffly.

The man indicated Michael should stand back, then he re-focused the beam to a pencil thinness and directed it at the frozen ground. A curl of steam

35

rose from the ice as the beam traced a circle. A cylindrical block of ice a meter in diameter and half as thick liquefied around the edges and dropped from sight.

"Home," the man said.

"Home?" Michael stepped carefully to the edge and craned to peer into the hole, the depths of which curved away in a tunnel and disappeared from view. The block of ice lay stuck on the floor. He wondered where the ice melt had gone.

"Into the caverns below the top ice," offered the metabase.

Caverns?

"You may think that all the ice you see is solid. But it is not, at least not at this latitude. Though it is on average ten meters thick, seasonally, the ice melts farther south and produces subterranean, rather sub-ice streams that course over the bedrock ground north to Lake Turk. These streams leave behind all manner of twisted and curved ice caverns."

I--

"Wait." The man grabbed Michael by the collar and yanked him back, then leapt into the hole. His ice razor flashed melting contoured steps into the sloping icy wall of the hole.

He climbed back out and stood over Michael. "Jamil," he said with a thump to his chest with his fist.

Michael stared in wonder. "Jamil?" Data flooded his mind.

"An Arabic name meaning handsome one."

36

Michael marveled at the odd collection of knowledge the Shepherd had provided. "Why did you refer to me, upon first greeting, as--"

Jamil grabbed Michael's arm, directed him to the hole, and before Michael could resist, shoved him over the edge.

He slipped on the steps and bounced washboard fashion the two meters to the base, landing on his backside.

Jamil ignored the steps, leapt down, hit and sprang upright. "No like steps."

"I like steps. I just don't like being pushed down them." Feeling bruised, Michael rolled to a sitting position and wrapped his arms around his chest, trying to conserve warmth if not also his self-esteem. It was still bitterly cold.

A glistening tunnel led away from him downward and to his right. Its icy walls curved seamlessly from floor to wall to ceiling. The tunnel was wide enough for two people to walk side-by-side, and tall enough so Michael, all of one meter-seventy centimeters in height would not have to bend over.

Diffuse sunlight filtered through the top ice. Yellow-orange, its glow was intense at the ceiling, then tapered off on the sides to blue, turning to an opaque white beneath.

Chattering voices echoed up the tunnel, followed by a clutch of beings not dissimilar to Jamil--an older male and female, possibly parents of Jamil, a female approximately the same age, and what looked like a male child, perhaps ten.

They crowded the tunnel, jostling for a look at Michael.

He shoved his heels against the slippery floor in a futile effort to back up against the wall. Feeling clumsy and foolish, he decided to relax and wait.

Jamil stepped forward. "Bad-Maraia." He waved his hand to include the others clogging the tunnel.

Metabase?

"*Bad-Maraia--A mix of Maraia and proto-humans, primitive hominids who have immigrated out of the ruins of ancient Nairob back to the north country, the original Maraia homeland.*"

Michael nodded and waved tentatively at the multitude. "Mixed?" he offered tentatively.

"Mixed." Jamil puffed out his chest. "Problem?"

What a fix. Michael looked for a way out but saw there was none. What was he to do, slip and slide up the passageway while Jamil and the others grabbed his ankles and pulled him back? "No problem."

The child came up to Jamil and insinuated himself under his protective arm.

"Your son?" Michael asked.

"Son. Jamani."

"Hello, Jamani," Michael said, but Jamani seemed shy and pulled back around Jamil. "I am Michael. I have come here to oversee the construction of A4-Ni."

Jamil looked at him with surprise. "A-far-en-i."

"Yes, A4-Ni." Michael's metabase told him he should be heading for the plateau, not explaining his purpose to a group of primitives. "I must be on my way."

Jamil patted Michael on the shoulder. "Good. A-far-en-i. Stay."

Michael thought about protesting, but decided against it. For now, it was better to sit tight and learn.

"Eat." Jamil pointed his finger at his mouth as though Michael were an idiot.

The other primitives let out an excited yelp and disappeared back down the tunnel.

Michael stood up and tested his knees. He had warmed up to the point where his joints hurt only a little. "I'm not hungry."

"Eat." Jamil took Michael by the arm and propelled him into the tunnel.

He stumbled forward almost losing his balance on the slippery surface. Twenty meters later, he came to an arching chamber with a large carpet made from animal skins spread across a flat floor of bare ground.

The others were already seated in a circle around a shallow parabolic vessel a meter in diameter and some centimeters deep made from what looked like hammered copper. It sat on a bed of glowing coals contained in a circle of stones. Steam rose off the surface of a stew.

Jamil directed Michael to an open space and made him sit.

The younger woman sat next to Jamil away from Michael.

He assumed the woman was Jamil's mate. "Who is this woman?"

Jamil glanced at the woman, then back at Michael and nodded. He pointed to the woman. "Rafiya." Then to the older woman and man. "Nina, Baba."

Without waiting for a response from Michael, they all clasped hands and bowed their heads.

Michael, feeling somewhat foolish, went along with what must be a coming prayer.

"Sedroth is great, Sedroth is good. Thanks be to Sedroth for this stew. And bless new man here."

Practically before the last word was out of Jamil's mouth, the others grabbed for wooden ladles that were stacked beside the vessel.

Rafiya picked up a ladle and shyly offered it to Michael, then when Jamil frowned, quickly picked up another ladle for him.

The ladle was crudely carved from a single piece of wood.

"*The nearest source of wood is Kanapoi.*" The metabase informed. "*And there, only available if it is stolen from Cardassin's compound.*"

"Eat." Jamil raised his ladle in front of Michael and moved it back and forth, as though trying to catch Michael's attention. Once Michael focused on the ladle, Jamil inserted it into the stew, with an encouraging nod.

Does he think I'm retarded? Dismayed, Michael followed Jamil's lead. Michael would have to ask the metabase to expand its answer on the origin of the wooden bowls later. He brought the ladle to his nose and sniffed the contents. "Fish?"

"Fish," Jamil answered.

"Where do the fish come from?"

Jamil pointed to an ice tunnel on the opposite the side of the room from where they had entered. "Lake."

The indicated tunnel led north. If that were the case, then Jamil was referring to Lake Turkana. "Lake Turkana?" Michael said.

Everyone, including Jamil, stopped eating and stared.

"Did I say something wrong?"

"You know?" Jamil asked.

"I was told the lake in that direction was known long ago as Lake Turkana."

"Who tell?"

"The Shepherd?" Michael wasn't sure what effect telling them about the Shepherd would produce, but he was curious, nevertheless.

Jamil smiled. The others all smiled. Jamil wrapped a strong arm around Michael and squeezed him tight. "We wait. Now, you come, again."

Me a prophet? Michael, feeling embarrassed, nodded and smiled, shoulders hunched, hands out to his sides. "Here I am."

The ice seemed to have been figuratively melted and everyone started talking at once to him and to each other. Michael tried to follow the fast-paced conversation, which was conducted in an archaic form of English. He failed and concentrated instead on finishing his fish stew.

At the end of the simple meal, the glow emanating from the chamber's ceiling darkened. The sun must have set on the plain above. Nina and

Baba left first, heading to what looked like an alcove melted into the side wall of the main space.

Rafiya followed, dragging a protesting Jamani by the hand.

"What's going on?" Michael asked.

"Night. Sleep."

Michael wasn't sure what to do. He didn't need to sleep. Maybe it was a good time to leave.

Jamil stood. "Close ice." He drew his ice razor.

So much for an open door.

Michael followed as Jamil plodded up the entrance corridor. At the far end, they came to the hole leading to the surface. That Jamil hadn't bothered to close the opening explained why it was still so cold down below. But everyone was fully bundled up making Michael wonder if they ever undressed.

"May I?" Michael indicated he wanted to look outside.

"Hurry." Jamil stepped aside.

Michael climbed the slippery steps. He pulled himself out of the hole and sat on its edge.

Though a stiff wind blew from the north, the sky was clear. A canopy of stars scintillated overhead. Low to the east, a full moon shone, its light enhanced by the omnipresent ice. The Loriyu Plateau stood in dark repose, its reflected image smeared on the sheet of ice before him.

A descending light flashed in the southern sky. *A meteorite*? No. Some sort of craft was coming down quickly, too quickly. It blazed a fiery trail, engines shrieking in a rising whine. A sleek craft

42

showed briefly, hit hard, tipped a guide wing into the ice and gouged the plain, raising a white plume of broken ice crystals. It came to a stop near the distant plateau. The icy tail fluffed and settled back to the ground.

"Jamil!" Michael looked back into the hole. "What was that?"

"Don't know."

"I'm going to investigate." Michael took a step toward the distant craft.

Jamil was out of the hole and at his side in an instant. "No. I go."

Michael was quickly coming to the end of his patience with this primitive, dinner host or not. "Then I'll come with you."

"No." Jamil grabbed him by his collar, hauled him unceremoniously to the hole and dumped him into the tunnel.

As Michael scampered to his feet, the searing light of the ice razor flashed, freeing a lens on one side of the hole and sending it across the opening.

The entrance sealed shut.

***

"What the fokk was that?" Cardassin stared at the lambskin carpeted floor around him, at the quivering canvas of the tent over him, then back at the bed he had just fallen out of.

"An earthquake, sire." An obsequious lump of putty-shaped flesh quivered nervously at his feet.

Cardassin gave the mass a kick.

Amoeba-like, it shaped away to a far corner.

"Cristina, *dawling*," he said addressing the shape, "that wasn't no earthquake. More like a

43

fokkin' crash of some sort. Where're my guards?" Cardassin pulled his white, silk robe about his thin body. His hands went to his face, drunkenly smoothed his short, rounded goatee and moved to his head where his fingers raked nervously through thin wisps of red hair.

This fokkin' body.

He couldn't remember why he had chosen the form he had. But there it was, and by now he was too lazy to change it to something else.

Besides, the sex is pretty good. Nothing like that on the outside. In fact there was nothing period on the outside, just potential.

And potential had never got him going.

Praise *Zug*! Surely He had his reasons for deploying players as He did. One here, one there. In and out of time. In and out of space. Immortal. All for what? Finding and destroying a tiny sphere, its transport the Shepherd, and the DNA of *Zug's* greatest foe--*Gilomir*.

At least I've done a pretty good job with the latter. Absently, Cardassin scratched his inner thigh. There weren't many Maraia left, and when they were gone his obligations here would be finished. Then what? Back to potential, he supposed. *Ick.*

A mewing emanated from Cristina followed by the cadenced thumping of Cardassin's guards as they humped into his sleeping chamber. All three came to ragged attention, limbs a-jingle, watery eyes drooping. Tatters of rotten clothing hung in odiferous disarray. Each guard carried a shiny

44

mag-steel razor rod in contrast to their otherwise ragtag appearance.

"Ma-justy," the tallest guard said, his speech slurred from overindulgence.

"Fokkin' idiot." Cardassin leaned to the edge of the bed and retrieved a blunt cylinder. He pointed it at the guard, thumbed a button, and grimaced as a cobalt-blue line of light shot from the business end of the ice razor, punched a hole through the tent wall on one side of the guard, and worked its smoldering way diagonally until it sliced him in half.

The guard crumpled to the floor, sheared neatly at the navel, both halves smoking in cauterized closure. The second guard kicked heavily at the half with legs still twitching and shuffled to his left to fill the space vacated by his erstwhile companion.

"Sire," the second guard said. "A *TrueMen* craft has crash-landed on the other side of the plateau."

"That's better." Cardassin waved the cylinder, now off, in a drunken spiral.

Sweat dribbled from beneath the tangled hairline of the second guard as he followed the path of the weapon with twitching eyes.

"They have come for the guardian," Cardassin said.

"We don't know that, sire. Only that a wandering mutant saw them crash."

"I knew they would come." Cardassin giggled. Spit slipped from his mouth, and he wiped it away awkwardly with his robe. "My decision to wait them out has proved to be prescient."

"Yes, sire."

"Go see what they're up to."

"Sire?"

"Idiot." The cylinder sizzled light that passed across guard number two rending him head to crotch. He split along the tarnished, gold-buttoned closure of his ancient vestment and toppled to both sides. The razor's light sputtered and went out.

The third guard quivered. "Sire, I will take some mutants to reconnoiter. If the *TrueMen* find the guardian, we will take it from them."

Cardassin smiled, musing at the jammed trigger of his razor. Frustrated, he shook it, then tossed it on the bed. "Good," he said, resigned that he would not be able to use the instrument again. "I am hearing what I want to hear. What did you say your name was?"

"I didn't my lord, but it is Igor."

Clever bastard. Cardassin waved his hand in dismissal.

Igor spun on his heel, listed heavily to the left and stumbled out of the tent.

Cardassin lay back on his bed, his head thrown back, eyes staring at the ceiling. He rolled to one side. "Lump of fokkin' Maraia flesh," he wheezed.

The lump vibrated, its expression of anticipation. "You desire something, my lord?"

"Come squeeze me."

The flesh slithered across the room, gained a purchase on the bed by pinching the sheet between pseudopodal clumps, and rose. After a moment of disorientation, it slid up Cardassin's leg to his groin and began a slow, pulsating rhythm.

46

Cardassin's eyes rolled beneath batting pink lashes. His tongue rattled inside his open mouth, sending flecked spittle to the edges of his lips. His muscles, what muscles he had, tensed in a rippling crescendo. He jerked spasmodically.

"*Zug* is great!"

He relaxed and breathed a sigh, a sowing wind rattling stiff reeds. *I really shouldn't use the Lord's name in vain, especially under the circumstances.* Cardassin giggled thinking of cir-come-stances. "Go," he commanded the flesh.

It withdrew to the far side of the room.

Cardassin swiveled off the pile of cushions, rubbing at a wet stain mid-robe. He slipped his feet into worn leather slippers and slapped his way across the carpet to the entrance where he pulled back the tent flap.

His tent sat on a slight rise above a hundred other tents randomly scattered on the ground before him. Fragrant acacias, with their feathery yellow flowers, mixed in dense competition with towering palms. Below them, bright, structured euphorbias and scarlet-tipped lobelias littered the ground. Out of this riotous tangle, like a scent on cool air, the sound of a bubbling brook carried between artificial lava-rock banks.

Nearer, tall palms clustered surrounded by cropped grass. Here and there, deciduous trees hung heavy with pomegranates, figs, and ripe plums. Water gurgled beside a path leading from his tent to co-mingle with other small streams and empty into a placid pond.

Marsh grass waved in a gentle breeze. Ducks, flamingos and other multicolored waterfowl swam in the still waters. Small birds, caricatures of their ancient forebears, flitted from tree to tree and arced high in the air.

An artificial sun shone brightly through a magnifying prism, warming the village. The sky beyond, a pastiche of blue with white clouds, looked as real as anything seen from a tropical isle of long ago.

Cardassin shielded his eyes. He must do something to adjust the intensity of the faux-sun. It kept Kanapoi warm, but the glare was annoying. "Habibi!" he screamed.

A misshapen boy club-footed up to him.

"Get rid of the bodies in my tent before that fokkin' Maraia lump eats them."

"Yes, sire."

Cardassin graced the boy with a leering smile. Was he fifteen or sixteen? Cardassin couldn't remember, but the youth sprouted appendages in multiple ways that no pure human Maraia could have supported. Indeed, he had two hearts, no stomach and three penises. Yes, Habibi served his master well.

A shuffling figure approached. "You seem to be in good form this morning."

Cardassin glanced at his seer, Trudal. The old Maraia looked like he'd slept in his clothes. His face was unshaven, his hair graying. "Fokk form."

"What a fine day," Trudal said peering up at the false sky.

48

"It's always like this. What do you know of fine days?"

"I have seen many, my lord. This one brings portent of great things to come. The Maraia *TrueMen* have landed. Better yet, they have crash-landed."

"Should I see some potential benefit from this information?"

"Yes, you should, sire. They come for the guardian. That is obvious. The myth of Sedroth's tomb does not permeate this region for naught."

"I know, I know. *Zug* willing, why else would I remain in this godforsaken place?" Cardassin doubled over in a coughing fit, hacked viscously, and spit into a dense tangle of pontederia that had left the waterway and sprawled next to the path. "I could be just about anywhere, any time. Instead, I have chosen this fokkin' frozen wilderness. If it weren't for these munificent nano-assemblers, life would be unbearable. It almost is anyway."

"Sire, you have done well to corrupt us and bring us into this abode. Kanapoi is reborn. Ancient history smiles upon what you have done to raise Kanapoi from frozen wastes to the paradise it once was."

"I don't think it ever was a fokkin' paradise, but it's certainly a lot more comfortable than living in an ice cave. What do you know of these *TrueMen*?"

The seer shuffled closer and sat down. "I had a vision--"

"Cut the crap, Trudal. What do you know?"

"They are led by our nemesis Doctor Gregory Rasmussen. It appears he has tired of being on the run, though one has to wonder that it took him twenty-five years to do so. I presume that he has now decided to cast caution aside and try to locate Sedroth's tomb with the few Maraia who remain. They intend to prevail or die trying. And die they will, since they resist all attempts to restructure their DNA."

"Is that surprising, given their creed?"

"Not at all. But there can be benefits to restructuring one's genomic pattern."

"Indeed." Cardassin laughed harshly, then sank into fits of coughing. His eyes watered. He swallowed hard. "Look at Habibi. You should have taken some advice from him. You might have been more productive."

Trudal smiled indulgently. "Sire, do you want me to continue?"

Cardassin drew his hand across his wet lips, catching a slime of mucous that played out into the light like a spider's web, glistening. He frowned, shook his hand in frustration, whipping the stubborn thread up and down, then wiped his hand on his robe. "Go on."

"Rasmussen is intent on building A4-Ni, the universal constructor of *TrueMen* myth. He has concluded no other way exists to save *TrueMen* than to construct this machine, prime it with their pure genome and send it out amongst the stars to breed *TrueMen* elsewhere, everywhen." Trudal smiled, presumably at his alliteration.

"He's going to do this without a fokkin' assembler? He's got no base for operations. I saw to that long ago. Is he going to hang out in the ruin and build this constructor from crumbling concrete?"

"I didn't say he was a practical man. Though the *TrueMen* eschew assemblers as a matter of faith, they are still a rather clever people. It is possible that the constructor can be put together with old fashioned Maraia sweat and tears."

Cardassin thought for a moment. "And what if they succeed?"

"Then your mission on Earth will have come to naught. Just as you are in the final stages of eradicating the *Gilomir* genome from remaining Maraia, a genius like Rasmussen rises up and points a way to save them. It must be most disconcerting."

"Genius, my fokkin' ass. He's an eccentric of no consequence. Still, he's managed to evade my mutants all these years. And when he can't evade them, he kills them and moves on. I don't understand it."

"Sire, with all due respect, the mutants you send against him are no more sober than you and yours are here."

Cardassin bristled, but the dull haze of indulgence slid over him and muted his anger. He supposed it was a good thing he had left the razor in his tent with its jammed trigger. Trudal could have paid for his impertinence. "They are all besotted idiots."

"The *TrueMen*, my lord?"

"No, the fokkin' mutants. I know what I'm going to do. When Gregory gets the guardian, I will steal it and complete the annihilation of the Maraia."

"How do you propose to do that, my Lord?"

"I'll think of something."

"The good Doctor travels with a party of nine including himself. One of your mutants, dull as you have characterized, was able to make contact with the protos of Nairob and give them ice razors and explosives. The latter armaments proved to be the deciding factor in convincing the good Doctor that he should come north again."

Cardassin waved his hand in a dismissive gesture. "I know, I know. One doesn't have to be a seer to learn this stuff. Tell me, is Gregory's daughter still with him?

"Yes sire."

"She's a peach. What I wouldn't give to have her lying beneath my loins."

"Yes, sire. She and the rest are all pure Maraia, or so I've been shown."

"Shown, shown?" Cardassin twitched. "Who showed you?"

"I dreamt it my lord."

"Fokkin' rubbish."

Chapter Three

Akilah gripped the crash rail so hard her knuckles turned white. She strained against the harness across her chest that pressed her into the cushioned captain's chair.

You're still alive, girl. Try to relax.

The craft had dropped on a shallow glide path and dug a groove three kilometers long before skidding to rest on the icy plain. Moonlight streamed through the bulkhead's ceiling, which had split down the middle like an overripe pea pod. Its ragged edges hung with fractured ceiling panels. Sparking cables flashed white in the dim red of the emergency lights. The smell of ozone drifted in the arctic air.

Her breath puffed billowing clouds.

Go ahead, hyperventilate and die. But the thought calmed her, almost as if she were a second person advising herself. Cautiously, she took mental stock of her body. No pain radiated from her extremities. She wiggled her toes in her crash boots, flexed her legs, and twisted her torso. Still no pain. She rolled her head on her neck and satisfied herself all her vertebra were in place. Then with an effort, she willed her fingers to uncoil. *Good.*

A groan emanated from the chair next to her.

"Father?"

Because he had swiveled away, she couldn't see if he was injured. She grasped her harness release between thumb and forefinger and gave it a sharp twist. It clicked open. The harness drew back into the seat, allowing her to stand. *At least something still works.*

Her father sat head-down, gray hair thrown forward as though it had been brushed to cover the bald spot on top. His arms dangled at his sides. His bony knees pressed against his khaki field pants. His boots remained locked into the crash clips.

Akilah placed both hands on his neck and probed. No swelling, a strong pulse. She raised his head.

His eyes flicked open, and he heaved a great sigh through an open mouth ringed by the graying muff of his beard.

"Water," he rasped, drawing his tongue over cracked lips.

Akilah located an insulated drinking cylinder resting against the forward console and handed the bottle to him.

Dayna stood on the other side of the console and moved her arm tentatively while checking her shoulder joint. She stopped mid-motion. "Ferral is bleeding."

Akilah stepped over to Ferral's crash chair. "He didn't get his harness buckled." Blood dripped from a wound on his forehead. The console in front of him was bloodied, indicating where he had hit upon impact.

"Get Nicholai up here to look at him," Akilah said. "You okay?"

"I'm fine. Stiff shoulder." Dayna started to duck into the hallway leading to the passenger compartment, then turned. "How's Doctor Rasmussen?"

Dayna the obsequious one. "He's conscious. Says he's thirsty."

"Thank Sedroth. Brrr!" Dayna rubbed her hands up and down her arms. Her taut body would offer little insulation against the cold. "We'll have to do something fast about shelter or we'll all freeze to death. I'll get Nicholai and check on the others."

Rasmussen sucked at the cylinder, coughed, and drew a shaky hand across his lips.

"Better." His eyes focused. He looked around for the first time and started to shiver. "The others?"

"We don't know, yet. But we have to get into the passenger compartment or we'll freeze." She unclipped his harness and helped him stand.

He draped an arm over her shoulder and leaned heavily.

They stumbled down the short hallway, making their way slowly on a floor tipped ten degrees starboard. At the far end Akilah pulled on the passenger compartment door, which slid open after some effort.

The compartment, a renovated cargo hold, smelled of stale breath. No air circulation. The one red emergency light flickered.

Someone walked toward Akilah in a stop frame motion caused by the stroboscopic flashing of the light. Hopefully it was Nicholai. They'd be in dire straits without their physician.

A small black satchel gripped in his hand, Nicholai stepped out of the passenger compartment and glanced at Rasmussen.

"Father doesn't seem to be hurt," Akilah said. "But Ferral banged his head on the console."

Nicholai eased past Akilah to the control room.

Dayna stood inside the passenger compartment. "Get in quick." She motioned.

As soon as Akilah and her father were inside, Dayna slid the door closed. It was warmer there, but not by much.

"I've got the auxiliary generator going," Dayna said. "We'll have heat and air in a minute."

The fans came on, and a breath of fresh air flooded the compartment. The temperature rose.

"What have we got here?" Akilah said.

"Two injured. Warren and Lorry." Showing no emotion Dayna zipped the collar on her tunic close about her neck. "They didn't get into their harnesses in time, either. Nothing life-threatening. Lorry is having a bit of a tough go, but she'll be okay once she gets her wind back. Everyone else is solid. Karin went to check the cargo."

"Warren and Lorry?" Rasmussen swayed unsupported. "Where are they?"

Dayna indicated the two, huddled together in one of the back rows. "They're probably suffering from shock. I gave them blankets. Nicholai can look at them after he's finished with Ferral."

"I understand." Rasmussen rubbed his forehead. He looked as though he was going to faint.

Akilah gripped his elbow. "You better sit down." She helped him to the armrest of one of the seats.

"We can't stay here," Dayna said. "The generator's only good for a few hours, then it's back to batteries for a few more. Any idea where we are?"

Akilah glanced toward one of the port windows, but it was dark outside. "I thought I saw the Loriyu Plateau off our left wing as we came down."

"*The* Loriyu Plateau?"

"Is that so strange?"

"I'd say that was pretty coincidental, us crashing so near the site." Dayna gave Rasmussen a questioning look, but he didn't register it.

Akilah decided to let Dayna's impertinence go unchallenged. "We're probably within walking distance. If the ruin still exists, it could prove to be a lifesaver."

"You don't sound hopeful."

"Hopeful? I wish I could be more hopeful. After twenty-five years, I can't imagine Cardassin leaving it intact."

"Child," Rasmussen said, lifting rummy eyes to her. "You don't give that player swine the credit he deserves. I'm sure he has calculated that we would eventually return to look for the guardian, and what better means to entice us here than to keep the ruin intact."

The door between the compartment and the control room slid open. Warmer compartment air puffed out an icy cloud into the hallway. Ferral, a

57

bandage wrapped tightly around his forehead, stood at the threshold.

"Come in, come in," Rasmussen said. "How do you feel?"

Nicholai crowded behind Ferral into the compartment and slid the door shut. "He'll be okay. The cut is superficial. Just a lot of blood."

"The controls were cut," Ferral said angrily, "just as I suspected."

Rasmussen's eyes widened. A vein on the side of his temple pulsed. "Cut? You mean we were sabotaged?"

"That's putting it simply. Someone knew what they were doing. Probably used time-delayed nano-dissemblers. Only the control lines to the critical thrusters were cut. Not thruster two. That caused us to veer close to the plateau. Pretty damn coincidental we crash-landed here."

"You're jumping to conclusions," Rasmussen said. "Are you implying we have a player spy amongst us?"

"I thought that was obvious."

"To think that one of us is a spy is beyond comprehension." Rasmussen sat down hard and stared at the floor. "We must be on our guard," he muttered. "First Jason, now this."

"Jason could have been infected before we took off," Dayna said. "For that matter, nano-dissemblers on the controls could have been planted months ago."

"Are you sure the control lines were cut?" Akilah asked.

Ferral stared at her. "You're doubting what I saw?"

Rasmussen waved his hands in the air. "No, no, of course we aren't. We're grasping at straws. I can't imagine someone would do something like that. We have all been so trusting. Everyone was free to wander through the control room at any time, either when one of us was there or the place was empty."

"Are you implying we are all under suspicion?" Ferral asked.

Rasmussen rose, clenching his fists. "This is an abomination. Someone so possessed by *Zug* will not be able to remain anonymous for long."

"Please, Father. Your blood pressure."

"Well, it's done," Ferral said. "Nothing we can do about it now, but watch our backs." He craned to see deeper into the passenger compartment. "What's the situation here?"

"Under control." Akilah marveled at how quickly Ferral put the suspected sabotage behind him. If there was a spy on board, remote as that possibility seemed, they had a major problem. Yet Ferral was prepared to move on. But that was just like him.

"How's your head?" Dayna asked, obviously trying to lower the tension.

Ferral touched the bandage gingerly. "I'll survive."

The rear door of the compartment banged open. Karin stepped out of the cargo hold, her arms laden with a bundle of insulated jumpsuits. "No need to worry about surviving--at least for a while." She dumped the suits on the floor. "If you put these on, we can reduce the load on the generators."

Akilah pulled at one of the jumpsuits. "They'll also enable us to explore outside."

"You're going outside?" Dayna asked.

"I'm going to the plateau to find the ruins. We can't just sit here."

Dayna reached for a suit. "I'm going with you."

***

Blowing ice crystals formed small drifts at the corners of the control room. The view out the port windows was gray-white.

"Doesn't look good," Akilah said.

Dayna nodded and snapped open the cover of a container recessed in the back of her chair. After rummaging around, she withdrew a small tablet-shaped device with a screen on one side.

"LPS." She offered the local positioning system up for Akilah to see. "We don't want to get lost out there."

Dayna switched on the LPS and examined the screen. "Plateau's about five hundred meters west of here. Assuming we get up the escarpment, the ruins should be another six hundred meters north. If we locate the ruins, we should be able to access the enclave." She tilted the screen so Akilah could see.

"You willing to give it a try?" Akilah asked.

"After you." Dayna stepped back.

Akilah smiled grimly and pulled goggles over her eyes, then shoved her hands into thick gloves. There was no need to open the main door. A crack in the bulkhead was big enough to step through.

She gripped the edge of the torn opening and hesitated. She'd have to drop to the ground below.

"It's about two meters down." She sat, then pushed off and landed, bending her knees to absorb the shock of the fall.

Dayna held the LPS out of the opening by its strap and let it dangle to Akilah's outstretched hands, then she dropped down beside her.

Akilah shoved a knob on the LPS with her gloved thumb and held the screen close to her face, focusing on the dim display. A stiff wind blew crystals of snow and ice across her view. "That way." She pointed west.

Walking side-by-side, heads down to protect from stinging ice crystals, they trudged toward the distant escarpment. Despite the insulated jumpsuits, the wind chilled their bodies. A low-lying layer of swirling white streamed over their boots, obscuring the ground. Weak moonlight glittered around them in a riot of prismatic color. After ten minutes of silent hiking, they came to the escarpment.

"Shit." Dayna slapped her hand against a sheer wall of ice. She cupped her mouth against the howling wind close to Akilah's ear. "How the hell are we going to climb this?"

"Let's move north," Akilah shouted back. "Look for any irregularities in the wall." She leaned into the wind with one hand extended to the ice wall as a guide. After a hundred meters she stopped.

"This might work." She squinted up at an angled groove in the steep escarpment. "The wind has carved a crease in the ice. "We can cut steps.

61

They'll be steep but better than trying to go straight up with axes."

Dayna took the LPS from Akilah and awkwardly pushed buttons on it with her thumbs. "That fixes the location so we can find it again. Let's get the hell out of here. I'm freezing."

Akilah shook her head vigorously. "I want to find the ruin."

Dayna held her gloved hand up to the wind as though testing its force. "Can't you wait? This storm might abate tomorrow. It would be easier then."

"I'm pressing on. If you want to return, then do so." Akilah stifled a rush of excitement, but still felt her voice waver at the prospect of finding the ruin. The aura of mystery surrounding the ruin loomed large. She had only heard tales from her father about the hallowed ground. Sedroth. Cathcar. Azizah. Legends all.

"Return without you? Are you nuts?"

Akilah smiled at the ready capitulation. Dayna was probably just as curious.

"You want to cut steps or should I?"

Dayna drew her ice razor from its holster. She thumbed the cylinder on, adjusted the beam, then directed it at the crease. "I'll do it. Stand back."

The focused light cut through the storm, puffing crystalline flakes into a gray vapor where they crossed the beam. She worked it back and forth, at first experimentally, raising a plume of steam that instantly chilled, collapsing sideways, as the cutter moved on. Having ascertained the depth and hardness of the ice, she snapped her razor more quickly, carving bulky steps, the runoff emptying over the side and freezing in layers like melted wax.

"I can only cut so high. We'll have to climb, establish a landing, then cut some more."

"I'll go first." Akilah played out a rope, knotted it to her belt and left a length, which she attached to her ice axe. When Dayna finished the steps, Akilah tested one of them with her boot. What was once a slick surface had frozen, capturing ice crystals out of the air to provide a semblance of texture.

She pressed her boot tentatively on the rough surface. When it held she buried her axe in the side wall, above her head, as far as she could reach.

The wind pushed her body against the hard wall. Akilah's grip slipped, and she fell back.

"Let me go first," Dayna said.

"The hell you will." Akilah pulled herself level with the attached rope, planted her feet and swung the axe higher. This time she was ready for the wind. She gave in to it, then renewed her climb.

Another slip, but no fall. There was no relief to her exertion. She was either climbing a step, swinging the ax higher, or pulling on the rope.

The steps grew shallower as she ascended.

She rested, her heart tripping rapidly, her breath puffing upward, fogging her goggles.

Damn wind. Damn ice. Damn. Damn. Damn.

A faint unintelligible cry came from Dayna below.

"I'm going to cut more steps," Akilah shouted, but the wind stole the sound of her voice. She tied herself off on the ax and fumbled for her ice razor. Leaning back as far as she could, she began

63

tediously cutting new steps. When the razor beam could no longer angle onto the groove, she resumed her climb.

After another repetition of step-cutting, Akilah lunged forward. This time her axe swooshed air. The summit.

Her limbs screaming in pain, she thrust with her legs the last meter over the top and lay panting with exhaustion. For once the stinging wind and its knifing ice were welcomed.

The rope tugged gently at her waist. Dayna. Akilah crawled to her knees and slammed the axe into the ice. She wrapped the rope around the shaft, then tugged strongly. When the rope went taut with Dayna's weight, Akilah lay back, feeling the quick chill of sweat turning to ice on her neck.

A rough shove.

"Akilah! Wake up."

She stirred, realizing she had almost passed out. The stress of the crash, the hike to the escarpment, the climb had taken their toll. "I'm okay. Just resting." *A lie*.

Dayna surveyed her with concern. She checked the closure on Akilah's jumpsuit, felt her neck, brushing ice away, then cinched tight her collar.

"Jeez, wish I could see something." Dayna shielded her goggles and peered into the wind. "It's a total white out."

Her attempt at distraction didn't fool Akilah. They were close to freezing to death. If they didn't find the ruin in the next ten minutes, they'd be turned to frozen stone, fossilized remains buried in layers of ice for some future generation of beings to find.

Bad thoughts. Focus. "I'll lead. Anchor me in case I fall." Akilah checked the LPS. "The ruins--" She pointed. "--two hundred meters."

Roped together, they trudged north. The wind blew more fiercely on top of the plateau, frosting their goggles and forcing them to wrap their scarves tightly around their mouths.

Akilah sensed Dayna's distress. "Just a little bit farther."

"What?"

The effort to speak exhausted Akilah. She checked the LPS. "I don't see anything. We should be there." She tried to hold up the LPS for Dayna to see, but the wind staggered her sideways.

Dayna hugged close to Akilah's ear. "It's buried!" She withdrew her razor. Holding it with both hands shaking, she fumbled for the switch.

The beam shot out, almost slicing Akilah, then steadied and began to bore a hole. Melted ice bubbled and froze away from the hot beam, leaving a narrow sloping tunnel that descended, then stopped.

Dayna played her flashlight into the razor's path. "I've hit rock or something."

Akilah pulled out her own light and examined the end of the tunnel. "It looks like concrete. Maybe we hit a wall."

She sat and slid feet first into the tunnel. "It's concrete all right!" Akilah could hardly contain her excitement. "I'm going to melt along it and see if I come to a window or door."

She directed the razor to the interface of the wall and the ice. Liquid puddled at her feet and quickly congealed, forcing her to raise her boots as she shone the beam ahead of her.

Dayna played out the rope. "I can't see you. Be careful."

"I'm through!"

Melted ice at her feet flowed away from her through an opening in the concrete. "I can see the inside."

"I'm coming down."

Akilah flashed her light into a dark space. *This is too good to be true*. She slid through the opening and dropped to a dry floor. Out of the shrieking wind, an eerie silence descended on her.

Caught in her light close up, chunks of concrete lay scattered randomly, casting darting shadows. Part of the collapsed roof. Its slab tilted to the floor at one end of the room. Remnants of what must have been roots, petrified or deep-frozen, snaked web-like across the floor.

Opposite walls defined an area twenty meters square. Along the perimeter lay regularly spaced rectangular openings for what must have been windows. Ice poured through them, hit the floor and froze into a white caricature of alluvial plains. Hoar frost on the concrete sent rainbows of light from her flash dancing about the room.

"This is amazing," Akilah said.

Dayna came up beside her. "Okay, you found it. Let's get back before we freeze to death."

"It's ten degrees warmer in here. We've got time. I want to see the tunnel."

66

"What tunnel?"

"You haven't read your scripture?"

Dayna sighed heavily. "Give me a break. It's enough that your father dumps on me at every turn. I don't need it coming from you."

"I'm sorry. In ancient times, a tunnel was bored through the plateau to facilitate travel east to west."

"So. Big deal."

"Well, it was a big deal. Real humans built the tunnel and this building, a research center, ten thousand years ago to study the first sighting of the Shepherd. She gazed around at the crumbling walls. "Sedroth walked these spaces. It was here that he dispatched the player Cathcar."

"Okay, it's important." She played here flash over the floor. "What's that?" She pointed to a square hole in the floor to one side of the room, giving onto an inky blackness.

"I think we're on a second level. That opening must have been for stairs leading to the ground level." Akilah walked over to the opening and directed her light. "There's a floor below this one. Let's investigate."

"How do you expect to get up after you're down?"

"Either you come with me and give me a boost or if you stay here, you can give me a hand up." Akilah sat and dangled her legs over the edge, then gripped it with both hands, extended and dropped to the floor below.

With obvious reluctance, Dayna followed.

"If this is the ground floor, then there must be a passage that leads to the tunnel below." Akilah played her light along the wall and stopped at a dark opening. "There."

"Sedroth only knows what they were thinking when they built this place," Dayna said.

"There wasn't a Sedroth when they built this place." Akilah entered a confining passageway, comfortably wide enough for one person. The darkness pressed around her, cut nearby by the white light of her flash. As she moved, the dark seemed to part, then flow back to a suffocating nothingness.

A nervous fear, or was it excitement, numbed her knees, making her feel weak. *Forward.* Her hand went out to her side of the passageway and trailed on the rough stone wall. With the light bobbing ahead, she felt her way slowly along the down-sloping corridor. Pock marks lined the rock wall at hip level where anchors for handrails must have rusted away long ago. In front of her, the darkness loomed, belying an indeterminable depth, swallowing her light. She stopped at a crumbling edge of concrete and swept her light down a shaft.

Dayna peered over her shoulder, almost tipping her into the void. "Sorry. Looks like this housed some sort of mechanism to raise and lower people and supplies between the floor of the tunnel and the floors above."

Akilah swung her light to her right. "The corridor continues over there." She continued along the passageway, following her light to another edge.

Dayna came up beside her, this time grabbing Akilah's sleeve as though to ensure she didn't fall. "Be careful."

Akilah shivered. "I feel Sedroth's presence everywhere about me. We are treading hallowed ground. The great evil, *Zug*, must be having fits."

"You and your father are too preoccupied with evil. Life is what it is. We must simply--"

"Stow it, Dayna. You've said that a hundred times before. I'll agree to put Sedroth and *Zug* to one side if you promise to concentrate on the moment." Akilah shone her light into a vast darkness. Nothing. She removed her glove and reached into a chest pocket to withdraw a flare. She broke the seal and, holding it away from her, pulled the activator strip.

A harsh sputtering light emitted from the stick. She turned her head away as she drew the flare back and heaved it into the void.

The flare tumbled end over end, casting quick sweeps of shadow and light on a rough rock ceiling and distant walls.

"It's huge," Dayna whispered. "Must be eight or ten meters floor to ceiling, maybe ten across. I gauge we're about four meters up. I hope you're not thinking of going down?"

"To think Sedroth stood here seeing what we are seeing." Akilah pointed to her left as the flare sputtered on the ground. "That's the blasted tunnel entrance the evil Cathcar dug through, and there--" She pointed a hundred and eighty degrees right. "--is the other sealed entrance, which became submerged beneath the lake."

"They're both submerged in ice now. Gives me the willies."

The flare dimmed, then winked out. The darkness that enveloped them was total.

"We'll be able to move the gear into the outer room." Akilah could have been talking to no one at all it was so dark. "Once we've got a way to access the tunnel, we can move it all down there...Dayna?"

"I'm right here."

Akilah turned on her flash. She felt Dayna's breath on her cheek. "I...I'll feel better knowing we've got a defensible space. There's no way we'd survive in the open."

"Time to go." Dayna grasped Akilah's hand and started back up the corridor.

"It's okay, Dayna, I can manage." Akilah withdrew her hand, but still felt the warmth of Dayna's grip.

They retraced their steps to the outside. Miraculously, the wind had stopped, and the sky had cleared.

"What a beautiful night," Akilah said.

Dayna came up close and with a shiver wrapped her arm around Akilah's shoulder. "So beautiful, yet so deadly. We're still stuck here."

"But we've always been stuck. Maybe this is for the best. You can be sure Cardassin knows we're here. He's not about to leave us alone. Better to go out with a fight."

Dayna lay her head aside Akilah's. "If it has to be this way, then I'm okay with it. At least I'm with you."

Akilah pulled away and put her hand on Dayna's cheek. It was wet with tears. "Poor Dayna.

If it makes you feel any better, I'm glad you're here, too."

They hiked back to the steps.

The wind picked up, depositing powdery snow.

"The steps have become slippery. We should rope together," Akilah said.

Dayna led off as Akilah looped the line around her waist, braced herself and played it out.

Dayna disappeared from view in the swirling flakes.

A yelp through the wind.

The rope raced through Akilah's gloved hands until she managed to slow and stop it. Dayna's weight on the other end threatened to drag Akilah over the edge. A moment later the load lightened. "What happened? Are you all right?" Akilah shouted.

"I slipped. I think I twisted my ankle."

"Secure yourself. I'm coming down." Akilah stepped down carefully, coiling the rope as she went. At a mid-elevation ledge she found Dayna, who sat with her back to the wall and rubbed her ankle.

"Can you walk?" Akilah asked, kneeling in front of her.

"I don't think it's too bad. Maybe I can work it out." She stood wincing and leaned on Akilah. "This is a fine mess."

"Take your time." She went first, bearing most of Dayna's weight on her back. It was slow progress, but they reached the bottom without further mishap.

Dayna tested her foot on the level ground. "It feels better. Ironically, the cold helps."

As Akilah started off toward the crashed Truman Light, the white swirl of ice crystals parted for an instant, flooding the area with moonlight. She gaped at a shadowy figure, five meters away.

"A man," Akilah whispered.

"Where?"

The wind gusted and came around.

"He was standing right there."

Dayna cupped her hands on either side of her eyes and tried to peer into the wind. "Are you sure?"

"Sure I'm sure.

"A mutant? Out here, at night?"

Akilah took out her ice razor. "Kanapoi's not that far on the other side of the plateau and mutants do go out at night."

"Not unless they're doped to attack," Dayna said. "Otherwise, they'd rather stay in their cozy little hovels."

"A primitive, then."

"We'll have to ask Doctor Rasmussen. But he's never mentioned primitives being in the area."

Akilah looked anxiously at Dayna. "We'd better get back."

***

The morning sun pierced one of the view ports, auguring a clear day. The wind, which had shrieked through the night, had stopped. With the direct sunshine and the laboring generators, the temperature inside the Truman Light had risen to two degrees Celsius. The walls of the passenger compartment gleamed slick with frozen condensate from the shuddering Maraia.

Akilah eased back as Dayna stirred where she had curled up and leaned against Akilah's chest. "We better get going." She stroked Dayna's hair.

Dayna sat up and stretched, her eyes squinched shut, her mouth drawn in an open yawn. She scrubbed her fingers through her hair and smiled, looking at Akilah. "I dreamt we were together in a warm place with liquid water, swimming naked in a heated pool."

A pleasant shiver coursed through Akilah at the thought, then it was replaced with an anxious darkness. "The only place you'll find that is in Cardassin's compound."

"We could have it here if *TrueMen* weren't so adverse to using nano-assemblers."

"My father would never permit it. He's got everyone believing assemblers are the source of all evil."

"Nothing in the myths says assemblers are evil. After all, *TrueMen* developed them. They're a tool. You just have to be careful not to abuse them."

"That's probably what he's worried about."

"But they can build anything you can conceive of."

Akilah looked askance at Dayna.

"Well, I know," Dayna said, "not everything. Obviously, they have their built-in fail-safes. Like, you can't get them to produce a nuclear weapon or anything. Just industrial scale--"

"Dayna, I know all that. So does Father. Enough with the things nano-assemblers can do."

Rasmussen entered the compartment.

Akilah distanced herself from Dayna. "You look worried, Father. Is something else bothering you besides being stranded here?" Akilah couldn't suppress her sarcasm. It wasn't that she disrespected her father, but there were times like this when his own preoccupations seemed to supercede those of the remaining Maraia.

Rasmussen gave her a sharp look. "I'm sorry I was asleep when you returned last night. What did you discover?"

"Lots of things." She thought to be coy, but when Father's face contorted in displeasure, she decided to play it straight. "We found a way up the escarpment. It's steep and slippery, but it works. Once we were on top of the plateau, we walked north, looking for the ruin. It was about two hundred meters from where we climbed to the top of the plateau."

"Did you go in?"

"How could we not? The ruin is under three meters of ice. We bored down. It was tight, but we squeezed through. There are two stories to the ruin, though the roof over the upper floor has collapsed at one end. The walls are intact all around."

"And the enclave?"

"We didn't get to the enclave or see a way in. We followed a passageway through the rock to a tunnel overlook. Maybe a four meter drop. We didn't try to descend, but we can rig something. The shaft adjacent to the end of the passageway is intact. It was very dark. Our flare didn't burn long enough for us to locate the entrance to the enclave."

Rubbing his hands together, Rasmussen looked upward, an ethereal expression on his face. "I'm assuming the only way into the tunnel is still from above."

"Exactly. It's a perfectly defensible space. Both ends are blocked as you've told us many times before. One can only surmise that the western end leads directly to frozen Lake Turk."

"So much potential." Rasmussen raised his hands in jubilation. "But there's no way to know if Cardassin has pillaged the enclave and destroyed it, or it remains intact."

"If it is not," Akilah said, "then building A4-Ni is going to difficult if not impossible."

Rasmussen's expression changed, a cloud blocking the sun. "There's no reason to despair. We are here. We've suffered no serious injuries...well, there's Jason, but that happened before we crashed. Most of our gear is intact. And now we've located the ruin. For a people who never contemplated coming out of this thing alive, I think we're in pretty good shape."

"Speaking of Jason--" Akilah crossed her hands across her chest, a *TrueMen* sign of Sedroth. "--what do you intend to do with his body? You can't just leave him sealed in the crew's quarters."

Rasmussen repeated the sign. "I don't want to sound cold, child, but what's the difference? Once we are settled in the ruin, we'll never return to this craft. Sealing him in the quarters is the same as placing him in an icy grave--and a lot safer for us."

"We saw a man out there last night," Dayna blurted. "At least Akilah saw him."

Rasmussen gave Dayna a lidded look, then turned to Akilah. "I think we're finished with the subject of Jason's disposition."

Akilah nodded.

"A man?" Rasmussen ignored Dayna and directed his question to Akilah. "What did he look like?"

Impulsive Dayna. Would she never learn to keep her mouth shut? "I only got a glimpse of him," Akilah said. "He was much shorter and stockier than Maraia men. We wondered if he could be a primitive."

"To my knowledge all the primitives in this area have been exterminated by Cardassin."

"God, this place is an abomination," Akilah said.

"I'm not going to argue with you, child. What's done is done. The sooner we get to work, the sooner we'll be able to look for the guardian. The sooner we'll build A4-Ni." Rasmussen closed the buckles on his coat. "I'll see you outside."

He shoved back the sliding door, forcing it until its stay engaged, then strode up the hallway toward the control room.

Akilah stared at his receding back. "I'm hungry!"

He spun around. "You shouldn't have slept so long. The others are all outside working. But there are energy bars in that box over there. We are on rations. One each for the time being." He walked down the hall and disappeared into the control room.

Akilah gave Dayna a hand up. She grabbed two energy bars and offered one to Dayna.

"That wasn't fair," Dayna said.

"He's under a lot of stress."

"That's a lame excuse. He carries on as though this were some survival exercise without any consequences. The mutants are going to discover us. Then we'll have to deal with Cardassin directly. It's only a matter of time."

Akilah unwrapped her energy bar and took a bite. "I feel like we've all been issued a death sentence."

"The good Doctor could at least have thanked us for finding the ruin."

"You don't know Father," Akilah said. "He has never thanked me or anyone else for anything in his life."

"Yet he's revered."

Akilah wasn't about to get into an argument with Dayna about Rasmussen. Dayna wasn't a *TrueMen*, so Dayna wouldn't understand what her father had accomplished, how he had held the remaining Maraia together through shear strength of spirit.

"We'd better join the others," Akilah said. "They'll think we're slackers even though we got to bed late." Akilah headed up the corridor, then stopped to check that Dayna had unlatched the sliding door and let it slide home.

Dayna gave her a palms-up as though she resented being suspected of forgetfulness.

Akilah stepped across the control room and lowered herself through the bulkhead opening, then dropped to the ground.

Rasmussen stood a couple of meters from where she landed, almost as though he had planned to be there. He turned a wizened look on her.

I'll be damned to Zug if I'll let him bully me. "What's the plan, Father?" Akilah stared at him.

Rasmussen brushed ice crystals from his sleeves. "Ferral put together a sledge from one of the doors. With two pulling, it should slide over the ice without difficulty. I estimate four or five trips to transport all our supplies to the escarpment. From there, we can winch the stuff up to the top. I've sent Warren and Lorry on ahead to enlarge a way into the ruin."

Akilah shaded her eyes. The distant outcropping loomed brilliantly in the low, angled light. Though she tried, she couldn't pinpoint Warren or Lorry. The snow swirled low across the ice surface, making anything shorter than four meters impossible to see. "Where's Karin?"

"Here." Karin came to the side of the craft where a gaping hole, minus its door, led to the cargo hold. She positioned a container at the edge.

"The blue containers are food stuff," Rasmussen said. "I thought we'd get them over to the ruins first."

"Looks like you have everything under control," Akilah said.

"As well as can be expected."

Akilah finished her energy bar and brushed crumbs from her gloved hands. "I'll go with Ferral. Dayna can help Karin."

Dayna dropped from the fuselage. "Did I hear my name?"

"I'm going with the sledge to the ruin," Akilah said. "You stay here and help Father and Karin."

Dayna stared, a hurt look on her face.

Without waiting for a response from Dayna, Akilah pulled goggles down over her eyes and nodded to Ferral, who had been standing by, holding two rope harnesses. She shrugged her shoulders into one of them, and when Ferral indicated he was ready, they both pulled.

The sledge resisted, then broke from the ice with a loud crack. Once it was free, it slid easily.

When they were out of earshot, Ferral glanced at her. "I sensed some tension between you and Doctor Rasmussen?"

"Father and I have a difference of opinion about the positive aspects of being here."

Ferral smiled. "Hey, I understand your disagreement. But there is an upside to all of this."

"Please, Ferral, I know where you are coming from. But he's my father. What am I to do? There are times I can hate him for his stubbornness."

"I'll not argue that. I've never gotten him to consider alternatives."

"He's driven." Akilah leaned into her harness hoping Ferral would leave the conversation alone.

"If you care about the remaining Maraia," Ferral said. "Then you'll help me find a way to convince him he is wasting his time."

Akilah stopped pulling and faced Ferral. "I think it's a bit late for that. We're all committed."

"I don't think we are all as committed as you think. Doctor Rasmussen jumped this adventure onto all of us at an emotional moment, burying Carol and Pierce. What was anyone going to do under those circumstances? Say they didn't want to continue to be a part of the Maraia?"

"I admit he bullied everyone, but 4-Ni is our only hope."

"I have always had other hopes, and you know it. At this rate the only thing we are committed to is dying for a useless cause."

There was no arguing with Ferral. Akilah shook her head and leaned into the harness, stifling further conversation. She squinted as bright sunlight reflected off the mirror-like ice. It offered some heat, but blinded her, creating psychedelic patterns against her closed lids.

After fifteen minutes, they came to the base of the escarpment and met up with Warren.

"Lorry's at the ruin," Warren said. "You want to haul this stuff up now?"

Akilah unbuckled the harness and dropped to her knees, breathing heavily. "Are you kidding? We've got maybe four more loads to haul. I suggest we get everything over here by mid-day, then hoist it up continuously."

"Sounds like a good plan." Warren indicated the ice wall. "I've deepened the steps. Climbing should be easier."

"After you." Akilah stepped back and let Warren and Ferral precede her up the icy staircase.

At the top, she looked around. The view stretched to the horizon in all directions. "I didn't realize the view from here was so extensive. All I saw last night were stars."

The crash site was clearly visible a kilometer away. The Truman Light rested at the end of a long scar in the ice but was otherwise surrounded by a frozen plain, flat and featureless. In the distant south, a white cinder cone mountain rose to break the line of the horizon.

Akilah pointed. "Is that Mt. Ken?"

"The same," Warren said. "Nairob is line of sight to the mountain about five hundred kilometers farther south."

"Too far to walk."

"You never give up, do you?" Ferral said.

Akilah gave him a half smile.

"Come on." Warren struck out, following a faint path of footprints in the dusting of snow.

Up ahead, a mound of frozen snow bulged from the otherwise flat surface, marking the location of the ruin. On the east side of the mound a gently sloping path in the ice descended toward an opening to the lower floor of the ruin. The dark hole contrasted against the smooth white exterior. Steam drifted from the hole and dissipated in the freezing air.

"Lorry's been busy." Akilah said.

Melted ice from the excavation had flowed over the edge of the escarpment and refrozen on its way down into an icefall.

Ferral stepped to the opening and guided his hand along the edge. "Looks like the first thing we'll need is a door."

Lorry emerged from the open doorway and switched off a light strapped around her forehead. "It's dark in there, but truly amazing. I feel transported knowing how old this place is and that it still exists."

"Dayna and I felt the same sense of awe," Akilah said.

"The inside is clean, just like you reported. It's a bit musty, hoar frost everywhere. Once we get a door installed, it shouldn't be too hard to keep the place warm. At least above zero."

Akilah acknowledged Lorry's housekeeping list with a nod, then turned from the entrance. She stepped to the edge of the plateau and shaded her eye against the glare. The midday sun beat down from a cloudless sky, dazzling, turning everything white.

Her eyes teared. She waited for them to adjust, then took out her binoculars and scanned the plain, coming to rest on two figures moving slowly away from the wreck.

"Who in Sedroth's name is that?" She handed the glasses to Ferral.

He peered through the binoculars. "Hard to tell at this distance. They're obviously two of ours, but what are they doing walking east?"

Chapter Four

When Akilah wanted to race back to the flyer, Ferral insisted they take the empty sledge with them.

"Are you crazy?" Akilah clenched her fists at her sides. "That's probably my father out there."

Ferral humped his shoulders into his harness. "Come on. It won't take much longer and will save us having to fetch it later."

Akilah shrugged into her harness and began pulling, trying to dissipate her anger. At the Truman Light, Akilah ripped off her harness and ran the last few meters to the broken hull. "Karin!"

She rounded the bulkhead. "They went exploring!" A frantic frown crumpled her face.

Akilah grabbed her by the shoulders. "Who's idea was that?"

"Doctor Rasmussen's." Karin twisted herself free, seemingly hysterical. "I told him it was a bad idea but he wouldn't listen. Dayna only went with him to make sure he didn't get into trouble. What are we to do now?" Tears started in her eyes.

Akilah slung and arm around Karin's shoulders and gave her a hug. "Calm down." Karin hadn't been herself since the crash and was obviously distraught. Now, she seemed to be bothered by every little thing, and when events got too complex, she simply broke down and cried.

Karin nodded and swallowed hard. "I was in the control room. Doctor Rasmussen came in and wanted the LPS. When I asked him why, he became angry. He said he wanted to pinpoint our position on the ancient maps." Karin's eyes stared wildly as she turned toward the Plateau. "But there's the plateau. What's to position?"

She's about to lose it. "Karin!"

Her gaze drifted back to Akilah. "He said he wanted to locate the river that cut a gorge through this area. He said primitives used to fish it. He was going to look for primitives!"

Akilah had a passing thought that her mention of primitives earlier had somehow set Father onto his present course of action. "Easy, girl. Was that the Kerio River he was looking for?"

Karin gulped a breath. "K...Kerio, I think so. He said the river flowed north into a lake."

God damn him. Akilah looked skyward. *What to do?* She walked over to Ferral. "Karin will take my place. You and she will continue hauling. I'm going to get them back."

"Maybe I should go after them," Ferral said.

"Thanks, but Father won't listen to you. I'm not even sure he'll listen to me."

Akilah grabbed an ice axe and a coil of rope, attached it to her belt and struck out after the two figures bobbing in the distance. She'd catch up easily given Father's bum knee. The stubborn fool. She hated it when he hunkered down on some trivial point, trivial to everyone else, but a big deal to him. She couldn't figure why finding primitives would be so important now. The ancient river was even more irrelevant to securing their safety. It was less than irrelevant, it was a dangerous aside.

Akilah came within shouting distance. "Dayna!"

Dayna stopped and turned around. She held tight to the rope that attached her to Rasmussen.

He didn't acknowledge the restraint at first. His boots pawed the snow-covered ice before he gave up and looked over his shoulder to see what held him.

"Akilah," he hailed.

She stomped up to him through twenty centimeters of impeding snow. "Where are you going?"

"No need to be so demanding. I'm looking for the Kerio River. It flows north to Lake Turkana and was a favorite fishing spot for primitives. I think you may have spotted one. And if they still exist, I want to find them."

"The man we saw could have been anybody...a mutant. What use can primitives possibly be to us now?"

"I know, I know. I have always discounted the primitives. In retrospect, I should have sought them out. After all they are or at least were able to survive out here, in these harsh conditions, while we Maraia toasted our feet in the Maraia enclave. If Cardassin hasn't exterminated them all by now, then they might come in handy...I'm simply looking ahead to unforeseen consequences."

"Can't it wait? To my mind we have far more pressing matters to attend to than searching out the remote possibility that primitives still exist and that their existence could possibly enhance our own."

"Do you always have to second guess me?" Rasmussen's hand shook as he fumbled with the LPS. "If the river exists, it shouldn't be far. I'd say about a kilometer in that direction." He pointed east.

"We can explore later."

"But we are almost there." His look was matter-of-fact, as if what he was about to do should seem obvious to anyone. "Are you coming with me or not?" Rasmussen looked from the indicator signal on the LPS to where it pointed. When Akilah made no move to join him, he smiled grimly and started off again.

Sedroth be damned. If Father goes alone I'm to blame if something happens. If I go with him, I'm to blame for not stopping him. Damn, damn, damn.

"Does this gorge really exist?" Dayna asked.

"Gorge, lake? How do I know? It's been a thousand years since anyone with any cognitive sense has seen it flowing. For much of the time that the Maraia were here, it's been covered in ice."

Dayna hide a smirk on her face with her hand, then started after Rasmussen, who slipped drunkenly across the ice with the LPS held out in front of him like a dousing rod.

Akilah followed them in silence.

Rasmussen stopped periodically to check his orientation.

"I think we must be very close," he called over his shoulder, his voice rising with excitement. The wind picked up, swirling ice crystals around them, higher and higher, until they were enveloped in a whiteout.

"Let me clip onto you." Akilah played out her coil of rope, looking ahead to the whitewashed figure of Dayna and her father. *That's all we need. To become separated.*

Dayna took the rope and attached it to her belt.

Rasmussen tugged on Dayna's rope. "What's holding us up?"

"Coming Doctor." Dayna shrugged.

He took another look at the LPS and stepped ahead boldly. His foot stumped through a crust of ice. As he stared at his leg, post-holed to the knee, a sharp crack split the air and a mass of ice and snow dropped out from under him.

Before Akilah could react she was yanked, then tumbled forward, dragged through snow, and dropped in a freefall. Seared in her mind was the faint image of Father disappearing in a shower of ice crystals followed by Dayna with her arms flailing. Now she was falling. *To where?*

Akilah came to an abrupt halt on a cushion of ice and snow. *A ledge.* She stabbed desperately with her ice axe. Just soft snow. She stabbed again.

This time the ax bit into the gray translucent ice and held.

She locked her arms around the haft of the axe. The rope clipped to her waist snapped taut, dragging at the steel ring coupled to her belt. For a moment she thought she would be torn in two by the combined weight of her father and Dayna.

Ice shards pin-wheeled, then clattered onto surfaces below out of sight. An eerie quiet descended, broken by a low moan from Rasmussen and the unnerving sound of rushing water farther down.

She looked up. Ten meters to the surface. Then around. A ledge. *Thank Sedroth.*

"Dayna!" Akilah prayed her ice ax would hold.

"I'm okay! Hang on!"

The ax shifted. "I can't."

"There's another ledge just below the Doctor. I'm going to cut him free and drop him onto it."

"Is he all right?"

"I can't tell."

The weight tearing at Akilah suddenly lessened, followed by a muffled thud. A moment later Dayna clawed her way up beside Akilah and lay next to her, breathing heavily.

"It's a wide ledge. I don't think he'll fall off."

Akilah peered overhead. Through swirls of wind blow snow, the sky shown a deep blue. "It's a wonder we weren't killed in the fall."

"How the hell are we going to get out? The wall slopes inward. We could never carve steps. Do you even have your razor?"

Akilah returned the accusing look. "I suppose you brought yours. I was hauling supplies when I spotted you and Father on this ill-conceived venture."

"It *wasn't* my idea!"

This bickering isn't helping. "I'm sorry. I know it wasn't your idea, and I know Father can be stubborn. Let's try to get to him."

Akilah reset the ice axe and added Dayna's ax for good measure. After tying the rope around both axes, she played the rope over the side. The rope reached to the ledge on which Rasmussen lay sprawled. "I'm going down." She threaded the line through rings clipped to her waist.

Dayna nodded and coiled the other end of the line around her back, wrapping it around both wrists. She braced her boots in a groove in the ice. "Ready."

As Dayna played out the line, Akilah eased over the edge and rappelled down the ice wall.

She reached the ledge. "I'm down!" she called up to Dayna.

Rasmussen lay immobile two meters from her, face down. His legs bent crookedly under his body. His left arm thrashed back and forth as he moaned in obvious pain.

Please don't die. I'm not ready for this.

Akilah rushed to his side. She stilled his arm and eased him onto his side, then straightened his legs.

He screamed. "Sedroth help me! They're broken." He ground his teeth. Tears streamed across his wrinkled cheeks.

"How about the rest of you?" She pulled at the double-stick closing the front of his jumpsuit and felt his chest and abdomen.

"That hurts," he said weakly as she moved her hand over his side.

Akilah felt a hard knot beneath the surface of his skin. "You're bleeding internally."

Rasmussen's face was gray and drawn. "I'm done for. Leave me here and save yourself."

"I'm not sure I can do that, even if I wanted to."

He gazed blankly at the bright spot of sky overhead. "Where am I?"

"You've fallen into a crevasse." She looked up. "I'm coming back up!" she called to Dayna.

"All right, I've got you."

Akilah climbed up the wall of ice.

Dayna helped her over the edge and they both sat, catching their breath and gazing at the rim of ice above. It seemed so out of reach, yet so inviting, a smooth arcing edge defining a blue, snow flurried sky.

"We're screwed," Dayna said. "They'll never find us."

"Ferral knows where I went. He'll find us."

Ice crystals streamed off the edge and floated in a glistening cascade toward them.

"Ferral?" Akilah shouted. She put hand to forehead and squinted at the bright sky.

"Somehow, I don't think that's Ferral," Dayna said apprehensively.

"Then who the hell is it?"

Something clattered over the edge of ice, fell in a rapid unrolling, and ended in a snap a meter above the ledge they were on.

"It's a rope ladder!" Dayna grabbed the bottom rung and pulled. It came on for another meter, then stopped. She leaned her weight onto it. "It holds."

"I'm not going to quibble with where it came from," Akilah said. "I'll stay with Father. You go up for help."

Dayna nodded and climbed the ladder. A moment later she gained the top and disappeared over the side. Her head reappeared. "There're boot prints all around here, but I don't see anybody. The end of the ladder is anchored into refrozen ice melt."

"Just get help. We'll figure this out later."

"What if this guy comes back after you?"

"I'm willing to take my chances."

Dayna disappeared, leaving Akilah alone on the ledge with her father below her. She tested the rope ladder. It still held firm. She checked again her rope around the ice axes, then rappelled down slick ice to where her father lay, looking like death.

"We're going to be all right," she whispered into his ear.

He didn't respond.

Great Sedroth, what have you gotten us into?

***

She stroked his forehead, her gaze unfocused, pushing out thoughts of death. *Damn these icy confines.* Gray walls closed in. The river's surging tumble masked any sounds that might have come from above.

Across the chasm something moved.

Akilah scanned back and forth, but all was still. Only three dark holes in the ice wall opposite. She played her flash over the holes. About a meter and a half in diameter, they sunk into the ice and curved out of sight.

Tunnels?

Her flash caught a pair of eyes, reflecting red in the light. They showed ever so briefly before whatever held them ducked back out of sight.

She shivered, realizing that the whole time she had been sitting there, someone or something had

91

been watching her. Thank Sedroth the tunnels terminated on the other side of the chasm.

"Hello!" A voice from above.

Ferral peered over the rim of the crevasse, his face and white bandage highlighted in ruddy orange from the setting sun.

"I'm here," she called grimly, thinking that being saved didn't necessarily improve her overall situation. She moved closer to the edge of the ice shelf and waved her arms above her head, making herself more visible in the gloomy depth. "We're still alive."

"I'm lowering a straight board. Can you strap Doctor Rasmussen onto it? Should I come down?"

"I can manage," she called back.

"Where'd this rope ladder come from?"

"Later. Let's get Father out of here first." She glanced over her shoulder at the tunnels, but all was quiet. The straight board tilted over the edge and descended slowly. It banged off the first ledge, setting free a shower of crystals, then after some jiggling by Ferral, it pitched over the side and lowered to where she could grab it.

"Okay, Father, time to move."

She lay the board parallel to his body, rocked him gently toward her and shoved the board under his back. He lay with his eyes fixed in a distant stare. His breath came in ragged catches. The great man looked so helpless, she almost cried. But it wouldn't do for the daughter of *the* Doctor Rasmussen to show emotion.

He'd pretty much bred that out of her. In a way he had to. How else could she have coped with having her mother disappear one awful night during a mutant attack? That they took her alive was odd. Maybe a show of force. Maybe a warning to the head of the *TrueMen* that if he didn't capitulate, his daughter would be next.

After arranging Rasmussen's broken legs as best she could, she buckled straps over him and cinched them tight.

He moaned.

Akilah jerked on the rope. "He's in."

The rope drew taut, and Rasmussen rose.

Akilah adjusted the ropes to level the board, then guided Rasmussen's free-hanging body away from the sides of the crevasse. She watched helplessly as he rose straight up, his lonely form silhouetted against the brilliant sky.

After assuring herself that he was safe, she stepped to the edge of the ledge and peered down. Dimly, in the deep recess, water churned north toward the distant lake, lifting a cool breeze on faintly humid air. She shivered. *What would have become of us if we had fallen all the way down.*

A closer look at the tunnels showed that they widened onto platforms. Could these be used by whomever dwelled there as places to fish the river below? Were primitives, if that is what they were, so clever?

"Akilah, I'm dropping a rope for you," Ferral called.

She could have climbed back up to the rope ladder using her own rope but welcomed the assist from above. She pressed against the icy wall. "Okay. Clear."

A coiled rope snaked through the space overhead and plopped at her feet. She wove it around her legs and mid-section. "I'm ready."

Immediately, the rope went taut and she felt herself lifted toward the opening above. A wonderful sense of freedom from impending doom swept over her. She leaned back in the harness as she entered a shaft of sunlight angling from above.

"You look fit to be tied," Ferral said as she came clear.

Akilah smiled at Ferral's awkward attempt at a pun. "I am. It was dreadful down there. Cold. With all that rushing water. How's Father doing?"

"We won't know until we get him back to the base, but I'm glad you're safe."

Akilah studied Ferral. "You care?"

Ferral shoved his ever present dark glasses up onto his forehead. "Yeah, I care. I really do."

That's a lot coming from Ferral. Akilah tried to stifle her surprise, knowing it showed anyway.

Ferral's features clouded. Then his eyes narrowed.

Akilah had seen the expression before. A prelude to things more sinister. This time she was at the receiving end. But the cloud seemed to pass.

"I'm sorry," he said. "It wasn't my place to--"

"Akilah!" Dayna rushed into Akilah and hugged her. "I worried leaving you behind, alone. Are you all right?"

"Yes, thank Sedroth." For once Dayna's exaggerated attention was welcomed. *A soft edge showing on Ferral?* "We should get Father to the ruin."

94

With a studied silence, Akilah and Ferral transferred Rasmussen to the sledge, while Dayna pulled the assorted equipment together.

"You say the rope ladder dropped from nowhere?" Ferral seemed to be trying to climb out of a character he was no where familiar with. "It was held in refrozen ice. Someone had an ice razor to do that."

"We don't know where it came from," Akilah said.

"I found boot prints," Ferral said. "None were ours."

"Akilah and I saw a man when we were investigating the plateau." Dayna shot Akilah a quick glance. "It could have been the same person. What do you think, Akilah?"

Thanks Dayna, just what I wanted. "Could have been." She hated herself for being drawn into this exchange. "While I was waiting to be rescued, something moved on the other side of the crevasse. Three tunnels led back into the ice. I swear, someone was watching me from one of them."

"The Doctor thought all primitive in this area had been exterminated by Cardassin," Ferral said. "I hope it wasn't a mutant." He finished knotting crude harnesses and handed them to Akilah and Dayna. "With three of us pulling it should be easy. The sooner we get back to the ruin the better I'll feel."

That caught Akilah's attention. She looked at him with concern. "You expect an attack?"

"What do you think?"

***

95

The frozen escarpment loomed large, its white face shooting upward, taunting, as if to ask, *how will you climb me with that broken man*?

Despite three pulling the sledge, Akilah was exhausted. She collapsed next to Dayna at the base of the snow-blown glistening wall. "I don't think I could have pulled another step." Akilah cupped handfuls of crystalline flakes and pressed them against her brow.

The sun shown as a pale disk, barely discernible above the horizon, giving no encouragement for warmth from its rays.

Dayna squinted in the direction of the fading light. Her jumpsuit caught the dying rays and stood out, an orange relief within a gray waste. "It's getting late. I can already feel the temperature dropping."

"Anyone checked the doctor?" Ferral stood over them, gloved hands tucked under his armpits.

Akilah crawled over to the sledge and felt for a pulse.

Ferral peered over her shoulder. "Is he still alive?"

"Are you suggesting our job would be simplified if he were dead?" As soon as Akilah spoke, she regretted it. Ferral didn't deserve that. *No, maybe Ferral did.* Sometimes it was hard to discern what he meant, but the first assumption was that his actions were self-serving.

"Of course not." Ferral looked away. His breath puffed in clouds, but he said nothing.

It's just like Ferral. Absorb a cynical remark and let it fester. "I'm sorry."

96

Ferral shrugged. "I was misunderstood."

Akilah nodded. *I can see through you, Ferral. You don't give a shit.* "You know my father is tough as nails. He's been through worse."

"We'd better get started." Dayna rolled to one knee and stood.

Ferral looked relieved, whether from the opportunity to get going or from Dayna's distraction from an uncomfortable confrontation with Akilah.

"I suggest we take it in stages." He unwound the harnesses methodically and re-tied the ropes to the front and back of the straight board. "Dayna and I can go up first. We'll pull the board and Doctor Rasmussen up level to us. Akilah, you can take this third rope and see that he doesn't bang against the side."

Akilah eased herself up to a standing position. "I can help pull Father up if one of you would rather stay here and guide him."

Ferral dropped the ropes and walked off a couple of meters.

"It's okay," Dayna said to Akilah. "You're exhausted. You don't have to prove anything to us."

With a sense of guilty relief, Akilah took the rope.

"Come on Ferral," Dayna called. "Stop being such an asshole."

Ferral and Dayna climbed the steps to a small landing about three meters above.

"Ready?" Dayna asked.

Akilah stepped back from the escarpment and dug her boots into the snow. "Ready."

The board lifted slowly while she pulled on the guide rope, keeping the board away from the wall. Once the board came abreast of the landing, Dayna secured it, then she and Ferral climbed the next segment.

Akilah came up to where her father lay. "We're almost there. Hang on," she whispered in his ear.

Rasmussen groaned, but didn't otherwise seem to know what was happening.

By the time they reached the summit. The sun was long gone. A deepening gloom surrounded them and a cold wind had kicked up.

After checking Father to see he was still breathing, Akilah slumped in the snow. Her arms ached. Her legs ached. Icicles of sweat formed off her brow, hung from her cheeks and chin. She brushed absently at them.

Ferral looked at her with disdain. "I'll go on ahead and see that the way is safe. I won't be long."

"Thank you, Ferral, for all you have done."

He stopped and looked at her with surprise, then his lips drew into a determined line. "Don't thank me. From what I'm told, Doctor Rasmussen is very important to the future of the Maraia."

Despite her exhaustion, Akilah felt the sting of his rebuke. She was sure he didn't mean it that way, or maybe he did. That was Ferral. Despite his attempts to censor what came out of his mouth, Akilah thought there was little filtering going on. She supposed he must think the same of her.

"Your word has been heard and taken to heart," she said levelly.

"If Doctor Rasmussen falters, the others all think you will take his place."

Yes, what if Father were to die? "Jeez, Ferral, Father's not dead yet and you're already thinking ahead?"

He studied her grimly, but said nothing..

"I might," she said, addressing his assursion, "but not in a way that you might approve."

Ferral smiled weakly, no, maybe a smirk. Akilah had trouble discerning his reaction in the dim light.

"Then let us hope Doctor Rasmussen doesn't falter," he said.

A wave of nausea swept over her, brought on by the threat to her father and Ferral's cynical remark. But she was too exhausted to retort. Let Ferral think what he would. He didn't matter in the scheme of things, anyway. Her father knew it, Dayna knew it. Ferral was just there--steadfast, but unimaginative and a bit unhinged. She thought to tell Ferral this, but he had already moved away to check the route to the ruin.

If Father could not lead, then it *would* be left to her. She was the daughter. Who else had the stature to oversee the final days of the Maraia? *The final days.* Everything her father preached led to the conclusion that those days had arrived.

***

Nicholai bent over Rasmussen, whom they had laid on a makeshift cot, which was pressed up against one wall of the ruin. The bare concrete, now dripping from the elevated heat, formed a dismal backdrop. The floor had become a dirt smeared mess from so many boots tracking over the thawing hoar frost.

Rasmussen stared blankly through one open eye, the other closed. His fingers laced over his chest, twitching reflexively. Onset of dementia, or just fatigue. His breathing labored, dry air sucked down a dryer throat.

"I've set his legs, but that's the least of my concerns," Nicholai said. "He's bleeding internally, and there's nothing I can do to stop it."

"Nothing?" Akilah had come to expect that medical science could right any wrong. She stared wondrously at her father. So strong and sure before all this, now just a quivering shell, the last barrier to an unfathomable future.

"I'm sorry." Nicholai slumped his shoulders. "He'll be dead in a matter of days. I could operate, but under these primitive conditions, I would only make matters worse."

Akilah took a faltering step back. Tears brimmed in her eyes. She had never thought of the world without her father. With her mother it had been different. She had been gone before Akilah could remember. But Father? "There must be something we can do for him."

"Too bad we don't have a nano-assembler."

Akilah brushed angrily at her tears. "That's perverse to even suggest it. You know how Father feels about nano-assemblers."

"But he's dying," Nicholai said.

Rasmussen's breathing stopped as he closed his mouth, then tried to wet his lips with his tongue.

He took a deep ragged breath and relapsed into a loud rhythm.

"Dayna, please get him some water." Akilah knelt beside her father and took his hand.

His stare roamed the ceiling of the ruin, down the wall, then came to rest on her. He struggled to raise his head, winced and fell back. "What happened?"

"You fell. Into a crevasse."

"I hurt."

"Your legs are broken. You're bleeding inside."

Rasmussen gave a slight nod.

Dayna returned with a water canister and tipped the cylinder so Rasmussen could drink.

His lips fumbled at the edge of the canister, wetting them, but most of the water dribbled down his chin. "How long do I have?"

Akilah glanced at Nicholai, seeking some indication from him as to how much she should tell her father.

Nicholai nodded.

"A matter of days." Akilah stroked her father's brow.

When Dayna offered more water, he pushed the canister away, seemingly exhausted by his exertions. "I feared it would come to this." With a limp hand, he motioned for Akilah to lean close.

"What is it, Father?"

"Promise...you'll pursue my dream." His voice was a disjointed whisper in her ear.

"To save the Maraia?"

Rasmussen coughed. A dribble of bloody saliva slid from his mouth. Color rose into his face.

"You know...only way to save the Maraia is...build A4-Ni."

"That's a fantasy. Why would you hold me to a false promise?"

"It's the only way....You will see."

Karen put a hand on Akilah's shoulder. "I'll sit with him for a while. Why don't you get some rest?"

"No, no, I should be here."

Karen squatted beside her. "You look beat. Please."

"I suppose I could use some rest," Akilah said.

Dayna gave her a hand up. "I'll go with you."

She led Akilah around a cargo container, where they could sit and be alone.

Akilah eased down, feeling every aching muscle in her legs and hips. "I *am* exhausted."

Dayna knelt and loosened Akilah's jumpsuit. "You're also flushed. I hope it's not the fever. We can't afford to have two leaders down." She put a hand to Akilah's forehead.

Akilah clasped Dayna's cool hand in hers and pressed it against her chest. "Dayna, Dayna. You're putting too much on my shoulders. My father is the leader. I could never take his place."

"Did you see the way the others looked at you? When Doctor Rasmussen dies, they will expect you to step forward."

"I can't."

"But would you try?"

"Building A4-Ni or whatever Father wants to call her is a dream. How can a dream stand up to Ferral's desire to go against Cardassin directly?

102

How could I argue that building A4-Ni is a better way to save our miserable souls?"

Chapter Five

Michael sat on his heels, his back pressed against the ice wall of the tunnel. Above him the sealed entrance was barely discernible.

I'm going to wait for Jamil to return, even if it cost me my outer limbs to frostbite.

There was work to do. The Maraia had arrived. They needed guidance. They wouldn't be able to construct A4-Ni without him.

Despite owing his life to Jamil's efforts, this detour into a primitive underworld was proving costly. More than costly. As far as Michael could tell, he was a virtual prisoner.

A plop of water from above alerted him to the tunnel entrance being reopened.

The opening widened, sending a small torrent of melted ice down the ducts paralleling the tunnel floor. The warmer air of the tunnel exhausted upward as Jamil slid down.

"You here?" He waved his ice razor at the side of the entrance and sealed it closed.

"Yes, of course I'm here. I've not moved since you left me. I have very important matters to attend to, and I don't like being shoved around and sealed up."

"Cold outside. You no survive."

"I appreciate your concern but I'm prepared to take my chances."

The metabase stirred. *"You are approaching this primitive negatively. Better to enhance his triumphs and minimize his defeats."*

Michael grimaced. *The metabase a counselor?*

Jamil pocketed his ice razor and trudged down the tunnel. "Flyer crash. Filled with *TrueMen*." Information tossed over his shoulder.

"Followers of the Cult of Truman."

The metabase again. "How many survived?"

"Find no dead. Maybe nine alive. Men and women. Two go to the ruin."

"The ruined research station on the plateau? You know about that?"

"Of course know. Know many things."

"Then tell me about the *TrueMen*. You seem not to like them."

"No like. Long ago, protos take Maraia. Make Bad-Maraia. TrueMen no like. Maraia no like. Bad-Maraia survive. Become us."

The metabase wound into high gear. *"The Shepherd was last here three thousand years ago and created the Maraia."*

A compressed stream of information injected into Michael's mind.

"The Shepherd provided them with a prophet and savior named Truman Justis, brought to the future from the past, the last true Homo sapiens. He almost martyred himself dispatching the player Cathcar and decreed that the Maraia should keep their genome pure. The surviving Maraia formed the cult of TrueMen.

"Everything went well until Cardassin appeared. Some Maraia survived in strength and

maintained their purity. They holed up in the ancient Maraia home, the Maraia enclave. Others became genetic platforms upon which Cardassin assembled the mutants. Still others fled south to the ancient city of Nairob where degraded Homo sapiens, the protos, dwelled in numbers. The protos kidnapped Maraia women. The result was Jamil's people, shunned by Maraia and protos alike."

"I begin to understand." Michael looked sympathetically at Jamil, whose expression never changed. He turned to leave.

"Don't you think it a lucky coincidence the Maraia crashed so near the ancient sites?" Michael asked.

"Don't know coin...cidence."

Michael smiled. *Patience.* "You followed the two who explored the ruins. What happened then?"

"They be long time in ruin. Very cold. When come out, cold even more. They climb down. Very, very cold on plain. One fall. Weak. They don't know cold. I think I help. They see me. Be afraid. Strong one point ice razor. I leave."

"Did they make it back to the crashed flyer?"

"Don't know. Don't care."

"But that must have happened yesterday. What did you do all day today?"

"I watch. Two go toward lake, but not know river and crevasse."

"The Kerio River?"

"Kerio. They fall. One hurt bad. Old man. I help. Throw ladder to get out."

"Did they see you?"

"No see. But female *TrueMen* see Jamani at fishing ledge."

"I don't understand."

"Tunnels end at crevasse. Form ledge. Sit to fish river."

"That must have confirmed to them that there are primitives--" Michael caught Jamil's sharp look. "--Bad-Maraia...in the area."

"Don't care."

"Well I do. If they think they might be threatened by your people as well as the mutants, then it's going to be that much harder for me to get to them without them trying to kill me."

"Don't care." Jamil started walking again down the tunnel.

Michael grabbed his arm. "So you've said. But I have a mission, and I'm not making any progress staying here."

Jamil looked disdainfully at Michael's hand on his sleeve. "Not safe outside. I tired. Sleep now. You, too."

"I wish I could."

Jamil grabbed Michael's coat and dragged him stumbling down the tunnel. They came to a curtain-draped entryway in the tunnel wall.

Jamil pulled back the curtain to reveal an oblong shaped space and shoved Michael through.

The curtain fell back into place, leaving Michael standing in the dark in what seemed to be a small room melted into the ice.

He searched his pockets and withdrew a small pen light, activated it and held it high, surveying the room.

It was more a cave than a room. Floor, walls and ceiling flowed together seamlessly. To one side lay a thin mat of some woven material. Must be a bed, no coverings. Don't they get cold at night? Maybe they never undressed, preferring to remain perpetually encased in their layers of clothing.

Next to the bed lay something wrapped in a rudimentary cloth, maybe food. Beside that sat a shaped vessel. Water? He picked it up and found that it was water, or had been before it froze.

No way I'm staying here. Michael pocketed the flash and stepped back into the tunnel. What to do? Maybe find a tool to hack his way through the entrance plug. No. The ice was at least a meter thick and hard as rock. He was trapped, better yet imprisoned, in an icy, underground labyrinth.

He paced. *Maybe I should sleep, or at least wait for a better opportunity.* Frustrated, he exited the room and started walking back up the tunnel.

A small figure hunched its way up the tunnel.

"Jamani?"

The miniature Jamil looked up at Michael from under heavy brows.

"Shouldn't you be in bed?"

"No sleepy."

"Then what are you doing out here? Maybe I should call Jamil?"

"No call. I walk. Get tired. Then sleep." Jamani stared at Michael questioningly. "You no sleep?"

"No. I'm not tired, either. In fact, I'd like very much to get out of here and have a walk around the surface. Maybe then I'd get tired enough to sleep."

"Good to walk. You go. I go." He turned to head back down the tunnel.

"But I can't," Michael blurted.

Jamani stopped and gave him an *are you stupid* look.

"The entrance is closed. I can't get out."

"I open."

"You can do that?"

Jamani stepped past Michael and pulled out an ice razor.

"Your father lets you carry one of those?"

"Doesn't know."

"Oh."

Michael shifted from foot-to-foot, slapping his gloved hands together impatiently while his diminutive benefactor took out his ice razor and played it around the former opening. Michael kept glancing over his shoulder, afraid that Jamil would round a bend and put an end to the whole enterprise.

"Okay?" Jamani stepped back, squishing his boots into the quickly freezing melt.

"Yeah," Michael said, amazed at how easy it had been. "That will do fine."

***

Michael stared through the opening at stars salted on a clear night sky. Not wanting to press his good fortune, he clambered up what remained of the slick steps and heaved himself onto the frozen plain.

The Loriyu plateau stuck out in clear silhouette against the heavenly backdrop. He inhaled the crisp air, felt it freeze the edges of his nostrils, then watched it puff when he exhaled.

He started off for the plateau, jogging methodically with his head down, concentrating on where his feet hit the frozen ground. Every once in a while, he would slip and fall, then right himself and press on.

Abruptly, he came to a deep gouge in the frozen waste. The flyer's mark, its last testament. It was over a meter deep, sides angling down to a constricted bottom. Must have been a wing or strut that had caught.

To his left, the groove ended after a hundred meters. The fuselage of the flyer gleamed dimly, a silvery trace in a silvery landscape. Jamil had said the occupants survived. Presumably, they had all gone to the ruin. Still, curiosity drew him to the scene of the crash.

He hadn't gone far when three shadowy figures stood out in silhouette against the plain, their gait erratic, humping.

"Mutants."

Thanks.

"Pathologically modified chromosome at chr6 hla hap1 est--"

I don't need that, now. Michael dropped to the ice and lay still, feeling fortunate he had seen them first. He crawled slowly toward the wreck. When the mutants came around and had their backs toward him, he stood and made faster progress.

Now close to the flyer, he lay down again and hugged the flat ice.

The three climbed the side of the flyer without hesitation. They disappeared through the ragged tear in the flyer's roof to tumble inside with dull thuds.

Michael lost sight of them momentarily, then one appeared, seen through the torn hull.

Muffled shouts reached Michael as they banged around the interior. Then they exited the hull, a drop of two meters that could have broken a normal human's neck. Rolling like excited dolls, they righted themselves and swaggered away drunkenly.

"Fokkin' great fuel. Better than *rub*," one of the mutants shouted above the soughing wind.

"Fokkin' right." A second mutant lifted a container to his lips and drank.

"Fokk this," the third mutant said. He activated his razor, caught the canister he was carrying on fire and heaved it at the wreck.

"And fokk Cardassin!"

Wild giggling as the canister shattered and spread quick flames throughout the forward control.

"He's a *player* all right!"

More giggling. Then together they sauntered off toward the plateau.

Once Michael thought they were well on their way, he hurried to the wreck, intent on putting out the fire.

"--fokk was that?" drifted to his ears.

Michael ducked.

"I'm not going back."

"Fokk it. Me neither."

This time they were gone. Michael climbed to the open ceiling and eased himself down to what must have been the control room. He stamped at the perimeter of the fire to keep it from spreading,

111

then as the rest of the jet fuel burned away or evaporated, he squatted in front of the dying flame and tried to warm himself.

After activating his flash, he panned the room. Crash chairs lay askew. Ceiling panels scattered on the floor, electrical cables dangled. Smashed computers and control sensors to the forward. Blood stains on a forward console. *Someone got hurt.*

He stepped to the console to examine the blood. A panel below the console stood ajar, the cables inside cut. *Sabotage? Help me.*

"Thrusters one, three and four were severed using nano-dissemblers. Thruster two is compromised but was still functional at impact."

An inside job?

"Probability seventy percent inside, twenty-two percent outside, eight percent random statistical noise."

A task made difficult, if the Maraia are infiltrated. Michael stood. Nothing more here.

An off-white colored hallway led to an after compartment. Two doors on opposing walls. Orange. Nice contrast. He tried the one to his right.

It opened onto a small room with a single bunk, a desk strewn with writing utensils, a metal chair, coiled design, powder-coated, wedged against a wall. Papers littered the floor. He picked some up and read...God's chosen people, the Maraia will...I declare in the face of the abomination that all *TrueMen* will from this day forward...

One man's room. Personal touches. A woman's two dimensional reproduction was taped to a wall.

He pulled it off the wall and turned it over. A smudged name and a date--*TrueMen 2980*. Twenty-five years ago. He tried to reattach the picture to the wall, but it wouldn't stick. Beneath it was another picture of a younger woman--dark hair framing a symmetrically featured face, teeth exposed.

"*A smile, an expression of endearment or mirth.*"

I know that.

He backed out of the room and tried the door opposite. Sealed. Odd. He followed a dark seam around the edges and came to a locking mechanism. *Help me.*

"*Six-five-eight-two-zero, stop, five-nine-nine, turn.*"

The seals cracked. The door swung ajar. The rancid smell of death drifted out. A quick survey. Dead person. Male. Caked pool of blood. Must have dripped from his extended index finger. One drop dried there. White sleeved shirt, soaked red. Head angled awkwardly. Upturned lips, bared teeth. *A smile*?

"*No.*"

Lacerated throat. Correction. A nano-gene separated throat. No wonder the door was locked. No signs of contamination, but they must have thought so.

Michael closed the door and proceeded to the after compartment. Empty. Nothing interesting. A cargo door stood ajar at the back. Empty seats. Debris littered the floor. Must have emptied the craft of everything useful. A sandal lay askew against the wall. Shucked off to receive a boot? A copper belt buckle, oxidized green. Small. Maybe a woman's.

He turned to leave, every joint in his body creaked. Very cold, now, as Jamil had said. No. Very, very cold.

Dumb. Too much attention to the wreck and not enough to my well-being. Hurry.

Michael jumped from the control room to the ice, then half-ran, half-stumbled toward the escarpment. His knees were the first joints to numb, then his fingers. The escarpment danced in and out of focus, then loomed suddenly. He crashed into it, fell and moaned at the pain in his hands after they hit the icy wall. His gloves seemed useless.

Now what? He fumbled numbly over the sheer, vertical surface.

"Head north."

How do you know that's the way to go? But he staggered north, trying not to slip and fall, and came to steps carved into the wall of ice.

He slapped his arms about his chest. But the action yielded no warmth, just more pain. *Colder than anticipated.* His grasp of reality faded in and out. *Should have heeded Jamil's warning. Waited for first light.*

He put one foot onto a step and then another like stacking dead stumps, but he rose, slowly. He lost his footing and slid all the way to the bottom

114

again to roll in the snow at the base. Cold. Snow stuck to his face. He had to keep trying.

Leaning forward, he pressed his face against the ice and resumed his ascent, stopping every few seconds to catch his breath, heavy puffs fogging the ice. His heart seemed it would burst from his chest.

"You can survive this degree of punishment, but do not exceed one-ninety-five heartbeats per minute for longer than five minutes."

That's reassuring. Michael knew his limitations.

After what seemed an eternity, he reached the summit and dragged himself over the edge. *Must keep going.* He tried to stand, but his legs refused to obey. He crumpled to his knees. Cramps locked his hamstrings. He rolled in agony.

Is this the end? He dragged himself forward, then pitched onto his face, sucking flakes through frozen nostrils. *Done.*

"Not done."

Don't care.

As if sensing a kill, the bitter cold reached icy fingers beneath his garments.

"Stubborn." A voice rasped in his ear.

"Jamil," Michael whispered. "How did you find me?"

"Not hard."

Jamil grabbed Michael's jacket with one hand and dragged him north, like some oversized bobbing doll.

The gray featureless ice gave way to a warm luminescence. Light filtered through what must be the ruin, giving it an eerie crystal palace glow.

Jamil slid down a slope and stumped up to a makeshift door. He pulled Michael to his feet, leaned him against the door and punched it hard a few times.

"Good-bye."

Panic. "Don't leave me." But Jamil was gone, slipping away as silently as he had come.

Voices muttered from the other side of the door, then were shushed quiet. The door opened inward and Michael toppled to the floor. He hit on his shoulder, rolled onto his back and stared up at a woman who held an ice axe above her head, ready to strike.

Michael brought an arm across his face. "Don't hurt me!"

**

From Michael's perspective on his back she looked tall, but his metabase said she was of average height. Her hair, which looked dark, was actually dark brown with lighter traces running through it. It drifted out from her face as though a breeze were pushing it to touch lightly on her shoulders. Brown, widely spaced eyes, peered at him from beneath delicate eyebrows. A strong nose gave onto dusky-pink lips with a subtle hint of a smile. She seemed a woman at ease with herself, the people around her and this situation.

What he could see of her figure led him to believe that she was fit, her skin silky smooth without blemish. Full breasts and a narrow waist, smooth hips. The orange jumpsuit she wore didn't do her justice. She was a younger version of the

116

woman in the picture taped to the wall of the flyer. *The daughter*?

"Who are you?" Jumpsuit said. The business end of the ice axe gleamed like a hungry smile in the flickering light.

"Michael, my name is Michael." The Shepherd had said nothing about the possibility of being hacked to death. Michael supposed if he had been programmed for a stronger emotional response this would qualify as a situation in which he would be afraid.

Half a dozen people in the room. The metabase had already given him the layout of the facility--two stories, ice-crammed windows, a passageway to the tunnel overlook running adjacent to an abandoned elevator shaft.

Most of the people stood at a distance, presumably engaged with unpacking cargo canisters brought from the flyer, at least until he had interrupted them. A computer and monitor were set up on one of the canisters. Wires from the computer snaked across the floor and up the walls to light niches, sunk into the ice where there were once windows. Other wires ended at the main door, presumably some sort of alarm system. Others fed infrared heaters. In a far back corner an ion generator hummed, providing power to the whole network.

Behind the woman an old man lay in some distress on a makeshift cot. He was being administered to by another man, possibly a physician.

Jumpsuit kicked Michael in the side. "You," she said when he locked eyes with her. "That's enough looking around. What are you doing here?"

"I'm here to help you. Can you put that thing away? You're making me nervous."

Jumpsuit glanced to her left at a tall man with a bandage on his head. Close cropped hair accented male pattern baldness. His loose clothing concealed a powerful build, giving him a hovering sense of menace. Not one to be provoked. His face was clammy with a sheen of sweat. Beneath what seemed a perpetual frown, his eyes bulged in their sockets, giving the impression that he was under constant stress and about to explode.

He came up beside her. "He looks Maraia."

Michael could almost sense the wheels turning in the man's mind, sifting possibilities, calculating probabilities.

"Don't be fooled, Ferral. He's no Maraia," the wizened old man said in a weak voice from the cot.

Ferral.

"*Feral--untamed, wild.*"

An apt name.

The splints on the old man's legs indicated that they were broken. He must have been the one hurt falling into the crevasse. Judging from his pale complexion and the flecks of blood on his lips, he was probably also bleeding internally.

Jumpsuit handed the ice ax to the one called Ferral and walked to the cot. She knelt beside it. "Don't tire yourself, Father. I'll handle this."

The old man raised himself onto an elbow. "Child, I know...Maraia." His voice weakened at the end of his statement.

Jumpsuit pressed gently at his shoulders, pushing him down on the cot. "You're overwrought. Rest."

The old man closed his eyes and breathed through an open mouth.

Jumpsuit returned and stood, hands on hips, surveying Michael.

"You had better be more specific," she said. "We're all that's left of the Maraia, and Father says you aren't Maraia. That makes you a player, a mutant or a primitive. You don't look like a mutant or a primitive. What are you?"

Michael glanced at Ferral, checking to see what hair trigger the man was on. He seemed to have relaxed slightly if that were possible. *No sense provoking him.* "I'm not a mutant or a primitive. And I'm certainly not a player." He searched his metabase for an appropriate response. "I'm Homo sapiens?"

Jumpsuit looked quizzically at Ferral, then back to Michael. "You don't sound too sure."

"He's lying," croaked the old man without moving or opening his eyes. "Homo sapiens have been extinct for five thousand years."

"We can settle this quickly enough," the man who might be a physician said. "Fetch a hair off his head and I'll run it through the sequencer."

Jumpsuit motioned to Ferral. When he stared back and didn't move she stepped to Michael, shoved back the hood of his parka and roughly plucked more than a few hairs from his head.

"Ouch! That hurt." Michael rubbed his scalp and glanced at Ferral. Given his size and bearing, Michael decided the man hadn't been afraid of approaching, but simply concluded there was nothing to be gained by putting himself out. Why embrace any risk if he could get someone else to do it?

"You're going to hurt a lot more if you don't test positive," Ferral said.

"He is a volatile man, obsessed with self-preservation, an anal retentive type, given to fits of violent anger when things don't go his way."

Thank you metabase, but I've already made the same assessment.

Jumpsuit handed the strands of hair to the physician, then wiped her hand on her hip.

Michael struggled to a sitting position. "What happened to the other Maraia?"

"We'll ask the questions," Ferral said.

Jumpsuit held up a hand to calm him. "Someone threw me a rope ladder today, at the crevasse. Was that you?"

Michael frowned, distracted by the tone of Jumpsuit's voice. It possessed a lyrical quality that resonated deep within his being.

"Not me."

Though such a seductive female, she obviously held some position of authority, at least higher than Ferral. Was the old man on top?

"Then it must have been a mutant," she said to Ferral.

120

"Why would a mutant want to throw you a ladder? A mutant would sooner see you die."

"A primitive then, or this one is lying." Jumpsuit eyed Michael. "If you aren't more explicit, the simplest solution will be to kill you. We can't be too careful."

"There are primitives in the area." Michael felt his way in the conversation. He sensed he could reason with Jumpsuit, but feared provoking Ferral with some inadvertent remark. "They are a mixed breed of proto-humans and Maraia."

"How do you know that?" Jumpsuit asked.

"I shared a dinner with them the night you crash-landed."

The old man stared at Michael, a gleam of professional interest burning bright for a moment despite his injuries. "*Truncus humanus*…their scientific name. What do they call themselves?"

"Bad-Maraia."

He started to chuckle, then gagged and spit up blood. He struggled to recover. "Not as bad as mutants…still bad."

"There is actually a small clan of them," Michael said, "a couple of kilometers east of your crash site."

"We're getting nowhere." Ferral drew back the ax. A sheen of sweat formed distinct droplets that slid down his cheeks. "I say he's a player and better off dead."

The metabase had issued a point alert. "*Say something that will catch their attention.*"

"Wait!" Michael shouted. "I have come to help you build *Afareni*."

The room became very still.

"Who's *Afareni*?" Ferral asked, swaying from one foot to the other, a nervous motion, a metronome set to a broken rhythm.

The old man began to shake, obviously fighting pain, but clearly distressed by what Michael had said. "I was...going to name A4-Ni, *Afareni*, in honor of the Earth mother...of ancient myth. I've...I've told no one."

Jumpsuit motioned to a similarly clad female, indicating she should attend to the old man.

He flopped back on the cot. "How does he know?" he mumbled weakly.

Michael craned to see the old man. "I know lots of things."

Ferral stepped ominously in his way. "Far enough--" then to jumpsuit, "--Somehow he's picked up on our history and stitched this thing together. *Afareni* isn't that hard to derive from A4-Ni. It's a coincidence. We should be done with him."

"Not so fast." Jumpsuit stayed Ferral's hand. "Something more is afoot here than player deceit. I'll admit A4-Ni is common scripture, but you can't seriously think Mike here came up with *Afareni* by reading scripture. As for looking like a Maraia, I doubt Cardassin has become so adept with designer-genes he could have come up with a Maraia look-like in the short time we've been here. Cardassin is better at tearing genomes apart than putting them back together."

"My question--*how does he know*?" The old man's voice drifted from the cot.

"As I said, I know a lot of things." Michael glanced apprehensively at Ferral. "Too bad you want to kill me."

Jumpsuit smirked. "Okay wiseass, tell us something we don't already know."

What would it take to convince these people he meant them no harm? "I know the location of Sedroth's tomb."

The old man coughed in surprise.

Jumpsuit stared at Michael with a renewed interest.

Ferral looked as though he hadn't heard. He focused his attention on the ax. One side of his face near his eye twitched.

Jumpsuit cast him a concerned glance. "Stow it, Ferral. Did you hear what he said?"

Ferral blinked. The twitching stopped, then started again. He opened his mouth to speak, but no words came out.

"*He is insane.*"

I decided that long ago. "I said I know where Sedroth's tomb is. You need to find the tomb to obtain the guardian. You need the guardian to build *Afareni*. I can guide you." Michael smiled hopefully.

"Father?"

"I...I don't know anymore. He could be bluffing."

"Let's all slow down a minute," the second jumpsuited woman said. Her hair was short and blond. Her body thin and taut, like a coiled spring. She had wondrous blue eyes.

"*A genetically perfect Maraia.*"

123

She joined the other two. "Akilah, I don't want to second guess you or Ferral, but let's look objectively at what we have here. If he guides us to the tomb, we have the guardian. If he doesn't, then we can dispose of him later. He's one man, unarmed as far as I can tell. There are eight of us."

Akilah.

"*Akilah, an ancient Swahili name meaning intelligent one, a person who reasons.*"

Not now.

Akilah seemed to ponder the alternatives. "It could be a trap to get us out of the ruin and into the open."

"I don't think so," the second woman said. "If the mutants want to attack us, they'd simply push through the door and start shooting."

"I have the results." The physician came up to the group. "He's Homo sapiens, just like he says. How in the name of Sedroth such a thing is possible is beyond me."

"If Cardassin is more clever than we think," Ferral said, "then it's possible."

"I vote for letting him show us Sedroth's tomb," the second woman said. "Let's put his origin aside for now and see if he can produce. What do you say, Ferral?"

"Agreed." Ferral said, though he looked disappointed.

"Okay, Mike," Akilah said, "show us what you've got."

Michael shifted onto one knee.

Except for Ferral, the others stepped back a pace.

124

"The tomb is about half a kilometer from here. It's on the eastern side of the plateau and approachable from the bottom of the escarpment. There's a fore cave filled solid with ice, then a large rock covering an inner chamber."

Ferral looked at Akilah. "We walked right by it."

"All right, this is what we're going to do," Akilah said. "Karin, Lorry and Nicholai will stay here with my father. Warren, you too. See if you can make this ice box more livable."

"I assume you want me to go with you to find the tomb." Ferral seemed very agitated, like nothing ever came easy to him.

"You can come, Ferral," Akilah said, obviously sensing the man's hypertension. "And you too, Dayna. We'll need an industrial strength razor to melt the ice. Bring your personal razors as well. If mutants are out there, we'll be outnumbered, but we might as well take a couple of them down with us."

"I pray to Sedroth that you're doing the right thing," the old man said from the cot.

"Father, I also pray to Sedroth that we're doing the right thing, for Mike's sake." Akilah bent over and offered her hand to Michael. "My name is Akilah Rasmussen."

Michael clasped her hand. She had a firm grip, direct, a woman in charge. He stood.

"An appropriate name."

"I have just managed to spare your life, Mike. Don't toy with me."

"Not at all." Michael shrugged his shoulders to adjust his parka. "In the Swahili language of the ancients who were once native to this area, Akilah means intelligent one, a person who reasons."

Akilah smiled. "I didn't know that."

Chapter Six

Outside, Michael led with Ferral not far behind, presumably with ice ax or ice razor at the ready should Michael decide to make a run for it.

He glanced around half-expecting Jamil to be waiting for him, but he wasn't. *No matter. I've simply left one controlled environment and exchanged it for another. I'm still a prisoner.* Hopefully, finding the tomb and the guardian would help him gain some trust. If not, then he didn't see how he was going to be able to help them build A4-Ni.

He didn't see how he was going to help them, anyway. No one seemed to have the required background or training to build something as complex as a universal constructor.

"*A self-replicating artificially intelligent machine capable of disseminating life from a genome, then remaining to nurture its development.*"

I know. Did the metabase think he was an idiot? No, the metabase didn't think, or did it? But that aside, even if these Maraia obtained a nano-assembler, those wonderful devices still had to be told what to do. *I suppose that's where I come in.*

At the base of the escarpment, he checked his internal guidance system and led them off again. After five minutes of walking, he stopped. "It's here."

The ice went white under the glare from their flashlights.

Ferral rubbed the ice wall with his gloved hand. "I don't see anything but ice."

"What gives, Mike?" Akilah asked.

"The ice here is three or four meters above ground level, the entrance to the cave. You will first have to clear a way down to the ground before boring into the ice clogged cave itself."

Ferral stepped back a couple of paces and cleared away shallow snow with swipes of his boot. "I'll set the razor here."

Dayna un-shouldered the tripod she was carrying and jammed its feet firmly into the cleared ice.

Once Ferral had the razor screwed to the top of the tripod, he directed it down at a steep angle, then toggled an on-switch. A shaft of violet light streaked from the razor's end, hit the ice and started boring a steaming hole. He adjusted the focus of the beam and turned up the gain.

Water boiled in a widening and deepening puddle, then the beam reached to the cavitated spaces below and suddenly all the water flowed out, leaving a gaping hole that penetrated to the ground below.

He withdrew a handheld razor and played it in concentric circles around the main bore to widen it. He sloped it at one side, and roughened it to facilitate climbing down.

The entrance to the cave gleamed in their lights.

"All right," Ferral directed. "Relocate the razor below and start boring horizontally."

Ten minutes later, with the razor set up on the ground, the ice in the outer cave was melted away.

"That's the rock." Michael pointed to the large stone that sat at the end of the shaft.

Ferral holstered his razor and stepped into the opening, ducking his head. He immediately lost his footing and lurched awkwardly against the wall of the shaft before sliding down in a sprawl to its bottom.

Dayna stifled a giggle with her hand.

Ferral glared at her.

Is he going to lose it here and now? The man seemed to struggle with his anger, shoving it down inside him, perhaps saving it for another time. He got to his feet carefully and tried again. This time he made it all the way to the back of the bore without falling. He ran his fingers around the rock where it met the wall. "We need a little more thaw," he said. "The rock is frozen at the back."

He retraced his steps and emerged, giving Dayna a sharp look.

"I'm sorry, Ferral, but it was comical."

"Maybe you'd care to be first in next time?" He didn't wait for Dayna to answer, but stepped to the mounted razor and turned it on.

After another five minutes the rock stopped steaming, indicating that any ice holding it in place had evaporated.

Dayna entered agilely and stepped to the back. She gave the rock a push. "It moves." She coiled a rope around the top of the rock and backed out again. "Give me a hand."

Together they pulled the rock toward them. Once it started to move on the floor of the ice tunnel, it slid easily. Its momentum carried it out the entrance where they gave it an extra push clear.

Light from Akilah's flashlight glistened off the sides of the shaft and disappeared into a dark hole that gaped at the far end. "That must be the chamber." Her face paled. "Any volunteers?"

"Mister Michael first," Ferral said. "This could all be a trick."

Michael shrugged and took the flashlight from Akilah, then stepped into the shaft. At the end, he got down on his hands and knees and inched forward through the hole.

"Is it Sedroth's tomb?" Akilah asked.

The nearness of her voice startled Michael. She had entered the shaft and now was close behind him.

"There's a skeleton lying on the floor against the back wall. No, two skeletons."

"Sedroth and his mistress?"

Michael pushed the flashlight through and crawled after it. The chamber was large enough for him to stand.

Akilah came though the opening next. Her flashlight played over the walls and came to rest on the skeletons.

"I assumed I was looking at two skeletons," Michael said. "There are two skulls. Otherwise the bones are pretty mixed."

From inside the jumble of bones, something reflected light.

Michael knelt and carefully picked some of the bones away to reveal a small sphere.

Akilah gasped. "The guardian?"

"Yes." Michael's metabase had already confirmed the find. "It must have rested on the chest of one of the bodies before it decomposed, then fell through the rib cage to the floor."

"It *is* Sedroth's tomb," she whispered reverently.

Michael retrieved the sphere. When he tried to hand it to Akilah, she pulled away.

"It's not going to hurt you," Michael said. "I thought you wanted to find it."

"Yes, of course. It's just that the magnitude of the moment is overwhelming." She reached a tentative hand to the guardian and took it. "It's so heavy for such a small object."

"It's made of exotic materials. Not native to Earth. Not native to this universe."

"You know that?"

Michael let the question stand, wondering how much he should be substantiating his knowledge with footnotes.

Akilah closed her hand tightly over the sphere. "I feel a vague tingling." Nervously, she opened her hand and offered the sphere to Michael.

"You keep it," Michael said. "It won't hurt you."

She looked skeptical but dropped the sphere into a pocket, then played her flashlight on the walls of the chamber. "Look at these paintings. They're beautiful."

"Juvenal was an artist."

"Juvenal?"

"A companion of Sedroth. Though Sedroth was the last true man, Juvenal was the first Maraia."

"I didn't know."

"You couldn't have." He was about to add *but the Shepherd told me*, then realized the absurdity of doing so.

Akilah gave Michael a skeptical look. "I'm not prepared to believe any of this until my father confirms it."

Michael smiled painfully at her continuing distrust. *What's it going to take to convince her*? He played his flashlight on the wall of the chamber. The drawings seemed to dance in the light, their colors undiminished from the time they were first painted. How long ago had that been? Three thousand years? The story was all there. Juvenal had painted well. The birth of the Maraia, Sedroth's appearance, the Shepherd, even the death of the player Cathcar who had killed Azizah, Sedroth's mistress. The detail evoked in Michael a twinge of sadness being in the presence of communications so old about events so tragic.

He stepped closer to the painted wall and traced his finger over an image. "This is the player Cathcar. He's the only one who looks Neanderthal."

"What is Neanderthal?"

"A primitive hominid species. Oddly, when Cathcar arrived three thousand years ago, he chose a Neanderthal's form, probably because they were very strong. He might have also thought to blend in with the other degraded humans in the area."

"Please, Michael, I don't want to sound dense, but...players...though we *TrueMen* talk about them all the time and rail against Cardassin, I've never known...I mean, I don't think anyone knows what they really are, or what they really want."

Total ignorance. How much do I tell her? "Players are *Zug*'s representatives on Earth, in this galaxy, in this universe."

"Our known universe?"

"Your known universe." *But not* the *universe. No, not now, not here.* "They are dispersed throughout time and space. Some in the past, some in the future, some overlapping. Cathcar's death alerted other players to this time and place. Only one thought it important enough to locate here. Cardassin."

Akilah stared. "How do you know all this?"

"I am probably speaking out of turn, but here we are in this cave, with the history of your people splashed across this rock wall. Listen to what I say, believe what you will and don't question the source. At least not now."

"You are not who you say you are?"

"No. But I am not a threat to you or your people. I don't know what I can do or say to convince you of that."

"You can stop lying to me."

"I haven't lied. I just haven't been forthcoming. I can't be."

Akilah studied him. "Okay, Mike. For the moment, I'm going to accept what you're saying as fact and trust that the picture will clarify as we learn more details."

133

"Thank you."

"So Cardassin came here based solely on what he suspected Cathcar was up against?"

Michael breathed an inner sigh of relief. "The primary mission of the players is to locate and destroy *Gilomir*. Since the guardian and the Shepherd are the sole entities that are entrusted with the safekeeping of *Gilomir*, the players pursue them as a way to get to *Gilomir*."

"I know we Maraia represent what is left of the human race. The Shepherd restored humans by restoring *Gilomir* in them. But I never understood why humans degraded in the first place."

"It's a long story," Michael said.

"Everything all right in there?" Dayna called from outside.

Akilah ducked down to the narrow crawl space. "We're okay. Just getting our bearing and sorting through what is in here. We'll be out in a few minutes."

"We better get back," Michael said.

"Look, Mike, you might think it's a long story, but I just gave you the benefit of the doubt, and I also asked a question. I expect you to answer it."

Michael surveyed the woman standing in front of him. Was she just bluff and bluster? A spoiled child living in the shadow of a dominant man, or was there something deeper and more fundamental to her character?

"I have been told--"

Akilah gave him a sharp glance.

Michael felt on the defensive. "Your scripture reveres *Gilomir*, but do you really know who he is and what he represents?"

"Of course I do. His genome is responsible for humans being human. Without him, we would have remained imbecilic hominids."

"I suspect that what you don't know is that the *Gilomir* genome and the base hominid genome are fundamentally incompatible. The latter takes every opportunity to eliminate the former. Without some mechanism in place to continually restore the *Gilomir* genome, it would be completely wiped out. The result would be the degradation of humans."

"So something maintained the *Gilomir* genome?"

"Something did, and when that something was removed, the hominid genome was free to eradicate the *Gilomir* genome. Humans degraded."

"So what was the mechanism?"

Michael searched in vain for an answer, but none was forthcoming. "I...I truly don't know."

"Gee, Mike, all this and now you come up short?"

Michael faltered. Up until now, the metabase had provided him with all the knowledge he sought and some he never thought he needed. That the metabase didn't know about the mechanism that kept *Gilomir* pure, or was unwilling to tell him, was most annoying.

"We're getting cold." Ferral called.

"We're coming," Akilah yelled back, then smiled at Michael. "Still thinking about my last question?"

"I thought I answered it."

"Look, I'm not naïve. When you figure out the why of my question, I expect you'll let me know. In the meantime, I'm going to think that you're being overtly secretive, despite the fact that we, no I, have been instrumental in assuring your continued existence."

"You have spoken well."

"I like your formality. I think we should return before Ferral comes in looking for us."

"You're right, of course."

She crawled out the opening.

Michael shut off his flash and followed. When he emerged, Akilah was already showing the others the small sphere. He hung back from the group, unable to share their excitement over the find. There was still so much left to be done with no clear indication how it was to be accomplished.

Dayna reached a trembling hand and touched the sphere Akilah proffered. "Is it really the guardian?"

"Michael says it is." Akilah turned to glance at him.

"I trust Doctor Rasmussen will be the final arbiter as to the authenticity of this bauble," Ferral said. "I suggest we not press our luck being out here in the open. The sooner we get back to the ruin the better."

"We must take samples from the skeletons," Akilah said.

"Skeletons?" Dayna asked.

"There are two skeletons lying in the inner chamber. Mike says they are Sedroth and his

136

mistress Azizah. I want to take samples and have Nicholai run them through the DNA sequencer. He'll be able to tell us if they are human." She turned to crawl back inside the cave.

"Don't be a fool." Dayna grabbed Akilah's jacket. "We are vulnerable out here."

Akilah shook her free. "I'm going back in. Wait for me."

Michael marveled at the temerity of this warrior-woman. Stunningly beautiful according to norms downloaded from his metabase, she also projected an inner strength, a conviction. When matched to other statistical parameters, she was at the high end of leadership scales. She really could take over from the old Doctor when he faltered. But the question was, did she really want to?

Even if she decided she wanted to, would it be in the best interest of the Maraia? Would it be in the best interests of the Shepherd?

The Shepherd must have thought all this through, or at least gained a perspective on events from the guardian at some time or place in the past.

Michael still didn't understand the full roll of the guardian. Was it just a benign protector as its name implied? Or was it more? It certainly seemed to have everything planned out. The Shepherd had said as much. *The guardian has a plan. We are all just cogs in its great wheel.*

At this point Michael didn't feel like a cog. He felt more like he was down in the midst of it, mucking around with detail. At any moment, things could go awry, and he would end up a mass of scattered cybernetic parts.

137

Be that as it may, events dictated that he do something. If not to control them, then at least he had to monitor them and bend them to his advantage.

Akilah re-emerged with a sample of bones in two small cloth bags. "Now we can go. This is Sedroth. This is Azizah." She held up the bags for Michael to see. "I took the samples from the skull fragments."

Michael stared at the bags. The Maraia *TrueMen* weren't going to be too happy about what they would learn from their analysis.

***

Cardassin blinked. He'd been sitting on the edge of the bed and staring at the floor for the last twenty minutes. Must have been especially good *rub*.

But what the fokk else was there to enjoy in this fokkin' place. Drugs, sex, death, destruction, not necessarily in that order.

The cascade of bells tied to the pole outside his tent rattled.

He cocked his head, listening for the tinkle bell, but it must have gone dead, or maybe a spider had built a nest in it, muting it. *What the fokk, no tinkle bell*?

The bells rattled again. This time more persistently.

"Come!"

Trudal pulled back the tent flap and stuck his head in, looking apprehensive, as well he should.

"Sire, the mutant scouts have returned and wish to report their findings."

138

"Well, show them in!"

"They are afraid, sire."

"Afraid?" Cardassin leaned back and reached for his robe. It wouldn't do to receive the guards in the nude.

"Yes, sire. They are afraid you might kill them."

Cardassin guffawed as he stood and slipped into his robe. Phlegm clogged his throat, and he doubled over in a hacking spasm. *Rub* will do that to you, too. *Thank Zug for* rub. *What the fokk would I do without it*?

He composed himself, though he didn't tie his robe, preferring to let it hang open in front. "In the name of *Zug*, get them in here. And if it makes them feel safer," he added in a wheedling voice, "I promise on my mother's grave, whatever the fokk that means, that I will not kill them."

"Thank you, sire, for your merciful beneficence. I will convey your words to the scouts. They are just outside."

Trudal ducked out of the tent.

Muffled voices carried through the heavy canvas, then the three scouts entered.

"Sire," one of the scouts said.

Giggling, Cardassin stiff-armed his ice razor, activated it, and punched a neat smoldering hole through the belly of the scout.

The scout's face purpled. He turned and teetered out of the tent, followed by a thud, presumably his body hitting the ground.

Trudal rushed in looking disappointed. "Sire, you promised."

"I lied."

"Most unfortunate. Most unfortunate," Trudal muttered.

"Now what?"

"Nothing, sire. Nothing. He was four months pregnant that's all."

"A pity. Now what do *you* have to report?" Cardassin played the end of the extinguished razor over the second scout. *When will they ever learn? I'm not rational. Should I be?*

The second scout was trying to speak.

Too fokkin' scared to talk? Cardassin sniffed. "What in the name of *Zug* have you been drinking?"

"Jet fuel, sire."

"Haven't I told you to stay away from that stuff?"

"Yes, sire, you have. If it wasn't for--" He thumbed over his shoulder indicating the death-departed first scout. "--I would never have indulged."

Cardassin stared at his razor, fumbling for the activating switch. *Why don't my fingers function?*

"Excuse me, sire," said the third scout. "If yaw persist in killing us awl, yaw will not know wot we have to report."

Cardassin looked up, eyes blinking rapidly, his mouth open in surprise. "Very wise. Very, very wise. I recognize your exaggerated speech. What *is* your name?"

"I'm Igor, sire. But I'm sure yaw already knew that."

"Igor. Yes, I do recall sending an Igor to investigate the crash. But you mutants all look

140

alike, at least to me. You can't expect me to keep you separate."

"No, sire."

Trudal stepped between the two remaining scouts. "Sire, you really should hear what Igor has to say."

Cardassin shook his head, trying to clear the *rub* from his mind. *Focus. It might be important.* "Yes, I suppose." He waved a hand at Igor, giving him permission to state his findings.

"Sire, we climbed up and over the escarpment and came onto the eastern plain. It was not hard to locate the crashed flyer. We entered and found it empty of awl sal...vage...able parts. The survivors, and awl must have survived for there were no dead persons left behind or they carried their dead away, which to my mind was a waste of en...er...gy, because after awl the dead are dead and what's the use of carrying them away to somewhere, anywhere, when leaving them there to rot, become putrid, worms in and worms out, would be just as--"

"Stop! You fokkin' idiot. Stick to the point, or I'll make a point out of you."

"Yes, sire. I'm sorry. I just thot with any of them being dead, they shouldn't have, at least I wouldn't have--"

"Igor," Trudal said quietly.

Igor blinked rapidly and started to suck his thumb.

Trudal reached and yanked the thumb out of the mutant's mouth. "If you want to survive this interview, you *will* have to stick to the subject. There. That's a good man. Now proceed."

Still blinking, Igor faced Cardassin. "After ass...certaining thot there was nothing left, we siphoned some flyer fuel and had a go. Once we were inerbraded, it seemed to us a good idea to set the craft on fire. We *proceeded* to do just thot, then we left. About a hundred meters from the burning flyer, we turned and saw a figure run into the craft and begin to stomp out the flames."

"Did you return?"

"No, sire. Since we did not know the strength of said figure, we decided it better to ensure ar survival and return with ar report."

Cardassin nodded sagely to Trudal. "Seems a wise decision."

Trudal nodded. "A wise decision."

"This figure you saw--" Cardassin stroked the cylinder of the ice razor absentmindedly. "--could it be a Maraia who came back for something?"

"I don't think so, sire. The Maraia stay together as a group. We saw a ple...thor...a of footprints heading for the plateau."

"Then maybe it's one of those fokkin' primitives that I failed to exterminate."

"Sire," Trudal said. "You have been very thorough in your extermination. I'm certain no primitives are left."

"Then who the fokk was it?"

"Sire, I had another dream last night."

"This better be fokkin' good. Don't test me, Trudal."

"Yes, sire. I mean, no sire. But it was a very good dream. I dreamt that the Shepherd had landed and produced a humanoid male person. It was he Igor saw entering the burning wreck."

"The Shepherd? Here? After all this time?" Cardassin made an elaborate show of pinching his arm. "Am I asleep? Could it be true?"

"All sarcasm aside, my lord," Trudal said, "but it is true. Hallelu--may the scouts go now?"

Cardassin crossed his eyes and frowned. *Damn rub.* "You still think I'm going to kill these two?" He struggled to bring his vision back into stereoscopic focus. First one eye rolled outward from his nose then the other, then they came to rest on Trudal.

"I did have some concern for their safety, my lord."

"Thanks be to *Zug*! I'm not in a killing mood...just yet. If the Shepherd is here and has loosed an agent upon these lands then I must know more about this." He placed both hands to his temples and squinted his eyes. "I have a plan."

"Very good, my lord. Do you wish to impart this plan to us now, or would you prefer we returned at a later time?"

Cardassin opened his eyes and blinked, marveling at the odd colors he perceived after applying pressure to the sides of his eyeballs. "Now is good."

Cardassin followed Igor's gaze to his open robe. "What the fokk are you looking at?"

"Yaw...yaw robe is untied, sire."

Cardassin shot him a sharp glance, pulled the edges around him and cinched a drawstring tight. "Didn't like what you saw?"

143

"I did, sire." Igor trembled. "Praise *Zug!*"

"That's better. Now to my plan. Igor, I want you to recruit a couple of mutants--" Cardassin waved a limp hand at the second mutant. "--this mute next to you, no pun intended, will do for one of them."

The second mutant giggled idiotically.

Cardassin slashed his hand in the air, shutting the mutant up mid-giggle.

"Thank you." Cardassin fumbled with his razor. *Why the fokk won't it work?* Exasperated, he shoved it in a pocket of his robe. "We will find out where the Maraia survivors have gone. I want to confront them and ascertain if they have found the guardian, or if they haven't, if they know where it is. If the Shepherd's agent is with them, we will kill him. If he's not with the Maraia, then he must be somewhere. He can't stay out in the cold forever. We'll send another team to look for a primitive nest. He must have tied up with one of them. I will *lead*, giving guidance and inspiration to my forces as needed."

Cardassin spun on one heel, avoided falling flat and recovered to sit heavily on his bed. He leaned over, reached under it and pulled out a flat box a half meter wide and one long. After sliding the lid off, he withdrew yellow colored boots that were trimmed around the top with purple fur. He shoved a bare foot into one of the boots and prepared to do the same with the other.

"Excuse me, my lord." Trudal rubbed his hands together nervously. "But I must counsel you that it is most dangerous that you lead this expedition. Although the Maraia are benign, we have no intelligence as to what powers the Shepherd's agent possesses. Better to go virtually."

Cardassin hung his head in his hands and gulped back a sob. The *rub* again. Exaggerated emotion. "You're right, of course." Then he brightened. "But I'll still be able to wear my uniform, won't I?"

"Yes, indeed, sire." Trudal clapped his hands, then stopped abruptly at a glance from Cardassin.

Cardassin pulled a nano-assembler from beneath his pillow. After fumbling with it, he leaned back satisfied and let five small pellets fall into his palm. He handed them to Igor. "I want you and dumbo here to each take one of these. Give the others to your recruits. I've designed genes to grow industrial strength razors on one of your arms for the duration of this expedition."

Igor took the pellets, popped one into his mouth and handed one to the second mutant. Igor looked at his arm expectantly.

"It will take a few minutes, you idiot." Cardassin motioned to Trudal, who handed Igor a small box-shaped device with a lens on it.

"You know how to use this, don't you?" Trudal asked Igor.

"Of course I do, yaw fokkin' idiot."

Trudal sighed. "Sire, it always distresses me that I don't command the respect of the mutants."

"Of course you don't." Carsassin giggled for no reason that he could ascertain. "You have chosen to retain much of your Maraia genome, whereas they have given themselves over to me entirely."

"But sire, you know I would gladly give up everything to be a better servant to your lordship."

"Cut the crap, Trudal. You know you're more use to me as you are than in the form of some fokkin' genetic freak."

"Thank you, sire. I truly would abhor being a fokkin' freak." Trudal smiled.

Cardassin waved his hand in dismissal. "I'm tired. Leave me."

Trudal and the two mutants bowed and backed out of the tent.

Thank Zug for small favors. If they hadn't left, I would have had to dissolve the lot of them. Why, why, have I come to this abominable life? I give, but I never get.

A bright light seemed to sear the inside of his skull. A bolt from out of the blue.

Cardassin dipped his head in a semblance of a bow.

Praise Zug. I suffer at your pleasure.

Stifling another giggle, He pulled on his other boot and leaned back on the bed. "Crist-tee-naa."

***

"The guardian?" Rasmussen seemed incredulous. "Are you sure?"

"We found it where Michael said it would be." Akilah's face showed a mixture of awe and fear at the magnitude of the find.

Rasmussen's gaze drifted to Michael. "You're new, aren't you?"

"*His mind is gone.*" The metabase.

You are premature. Listen to what he has to say.

146

"I have waited...for this moment." Rasmussen's voice broke. He took the sphere and held it in one hand while caressing it with the other.

"Okay, we've got the sphere, now what?" Ferral's cheek began to twitch.

"I will use it," Rasmussen wheezed. "It will tell me...how to build *Afareni*."

"Hold on!" Ferral stared at Rasmussen, his face contorted as he worked to control the stress he was obviously under. "How do we know this isn't some elaborate ruse! We know nothing of this man." He gestured wildly at Michael, drawing his other arm across his brow, smearing sweat across his balding scalp. "He comes out of nowhere, leads us to a frozen cave that only he knows about, so we can find a sphere that no one can figure out how to use."

Akilah stepped between Ferral and her father. "I see you've--"

"I'm not finished! When you add a pressing population of mutants led by a fiendish player just itching to climb the plateau and wipe us all out, we are in a hopelessly weak position!"

"I see you've been giving this some thought." Akilah patted Ferral's arm as if she wasn't the least bit bothered by his outburst. "But you are taking the extreme view of events. It is entirely possible that Mike is genuinely interested in helping us build *Afareni* and has come by his knowledge in a way that, although unknown to us, is neither sinister nor threatening."

Are they all so far gone that they tolerate this kind of behavior without being disturbed? The man was obviously unhinged, routinely visiting angry outbursts upon people who were presumably his friends. There seemed no limit to whom he would attack next, so long as it buttressed his own stature. Are the other Maraia similarly afflicted?

A combination of inbreeding and the stress of living under a player threat has produced in this population the seeds of communal mental disorder.

Can I work with these people? No. Don't answer that, I don't want to know.

"*Biiizzzz bup.*" The metabase shut down.

"May I make a suggestion?" Nicholai asked.

"What?" Akilah snapped.

"You have collected samples from the skeletons in the cave. I could analyze them to determine if their DNA correlates with known parameters for the prophet Sedroth and his mistress. We believe they were the last true Homo sapiens. If I obtain a positive correlation, then we could presume that what Doctor Rasmussen holds--" He indicated the guardian. "--is in fact the guardian and not some bauble planted by Cardassin."

"That won't cut it for me, Nicholai," Ferral sneered. "My guess is that if mister Michael can fool a DNA sequencer into thinking he's a Homo sapiens, then it's not much more of a stretch that those bones are doctored as well."

"Ferral," Akilah said, "I'm going to ask you to put a lid on your paranoia. It's not helping the situation." She looked around at the others. "We shouldn't rush to judgment. In the short time that we've been here, it's unlikely Cardassin could have stashed the skeletons of two Homo sapiens in an ice cave and then sent Michael to help us find it. Presumably, no one even knew we were coming."

Ferral tossed his head back and cut loose an explosive laugh. He clamped his mouth shut, and glared at Akilah. "Don't be stupid. What if the player spy who cut the cables and corrupted Jason is still amongst us?"

Akilah fixed Ferral with a steely gaze. "As far as I'm concerned, that's more paranoia. I grew up with all of you, and I can't imagine that any one of you has become a player spy. There are other explanations for what happened than to insinuate that one of us is in league with Cardassin. As for being stupid, I'll thank you to keep your personal opinions of me to yourself."

Ferral's face turned a shade of purple, but he maintained his silence.

"Good. I suggest we move on. We will put these bones--" She held up the two bags from the cave. "--through the sequencer as Nicholai has suggested. Knowing they are Homo sapiens will dispel our misgivings about the authenticity of the guardian." She handed the two sacks of bones to Nicholai.

Nicholai glanced nervously at Ferral, but took the two bags. "It will only take a minute."

A heavy silence fell over the ruin.

What a divisive group, Michael thought. They all had different agendas, at odds with each other. The only person they seemed to respect in common was the Doctor. When he died, Akilah could presumably take the lead, but she'd be up against

Ferral and his hair-brained idea that the Maraia could take back the planet.

Nicholai rejoined the group.

"Well?" Akilah said.

"This bag--" He held up the bag with bone fragment from the larger of the two skulls. "-- contains bones that correlate ninety-nine percent to a Homo sapiens. Presumably that means they are Sedroth's.

"This bag--" He held up the other bag. "-- contains bones belonging to a player."

Ferral stopped his pacing and stared dumbstruck at Nicholai. "Azizah was a player?"

"It can't be true," Rasmussen muttered, staring at the guardian.

Akilah raised her eyebrows. "Are you sure?"

"I'm sure. Although Homo sapiens DNA predominate, that DNA exists on an underlying matrix of player DNA."

"What the hell does that say about the scriptures we've all been told to revere as gospel? Sedroth consorting with a player whore?" Ferral practically screamed. "What does that say about...about the guardian, about building A4-Ni or *Afareni* or whatever you want to call it. The players have been in on this from the beginning."

"Blasphemy!" Rasmussen wheezed from his cot, then degenerated into a coughing fit.

"Father, please. Everyone try to calm down." Akilah brushed her hand over Rasmussen's forehead. For a moment, Michael thought she might clamp her hand over his mouth to shut him up. "This makes no sense."

"If I may," Michael said.

They all turned to him, seemingly dumbfounded.

"What difference does it make if Azizah was a player? Your scripture says they trusted one another, enough that they were buried together. The important point, now, is to establish whether or not Doctor Rasmussen can use the guardian, and if so, whether it gives him some way to confirm that it is genuinely the guardian." Michael sensed their hostility. "It's only a suggestion."

"Michael's right." Akilah stepped to the center of the ruin. "This is all ancient history. If Father can divine the plans for constructing A4-Ni from the guardian, why should we debate whether or not Azizah was a player? Personally, I don't give a damn."

A choking gasp from Rasmussen drew all their attention. His face turned an apoplectic purple.

"I don't think Doctor Rasmussen agrees with you," Ferral said. "The genealogy of Sedroth's mistress bears on everything we will do with the guardian. Once a player, always a player, I say. How do we know what insinuations she pushed forward while Sedroth was still alive. Did any of these pollute what the guardian will tell us?"

Paranoid man. Michael marveled at the way Ferral swam the currents of opinion coursing through this assembly. Where they coincided with his own, he reinforced. Where they diverged, he heaped scorn. "I think Ferral is being overly cautious."

"Who asked you!" Ferral spun on Michael, riveting him with such a penetrating glare that Michael took an involuntary step back.

Akilah stepped quickly between the two of them. "Easy, boys. We've got a more basic problem here. Do we know how to use the guardian, even if it is the guardian of the scriptures."

Ferral peered at the sphere. "I don't see any switches or controls.

Rasmussen's fingers trembled as he lay back on the cot and closed his hand over the sphere. "I think...I just hold it."

Minutes passed.

Ferral paced. "Anything?"

Akilah grabbed his shoulder and spun him around. "Calm down, damn it, you're making us all nervous."

"Nothing," Rasmussen said, looking bewildered.

"Perhaps Doctor Rasmussen should try again," Michael said.

Akilah looked at him blankly, then turned to her father. "Are you strong enough to give it another try?"

Rasmussen had begun to breathe more regularly. "I will give my dying breath to bring A4-Ni from a dream to a reality."

He clutched the sphere in a tight fist, brought it against his chest and closed his eyes. He stiffened. His eyelids fluttered. After an interminable period, he twitched , as though coming out of a trace, then stilled.

"Great Sedroth! It killed him," Ferral said.

"Stow it, Ferral." Akilah knelt by Rasmussen's side and pried the guardian from his grasp. She shook him and he responded groggily. "Are you all right?"

"I...I have seen the future."

Everyone except Michael and Ferral leaned forward expectantly.

"The designs for A4-Ni flashed before my eyes. I could not absorb it all...so complex." He buried his head in his hands.

"Then what use is it?" Ferral stood over Rasmussen. "You've come all this way, expecting that finding the guardian will solve our problems, and what happens? You have the guardian but cannot understand what it is trying to tell you. And if Nicholai is right, you'll be dead by morning, which will leave the rest of us to figure a way out of this abominable situation you have placed us in."

"I've had enough of you, Ferral," Akilah said. "My father is critically injured, but he's still trying to help us. It might prove difficult to tie and gag you, but by Sedroth, I'll give it a try if you don't shut up."

Ferral glanced at the others.

For a moment Michael thought that the argument between Akilah and Ferral was about to break out in a physical free for all.

Akilah knelt beside her father and closed her hand over his. "Try again, Father. How do you know when it is working?"

"I only close my palm and a little later, I feel open to everything. I suppose it senses me." He stiffened and fell back on the cot.

"Here we go again." Ferral looked at the pock-marked ceiling.

Concerned, Nicholai stepped toward Rasmussen, but stopped when Akilah held out a restraining hand.

Rasmussen steadied. He opened his eyes and handed the guardian to Akilah. "It was better this time. Somehow the visions slowed. It was almost as if the guardian was asking me for information. So I just thought about what I have always envisioned A4-Ni to be. Then there was a flood of information. Some of my assumptions for building A4-Ni were incorrect."

She put her hands on her hips and stood over her father. "The question remains, do you now know how to construct A4-Ni?"

Rasmussen rubbed his eyes. "Yes, daughter, but it is all far more complex than I anticipated. It could take years."

Ferral smiled for the first time since Rasmussen had tried to use the guardian. "I think that settles it. We don't have years. We don't even have months. Given the time we do have, we need another plan!"

The situation was quickly veering out of control. Michael stepped to Rasmussen's side and gently removed the guardian from his hand.

The others immediately began to protest.

Michael raised his hand. "I think I can help. I may be able to gain the blueprints for building A4-Ni directly."

"No." Rasmussen reached for the guardian. "It is written that a Maraia must listen to the guardian and divine its message."

"Whatever's written has become suspect, Father, and you know it," Akilah said. "Maybe Michael is in a better position to understand the blueprints."

"I do not question scripture and neither should you, child." Rasmussen reached feebly for the sphere.

Michael closed his hand around the guardian. He felt an odd tingling from the sphere, then experienced a blinding flash. The sensation lasted for no more than a second. He didn't know what had happened, but then he knew something. *I know how to build A4-Ni.* It was all there, not as reams of schematics and specifications, but simply a confidence that given the time and material, he saw a beginning and an end and the way in-between. He also saw a problem.

"The Doctor is withholding information," Michael said.

The others looked at him in surprise, then at Rasmussen.

"Is that true, Father?"

Rasmussen fidgeted. "There is one irrelevant point. The guardian's plan to build A4-Ni requires the use of a nano-assembler."

"Well, well, we've come up against an abomination," Ferral said.

"Amen," Rasmussen rasped. "It is a cruel twist along the path to realizing something that is pre-ordained."

"Are you all blind," Dayna interjected, nearly shouting, her face flushed such was her frustration..

Everyone looked at her.

"Please, Dayna," Akilah said. "If you have something to say, you don't have to shout. Please have some decorum."

"Decorum, be damned," Dayna said heatedly. "You *TrueMen* are so caught up in scripture that you cannot see that the only way to save our precious genome is to forego your aversion to a nano-assembler and build A4-Ni."

"Never!" Rasmussen shouted from his cot.

"We cannot." Akilah spread her hands in despair.

"Then we are doomed," Dayna said.

"We could get a nano-assembler from Cardassin's enclave," Michael suggested.

"You really don't get the point," Akilah said. "We don't use nano-assemblers, ever."

Michael handed the guardian to Akilah. "Then A4-Ni will never be--"

A sizzling crackle rattled the ruin's makeshift door. The plas-steel from the ship's cargo hold vibrated. Its smooth surface dimpled. With a loud bang, it blew off its primitive hinges and exploded across the room to clang against the far wall.

Chapter Seven

Five mutants barged into the ruin.

Bloodshot eyes gleamed, mouths slacked open, ragged clothing hung in tatters. Their right arms sagged at their sides. From their left shoulders grew industrial strength razors.

What wonders nano-assemblers can produce. Michael felt an odd detachment from what was fast becoming a surreal situation.

Muzzle still smoking, the lead mutant swung his razor in a slow arc across the Maraia. His lips curled into what must have been a mutant smile, blocky rows of stained teeth, sucking an overflow of saliva. His eyes narrowed in forced concentration. No doubt this predator meant business.

Warren must not have received the same message as Michael. The idiot lunged for a razor atop one of the cargo canisters that sat three meters away.

The lead mutant grunted, leaned back as though levering a heavy weight and fired the tip of his razor from waist height.

"Like a six-shooter." The metabase.

What's that?

A blue beam of phase coherent light first scoured a black groove in the concrete floor, then panned left to right, catching up to the flailing Warren.

He made it to the canister and nearly to the razor before the heat neatly sizzled a crosscut through his legs. They clumped to the floor, odd looking body parts. Neither one of them fell over, but stood upright like boots waiting to be put back on. The rest of his body, with nothing to hold it up, pitched forward.

Upper Warren crashed to the floor, his eyes wide with surprise, his mouth open in blubbering agony, his hands raking the two smoking stumps extending from below his hips. Still hot, they seared his fingers, loosing in the air the stench of burnt flesh.

Nicholai twitched in Warren's direction, then probably thought better of it.

"No bah...dy moves!" slurred the lead mutant. The blue flash sucked silently into the cylinder. He gazed at the razor's end, puffed a breath to dispel a tailing of smoke and shifted his mutated arm to cover the stunned Maraia. "Next?"

The other mutants fanned out beside the number one mutant, razors at the ready. One of them stepped forward and handed him a slim, clam-shell shaped device with a small stub of an antenna.

The lead mutant flipped the device open, thumbed some colored buttons and pressed the device to his ear. When nothing seemed to happen, he grunted and stabbed more forcefully. This time a connection must have been made.

"We got'em covered," he said to someone at the other end of the communication. After a moment of attentive listening from the mutant, he clapped the device shut and motioned to number two.

Number two reached into a pack on his back and withdrew a small black box with a shiny lens on its top side. He placed the box on the floor, pressed a group of flush-set buttons in sequence, then stepped back.

The air above the box condensed to a whitish blur. Slowly it cleared and an image appeared. It steadied and focused to reveal a holographic projection, the surrounding white cloud now entirely gone.

The image of a wretchedly thin man hovered four centimeters above the floor in the middle of the ruin. With skeletal arms akimbo, his posture was haughtily erect, his feet planted in oversized yellow boots trimmed with some sort of animal's fur dyed purple. One hand was shoved pretentiously into a wide black belt that wrapped his waist, cinched tight by a large, square brass buckle. He wore a high-collared red jacket with gold buttons lined down the front, flanked on his chest by rows of brightly colored ribbon medals.

He wasn't wearing any pants as far as Michael could tell. Either he'd forgotten to put them on, or simply always dressed that way.

The caricature might have been amusing, but that was before Michael stared at the man's eyes. No hint of clown there, just a steely black deadness, like looking at a predator who was about to bite through a rabbit and eat it guts and all.

"Hello, Gregory," the image said. "And you all." He waved his free hand vaguely at the others.

"Cardassin," Rasmussen wheezed. "You butcher."

Warren twitched on the floor, his vital fluids leaking out in a swirling pool of clear plasma laced with streaks of blood.

Cardassin squinted in the general direction of Warren, but not directly at him, off to the right. He must have been looking at a monitored projection of the room. "Ick." He snapped his fingers at the lead mutant, a bit off line of center. "Igor, please end him."

A blinding flash erupted from Igor's razor, and Warren's head rolled on the floor.

"Tsk, tsk," Cardassin said. "The man's distress was becoming distracting, though I do admit to being captivated by the play of colors in his effluent." Cardassin sniffed and cupped his hand to his crotch adjusting something beneath the edge of his jacket.

"Thrilling." His eyes bulged momentarily before the predation returned. "Now...where's the guardian?"

Lest he give away who had the guardian, Michael dared not let his eyes wander from this horrible little man.

"Come, come. I've not got all night." Cardassin motioned to Igor.

He stepped through the hologram to Warren's still smoldering head to kick it out of the way. As he did so, his boot toe lodged in Warren's gaping mouth. The mutant shucked the head free, letting two of Warren's teeth rattle out and hit the floor, spinning. Igor steadied himself before dragging on the edge of a cargo container, spilling its contents to the floor. "Do I haff to search all of them?"

160

"We know nothing of the guardian." Ferral edged slightly behind Akilah. "We're lucky to be alive after crashing on the plain."

Cardassin let loose a high pitched giggle that sent him grabbing his throat as his outburst degraded into choking. He recovered and looked off line at Rasmussen. "Gregory, who is this impertinent man? I want the guardian, now. Puh-leeze!"

When Rasmussen failed to respond, Cardassin snapped his fingers.

Igor came to limp attention and extended one hand, palm up, out to his side to mutant number two.

The second mutant hurried forward and placed a cylinder rounded at both ends in Igor's hand.

Dayna gasped. "A nano-assembler."

Cardassin cast her a droopy-eyed look. "Well, hello, little lady. I'm surprised *TrueMen* even know what one looks like."

"I am not--"

"Shut up Dayna," Akilah said.

"Hottie, tottie," Cardassin eyed Akilah lasciviously. "You must be the daughter all grown up, now." He bit one of his fingernails and spit the clipping out the side of his mouth. "Wanna fokk?"

Akilah kept cool, standing her ground and staring at the player, but she was shaking. In fear or rage, Michael couldn't tell.

"I thought not," Cardassin drawled. "Now Greg, I'll ask once more for the guardian, and if it isn't produced things will get messy, as they say." He thrust out his hand and waited as though he would have been capable, as a projected image, of receiving the guardian had it been produced. His red enameled fingernails flashed in dim light.

Rasmussen spit at Cardassin's image and glared. "You don't scare me."

Cardassin peered down at his fluffy boots as if Rasmussen's spittle had actually soiled them. "What a mess you've made." A nod to Igor.

He withdrew a small pellet from the end of the nano-assembler. "Do you know wot this is?"

"You wouldn't dare." Rasmussen raised his arms across his face, the protective sign of Sedroth lying prone.

Michael had to admire Cardassin's audacity. All the doctor stood for was anchored in the purity of his genome, and now this Cardassin was threatening to corrupt it with designer genes.

Akilah rushed forward. "I'll give you the guardian! Leave him alone."

"She knows nothing," Rasmussen cried.

"You are testing my patience," Cardassin said. "Igor, I think Greg here wants a taste of diversity."

Igor nodded to mutant number two, who straddled Rasmussen, grabbed the doctor's cheeks in a massive hand and squeezed his jaw open.

With Rasmussen's tongue lashing back and forth in an effort to ward off what was coming, Igor shoved the pellet deep into Rasmussen's mouth, tamped it down his throat with a rough finger, then had mutant number two clamp Rasmussen's jaw shut until he swallowed.

162

When released, Rasmussen gasped, trying in vain to cough up the pellet. "You won't get away with this. Where's your sense of decency?"

"Fokk decency," Cardassin said. "And I intend to get away with this."

"You are truly barbaric."

"Yes, but I am winning."

Akilah rushed to her father's side. She cupped his face in her hands. "We'll get it out. Nicholai will pump your stomach." She cast a hopeful glance at Nicholai, who shook his head sadly.

"I'll see you dead for this!" Akilah shouted at Cardassin.

He turned a steely gaze to Akilah.

Then the lights went out.

His image glowed for an instant in the dark, then flickered and vanished.

Someone loomed massively in the entrance, then slid off to one side into the dark. Two ice razors hissed in resonance from a barely perceptible source within the gloom.

Michael dove for Akilah and knocked her off her feet. They crashed behind a stack of containers.

She struggled. "Get off me! I've got to help Father."

Michael cupped a hand over her mouth.

Streaks of light gleamed in quick crossing patterns.

A bluish streak sliced the second mutant's body in three before the pieces hit the floor.

Maraia razors blue and red crackled through the air at maximum power, ricocheting off walls, sending concrete chips flying.

The mutants' industrial razors fired up and hummed, sending out pulses of light, peppering the walls and exploding anything else that got in their way.

"Out!" Igor shouted above the din.

The flash of mutant razors concentrated toward the entrance.

Defensive beams collided with incoming. Shattered bursts from intersecting photons buzzed out of phase.

Humped shapes slid to the entrance, then they were gone.

Darkness returned accompanied by an eerie silence. The smell of burnt flesh pervaded throughout.

A lone being stepped to the entrance, his figure silhouetted against weak starlight. He snapped off razors held in both hands and pocketed the tools.

The lights came on.

"Jamil!" Michael shouted.

"Who's Jamil?" Akilah craned to see from her prone position.

"The computer's recycled the circuits," Ferral said. "I don't know how they went off in the first-- who's that?"

Jamil stomped over to the fallen mutant and stepped hard on his fingers. The mutant remained still. "Dead."

"Of course he's dead," Ferral said. "You cut him in three."

"Make sure." Jamil moved back to the shadow of the entrance and squatted on the floor. He pulled the hood of his parka down over his forehead. His

164

eyes darted keenly as he regarded the confusion in the room with curiosity.

"Is he dangerous?" Ferral fumbled for one of the razors that had spiraled away in the confusion and lay against a wall.

Jamil's head jerked up. He reached to his pocket.

"Ferral!" Akilah shouted. "He just saved our lives." She hurried to her father's bedside. "Is there anything we can do?"

"I feel nothing untoward, child. Perhaps the designer gene failed to take effect."

"That would be a first." Ferral clutched his upper arm. Blood seeped through his fingers.

"You're hurt," Akilah said.

"It's nothing."

"Let's have a look." Nicholai pried Ferral's hand off the wound. "Nothing? You're lucky the razor didn't sever your humerus. This will need stitches."

"Then stitch it." Ferral sat heavily on one of the low canisters and regarded Jamil in what almost became a staring contest.

"Jamil is one of the primitives I spoke of earlier," Michael said. "He's the one who dropped Akilah the rope ladder."

"Then we owe you thanks for helping to save our lives." Rasmussen spoke to Jamil in his ancient language.

As far as Michael could ascertain, Rasmussen seemed okay. Maybe the designer gene pellet *had* been a dud.

"Come closer, Jamil," Rasmussen coaxed. "Let me look at you."

"No, I go." Jamil stood to leave.

"He's a bit shy," Michael said.

Rasmussen said something more to Jamil. Then he turned to the others. "After the Maraia were created, Cardassin did his best to eradicate them and the *Gilomir* genome they carried. Some Maraia fled south only to be assaulted by proto humans. Kidnapped Maraia were forced into cohabitation and the result was--"

"I'm sorry Doctor Rasmussen, but enough of this anthropology lesson for now." Ferral flexed his arm, then pushed Nicholai away when he tried to re-examine a stitch that came free.

Nicholai looked insulted. "I'm not done."

"Ferral, you've got to let Nicholai finish," Akilah said.

Ferral ignored her and reached for one of Warren's arms, which had risen stiffly off the floor. "I suppose you are prepared to--God that hurts." Ferral winced and stopped pulling on Warren's arm.

"We'll clear the remains," Akilah said. "I suggest you let Nicholai finish his doctoring."

Ferral glared.

Akilah turned to the others. "I want a perimeter set up, the door repaired, and all these body parts cleared outside before they begin to decompose."

Dayna, probably also seeing the tension between Ferral and Akilah, pulled Warren's head toward the door by the hair. "Poor Warren. He always meant well. He was just a bit too eager and got himself killed." She wrinkled her nose. "It's heavier than I thought."

"Looks like the son-of-a-bitch is still grinning," Ferral said from his seated position across the room..

"That's not funny, Ferral." Akilah turned her back on him and dragged one of Warren's severed legs to the door and placed it outside. "I hate to leave Warren like this," Akilah said. "But it's twenty below out here. I suppose he'll keep. We'll see about burial come first light."

***

Michael counted three trips to clear the ruin, not that it mattered, but it was in his nature to keep track. Two trips for Warren's scattered parts and one for the mutant's remains.

Outside, following Akilah's instructions, they arranged Warren to one side of the entrance and piled the mutant on the other.

In an odd way, Michael could admire the forthrightness of Rasmussen's daughter. She obviously knew her place amongst these people. Yet, she seemed reluctant to step forward forcefully, especially when it involved putting Ferral in his place.

Back inside, the scene had almost quieted down. Karin comforted Lorry, the latter sobbing uncontrollably as Karin caressed her hair, whispering to her, obviously trying to keep her from dissolving further into hysteria.

Dayna had retreated to one of the canisters and leaned against it with her arms folded across her chest.

167

Rasmussen lay, staring glassy-eyed at the ceiling. He seemed to be oblivious to what had happened.

Okay, Michael thought. *Maybe we can all calm down and pull this effort together in one direction.*

Rasmussen's skin darkened, then started turning green.

"What have they done to my father?"

"Diversity," Ferral said sarcastically.

"Have you no heart?" Akilah rushed to her father's side.

"I resent that," Ferral said, obviously still engaged in his last exchange with Akilah.

"I've no time for this, Ferral.

Rasmussen moaned. "Kill me."

"Can't we do something?" Akilah searched the peering faces around her.

Why the panic? Michael thought. *He can be cured. They just need a nano-assembler.*

Rasmussen screamed. A sound laced with self-loathing, remorse, emptiness.

"We'll think of something, Father."

"I could run some tests with the sequencer," Nicholai said, "but that would only confirm what we already know. If we had a nano-assembler to clear the anomalies, we could save him."

Finally.

"I can understand you saying that as a doctor," Akilah said, "but that is not an option. Father would never use a nano-assembler. He'd rather die."

Nicholai refused to be bullied. "Would you let Doctor Rasmussen die without trying?"

"Even if I thought it would save his life," Akilah said, color rising in her cheeks, "we all know the only place we would be able to obtain a nano-assembler is from Cardassin's compound and then we'd probably have to kidnap one of his mutants to show us how to use it."

"I thought their use was intuitive?" Ferral said.

Akilah gave him a thoughtful look. "To some extent, but in unskilled hands you can see the results. Mutants."

"You're both getting way ahead of yourself," Dayna said. "The first step is to figure out how to obtain a nano-assembler, and I will remind you that those mutants who just attacked us carried one. If we caught up to them, we might be able to get it. The dimwits move slow enough."

"We might be able to catch up to them," Akilah said, "but we'd never take them by surprise. We'd stick out like sore thumbs on the flat ice."

"Blasphemy!" Rasmussen croaked.

"Father, please. You're only making matters worse."

"We need to focus on building *Afareni*!" Rasmussen shouted. "We--" He choked and spit up green bile mixed with streaks of blood, then fell back on the cot, his cheeks and chest stained, his breathing labored. Small tendrils, green with chlorophyll, budded on his skin.

Dayna stared aghast. "We can't just stand by and watch him die."

Akilah tore her gaze away from Rasmussen, her face contorted with anxiety. "All right. At this point, we have a convergence of need. According to what Michael has said and Father has confirmed, we need a nano-assembler to build A4-Ni. If we had a nano-assembler, it could also be used to save my father."

"But he'd never--"

"Dayna, please. I'm well aware of the odds that Father would ever accede to the use of a nano-assembler even if his life depended on it. I'm only looking at our options and trying to put the best face on them that I can."

This is getting out of hand.

"The *odds of success are 52%, failure 38%, random dispersion 10%.*"

Thank you metabase. I think they and we have no choice but to pursue a nano-assembler. It is dangerous, but A4-Ni won't get built otherwise.

"I think going after the mutants to procure their nano-assembler is a good idea," Michael said.

"Who asked you?" Ferral snapped.

Akilah raised her hands to calm everyone down. "Thanks, Mike. I'm glad someone agrees with me. I know it would be a dangerous undertaking. We could all be killed. But without a nano-assembler our options are nil to none. Any objections?"

"Just the obvious one," Dayna said. "How do you propose sneaking up on the mutants?"

"It's a risk we'll have to take. I don't know how else to do it."

"Tunnel." Jamil stirred by the entrance.

"The forgotten man," Ferral said. "Or should I say, half man?"

"I think he's trying to help us, Ferral," Akilah said. "Can't you think positively for a change?"

Ferral looked like he might say something, but then decided against it.

"Ice tunnel. I make," Jamil said.

Michael stepped over to Jamil and squatted in front of him.

"What tunnel are you talking about?"

"Under ice. To Kanapoi. I go, many times. Steal from Cardassin. Mutants eat drugs, drink fire, sleep. Easy to steal."

Michael stood and returned to the others. "It seems there's a tunnel under the ice. Jamil has used it to steal things from Kanapoi. Cardassin and his mutants are so out of it they never know the stuff is disappearing."

Ferral waved his hands in the air. The gesture would have seemed ludicrous if the man producing it wasn't so sinister. "You're suggesting we just waltz in there and help ourselves to a nano-assembler?"

"I'm simply repeating what Jamil has said. You've already indicated that it's not my place to suggest anything." Michael hoped Akilah would take the lead.

Dayna wheeled on Michael. "I don't like the way you step in and steer the discussion at critical moments. It strikes me as too opportunistic. You haven't done anything to prove you aren't one of Cardassin's agents."

"Though we don't know who he is," Akilah said, "I'm fairly certain he is not one of Cardassin's agents. Mike, I'd like to hear what you have to say."

"All right. If you want an opinion, then I have to agree with Akilah. Your options are severely limited without a nano-assembler. Logically, you would be better off waiting and concentrating your efforts on fortifying your existing location. But Doctor Rasmussen's life hangs in the balance. You need not commit all of your manpower to the mission. The odds of failure are high, but success is possible."

"Thank you, Michael," Akilah said.

"Well, well," Dayna said. "He has an opinion after all."

Akilah wheeled on Dayna. "It's all well and good that you can make light of this conversation, but I've already compromised much of what I believe to even consider a foray that might secure us a nano-assembler. If you are so opposed then I don't expect you to volunteer."

"Akilah, I would never--"

"I know you would never, whatever. I'm asking for volunteers!" She stood, shaking, emotion coursing through her.

No one moved.

Akilah smiled grimly. "Okay. I guess that shows the commitment of the assembled to my father's goal."

"Screw commitment," Ferral said. "It's common sense. This whole A4-Ni thing is a boondoggle."

172

Akilah blinked rapidly. "Really? Really? Then, Sedroth damn you, Ferral. You can stay here."

Ferral stood his ground, defiant. "You do me wrong."

Akilah glared at him. "We don't have to debate this to death. Your wound precludes your participation. Besides, I can think of no one more qualified to step forward and lead the Maraia if I perish going after a nano-assembler."

The others gasped.

Akilah dug into her pocket and produced the guardian. She tossed it to Ferral. "Keep it safe."

"You're thinking of going alone?" Michael asked.

"If I have to."

Michael saw baleful faces, faces that looked away, faces that showed fear. "I'll go with you."

"Me, too," Dayna said.

Jamil grunted and rose to his feet. "I go, too."

Karin stepped forward.

"What is it, Karin?" Akilah snapped.

"We might need you."

"With all due respect, if we don't have a nano-assembler we'll not need anybody. Besides, apart from being my father's daughter, I have no more claim to leading the *TrueMen* than Ferral here has in misleading them in a futile attempt to regain the planet."

Ferral seemed to want to counter what Akilah had said. Instead, he palmed the guardian and folded his arms across his chest, a twitch of a smile on his lips.

173

"He will make his move soon," the metabase said.

But how soon?

"Two days."

***

"Okay, Jamil, lead the way." Akilah stepped away from the door that led to the passageway.

He glanced at her, but showed no other reaction. Instead, he stepped onto the stair landing, his massive build filling the space side to side.

The others lined up behind him and waited until there was room to advance. After Jamil, Dayna pressed forward eagerly, then Michael, with Akilah bringing up the rear.

Michael could have predicted the order. Dayna out front. Ready to take on anything that came her way. Akilah, more cautious, but no less fearless would bring up the rear. She would want to know what lay behind her, while keeping her sights on those in front.

Michael still didn't have a good grasp of what motivated the two females. Sometimes Akilah seemed very eager to further her father's goal and at other times she seemed to waver.

Dayna on the other hand was a complete unknown. She seemed high on energy, but used it to mask some other ulterior motives.

Ferral remained in the ruin with the others as Akilah had instructed. He hadn't showed any disappointment about being left behind. Indeed, he might have even thought, *thank Sedroth.*

Doctor Rasmussen was in some sort of mental and physical limbo.

As far as Michael was concerned, this was playing out well. At least he would be able to control the situation with Ferral out of this improbable pursuit.

How interesting the Maraia had become. Michael wondered if he would ever understand them. Of course, the endeavor became moot. The Shepherd's directive didn't give him a whole lot of time for understanding.

Jamil came to the elevator shaft and stopped. "We go here."

Dayna peered down the shaft. "How?" She picked up a loose pebble and dropped it into the darkness. A moment later the stone rattled on the bottom. "It's not a long way but will take some doing."

Akilah glanced down the shaft, then at Jamil. "You got a rope?"

But Jamil already had his rope out and was playing it over the side.

"I should have known," Akilah said. "I'll go first. Mike will belay me."

Michael nodded, admiring the way Akilah stepped forward to take charge.

When the rope hit bottom, Jamil handed one end to Michael.

Akilah waited for him to secure the rope, then went over the edge.

Dayna followed, then Jamil, forcing Michael to sit and brace his feet against a low concrete lip at the edge of the shaft opening.

"How am I supposed to get down?" Michael said, peering down the shaft at the others looking up at him.

"Jump." Jamil stepped apart from the others and spread his arms.

"You've got to be kidding."

"No kid."

Michael squinted his eyes closed and stepped off the edge.

A moment later he was cradled in Jamil's arms, looking up at his toothy grin.

"I owe you one," Michael said.

Jamil set him down, seemingly not understanding Michael's comment. Instead, he disappeared into the main tunnel.

They all switched on flashlights, playing the beams into the darkness, crisscrossing, then fixing on Jamil.

He waved his hand directing them to lower their beams to keep from blinding him. Then he headed toward the western end of the tunnel.

The others grouped together hesitantly.

"How does he expect to get us out of here?" Dayna asked. "Both ends of the tunnel are blocked, not only with ice but fallen rocks, have been for centuries."

"He's pulling the rocks aside," Akilah said. "I suppose if he can clear a path to the ice, he can cut us a way out."

Michael crossed the tunnel floor and helped Jamil roll stones out of the way. "You think there are a lot of these?"

Jamil stopped. "Not many." He looked at Michael as though he couldn't count.

Little by little a solid wall of outside ice began to reveal itself.

"How deep is the ice here?" Michael asked.

"Ten meter."

"You're sure there's a tunnel out there?"

"Sure." Jamil tossed a final stone aside and stood back. He drew his ice razor, activated it and played the beam on the flat white wall. After boring a shaft two meters horizontally, he stepped in and started melting a shaft at an angle upward and to his right.

Michael peered into the round, sleek tunnel. Water slid down the bottom of the shaft with a whiff of steam drifting over it. "How do you know where you're going?"

"Don't know."

Akilah came up behind Michael. "He doesn't sound too confident."

"Please be patient," Michael said.

Jamil turned off his ice razor. "Wrong way." He swiveled ninety degrees and began boring into the opposite ice wall.

"This is a waste of time," Dayna said. "The primitive is casting about for something he doesn't seem sure exists. We'd be better off concentrating on reinforcing our position in the ruin and waiting the mutants out."

Akilah glanced at Michael but remained calm.

"Are you so quick to lose your resolve?" Michael asked Dayna.

"Our collective lives are at stake," Dayna countered. "You've only got your own to think about."

"But I take my life very seriously. Besides you agreed to this course of action. Let's give Jamil a chance."

"Through," Jamil said matter-of-factly.

"I'll be damned." Akilah gave a sigh of relief as she strode over to the shaft.

Michael came up behind her. From where he stood, the shaft penetrated straight in, then curved up to the left. A faint glow emanated from somewhere ahead.

"Main tunnel." Jamil pointed, pocketing his razor. "We go."

Jamil had roughened the slope, making it possible to gain a footing. Soon they were standing in a tight tunnel that sloped gently downward to the west.

"Slide." Jamil sat on the tunnel floor, leaned back and gave himself a starting push. He picked up speed and disappeared a hundred meters down into the darkness.

"I guess we're to follow." Michael sat down and pushed off. He picked up speed and was soon at the bottom. Jamil was nowhere in sight. "Jamil?"

"Here."

Michael looked up. Jamil had climbed three meters up a vertical shaft. He played his flashlight down on Michael.

Akilah came down the slide and bumped into Michael. "Where's Jamil?"

Michael pointed.

"I get it," Akilah said. "We slide, then climb and slide again. Very clever. We'll be able to get ahead of the mutants easily."

Michael climbed up and gave Akilah a hand. Dayna arrived and made her way up the shaft.

After four such sliding and climbing trips, Jamil raised his hand, indicating that the others should stand back. He bore an angled hole with his razor. Melted ice coursed down the hole to the tunnel and disappeared out of sight. With a faint crackle, the ceiling ice grew transparent, shattered and fell, creating an opening to the night sky.

He climbed out and lay low to the ice.

A full moon punched a white hole in the dark sky. The ice about them gleamed black and white. The plateau rose above the plain a half kilometer away.

"I don't see them," Akilah whispered.

"There." Michael pointed.

Four hunched figured lurched ten degrees off Michael's line of sight to the plateau. Jamil had indeed brought them out ahead of the mutants. Now to set up an ambush. Not much time.

Akilah motioned for Dayna to fan out to her right, then indicated that Michael should take the left side with Jamil. She would stay at the center. "Fire when I do," she whispered.

The mutants lumbered straight toward them.

Dayna moved a fraction, but it must have caught the attention of the lead mutant.

"Ambrush!" he shouted.

"Damn it, Dayna." Akilah fired her razor. The beam lanced forward and was swallowed up in the dark.

The others opened fire.

The mutants dispersed, going in four different directions without returning fire.

Dayna stood and pocketed her razor. "We can forget it. They're out of range. No telling which one has the nano-assembler."

"We had them until you moved." Akilah glared at Dayna.

"I'm sorry. I shouldn't have moved. I thought they--"

Akilah waved her hand. "The damage is done. Now what?"

"We could split up and go after them," Dayna said.

"I don't think so." Akilah glanced at Michael. "I wouldn't want to go one on one with a mutant out there. Mike?"

"We could keep trying," Michael said. "They'll probably come back together before getting to Kanapoi."

"How much farther is that?" Akilah said.

Jamil rested on his haunches, eyeing them critically. "Ten kilometers."

"Does this tunnel go that far?" Michael asked.

"Far," Jamil said.

Akilah pressed her hands to her forehead. "What if they get to Kanapoi first?"

"I guess that's the end of it," Dayna said. "There's no way the four of us are going to penetrate Cardassin's lair, steal a nano-assembler and get away with it."

"Not hard."

Akilah looked surprised. "I forgot. You've been there before."

"Many time. Go quiet. Take anything. Mutants never know. Cardassin never know."

"Let's hope it doesn't come to that." Akilah looked around. "We'll keep going. Who wants to lead the way?"

"I will," Dayna said.

They roped themselves together, then Dayna stepped to the shaft leading to the next slide. She sat and prepared to lower herself into it, then stopped. "What's that sound?"

Jamil cocked an ear. "Waterfall."

"A waterfall? In the tunnel?" Dayna sounded incredulous. "I thought you said the tunnel went all the way to Kanapoi."

"Waterfall new."

"Great." Dayna tied the rope about her waist. "Someone belay me. I'm going to have a look."

Akilah grabbed the rope and coiled it around her waist, then anchored her cleated boots into the ice.

Dayna eased over the edge and disappeared down the shaft with Akilah playing out the rope.

The rope went taut.

Akilah lost her footing and was dragged into the shaft.

"*You have but seconds before you will be pulled after her,*" the metabase offered.

The rope jerked Michael into the tunnel after Akilah. Up ahead she flailed wildly with one hand as she hung onto the rope with the other. Down the shaft she shot.

The dark and the roar of the water was nearly suffocating.

Despite Michael's attempt to dig in the cleats on his boots, the floor of the tunnel slid beneath him. He was in freefall, disorientated.

A splash sounded from up front.

He ground his heels harder, groped for his ice ax, and after fumbling to clear it from his belt, swung it into the ice.

A high whine of ax point grooving ice, flakes shattering upward, then finally a grinding halt.

Michael secured the main rope around the haft of the ax.

The rope around his waist drew tight, threatening to cut him in two. Dayna must be in the water and possibly Akilah.

Michael grimaced. His boots dug deep. The sound of rushing water blotted out everything, even thought.

His eyes focused. A dim edge divided white on black in front of him. The tunnel had ended abruptly.

Chapter Eight

Michael craned forward and could just see the top of Akilah's head. He dared not lean more for fear of losing his purchase on the ice. A dark river raged five meters below Akilah. He took out his flash, turned it on and set it on end to shine on the roof overhead. Light reflected off the glistening walls and illuminated the river below..

Dayna bobbed like a cork on a string, dipping in and out up to her waist. Each time the river took her legs in, a biting spray rose and washed over the rest of her.

"Where's Jamil?" Akilah called.

"He's still up top," Michael yelled above the roar of water. "His rope is the only thing keeping the three of us out of the river."

"I'm cutting myself free!" Dayna screamed. Her voice was chattering, as if the icy water had frozen her jaw, numbed her tongue.

"You'll do no such thing," Akilah yelled. "I don't want you to die."

"It's either that, or we all die." Dayna fumbled at her belt for her knife.

The river churned and swallowed her legs up to her hips.

She struggled to keep her head above water as her knife flashed briefly before being slapped away.

"Dayna!" Akilah pulled on the rope connecting them to no avail.

"God, that's cold. I lost my knife. I'll have to untie myself."

"Stow it, Dayna! Here's what we're going to do. Michael, are you listening!"

"I'm here, but I don't know how long Jamil can hold us." He looked anxiously back up the tunnel. "Jamil!"

No answer.

"Forget Jamil. Lower the end of your spare rope to me." Akilah didn't look up, her gaze set on Dayna below her.

"How's that going to help?"

"God damn it, Michael, just do it."

Michael played out his rope. It snaked down, drifting to the right as currents of air stirred by the river's flow picked it up.

Akilah reached out both hands blindly, not able to see where the rope had gone. "Where is it?"

"Farther to your right. There. Reach up."

She snagged the rope and pulled down extra line.

"What are you doing?" Michael shouted.

"The only thing I can do, buy time." She knotted the end of the rope, coiled the rest and threw it into the river upstream from Dayna. "Grab the end!"

Dayna flailed. "I've got it."

"Tie it around your waist. Quickly."

Dayna fumbled with the rope. "I can't. My hands are frozen stiff."

"All right. Plan B." Akilah pulled back Michael's rope until she had the loose end, then with a strain, she leaned back and pulled on the rope to

Dayna. Once she had some slack she formed a loop and shoved the end of Michael's rope through, quickly half-hitching it above and below the loop. "Okay, Michael, are we secured to your ice axe?"

"Yeah. The axe is buried and frozen in solid. I've hooked myself to it, in case Jamil's rope fails."

"Excellent. Now, take up the slack and tie Dayna off on Jamil's rope. Hurry."

Michael could hear the strain in her voice. Then he knew what she was up to. "This isn't going to work!"

"What? I can't hear you. Tell me when you're done."

"I said this isn't--never mind. His left foot slipped and for the first time his entire weight and that of the women was on the ice ax.

It held.

"Dayna!" Akilah's voice was ragged with fear.

No answer.

"Dayna, God damn it, don't fade on me, we're going to get you out."

"I can't move." Dayna called weakly. "My legs are gone. I--"

The rest of what she wanted to say was washed out by another dunking. She came up sputtering, unable to wipe water from her hair and face.

Michael attached the end of the spare rope to the clip at his waist that led to Jamil's rope. "It's tied."

"I pray to Sedroth that this holds," Akilah said.

"You better pray to Sedroth that Jamil is quick footed."

"Now, free yourself from the clip."

"I'm free. I still don't think this is--"

"I'm cutting us free of Dayna."

Jamil's rope jerked suddenly with the transfer of Dayna's weight to it. The knot Michael had tied slipped, then held, turning as it tensed. The rope rose stiffly off the floor.

A muffled scream echoed down from the top of the tunnel.

The other the rope holding Akilah lessened its weight on Michael by half.

The rope to Jamil moved down, gaining speed in the direction of the waterfall.

"He's lost his footing!" Michael yelled.

Akilah twisted around to see what was happening. "Hang on!"

"He's going to hit me hard. We're all going over."

"Have faith. Dayna?"

No answer.

"She's finished!" Michael shouted. "Cut her loose. It's her or all of us."

"Never!"

Jamil's rope sizzled by Michael. He turned.

Jamil slid out of control toward him, his ice ax in one hand, his boots grooving desperately against the sides of the tunnel.

Michael resigned himself to being hit and propelled over the edge. The icy water would close over him. At first he would feel nothing but its speed, then seepage through his parka and pants, his boots, into his ears, nose and mouth. He'd try to scream, but water would pour into his lungs,

186

freezing his breath, stilling his heart, then a void, dark, an abyss without bottom.

Nothing.

"Stupid."

Jamil's voice was practically at Michael's ear, his breath heaving warmly on Michael's cheek.

Both ropes hummed taut.

Jamil gulped air, trying to recover from his fall. He shifted his weight to get a better anchoring position. He spat onto the ice in front of Michael. "*TrueMen.*"

"I know you don't like them," Michael said through clenched teeth as he felt again the strain of holding Akilah out of the water, "but now what do we do?"

Jamil tugged on his ice ax to satisfy himself that he was well anchored, then he pulled arm-over-arm on the rope to reel Dayna in. Her body skimmed over the surface of the river, alternately merging and submerging in the freezing water. She finally rose free and slapped limply against the side wall of ice next to Akilah.

She grasped Dayna, then shook her. "She looks dead."

Jamil pulled Dayna's still form over the edge and shoved her farther up the tunnel and out of the way.

"Now help." Jamil leaned over and grabbed Michael's rope in one massive hand and pulled. Together they brought Akilah up to the ledge. She flopped onto it, her face blue. "Where's Dayna," she gasped.

187

Jamil sat back on his haunches and leaned against the tunnel wall. Between gulps for air, he pointed up the tunnel.

Ripping off her gloves, Akilah scrambled over to Dayna. She rubbed Dayna's exposed hands and slapped her face gently. "Dayna, Dayna, don't die on me."

With a look of disgust, Jamil heaved himself upright and strode over to them, ice razor out.

"Move."

He aimed at a far wall, activated the razor, then quickly tamped its beam down to a very diffuse glow. He played the dim light over Dayna, while Akilah kept rubbing her legs and arms.

"That feels good," Akilah said. "She's still breathing."

"Not dead."

Michael coiled the ropes. He shuddered, thinking about what might have been.

Dayna groaned. Her eyes flickered open. "Am I in heaven?"

"No, but the next best thing," Akilah said. "We're all safe."

"I don't feel too good." Dayna leaned sideways, gagged and spit up water. She coughed to clear her lungs. "I don't know if it's better to drown or freeze to death."

Akilah hugged her. "I thought I'd lost you."

Michael finished with the ropes and stacked them in a neat pile. "That was quick thinking," he said to Akilah.

She loosened her embrace of Dayna and looked up at him. "If you and Jamil hadn't been able to hold us, no amount of my thinking would have saved us." She stood and offered Michael her hand. "Thanks. I owe you one. And Jamil, too." She glanced at Jamil, who ignored her and concentrated on warming Dayna.

Michael took her hand. It was still cold. "You're bleeding." He reached into his pack for a first aid wrap and disinfectant.

"That can wait. I want to make sure Dayna is all right." She returned to Dayna and helped her sit up.

"It's getting right balmy in here." Dayna spread her hands and clasped her fingers, obviously enjoying the warmth from Jamil's razor.

"Are you strong enough to walk?"

"I think so." Dayna waved Jamil's razor away and tried to stand. She managed to stay erect, though not very stable. "At least my clothes have dried." She leaned against the wall. "I guess that does it for the nano-assembler. We'll have to take to the surface, and there we'll not stand a chance against the mutants. I vote we abort and return to the ruin."

Akilah glanced from Michael to Jamil. "I thought this tunnel went all the way to Kanapoi."

"It does," Michael said. "So we don't have to surface but how do we get past this waterfall?"

"No problem," Jamil said.

Akilah gawked.

Jamil waved them back, then refocused his razor and pointed it at the side of the tunnel.

The light penetrated in and upward, opening a shaft.

They retreated dodging the ice melt that quickly formed and ran down the shaft to the tunnel and over the edge into the river.

Jamil stepped purposely into the shaft as it deepened. After he had angled up about three meters, he turned and began to bore a hole through the vaulted ceiling ice over the chasm. Michael estimated there was a meter of ice between the floor of the bore and the ceiling, preventing them from dropping through.

"Smart man," Akilah said.

"Probably done it a million times," Michael said grudgingly. "I'll go first this time. I suggest Dayna follow, then you. We shouldn't all be in the bridging tunnel at the same time."

They nodded.

Michael climbed up the sloping shaft to where he could see Jamil boring his way across.

Jamil stopped going forward. He focused his razor to a pencil thinness and directed it down at the ice.

At first Michael wondered what he was doing, but then realized that Jamil couldn't bore a downward sloping shaft until he had a drain hole for the ice melt.

Steam rose from the boiling melt. A moment later, the bubbling stopped. The melt sank into the ice and disappeared below. Jamil had bored through. The sound of the raging stream drifted up out of the hole to mingle with the greater sound coming from behind him.

Jamil quickly widened the hole into a shaft they could fit through. He turned to look at Michael across the bridge tunnel. "Easy."

"For you." Michael crawled on hands and knees, fearing that with each forward motion, he'd crack the floor below and plunge into the water. But Jamil had done his job well. Michael reached the other side. "Dayna, you can come now." Without waiting for her, he slid down the shaft and stood beside Jamil.

"Nice work."

"No work." Jamil grinned. "Fun."

Michael shook his head.

Dayna came down the shaft feet first, hit the tunnel floor and crumpled. "I guess I'm not as strong as I thought."

Michael reached to give her a hand up, but she waved it away and continued to sit on the ice. "And I hoped we'd be returning to the ruin."

Akilah slid down beside her. "Dayna?"

"We can go back." Dayna looked hopeful.

"We don't have a choice, now, but to move forward," Akilah said. "Everything Father has lived for is at stake, not to mention his life."

"We go," Jamil said. "Not good stay here. Mutants find."

"I agree," Michael said. "The mutants might have doubled back and are waiting for us to backtrack. It's better we proceed."

Akilah reached to steady Dayna. "I'll help you."

Dayna smiled weakly. "I'll manage. Just don't leave me behind."

191

***

The tunnel continued on a downward slope, its glistening walls disappearing quickly into a bottomless gloom.

Michael pressed against the side, feeling the slick cold penetrate his parka. "You first this time," he said to Jamil. "Then Dayna and Akilah. I'll bring up the rear."

Akilah handed the end of the rope attached to her waist to Michael, then clipped Dayna's rope to her belt and stepped behind her.

Jamil gave them a glance as if assuring himself that they were ready, then slid down the remaining tunnel segment. The light brown of his parka shown in the dim light, then fell away to be enveloped by the dark. A faint flash from the light strapped to his forehead reflected off one wall and then was gone.

Dayna stood ready, feet planted apart, playing out Jamil's rope. As it grew taut, she gave an apprehensive glance over her shoulder to Akilah. Dayna eased herself over the threshold, landed on her backside and slid forward, arms held straight out above her head.

Akilah stepped up to take her turn. She stared glumly down the tunnel, then up to Michael.

"What is it?" he asked.

"If this doesn't work out," she whispered, "Remember I saved your life once."

"What's that supposed to mean?"

Her rope tightened, and she stepped off without a backward glance.

"She's a complex Maraia female."

192

That doesn't tell me anything more than I already know.

"*Hominid emotions.*"

Enlighten me.

"*I can't. We have no baseline for evaluating emotions. You might. You're mostly hominid.*"

The metabase spoke in riddles.

The rope securing him to Akilah snapped tight and jerked him into the tunnel. He floundered on his belly, feeling awkward and foolish.

"*You should pay more attention to your surroundings.*"

Shut up. Michael slid headfirst. The darkness a welcome respite. He closed his eyes. Moments of weightlessness. Moments only to question his own motives--assist in the construction of A4-Ni. But aside from that he had no guidelines for what he was supposed to do, or how he was supposed to act. He could gauge risk as it pertained to his goal, but what good was that when the goal had obviously been met? Did it mean that he could do anything and things would turn out well despite his behavior?

"*A profound philosophical question.*"

Do you have the answer for me?

"*It is better you discover it for yourself.*"

The others were grouped together at the end of the tunnel, waiting for his arrival. They looked up puzzled, then he careened into them head first.

Dayna cut a laugh short by covering her mouth with her hand.

Jamil shook his head in disapproval and ascended the ice to the start of another tunnel.

Akilah helped Michael to his feet. "Daydreaming?"

They repeated the maneuver without incident until they came to the end of the third tunnel.

Jamil stood with his hand up as he peered forward.

"What is it?" Michael whispered.

"Not here before."

"Neither was the waterfall." Michael looked over Jamil's shoulder.

The tunnel opened into the side of a large bowl-shaped depression. The night sky domed overhead. The air was crisp with the dry cold of the outside, not like the dank interior of the tunnels. The rest of the tunnel continued on the far side of the bowl about fifty meters away.

The full moon shown against the black sky, peppered by hard points of light from the brighter stars. Moonlight defined the perimeter of the bowl where it met the ice plain above. The sides of the bowl glistened, shading around from white to dark gray, then black. There were no noticeable irregularities to the bowl's surface. It would be easy enough to slide into the bowl, but take time to climb up the other side to the safety of the opposing tunnel.

"I don't like this," Akilah said once she had surveyed the scene. "We're sitting ducks out there if the mutants have planned an ambush."

"No like ducks."

"Okay, Jamil, you don't like ducks," Michael said. "How are we going to get across?"

"I go. Then you go."

Before Michael could argue, Jamil had freed himself from Dayna's rope and stepped over the threshold. He slid to the bottom of the bowl, then using his ice ax and jamming his cleated boots into the smooth ice, quickly hauled himself up the far side and disappeared into the opaque dark of the tunnel. His traverse took only seconds. Nothing else moved in or around the bowl. He emerged halfway into moonlight and waved them on.

"You two first," Michael said. "I'll cover you and bring up the rear."

"Are you up for this?" Akilah asked Dayna.

She nodded, but didn't look at all convinced. She had lagged behind alarmingly at the transition between the last two tunnels.

Akilah took her hand and together they slid to the bottom of the bowl.

They drew their ice axes and were about to climb the other side when crisscrossing razor beams formed a spider web of light around them, preventing them from moving without getting sliced in two.

Jamil's razor penciled light toward the sources of the attacking beams.

When Michael swung his razor toward the rim, a mutant popped through a thin layer of ice at the bottom of the bowl, shoved Dayna out of the way and threw a rough clad arm around Akilah's neck.

The incoming razor fire ceased, leaving deep grooves in the ice and a slow trickle of quickly solidifying melt.

The mutant backed his way up the side using Akilah as a shield.

A surreal silence fell on the scene. No razor fire, no shouts, no movement except the mutant as he struggled to hold Akilah, each boot stamping deliberately at the ice surface, jamming cleats in deep.

"Help me!" Akilah screamed.

Dayna hesitated, probably saw that she couldn't get a clean shot, then beat a retreat to Michael.

The spell having been broken by Akilah's plaintive cry, razors from the top perimeter wove a deadly pattern around Dayna. She scrambled desperately, flailing the ice with her ax until she flopped into the tunnel beside Michael.

The bottom edge of her parka smoldered from a near hit. "They've got Akilah." Her voice was dry with fear.

"I can see that." Michael peered around the edge of the tunnel entrance, hoping to get a shot, but feared hitting Akilah. Jamil must have thought the same thing. He stood motionless, half concealed by the tunnel wall.

Akilah's struggles weakened, her pleas for help reduced to hoarse whispers, then the mutant backed over the top edge of the bowl and tumbled out of sight onto the plain above.

A dark shape rose and stood at the bowl's edge, hands on his hips, legs spread apart. "We gonna kill the girl if yaw don't surrender."

"It's the one Cardassin called Igor," Dayna said.

"Not too smart showing himself like that." Michael and Jamil fired their razors simultaneously. Both missed.

Igor stood his ground.

A third mutant ninety degrees around the bowl perimeter fired at Jamil.

The bolt of light hit him mid-chest.

He grunted, clutched his chest with both hands and pitched forward onto the sloping ice. With legs splayed out, boot toes pressing ineffectually into the side, he slid face down to the bottom of the bowl and came to rest at the edge of the mutant's spider hole.

"Back off," Igor yelled to Michael, "Or yaw lady friend is good as fried."

"We've got to save her." Dayna lunged out of the tunnel.

Michael grabbed her arm, and when she struggled, grappled her.

She tipped back into the tunnel.

Michael twisted her around and fell on top of her.

"I can appreciate that you want to save Akilah," he said, breathing heavily. "But right now, there's nothing we can do."

Igor hefted his industrial razor, and pointing it in the general direction of Michael and Dayna, slid agilely down the bowl to Jamil. He kicked Jamil in the stomach. When he didn't move, Igor grabbed the back of the primitive's parka and dragged him to the lip of the spider hole, then used his boot to roll him into the pit.

Jamil's body sank a half meter and wedged tight. All that could be seen was his back.

Igor clumped laboriously to the top of the bowl and sat on the edge. He shot a burst of light across the bowl, held the beam steady for a few seconds then turned it off.

Melted ice flowed to the bottom of the bowl, some of it reaching the spider hole before freezing.

"Give up?" Igor called.

"He's going to bury Jamil alive," Dayna said.

Michael wondered about that. If Jamil was to be buried alive, then he wasn't dead. A good thing. But if he was already dead, he couldn't be buried alive. Either way, there wasn't much Michael could do. Igor held all the options.

"*Odds are seventy-five percent Jamil is dead. Twenty-five alive.*"

Odds are that they will kill Akilah, too. Surrendering will only give the mutants two more bodies to play with.

"I don't got all night," Igor shouted.

"We have to do something," Dayna said.

"No heroics, Dayna. We buy time. Odds are that Jamil is dead, so no point running out there to save him. Igor would incinerate us as soon as look at us. Better to wait until they leave, then plan a counterattack. They probably won't try to come after us. The tunnel is too constricted and easily defended."

"How can you be so clinical," Dayna said, eyeing Michael. "I thought Jamil was your friend."

"Clinical? I don't know as what I feel is clinical or not. I do feel his loss. I find it difficult to find words to express that loss. Is that clinical?"

"Bye, bye." Igor played his razor at the ice, and with a little guidance from a groove he cut, funneled the melt to the spider hole.

After a few seconds the water leveled at the top of the hole, spilled out into the bowl, then congealed.

Igor cut his razor beam and moved off out of sight.

Michael brushed at his eyes, suddenly wet with tears.

Minutes passed. No sounds came from the outside.

Michael ventured forward and peered out. The bowl was deserted. "I think they're gone."

"Should we try to save Jamil, now?" Dayna asked.

Michael stared at her.

"It's a sarcastic question." The metabase.

What's sarcastic?

"The obvious meaning to her words is to be ignored. Look for an underlying meaning."

"We're probably too late. And we have no way to dispose of the ice melt if we thaw the ice around him. It will freeze back in place as fast as we can melt it."

"Then how did they form this God damn bowl?" Dayna screamed.

"You forget that they have industrial strength razors capable of quickly melting the ice through to the underlying cavities. Our personal razors aren't up to the job."

"I'm going to kill every single one--"

A whoosh of air coming from the back of the tunnel caught them by surprise.

"What in the name of Sed--"

199

"Water!" Michael yelled. "They're melting the far end of the tunnel. Out. Out. Quick."

Dayna swung her ax around the edge of the tunnel entrance and dug her cleats deep into the side of the bowl, straining, she pressed her face close to the icy surface.

Michael did the same on the opposite side and climbed.

With a roar, water coursed down the tunnel and exploded into the bowl. The melt spewed across the bowl, hit the other side and swirled to the bottom. The bowl started to fill.

"We've got to climb higher," Michael said. "The water won't rise farther than the height of the tunnel's back end."

But the water didn't even rise that far. After the initial flood, the flow decreased rapidly then stopped altogether, leaving the center of the bowl under another three meters of quickly freezing water.

"I guess that was just a parting shot," Dayna said as she gained the top of the bowl.

"Hold it here," Michael cautioned. "Let's make sure it's safe." He peered over the edge. "They're moving off. I count four mutants and Akilah."

"You hold it!" Dayna rose to her feet and sprinted after the retreating mutants.

Stubborn. Michael caught up to her and pulled her down.

She struggled to free herself, then gave up and lay limply, gulping for air.

"We've got to think this through," Michael hissed in her ear.

"Okay, think. For starters, you can get off me."

Michael rolled to his knees. "Rushing after them now isn't the answer."

"So what do you propose," Dayna said, obviously irritated, "sitting here and freezing to death?"

"I suggest we return to the ruin and regroup. If we still think we can penetrate Cardassin's compound then let's do it with some force."

"Negative. If the mutants are all as inebriated as Jamil has said, then we should still be able to make it to the compound through the tunnel. We breech the perimeter, and once inside, we find Akilah, kill any mutants that get in the way, grab a nano-assembler and escape."

Michael regarded her with surprise. *She won't give up. Is it the nano-assembler for Doctor Rasmussen or her loyalty to Akilah?* Whichever, she was going to get them both killed. And that would be the end of building A4-Ni.

"The odds are not with us," Michael said.

"Now *you* are thinking too much. This way we have the element of surprise. They'd never, ever expect us to persevere."

You've got that right.

The only thing giving Michael any confidence was the knowledge that the Shepherd existed, so A4-Ni must have been built, and since his mission was to assist in that construction, then he must surely survive...unless someone else used the guardian, and he wasn't needed.

201

Chapter Nine

Like a caged tiger, Cardassin paced inside his tent, five strides to the east wall until he came up against a hanging black-on-red tapestry depicting a smiling Buddha, something his nano-assembler had spit out from ancient DNA lodged in its memory. Then he'd turn, five strides to the west where there was nothing except bare canvas.

If I keep this up I'll wear a tread in this fine carpet.

Not that he could remember why it was fine. Someone had given it to him after it had been mistakenly created by another nano-assembler. One never knew what lurked in these tubes from previous unsupervised use.

The bells outside the tent, minus tinkle bell, rattled.

"Come."

Trudal stepped in and threw back the hood of his cassock-like robe to reveal a triumphant smile. "We have prevailed, sire."

Cardassin perused Trudal's finely woven cloak, gray with black pin-striping and compared it to his own plain white robe.

I'll have to ask him where he got it. "Excellent. Please do tell me over what we have prevailed?"

"We have neutralize--"

"Fokk the big words, Trudal. I want to know what you have."

"Yes, sire. We have Doctor Rasmussen's daughter. More accurately, she is in the custody of Igor, who is eager to report." Trudal paused, perhaps considering his play on words, but must have quickly thought better of it when Cardassin glared at him. "The man-being I dreamt was created by the Shepherd is dead, along with a primitive and a nameless Maraia female."

"Where are the bodies?"

"Bodies? Sire, the bodies could not be recovered as they were drowned in ice melt that quickly turned solid."

"So, the only thing you know for sure is that you have Rasmussen's daughter."

The amoebic lump quivered. A tear formed at the corner of Cristina's one eye and slid to the floor.

"Observe, Trudal, the mention of Greg's fair daughter has brought a tear to Cristina's eye. How touching."

"Excuse me, sire. Perhaps I have been too explicit."

Cardassin started pacing again, staring at the intricately patterned carpet and trying not to step on any yellow lines. When Cristina didn't get out of his way, he kicked, feeling his bare toes sink into her putty-like flesh before she rebounded across the room and plunked slug-like against the Buddha-draped wall. "I want a full report from this Igor, then I'll see the daughter." He grabbed his crotch and scratched.

"Yes, sire. Igor first, then the daughter. That would have been my choice, too. See what he knows, then see what she knows."

Cardassin waved his hand in dismissal.

Trudal bowed out of the tent.

Where to sit? The bed wouldn't do, despite being the preferred location. Maybe the big chair. It sat regally to one side. Its seat, upholstered in red velvet, hovered a meter off the floor. Ornately carved wooden legs curled into arm rests with royal-purple cushions. The back rest panel was carved with the likeness of a lion eating a snake.

I'll have to do something about the big chair. He hated sitting on it because his feet didn't touch the ground. But at least it enabled him to look down on anyone who came before him.

The bells rattled again.

"Come!" *Save me Zug, from these awful formalities.*

Igor shambled in and stood, looking apprehensive. "Yaw won't kill me, will you, sire?"

"Tsk, tsk, Igor. You're my man!" Cardassin buried his forehead in his hand and shook his head, stifling a giggle. But it wouldn't do to seem too detached from the proceedings. Might weaken morale. "Fear not. I've a long list of things I'd like you to do for me. And right now, number one is-- what the fokk happened out there!!"

Igor blushed. "I like lists, sire."

Cardassin despaired. The poor sap was petrified. Such an irony coming from a hulk who could have twisted him into a pretzel. Cardassin projected an air of infinite patience. "Puh--leeze, Igor, proceed."

"Well, we were doing well after establishing ourselves within the *TrueMen* stronghold, when this

204

insane primitive barged in and started cutting us up. It was all the four of us could do to escape. My second in command was cut in three."

"I know, I know all that. I was there, you fokkin' idiot. Well, not really there, but you know what I mean."

"Yes, sire. After that we retreated. Better to wait another day or night to confront wot appeared to us to be superior numbers. We hadn't gone a few klicks when a force of Maraia popped out of the ice ahead of us and started shooting. Fortunately, I had noticed a movement and suspected an ambush. I was able to alert the others, and we escaped without incident."

"Could you pul--leeze speed this up?"

"Yes, sire. The mutants were traveling the primitive's raiding tunnels, so we set up an ambush. We kidnapped Rasmussen's daughter, killed the primitive outright and flushed the other two Maraia into an ice bowl we had created and froze them all alive."

"Two Maraia? Trudal said you had killed the synthetic man sent by the Shepherd."

"The who?"

"Never mind. Thank you Igor." Cardassin waved him away.

Igor hesitated.

"Yes, Igor," Cardassin drawled.

"My arm, sire."

Cardassin peered. "What about your arm?"

"It's gone limp, sire. I can't finger the trigger, flash the badge, cock the cock."

Zug give me strength. "The designer gene has run its course. I'm afraid you'll have to be content with whatever was previously at the end of your shoulder."

"Yes, sire." With a sidelong glare at Trudal, Igor exited the tent.

"A most impertinent mutant, if I don't say so myself," Trudal piped.

"Shove it, Trudal. I'll see the bitch, now."

"Yes, sire." Trudal ducked outside.

Cardassin climbed up into the chair, and had just struck an imperial pose, when Trudal shoved the female into the center of the tent.

She staggered forward, came up abruptly and stood, clutching her arms across her chest.

Odd they do that, Cardassin thought. *But most comely.*

"What have we here?" Cardassin said loudly, though he knew full well what he had.

"Sire, I give you Rasmussen's daughter--Akilah."

Cardassin winced. "Great seer that you are, pul--leeze don't tell me what I already know."

"Yes, sire."

Cardassin pulled his robe across his knees when he noticed the hostage was distracted by what lay between his legs. "So, Miss Rasmussen, or should we be on a first name basis? You can call me Card-Ass."

"I demand to be released."

"Fair Akilah, you disappoint me. Do you truly think that you can shoot up my mutants, allow yourself to be kidnapped and then dragged into my

206

compound with only the minimum of resistance, and demand to be released? Whatever happened to personal responsibility? You fokked up, my dear. You can't be serious in thinking that I will let you go...Scot free!"

He turned to Trudal. "I believe that is the ancient term. Is it not?"

"Yes, sire. You have it right."

Akilah's arms had left her chest, perhaps an indication that she would not let her body language project the way she felt. Her hands were now at her sides, fists clenched. *She's got fiber, this one.*

"I am but one of few remaining pure Maraia. We hold to beliefs in the *TrueMen*. What is it to you if we pursue our perceived destiny? You have paradise here. We have nothing. You have killed my companions. My father lies dying. Let me go that I may be at his bedside when he perishes."

"Miss Akilah--" Cardassin drew a powder blue handkerchief from a container at the side of the chair and patted his eyes as if drying them of tears. "--a most impassioned speech. You have almost convinced me that it would be in my interest to--" He squirmed trying to subdue an itch that was maliciously tickling his anus. "--I must admit that I really don't have a whole lot of interest in you. I am more interested in knowing about the Shepherd."

"Shepherd? He plays a role in Maraia myths. Surely you are well versed in those."

"I am, but I mean here and now."

"I don't know what you're talking about."

"Don't play cute with me. It could result in some sort of unfortunate incident." Cardassin rubbed his inner thigh, scratched his armpits, then examined his nails. *Nothing. Must have bathed well. Will have to complement Habibi.* "Now as to the Shepherd, I want you to--" Cardassin stood abruptly. "--Excuse me, my dear. I really must do something about an itch."

***

Akilah didn't know whether to be shocked or disappointed. The player was obviously insane, or putting on a good show. Perhaps Ferral did have the right strategy. Take back the planet. How hard could it be to go up against combatants like this?

Trudal wrung his hands. "Miss Akilah, perhaps you would like to sit down until our lord returns."

"Shut up, you odious low life. You look Maraia. What happened?"

Trudal shrugged. "I have tried to survive."

"Haven't we all."

Trudal looked anxiously to where Cardassin had exited. "You are still young. I cannot expect you to understand."

"And you're so much older? You look to be--"

"I'm one hundred years old."

Akilah gasped. "How...?"

"Cardassin. Nano-assemblers. There's an ancient saying...*I have eaten more salt than you have flour.* You know me not. But I know you. Please." He gestured to the bed.

Akilah shook her head. "For a moment you had me going, Trudal."

He smiled, a knowing smile. His bubble had burst, and he pulled his cloak tighter about him.

Akilah scanned the room. One large bed, enough to sleep six, covered with a red, silken bedspread with a black dragon figure finely stitched across its field. A garish carpet underneath. Plush pillows, pastels in silk, crammed the four corners, and that ridiculous chair.

Her scan returned to the chair that Cardassin had vacated and focused on what appeared to be an ice razor lying snug between the seat and the upright arm rest.

"That wouldn't be an ice razor sitting there would it?" She edged between Trudal and the chair.

"You don't want to even think about using that, Miss. Especially not here. Lord Cardassin would be most upset."

Akilah stepped over to the chair and hefted the razor. "We'll see about Lord Cardassin."

An amoebic lump slithered from under a pile of pillows, causing them to cascade, bounce and roll out onto the carpet.

"Kill me. Kill me. Have mercy and kill me."

Akilah stepped back, startled. "Good Sedroth, what is that?"

"One of Cardassin's toys. Ignore her," Trudal said. "She gets out of hand with strangers. Why? We've never been able to find out. This death wish. My lord feeds her well. Most unsettling."

Akilah tried to mask her disgust. "What is she?"

The lump squiggled over to Akilah. One obvious eye let go a large tear. "I was Maraia. Now, I am nothing. I beg you. Kill me." She extended a fine pseudopod toward Akilah.

209

Dispite her revulsion, Akilah let the thing touch her finger. *An odd pleasantness to the touch.* Encounters with corrupted Maraia were often like this, unlike the bombast of the obsequious Trudal. Maraia so compromised would plead for termination with the last breath of their deteriorating sanity. One got used to mercy killings. Unfortunately. "Are you sure you want to die?"

"If I could activate that razor I would do it myself." The psuedopod slid from Akilah's hand to the razor and stuffed its business end into her like a stick plunging into thick dough.

Akilah gazed for a moment at the closed eye, the slick surface wet with tears, then she pulled the trigger.

The razor flashed.

"Sedroth!" The lump sputtered as it was sliced in two, loosing the stench of burnt flesh and a puddle of clear fluid that quickly seeped into the carpeted floor.

Akilah stared, wondering if she had done the right thing.

Trudal never flinched, but pulled his hooded cassock low across his brow, hiding his face.

Scratching his bottom, Cardassin re-entered the main room of the tent. When he saw the amoeba's smoldering remains, he stopped, put hands to thin hips and looked to the tent's ceiling. "Who has done this dastardly thing?" Then he stifled a laugh by pinching his nose, but snorted anyway.

Trudal threw back his cassock and smiled.

Akilah pointed the razor at Cardassin. "I did it. It was an act of mercy."

210

Cardassin clapped his hands over his mouth. "Trudal?" A mumbled question.

"Perfect, sire," Trudal said.

"What's perfect?" Akilah demanded. "I'm about to end you and this pervert, too. What the hell do you think is perfect?"

Trudal shrugged, palms up, then dissolved into giggles.

Akilah pointed the razor at Cardassin and pulled the trigger.

Nothing.

Cardassin whooped. "One shot's all you got."

Akilah threw the razor at Cardassin's feet. "Then it was one shot well taken. I delivered a Maraia from misery."

"Ah, the irony."

"I see no irony in the situation," Akilah said.

"Cristina was very good at what she did. The name, does it ring a bell?"

"No bells, Cardassin."

Cardassin looked disappointed. "I see. Maybe the name Cristina Rasmussen might ring your bell."

Akilah blanched. "My mother."

"Yes. Such a waste. Daughter and mother reunited after all these years, only to have daughter slaughter mother. There's something oedipalistic about that."

Akilah rushed him, fists flailing. She hit him hard, and they both went down.

"Trudal," Cardassin waved as he fell to the floor.

Trudal hurried forward and grabbed Akilah around the neck, straining to pull her off Cardassin, who flopped on the floor giggling, his hands groping her in intimate places.

"You'll do well, my pretty. Good squeezers are hard to come by, if you get my drift."

**

Michael's hands slammed against the gleaming walls flashing by him. His head lamp bobbled, giving little comfort and no forward vision at all.

Suddenly, Dayna loomed into view, her head up in surprise, an arm raised protectively across her chest.

He careened into her, caught one of her booted feet in his stomach and let out a whoosh of air as he tumbled to a stop.

"I tried to warn you," she said.

Michael gulped. "I know. Sorry, I should have been more careful. The tunnels had to end sometime. I didn't think we were that close." He rubbed both hands over bruised ribs.

Dayna tore the lamp from her forehead and shoved it close to a brown, textured membrane that ended the tunnel. "Do you think this is the perimeter of Kanapoi?"

"It seems like we've traveled far enough. Why else would a membrane be sealing the end of the tunnel?" Michael untangled himself, pulled off his glove and placed his hand on the membrane. "It's organic, I can feel it move. Probably some sort of replicating structure."

Michael took out his knife and cut a small slit into the brown barrier.

It parted slightly, then the edges immediately sealed back together.

"I saw dirt on the other side," Dayna said.

"I saw it, too. There's no other place in all of Kenya but Cardassin's compound where loose dirt could exist."

"Kenya?"

"It's the ancient name for this land."

Dayna nodded, probably wondering how Michael knew. "How are we to get through? The membrane grew back so quickly."

"I'm more worried that it's rigged to send an alarm if breached."

"If it was rigged, then an alarm has already been sent. We're committed."

Not entirely. "If we cut a large enough piece and dig, even though it grows back, we can repeat the procedure until we have dug deep enough to get into the other side."

"Sounds like a plan. I'll back you up and pull dirt out of the way as you dig."

Michael slashed his knife in a wide circle almost to the edges of the tunnel, pulled the membrane away and then furiously scooped handfuls of loose dirt. He dug about a half meter into the other side before the membrane began to close, forcing him to pull back into the tunnel.

"That's not too bad," Michael said, exhaling a puff of frosty breath. "The membrane re-grows slowly enough that we'll only have to do this a couple of times before we are through."

Ten minutes later he had a short tunnel bored into the dirt, enough for him and Dayna with room to spare. They crawled in and watched apprehensively as the membrane closed behind them.

"Okay, now we head for the surface and hope that it isn't too far above us."

Michael scooped dirt and shoved it between his legs and behind him where Dayna caught it and pushed it farther back. The air quickly fouled with their exertions. Michael stopped periodically to wipe sweat from his eyes. They advanced upward until they came to roots.

Michael angled his head lamp upward.

Roots fingered down from thick stems, then branched again and again to smaller ones until they ended in bushy filaments. "From the size of these, we must be under a tree or large shrub."

Dayna took out her knife and prepared to slice the hanging ends.

Michael stayed her hand. "We should go around them. If we cut through, the foliage above may somehow suffer and give us away."

"I hadn't thought of that," Dayna said. "Everything about Cardassin's compound is nano-assembler driven. I assumed they would just regenerate."

Michael dug around the roots and up. The earth gave way, and light streamed in. "We're through."

Cautiously, he peered out the opening. The air was warm and humid. Light seemed to be coming from an artificial sun overhead. He assumed it was artificial since the last time they had been outside, it had been night. A low mist lay over the sloped ground, drifting from an uphill source, down toward a large pond. Swans and ducks with ducklings swam lazily across the water. Trees, with hanging branches dipping to the water's surface, lined the edge of the pond.

"Salix, part of the willow family Salicaceae. Commonly known as Weeping Willows."

And what are those over there? High up against the perimeter. So majestic.

"Coniferous trees of the genus Pseudotsuga in the family Pinaceae. Douglas firs. Extinct for one thousand years."

Worn paths traveled up from the water's edge, snaking through dense greenery and ending at gaudily colored tents that seemed pitched almost carnival-like. One tent stood out from the rest, bigger, brighter, more ornate.

Michael ducked his head down. "It's a paradise."

"If I could see it, too, I might have the same opinion."

Michael squirmed down past Dayna. "I'm sorry. See for yourself."

She poked her head out and returned. "You're right. But for a paradise, it doesn't look like anyone is around to enjoy it. I'm climbing out."

"No." Michael grabbed her foot and pulled her back into the hole.

She glared at him. "What's the problem?"

"We need a plan."

"Okay, plan."

Michael didn't like her cavalier attitude. If she were truly committed to Akilah and the other Maraia, then she might show a bit more caution.

"As I understand it, Cardassin has ten or twenty mutants hanging around at any one time. That we don't see any of them probably confirms what Jamil said about them all being too inebriated to be a threat. You saw the big tent on the hill?"

"I did. I assume it's Cardassin's."

"If I had just kidnapped the daughter of the leader of *TrueMen*, then I'd be making my report about now and handing over my hostage."

"But a lot of time has passed. Maybe Akilah is in that tent and that brute Igor is somewhere else."

"Possibly. With all due respect, I think we should check out my initial premise. I'll go first and see if I draw any attention. Cover me."

"Negative."

"What?"

"Look, Michael. From what I've seen, you know more than you're willing to tell. That makes you more important to this mission than me. So I'll go first. You bring up the rear."

Michael couldn't find a good argument for saying otherwise. "Okay, but be careful."

Dayna gave him a *thank you, but I'm not dumb* look. She climbed out of the hole and squirmed forward on her stomach, pulling with her elbows.

Michael followed. Still no one in sight.

Dayna rose to her feet and stepped quickly up the path that led to the big tent. The mist closed in around her.

Michael trailed ten meters behind, razor drawn. Once he was out of the mist, he could see Dayna forging ahead of him. But where once he had thought that no one was around, the hill above the mist teemed with tens of mutants.

Some lay flat on the ground. Others staggered about in drunken fashion. Some quarreled.

A razor flashed and a mutant convulsed and lay still, presumably ending the quarrel.

Other mutants, stretching the definition of male and female, engaged in convulsive, grotesque trysts, almost as if they had lost all knowledge of how the act was to be performed.

Dayna pinched her nose and waved to him to continue, a bit too brazenly for Michael's taste, up the path to the big tent.

She passed a large mutant sprawled on the grass outside the approach to the tent. She pointed, but kept moving.

Michael came up to the mutant and realized that it was Igor, asleep, or drunk, or drugged. He seemed to be breathing, but was otherwise immobile.

A nano-assembler hung loosely from his belt.

Can it be this easy?

Gingerly, Michael unclipped the short tube and stuffed it down the top of his boot. *Objective realized, now for Akilah.*

Dayna was up to the front of the tent. She leaned close, listening, motioning for Michael to slow down or stop.

Before he had a chance to do either, he was hit sideways from behind. He went down.

Igor pressed on top of him.

Michael thrust up with his knee to Igor's groin but did not produce the desired agony, instead more of a mewing pleasure.

Michael rolled free, leapt to his feet and raised his razor.

As if Igor's assault had been a signal, mutants lumbered out from just about everywhere. Flailing razors, they fired erratically. Burnt creases seared the grass. Holes punched open the membranous dome overhead. Severed palms crashed to the ground, setting bushes smoking before everything quickly reconstructed.

While Igor struggled to his feet, Michael cut down two mutants who staggered too close. Dayna was nowhere in sight. The mutants in front of him fired their razors and bumped into one another. After much of what seemed to be their operative mode, they fell down.

Where the hell's Dayna? Michael stood. Maybe she made it into the tent, and all he had to do was find Akilah. Certainly Cardassin would be more or less defenseless with this inebriated tribe protecting him.

A crushing grip clamped around Michael's chest.

"Yaw thot yaw could fool me?"

Chapter Ten

Cardassin rubbed his sandaled foot back and forth over the dark stain on the carpet. "The bitch ruined my carpet."

The mutant who had been collecting the shriveled pieces of Cristina looked up. "But she's dead."

Cardassin frowned, confused. Then realized the mutant was referring to Cristina and not her daughter. "Never mind."

"Yes, sire." The mutant dumped Cristina's remains into a cloth sack and dragged it out of the tent.

Trudal rattled the bells, entered and bowed slightly at the waist. "A pity about the carpet, sire."

Cardassin stroked his short goatee preferring to ignore the carpet. He'd sprinkle it with DNA cleaners and it would be as good as new. "My dear Trudal."

"Yes, sire."

"It appears that you have a report to correct."

"Thank you, sire. I do indeed wish to correct an earlier report."

Cardassin gazed at the ceiling of the tent, rolling his eyes, but then felt dizzy and decided the overt display of his displeasure might induce nausea.

"The synthetic man is not dead but has been restrained by Igor. The former, with the aid of a

Maraia female, were trying to assault our compound."

Cardassin buried his head in his hands in despair. "First I'm told that all these lovely folks are nothing more than popsicles. Now these popsicles are alive and storming my paradise?"

"That seems to be the case." Trudal fidgeted. "But we have prevailed and now hold them both in custody."

Cardassin wagged a finger at Trudal. "I often wonder why I tolerate you as my seer if you cannot see the obvious truths that exist in the present, let alone those truths that lurk in the ephemeral future."

"Sire, I can only see what I can see. You may rest assured that there is no subterfuge to my foresight. I report only what I think I see."

"Horse poop, Trudal. Your mouth moves, and the same stuff comes out in permutated fashion. You know you make it up as you go along. But I like you. So I tolerate you. So I--"

"Sire, I am devastated by such accusations."

"Well you might be. But let's move on. What are the results of the tests you have performed on this miscreant?"

"Thank you, sire...for moving on. The tests are most interesting. Our subject is indeed a mix of hominid DNA and synthetic parts."

"You merely have confirmed what I have always believed. I should *ick* you right now for your incompetence."

"Obviously, sire, you can *ick* me at will, but I beg you to persevere and hear out my full report."

Cardassin fiddled.

"His hominid base is dominant. That's a surprise to me, since I would have thought that the Shepherd would have given him a greater capacity, knowing what he would be up against."

"You idiot. You know full well that everything about this godforsaken place is preordained. The Shepherd is only acting minimally to further what he knows will already transpire."

"But that is horrible, sire."

"What the fokk is horrible?"

"We have no self-determination."

"Get a life, Trudal. I've told you this before."

"Yes, sire. Now that you mention it, I seem to remember. Something about our worldlines being closed."

"Very good, Trudal. I think we can leave it at that right now. Is there anything else in your report?"

Trudal looked crestfallen. "No, sire."

"Then please, show in the synthetic man."

***

The rope around Michael's neck tightened.

"Get the fokk up!" Igor was in a good mood.

Michael stood, wondering what lay before him. Dayna gone. Akilah nowhere in sight. And a foul-mouthed Igor jerking him toward the big tent.

Igor raised the tent flap and shoved Michael inside onto a carpeted floor.

Michael wrinkled his nose at an odor of burnt flesh rising from the carpet, then looked up from his prone position.

Cardassin stood two meters away, hands on hips, legs planted firmly, knobby knees showing bare below his robe. To his right stood another person, a corrupted Maraia from the looks of him, but well kept, given the quality of his outer garment.

"I don't believe we've been formally introduced," Cardassin said. "My name is Cardassin, and this here is Trudal, my trusted counselor. I'm sorry, I didn't get your name."

Michael stood with a sidelong glance at Igor and Trudal, then turned to Cardassin. "My name is Michael."

"No surname?"

"Surname?"

"*A last name. Tell him Blue. Better that than trying to explain.*"

"...Blue. My surname is Blue."

"How truly colorful."

"I don't think color is what you have on your mind at the moment."

"Why no, Mister Blue. How perceptive of you." Cardassin wrinkled his nose. "Do you smell that?"

"Yeah, it stinks in here."

"Most regrettable. We've had a death, and the stench hasn't cleared out. Trudal, be a good man and raise the tent flap."

Trudal scurried to the entrance and heaved back the flap. While there he sucked in some fresh air.

"Now where was I?" Cardassin said. "Ah, yes, I don't give a fokk about your name, your origin, your relationship with these miserable Maraia or why you've come all this way to kill my mutants. I am simply and most attentively interested in the

Shepherd. Period. End of story. Bring down the curtain. Do you get my drift?"

"You've been more than explicit."

Besides the front entrance, a rear drape of cloth shielded another room, now dark. Could Dayna and Akilah be in there? No way to tell, but a high probability. Why would Cardassin keep them anywhere else?

"The Shepherd?" Cardassin moved to a large ornate chair and sat down.

"I'm sorry, I was looking for a way out of here."

"I thought you might be." Cardassin smiled and rubbed his big toe on the foot he had crossed over his knee. "The Shepherd?"

"I don't know what you're talking about."

Cardassin wrenched his toe in anger and winced when he realized he had only hurt himself. "Then do tell, what about *Gilomir*?"

"*The name of our lord*."

He knows. Michael was stunned.

"Cat got your tongue?"

"No," Michael recovered quickly. "You said something just then, and I didn't know what it meant."

"Ah, such evasion. I know that you do know what it meant. I saw it in your face. Now, please, tell me where the Shepherd is."

"I don't know."

"Well, well, that's a step up from *I don't know what you're talking about*. Let's take a stroll outside. This tent is getting claustrophobic." Cardassin leapt off the chair and slid his hand around Michael's elbow, then guided him out the entrance.

"Sire," Trudal called.

"Excuse me, Blue." Cardassin let go Michael's arm and turned back to the anxious seer. "What is it for fokk's sake?"

"I don't think it wise to walk unescorted with the unknown."

"Unknown to you, my dear inept seer, but well known to me." Cardassin reattached himself to Michael, and they proceeded down the path. "Isn't this a lovely place?"

"You have built a paradise here," Michael said. "Are those really live birds?"

"Of course they are. Thank *Zug* the nano-assemblers still had records of their DNA. Now where were we?"

"You're asking me?"

"No, I suppose I should keep track of my own conversation. I like you Michael. Very direct. No pretense. Not like the insufferable idiots I have to contend with every day."

"I wouldn't know."

"No, of course you wouldn't, you're synthetic."

"I wouldn't know about that either."

"Come, come, of course you know." Cardassin squeezed Michael's arm and leaned into him. "I will offer you a deal. You tell me where the Shepherd is and I will make you human."

"I don't know what you're talking about."

Cardassin sighed. "There you go again."

"I wish I could."

Cardassin stopped and spun Michael around. He pushed his face close to Michael's. "Just because you see a lot of inebriated mutants in my employ doesn't mean I'm also stupid. I've checked your DNA and though most of it is hominid, a lot of it is manufactured."

"I know nothing about your methods or equipment."

"No, of course you don't. Perhaps I should ask Akilah?"

Michael gazed at the pinch-faced man staring at him. "If you have Akilah, then we'd like to have her back."

"If I had her that might be a possibility, given that I might want something in exchange."

"So you do have her?"

"Are you daft?" Cardassin looked perplexed. "I thought I was quite clear about what I have and don't have. I presume we are still speaking the same language."

"Then you're bluffing."

"What would you give to find out?"

Michael paused. "I have nothing to bargain with."

"Ah...but you do." A smile twitched at the corners of Cardassin's lips. "That brings us full circle to the Shepherd."

"And the end of this conversation."

Cardassin made a clicking sound with his tongue against his palate as though he were in deep thought. "Then we shall widen the discussion." Cardassin let go of Michael and stomped back to the tent.

Igor, who had been following close behind, took hold of Michael's parka. "Yaw aren't thinking of running away, are yaw?" He dragged Michael to the tent and shoved him inside.

"Trudal!" Cardassin shouted. "I want to see the Doctor's daughter. Now!"

***

I killed my mother. The searing reality replayed in Akilah's head again and again, without beginning or end. *I killed my mother.*

"Akilah, my dear, so good of you to come," Cardassin said. "Oh, I'm sorry, I see you're looking a bit glum, as well you might be having just offed Mom."

Akilah raised her head and tried to concentrate on what was around her. Cardassin sat in his high chair. Trudal stood to his left, hands tucked into the sleeves of his cassock. Igor was picking his teeth with his thumb nail. And...

"Mike! Thank Sedroth you're all right." She broke away from the mutant that had guided her into the tent and ran to Michael.

He took her in his arms, an awkward embrace, but still an embrace. "Jamil is dead."

"Jamil? How?"

"After they kidnapped you."

Tears welled into her eyes. The pain she felt was almost too much to bear. Death upon death. Then back to the memory of her razor flashing, the neat parting of her mother's flesh, the welling of blood turned to steam, the stench. Her knees buckled, and she sagged against Michael.

226

"What have you done to her?" Michael said to Cardassin.

Michael's voice seemed to wander to her from a hundred kilometers away.

"I have done nothing," Cardassin said. "It is she who has taken it upon herself to act in a godless way and deliver others from perceived misery only to find that she made a mistake."

"You're not making a lot of sense."

"She killed her mother." Cardassin smiled, then picked his nose and concentrated on flicking the find off his finger. When the booger refused to fly, he removed it with his mouth and spit it in Michael's general direction. "Need I be more explicit?"

Akilah's strength flowed from her body as though someone had cut a hole in her leg and now all her energy was gurgling out. She sat on the bed, letting her head hang. *When will this end?*

"My dear, we don't have time for remorse. What's done is done. I have more pressing business than worrying about a dead sex toy. After all, they aren't that hard to come by." Cardassin giggled, then stopped abruptly. "Please tell me where the Shepherd is."

Akilah brushed tears and glared at him. "What are you talking about? The Shepherd plays in our mythology. You think he's here?"

Cardassin pointed to Michael. "*He's* here. Don't play cute with me. You seem to be taken by this *being*. Did you know that he's not human?"

"You're insane."

"I can see I'm not making myself very clear. I really do want an answer. Perhaps I can energize you somewhat." He motioned to the mutant.

The man ducked out of the tent and returned a moment later with Dayna.

She stared blankly, her walk reduced to a shuffle.

She's alive, but look at her.

"She's actually somewhere else at the moment," Cardassin said. "I suspect she wouldn't want to be a real part of this." He snapped his finger.

Igor lumbered forward, reached inside his shirt and removed a length of flexible wire. He coiled it around Dayna's neck and began twisting, stopped once to scratch his nose, then continued.

Dayna's mouth opened in forced agony. Her breath wheezed. Her eyes bugged.

"Stop!" Akilah screamed. "I'll tell you what you want to know."

"My, my how quickly we come to our senses. Igor." A desisting wave of a hand.

Looking disappointed, Igor methodically removed the wire and tucked it back inside his shirt.

Dayna collapsed on the carpet, where she lay unattended, gasping for air.

"Well, I'm waiting."

Akilah tore her gaze from Dayna and glanced at Michael, who stood stoically. She could almost feel his anguish, almost hear his thoughts calculating how to get them out of this mess.

She stared at Cardassin. The wretched man sat rubbing his thigh distractedly, no doubt enjoying every bit of their misery.

"The Shepherd is here, or at least he was two nights ago when we crash landed. We believe our flyer would have come apart upon impact had it not been for the cushioning effect of a mysterious force field that we later were able to attribute to the Shepherd. When we searched the area afterward, we came upon the Shepherd in a swirling storm. He gave us provisions and clothes and told us to--"

"Oh, please do shut up. This isn't worth listening to. Trudal!"

"Yes, sire, she is most definitely lying, and you are getting nowhere with this interview."

"And pray tell, how am I to get somewhere? Dismembering our resident female zombie here would only produce more lies."

Trudal proffered a nano-assembler. "It's worked before." He smiled.

Fear turned Akilah's blood cold. She could almost feel it grow hard and labor to push through her veins. Her hands felt clammy, but she refused to wipe them on her pants lest she give away her emotion. They seemed to enjoy using DNA from the nano-assembler as a last resort.

Cardassin gave her a droopy look. "It's not you I'm going to enhance, my dear." He looked at Michael.

Akilah gave a start.

"And it's not him." Cardassin chuckled. He fiddled with the nano-assembler, then handed a pill to Trudal. "I do believe I've detected a strong attachment between Miss Akilah and this spaced-out female. Friends, or should I be so bold as to say, *lovers*?"

Words clogged on the way to Akilah's lips.

Cardassin patted her hand. "This little pellet here could actually improve your pal. Transform her into something that would make your experiences with her all the more pleasurable."

"Don't you dare."

"I love dares, darling. Trudal, please administer the inducements and let's sit back and watch the play begin."

Trudal stepped over to Dayna and motioned for the mutant to raise her off the floor.

What am I to do? Lie again? "Wait. I'm sorry. I lied. I'll tell you anything you want to know, just leave Dayna alone."

"Dayna? What a lovely name. Now, where were we? The Shepherd. In your fantasy he was helping you, but...in reality he was..." Cardassin gestured for Akilah to speak.

"In reality, I know nothing of this Shepherd. Michael...Michael here appeared two nights ago at the door of the ruin, alone. We took him in and--"

Cardassin leapt from the chair, drew his razor in one smooth motion and flicked it on. "More lies!" In a motion that defied his emaciated state, the razor's beam flashed across the room, missed everything else, but neatly severed Akilah's raised hand at the wrist.

Michael started forward, only to be pinned to the spot when Cardassin pointed his razor at Michael's mid-section.

Akilah grabbed her smoking stump and stared aghast at her left hand lying at her feet.

Cardassin marched toward her and gave her a push with the razor that sent her sprawling on the bed. He stooped painfully and picked up her hand by its pinky. "Properly cured, this will make a fine purse, or perhaps some foreskins for Habibi." Cardassin leered close and examined the thumb. "Although this one might be a bit small."

Akilah struggled to her feet, clutching her mutilated arm at the wrist. "I'll see you dead for this."

"You will see nothing of the kind."

Michael came to her side and put a comforting arm around her shoulders. "Leave her be, Cardassin. I'll tell you anything you want to know. Just let them go."

"Ah, now we are getting somewhere. But how am I to tell if you aren't lying, too?"

Wild shouts from outside punched the stillness inside the tent, followed by the hiss of razors.

"Trudal." Cardassin motioned for Trudal to see what was happening.

The seer rushed to the entrance and peered out.

A mutant staggered in, brushing Trudal aside.

"What is it?" Cardassin snapped.

"A primitive has appeared. He's killing everyone in sight!"

"Ah, jeez. What did you expect? Most all of them are drunk."

Trudal struggled off the floor. "What are we to do?"

"Well, we'll have to think of something." Cardassin stroked his goatee. "I know, we'll offer him a deal. If he spares me and the rest of you,

231

we'll give him back these fine people. Ah, Trudal, be a good chap and call him over here."

Trudal gaped. "Me, sire?"

Cardassin looked over his shoulder. "Well I certainly can't send him--" He jabbed a thumb at Mike. "--and if I don't send him, then I can't send them--" He indicated Igor and the guard.

Trudal nodded resignedly and pulled a white cloth from his robe. "I've been told they respond passively to white."

"Get going!"

Chapter Eleven

A razor beam punched a smoking hole in the tent wall, entering one side and exiting out the other.

Akilah flinched. Though her arm ached, Cardassin's razor had cauterized the wound as it sliced.

"Damned incompetent mutants," Cardassin raged. "A primitive force of one is giving them fits. I should have inbred more resolve, but then they might have taken a fancy to turn on their esteemed leader." He whirled. "Miss Akilah, do you agree?"

She eyed Cardassin, her blackened stump, and put on a stalwart face. "Are you suffering a crisis of confidence?"

Cardassin seemed about to respond, when the firing stopped. He listened, then breathed a sigh.

Trudal stumbled into the tent, a smoking hole in his white flag. "I think he means to kill us all!"

"Igor!" Cardassin shouted. "Sic'em!"

Igor drew his razor and charged outside.

A sizzling pop, and Igor sailed back through the entrance onto his back, his right arm missing to the shoulder. "My arm!"

"It can be fixed later." Cardassin scampered to the other side of the bed and aimed his razor at Akilah and Michael. "I do believe we're about to have company."

Jamil loomed in the opening. A charred hole gaped in the outer garment of his chest.

Trudal flattened himself onto the carpet.

"Jamil!" Akilah couldn't contain her joy.

"He's alive," Michael said incredulously. He started to rise, but was shoved back onto the bed by Cardassin.

"Let's all just sit tight until we work this thing out," he said.

Jamil oriented himself with a quick scan, then, aimed his dual razors at Cardassin. "All stop. Now."

Cardassin cleared his throat. "Come, come, my cute primitive, don't you know that you can't kill a player?"

"Find out."

"No, no, no that's too wasteful, recycling and all that, never sure if I get it right, have to choose a new body. Contrary to what you might think, I actually enjoy this body. So let's forget the *killing*! I'll let you all go this time. Time, time? I love that word. It has such an ephemeral quality."

"No time. We go. Now."

"I do believe this is what is called a standoff. You could try to kill me, but I'd off these two first. I hate dilemmas. What shall we do?"

"We go. You stay. No harm."

"That's all well and good in theory, but if I let you all go what assurances do I have that you won't simply kill me and my precious hoard here on the way out?"

"Deal a deal."

"Yes, yes, I know. In the old days it used to be like that, handshake and all, but nowadays, one can't be too sure." Cardasiin looked imploringly at

234

Akilah. "My dear, couldn't you add a word in here edgewise?"

"You have my word, we'll not harm you or your men on our way out."

Cardassin drummed his fingers on his teeth. "Another promise, but I suppose a mutual withdrawal can be accomplished. We'll simply back away from each other...razors drawn, and hope that no one gets an itchy finger."

"Sounds like a plan," Akilah said.

"How about you Mike?" Cardassin asked. "She does call you Mike doesn't she? Terms of endearment, or is it--"

"Don't press your luck, Cardassin." Akilah nodded to Michael that he should attend to Dayna who had remained crumpled in a swoon. "We'll be out of here in a sec. After that all bets are off."

"Of course. That is most understood. Trudal, please get up off the floor. It's most unseemly of you."

***

A man-sized orifice opened in the membrane that encapsulated Kanapoi.

Akilah stepped through, cradling her severed forearem, followed by Michael, who steadied Dayna, then Jamil, razors still trained on Cardassin and now Igor, who held a razor awkwardly in his left hand minus his right.

"Bye, bye." Cardassin waved, stepping back from cold air that seeped into the compound. He tugged on what must have been a faux fox fur around his neck.

Why he hadn't put on more than that Akilah couldn't imagine, but then there wasn't much about Cardassin that she could imagine.

Warm air billowed from the orifice, strangling down to a trickle. The membrane, which had lit up to produce a glowing light, dimmed and went out.

They stood in almost total darkness.

"We'd better hurry," Akilah said, "before he thinks of a way to double-cross us."

"Storm come." Jamil waved one of his razors to the north.

Dark clouds obscured the moon, plunging the ice sheet into darkness. Overhead, the stars still shone brightly enough to give them a bearing on the plateau that loomed far away to the east.

Akilah started a fast walk. "Pick up the pace," she called, looking over her shoulder when the others lagged. She drew in a deep breath and felt the cold air tingle her nose, throat and lungs. Thankfully, it had a numbing effect on her stump.

The wind increased ahead of the approaching storm. Ice crystals kicked up by her boots swirled out in front of her only to be brushed back into her face. She pulled the hood of her parka close, annoyed by the constant stinging.

Her cheeks felt cold, and she realized she was crying. The crushing memory of her dead mother rose and occupied her consciousness. *Let it out.* She dissected the memory, searching in vain for a mistake, something she could have done differently. It didn't matter that she had been set up to kill Cristina by Trudal and Cardassin. She had listened to what Cristina had said and then made a decision. She'd have to live with that.

She shuddered thinking what her mother had been through all these years. Father had never talked much about her. Mom was simply a photograph.

Dayna groaned.

Akilah stopped and let Jamil, who had taken over carrying Dayna, catch up. He held her draped across both arms, her head lolling back.

Dayna. Dayna. What you have gone through for me. Akilah stroked Dayna's brow. "Can you hear me?"

A weak breath fogged in the arctic air.

What has Cardassin done to you? Akilah turned to Michael. "Will she be all right?" Michael was the only one who knew the big picture.

"It's hard to tell," Michael said. "I don't think Cardassin would have gone so far as to feed her mutated genes in the short time he had us. Plus he wouldn't necessarily want to preclude his options if things took an unexpected turn. Still…"

"I hope you're right. She's like a sister and has been with me through so much." Akilah noted a flicker of doubt that chased across Michael's brow. But she wasn't about to challenge him now. "How long before we can get her home?"

"I'd guess we have another nine kilometers. It'll be at least a couple of hours."

"Awake," Jamil said.

Akilah stepped over to Dayna caressed her cheek. "You're going to be all right."

Dayna blinked. "What happened? I don't remember anything after I came up to Cardassin's tent. Something hit me, and--Jamil's alive?"

"We all are, thank Sedroth. You've probably been drugged. At least we think that's the least Cardassin has done to you."

"Dear god, your hand is missing."

Akilah held up her stump and eyed it appreciatively. "It's probably a good thing you don't remember any of what happened. It was pretty ugly."

"But your hand."

"It could have been your life. It could have been all our lives. We are safe now and soon home. Rest."

"I...I want to walk. It might help to clear the cobwebs."

Jamil eased her to her feet but still supported her at her waist to keep her from falling over.

"How...Jamil...how did you survive?"

"Not hard."

Dayna threw a quizzical glance at Michael, who nodded. "I'll find out." He spoke rapidly to Jamil in the primitive's language.

Snow began to fall, large hard-edged flakes that caught in the driving wind, piled into the creases of their parkas and obscured the toes of their boots.

Shielding his face from the storm, Michael motioned Akilah to huddle next to Dayna. "He says the razor that struck him only stunned him. He was momentarily incapacitated, and before he could recover, Igor shoved him in the spider hole.

Fortunately, Jamil fell face down in the hole and his bulk sealed the edges, leaving an air pocket below.

"After the ice was melted above him, and later when the flow came out of the tunnel, he simply waited, then drilled through the thin plug beneath him with his razor. The drain shaft for the bowl dropped into the ice caverns below. Once he had the drain open, he disengaged himself, turned his razors upward and melted his way topside." Michael clapped his gloved hands across his chest and clamped them under his armpits. "We better keep moving. We only have a few minutes of lead time if Cardassin unleashes his mutants against us."

"Has he no sense of morality?" Akilah said.

"He doesn't even know what the word means," Michael said.

***

"Trudal!" Cardassin screamed from his bed as he clutched at thin covers. "I'm cold! Where are the fokkin' nano-assemblers?"

"I have one here, sire."

"One?!"

"Yes, sire. I'm sorry to report that the nano-assembler carried by Igor is missing."

"Missing?"

"Yes sire. I fear that when Igor lost his arm, he was so distracted that he also lost sight of the nano-assembler that had been entrusted to him."

Cardassin buried his head in his hands. Such was the force of his thrust that he almost lost his balance. "Igor! He was my man! Where the fokk is he?"

"He's sitting outside your tent, sire. He's feeling very contrite."

"Fokk contrite. I want a word with him."

"Yes, sire." Trudal stepped to the entrance and said something to someone, presumably Igor outside, then stepped back as if to get out of the way.

Igor staggered into the tent, steadied himself, and tried to focus on Cardassin.

"Igor! What do you have to say for yourself?"

Igor's eyes were bloodshot and watery. "My arm, sire. Yaw promised."

Cardassin felt his cheek twitch, his brows knot, his fists clench. "That was when you still had the nano-assembler!"

"Yaw don't have to shout at me, sire. I can hear yaw quite well."

"No, I suppose I don't. I can be reasonable, too, you know."

"Yes, sire. I have always considered yaw a reasonable person."

"Stuff it, Igor. You know full well I am not a person. Let's stick to the point here. I'm most concerned about our little nano-assembler that has disappeared."

"My arm, sire. Yaw promised."

Cardassin pressed the heels of his hands to his temples in frustration. "Trudal."

"Sire."

"Pul...eeze, fix this inebriate's arm."

"Yes, sire." Trudal fumbled with the nano-assembler for some minutes, then shook out a pellet. "Here, take this." He thrust the pill at Igor.

240

The brute swallowed it and smiled winsomely when small, fleshy buds sprouted from the stump of his shoulder, elongated, wove together and began to fill out an arm.

"Thank you, sire." Igor's smile sagged. "But...but I already have a left arm."

"For *Zug*'s sake, Trudal. Can't you get anything right?"

"The arm does indeed seem to be a left. What shall we do?"

"Nothing, you idiot. Right, left it doesn't matter, does it, Igor?"

"No, sire, I suppose it don't."

"Good. Now, the whereabouts of the nano-assembler."

"It's gone, sire," Igor said. "Truly, beyond belief, I let it get away from me."

"But you were my man! I had great plans for you."

"With all due respect, sire, I am still your man, even more so now that I have two left arms."

"Fokk this!" Cardassin fluttered his hands in frustration. "We're in a real pickle now. Trudal!"

"Yes, sire." Trudal stepped between Cardassin and Igor. "I understand completely the fermented complications. If the *TrueMen* do indeed have the missing nano-assembler, then they can do what we can do. They can't even be starved out of the ruin. They might even be able to find a way to open the sealed entrance to the enclave."

Cardassin waved his hand dismissively. "A minor consideration. I'm still thinking we should set up a siege around the ruin, around the plateau, if you get my drift."

"Yes, sire."

"I'm talking knights of old. Very old, Trudal. We will encircle the Maraia...don't look at me that way. We can't very well assault them if they have a nano-assembler. We will starve...no that won't work either as you've already said. We will wait them out."

Trudal wrung his hands nervously. "Excuse my impertinence sire, if Maraia have a nano-assembler, we could be there for a very long time."

"Yes, yes, I realize that. Then we will camp out around them for the heck of it. We'll party. Have a good time."

"Yes, sire." Trudal bowed. "Party. You are very wise."

"But this has to have a plan." Cardassin glanced around and focused on Igor, who was still standing off to one side, flexing his repaired arm. "Igor. I want you to lead this operation."

Igor snapped to attention. "Yes, sire. I can do that. Put me on the list." He was about to salute with his right arm, then probably realized it was left-handed and stared at it bewildered.

"What list?" Then Cardassin remembered that Igor was his man and the list of things that Igor could do for him was long. "Do you have any suggestions as to how we should deploy?"

"Yes, sire." Igor began hopping from one foot to the other in obvious anticipation of the venture to come. "Given our current strength of mutant supplicants, it would be possible to rim the plateau with parabolic arcs of manned tents. No Maraia could get out, and at the same time we could all have a good time. We'd grow tubular membranes long enough and big enough around to encompass our tents. The tubes could be interconnected with smaller tubes, so we could get from one to the other without having to go outside."

"Splendid. You're smarter than I thought. Trudal, don't just stand there. Call out the guard! Assemble the troops! I'll lead the way, and don't forget to bring the tents!"

Chapter Twelve

Akilah pressed her cheek against the ice on the western wall of the plateau. The cold produced a welcome numbness. Her breath puffed. With stiff fingers, she shoved her fogged goggles onto her forehead and squinted at the steep escarpment that towered above her.

Halfway up.

The storm slewed around her. A malicious wind laced with ice-crystals piled snow against the wall.

She repositioned her goggles, then yanked her ice ax free and swung it higher. When it caught, she brought up one cleated boot and dug into the ice, followed by the other. Her amputated forearm pressed painfully, slipping with no grip, but adding incrementally to the hard won friction of her ascent. Slowly, she made her way up an angled crease.

The others had long ago disappeared off to her right, Jamil and Michael relaying up the ice, pulling Dayna between them.

Exhausted, Akilah dragged herself over the top edge and lay on her back, mouth open, gasping for breath. Up ahead, a glow of light through the top ice marked the location of the ruin. Only two days and it already seemed like home.

Michael crunched over to her across frozen snow. "Dayna's safe. I'm sorry I didn't help you. I thought you would want Dayna taken care of first, then for me to come for you. But you've made it on your own." He patted her back, which annoyed her.

I made it on my own, period. "Get me inside. My parka's soaked. I don't want to freeze to death this close to home."

She leaned heavily on his shoulder as he led her to the eastern side of the plateau where the entrance to the ruin had been bored through the ice.

She slid down the shaft and emerged into bright light.

Jamil squatted to her right. Dayna lay prostrate, conscious but looking woozy as Nicholai hovered over her.

Ferral faced her with Lorry and Karin just behind him.

"Well?" Ferral asked.

Akilah cringed. *You don't mince words, do you?* Ferral had suffered a few stitches. She had lost her mother and her hand.

"I want a private minute with my father." Akilah hid her mutilated arm behind her hip.

Ferral gave Nicholai a side glance. "We have more pressing issues to discuss, but if you want a minute, I don't see that it will make a difference. The good Doctor hasn't stirred since you left."

What an ass. She walked over to her father and knelt. "Can you hear me?"

He lay on his back, his mouth open, dry air wheezing in and out. Not a hint of recognition or cognizance.

"I told you." Ferral said.

She stood awkwardly, her amputated arm throbbing.

245

Ferral squinted. "Are you all right?"

"No." Defiantly, she held up her arm.

Ferral smiled, then transmuted whatever quivered on his lips into a wince.

"Cardassin cut it off when we refused to give up the location of the Shepherd."

"The Shepherd? But you couldn't have. We know nothing of the Shepherd."

"Yes, Ferral. That's what I told Cardassin, but he didn't believe me."

Ferral squared on Michael, who had taken up a position on a far wall along with Jamil. "It's all about you."

"Yes, it's about Michael." Akilah held her arm out to an attentive Nicholai while never breaking eye contact with Ferral. She wasn't about to show a reaction that he might interpret as weakness. "It's my opinion that the Shepherd has been here recently and deposited Michael amongst us, supposedly to help us."

Ferral snorted a laugh. "You expect me to believe that! You *TrueMen* always amaze me, how much faith you put in the old scriptures and myths. It would be easier to believe that Cardassin created this…this freak, than to embrace the Shepherd as his creator. Next you'll be telling me that Sedroth is standing outside."

Michael blanched. "I'm…I'm not a freak and you know it."

"Stow it, you guys. I can't deal with a pissing contest right now. I've got an arm that needs attending to."

246

Nicholai turned her arm toward the light and examined the blackened end. "It's sealed, cauterized by the razor. The nerves will be sensitive for some time. I can give you a pain killer."

Akilah pulled her arm from his grasp. "I'll manage." She didn't feel like accommodating anyone, not even at her own expense.

Ferral pulled a rag from his pocket and wiped sweat from his brow. "Look, I'm sorry you lost your hand, but there's something we've got to talk about."

Oh, oh. Just like Ferral to make his move while I'm away. Father at the edge of his grave. Michael an enigma. She glanced around the room. Nicholai, Lorry and Karin caught her gaze then stared sheepishly at their hands clasped in front of them. "Okay, what's up?"

"We've decided," Ferral said with a wave of his hand at the others, "that my view of things is the stronger way to go. Things are getting desperate."

"I think things are beyond desperate at this point." Akilah quickly surveyed all of them. "I come to this conclusion reluctantly. We are doomed."

"Precisely,   you've just returned from Cardassin's compound empty handed--" Ferral blurted a laugh, but quickly recovered. "--In order to even consider realizing Doctor Rasmussen's goal, you needed a nano-assembler."

"I can't argue that."

"So, this is what we have decided on."

"You've already decided?"

"You had your chance." Ferral's cheek twitched. "You failed. I think you should now consider what I am about to propose."

"Okay, Ferral. Propose."

"Rather than trying to build A4-Ni, or whatever our esteemed leader wants to call it, or is it to be a her, I propose that we repair the flyer, retreat to Nairob and regroup."

Akilah shook her head in despair. "Repairing the flyer is a pipe dream. Regrouping is more than a pipe dream...there are only six of us left."

"Hear me out. You weren't able to steal a nano-assembler from Cardassin, but one might be bartered from him."

"Bartered?" Akilah stared at Ferral incredulously. "What do we have that Cardassin wants so badly that he would give up a nano-assembler?"

Ferral reached into his pocket and removed the guardian. "This."

"Ferral, you're insane. We can't give him the guardian. It's our only hope for salvation."

"I couldn't agree more. Once we've used it to obtain a nano-assembler we can easily repair the flyer. Once we're back in Nairob we regroup...you know, start to rebuild our population."

Akilah winced. "That's grotesque."

"Grotesque?"

"God dammit, Ferral, what does it take to lay it out for you? Have you forgotten what amateurish use of a nano-assembler can produce."

"Those so called amateurs manipulated their DNA for self-gratification," Ferral said. "We'd be working with pure Maraia DNA with the sole purpose of increasing our numbers. You wouldn't mind having a couple dozen of yourself running around would you? I wouldn't mind."

Wouldn't mind a dozen more Ferrals either, or mind more of me for that matter? The idea is repulsive. "I'm not going to stand here and engage in this specious debate."

Ferral glared at her. "If you don't want to be part of the solution, then so be it. Certainly the four of us have DNA as pure as any you might contribute. I wouldn't even get near whatever Michael might be carrying."

"You disgust me," Akilah said. "I've been to the player's lair. I've seen what he can do. He's invincible. You might quash him here, but he will reappear there. You might think you can barter with him, but he plays by his own rules."

"Tell you what." Ferral drew his razor and held it casually in front of him. "I'm going to slip out and confront our evil player. I'm confident he'll want this bauble badly enough to fork over a nano-assembler. I'll take my chances that he might deceive me. After all I'm not some stupid low life mutant." He looked to Lorry, Karin and Nicholai. "Any of you want to come with me?"

Nicholai glanced at the two women, then shook his head, a motion of negativity or simply confusion..

"You don't seem to have command of your recruits." Akilah didn't mind seeing Ferral squirm.

Ferral reddened. "Damn you all." He pulled on his parka, zipped it up tight and headed for the door.

"Ferral, don't be stupid," Akilah called.

He turned and gave her a condescending look. "I am the only one with a plan to get us out of here alive."

***

"Fokk this!" Cardassin pulled the faux fox scarf tightly around his neck. He pumped his goggles out and in from his face hoping to clear the fog that had collected on them. "I'm freezing to death."

The storm that had dogged his progress from the comfort of Kanapoi to the plateau had abated, leaving behind knee high snow. His sledge sat like some oversized ornament from an ancient holiday tree, runners curling up fore and aft like the boot toes of elves. At the middle of the sledge, Cardassin sat wrapped in layers of woolen blankets.

He would have preferred to wait until a nano-assembler could have been programmed to grow a proper, more appropriate snow-vehicle, but that would have taken too much time and provided a window of opportunity for the Maraia to escape or plan some other dissembling activity. Since the nano-assemblers had been created when things were a lot warmer, they contained no stored programs for vehicles capable of coping with arctic elements, anyway. Hence, the hastily improvised sledge.

"Sire," Trudal said. "the mutants are working as fast as they can. We have already made good progress seeding the western side of the plateau and rounding the north. Now all we have to do is seed south along the eastern flank, and we'll have them surrounded."

250

"What about the south? We haven't seeded the south. They can get out that way."

"Quite right, sire. But since that is up and over the plateau, I thought we could seal it off with a few well-placed warriors, rather than awkwardly extending our membranous tubes there."

"Good thinking, Trudal. Do we actually have warriors?"

"Excuse me, sire, if I have exaggerated for effect. But the concept still stands."

"How long is it going to take for these tubes to grow? I'll be a popsicle before long."

"Ten minutes from seeding. Already the earlier seeds have closed in on themselves and provided the necessary cover for our hoards to pitch their tents."

Cardassin turned painfully to look over his shoulder. Indeed, the membrane was growing wonderfully. Already, tents stood scattered throughout its vast interior. Multicolored lights twinkled from canvas seams, down guy ropes and between tent poles, giving the whole array a gaudy carnival-like appearance minus the music.

"I kind of like it," Cardassin said. "It makes me want to party."

"And party we shall, as soon as we have them surrounded."

"Have you brought the women?"

"Me? Personally, no, sire. You are aware that I prefer men, as does your hindship. But I have instructed Igor to garner a sufficient number of wenches to keep every man well coupled."

"Good, good. We shall have a wonderful time, despite you and me having to fend for ourselves."

Trudal signaled for two attending mutants to move the sledge to keep ahead of the growing membrane. "Sire, please tell me where you intend to pitch your tent. I hope I am not too bold to suggest a site on the eastern side of the plateau directly opposite the ancient ruin."

"Splendid. From there I will have a direct view of Maraia comings and goings. They are indeed a sneaky lot, don't you agree, Trudal? Conspiring to steal one of my nano-assemblers, then hunkering down in their ruin. Has anyone seen or heard anything?"

"No sire. But I can assure you that they will soon think of something."

"Eh? Whose side are you on, anyway?"

"You do me wrong, sire. I merely meant to suggest that the Maraia are driven to construct a universal constructor to save their souls, and that such an undertaking will require no small amount of reshaping the top of the plateau and transforming its insides."

Cardassin tried to yawn, but found his jaw was too stiff from the cold. "You wouldn't be pulling my short hairs would you, Trudal?"

"You jest sire. Everyone knows you have no short hairs to pull, not that I would be so inclined, anyway. Indeed. It has been shown to me that the Maraia will build the universal constructor A4-Ni, christen it *Afareni*, a female appellation, and launch it into the grand void with their last remaining genomic code on board."

A warming shiver of fear tingled head to toe. The Shepherd so close. The guardian near. An object so sought after, that having it now in his possession would give him an overwhelming sense of anticipation. Oh, to hold it in his hand for as long as possible before giving in and tasting its fruits. "Trudal, you'll excuse me, but for now, my foremost concern is seeing that we have successfully encircled the plateau."

Cardassin waited impatiently as the membrane caught up to him, grew wispy tendrils high on either side of him and closed overhead in a streaming basket weave that quickly melded together into a seamless fabric.

Equally spaced white lights came on overhead, supplemented by colored decorations lower down. The air warmed perceptibly, so much so that Cardassin began to shed layers, finally stepping out of the pile and off the sledge. He ran his fingers through mussed hair, then smoothed a wrinkle in the green and black splattered design of his camouflage pajamas.

Trudal raised an eyebrow, then quickly a hand to scratch it with.

Does he think I'm a fool? "You don't approve of my attire?"

"On the contrary, sire. Green and black will hide you well in the frozen waste."

"They appear green and black here. If we ever exit, they will change to suit the surroundings. Clever don't you think." Cardassin held up his hand. "Forget it. You always agree with me. Is my tent being attended to? I feel like retiring. It's been a long day."

Igor lunged into the tent, tripped and sprawled before Cardassin. "Sire!"

Reluctantly, Cardassin let go his anticipation of dreams of young boys cavorting naked to the rhythms of stringed instruments and drums. "What is it Igor?"

"I have reports that the synthetic human has left the Maraia compound."

***

Akilah stared somberly at the entrance Ferral had just stepped through. *He's right. What alternative do I have to offer but Father's dream of Afareni?*

"I'm glad he's gone." Dayna struggled to a sitting position and leaned back against one of the containers. She took a deep breath, composing herself. "And I'm surprised that you all--" she pointed at Karin, Lorry and Nicholai. "--would be so easily swayed by such a low probability solution to our problem."

"He didn't let us speak," Karin blurted, hands shoved deep into her pockets. "I, for one, had doubts from the beginning about his plans."

"That's not the way it looked to me." Nicholai called over his shoulder as he struggled to close the makeshift door.

Lorry moved to grasp Nicholai's arm in a show of solidarity. "Nor I."

"I'm not surprised you're divided," Akilah said. "I really don't care why you ended up agreeing with Ferral. He can be intimidating. But the reality is that he's gone on his insane quest, and we are all stuck here."

Michael cleared his throat. "Excuse me, if I may?"

"What is it now Michael," Akilah said impatiently.

He reached to his boot and withdrew a slender cylinder.

Dayna gasped. "That's a nano-assembler."

"Yes," Michael said. "I took it off the inebriated Igor before he came to his senses and overwhelmed me."

"Then we are saved!" Lorry shouted, crossing her heart with her hands.

Akilah gave Michael a questioning look. "Are we?"

"The assembler is damaged, but I may be able to fix it."

Dayna coughed a painful laugh. "This is great, Akilah. But last I heard neither you nor I nor any of the other *TrueMen* know how to use a nano-assembler. So mystery boy here must know, especially if he says he can fix it. Are we to put our faith into an unknown?"

"I'm well aware of our differences," Akilah said. "You needn't bring *TrueMen* into the argument."

"Small comfort. You *TrueMen* have shunned us for decades."

"Do we have to get into that now?"

"I suppose in my obtuse way," Dayna said with resignation. "I'm just trying to level some old scores."

Poor Dayna. Still so troubled. After all these years. "I realize that. We are nowhere unless Michael can fix the assembler. Let's go from there."

Michael sat on a low canister, looking as though he were waiting until their attention shifted his way. When it did, he pulled a light close to bear on the nano-assembler. "Does anyone have an enlarging glass?"

"Nicholai, you must have one in your kit," Akilah said.

Nicholai nodded and rummaged in his satchel to produce a clear, bi-convexed lens, its edge wrapped with a metal band and attached to a black handle.

"That will do," Michael said. "Rather mundanely primitive, but functional."

"Do you want it or not?" Nicholai said defensively.

Michael took the lens without comment. Then holding it steady above the nano-assembler, he felt along its length and found a seam. With a firm press, the assembler split open to reveal an intricate inside.

"How are you going to be able to repair that?" Akilah said. The guts of the assembler looked far too complicated for anyone without very sophisticated equipment, or knowledge, to fix.

"The core of the nano-assembler is sealed and practically indestructible, so I'm not worried about it. What we see here--" He indicated a fine clockwork-like construction. "--is the mechanical part of the tool. Much more subject to damage, but also more easily fixed."

He fussed with the innards for some minutes, poking with a pin-like instrument, then pouring over the construct with the lens.

"I think that will do it." He snapped the housing home and thumbed a switch.

The nano-assembler flashed a couple of lights. An orifice at its end puckered and moved through the motions of expelling a pellet, though none was actually expelled.

He handed the assembler to Akilah. "It's all yours."

She drew back. "I...I don't want it. I don't even know how to use it."

"I could show you," Michael said, looking disappointed. "I think your father might trust a cure more if it came from you."

"Dayna?" Akilah felt unsure of herself.

"I don't think it matters who operates the nano-assembler. We don't even know if Doctor Rasmussen will accept a cure much less if we can even find one."

Akilah moved to stand beside Rasmussen's cot and reached for his hand.

He lay with his mouth open, his breathing labored, his eyes closed. "Akliah. You've come back," he said weakly.

"Please Father, I've not left you." She stroked his brow. "I've seen my mother."

Rasmussen's lower lip quivered. His tongue peeked out of his mouth and ran over dry scabs. He swallowed with difficulty. "I couldn't bear to tell you."

"You knew?"

257

"I was powerless." He coughed. "Cardassin taunted me with her. Even if I could have saved her, there's no way I could have restored her."

"She asked me to kill her, and I did."

Tears leaked out the side of Rasmussen's closed eyes. He turned his head toward the wall.

"I'm sorry, Father."

A limp wave of his hand indicated he wanted to be left alone.

"Father, we have the ability to cure you." She held up the nano-assembler.

He turned back. His eyes fluttered open. His skin was pale, his breathing shallow. "Get that thing away from me."

"Father, you're being unreasonable. It was a nano-assembler that put you into this state in the first place. There's no harm done in letting a nano-assembler get you out."

"I would rather die."

"What's he saying?" Dayna leaned close.

"He wants to die." Akilah put her hand on her father's shoulder. "Please."

He shrugged off her hand and turned back to the wall.

She rose, handing the nano-assembler to Michael. "I really can't blame him, I don't like it either."

Dayna sat on a nearby stool and let out and exhausted sigh. "So here we are. Doctor Rasmussen refuses a cure from the nano-assembler on purely theological grounds. I can accept that but I wonder if he's willing to accept what will happen to him. Ferral wants the nano-assembler to repair the flyer so he can further his own vision of taking back the planet. I can accept that, and I don't think his using the nano-assembler to fix the flyer is contrary to anything in scripture. That leaves you, Akilah. You have to come to a decision regarding the restoration of your hand. I will accept that decision, but I'd sure like to know the reasoning behind a refusal to do so."

Akilah stared at Dayna in disbelief. "That's quite a speech."

Dayna stood and staggered into Akilah's arms in a heartfelt embrace.

Dayna withdrew, tears in her eyes. "And your hand?"

Should I? Against all my upbringing? "Dear Dayna, I know your intentions are sincere, but you've been amongst us long enough to know that our beliefs are not a matter of accommodation. *TrueMen* live in the present, in reality. I've lost my hand. So be it. I respect Father's decision. It's the same as mine."

Chapter Thirteen

Hands on hips, Cardassin stood over the prone Igor. "The last time you told me about the synthetic human he was supposed to be encased in ice, then he showed up in Kanapoi to threaten me. Have you forgotten? Are you sure this time?"

"Sure, I'm sure." Igor struggled to his feet, brushing himself off awkwardly with his extra left hand. "He's headed di...rect...ly for the flyer."

"That's neither here nor there. Any idiot could go directly to the flyer."

"Quite so, sire. Wot yaw want us to do?"

Fokk, I have to make a decision. Cardassin supposed it didn't really matter whether or not this guy was his guy or not. "Bring him in."

"Yes, sire. Thot we'll do."

Igor clumped out of the tent, shouting orders to his compatriots.

"Trudal!" Cardassin called.

"Sire."

"Where have you been?"

"I haven't been anywhere but here, sire. Didn't you notice me?"

"No, I did not. Now that you're here, what do you make of this intelligence about the synthetic slinking off to the flyer?"

"It's clear to me, sire, that the Maraia have sent him to assess the damage to the flyer. I would be their intention to repair the flyer and beat a retreat to

Nairob, there to regroup and launch an assault on you and yours."

"How can you possibly know that?"

"My dreams, sire. Indeed, I am told that--"

"Stop! I'm not interested in your dreams any longer. I want real intelligence. And I don't mean the kind that exists in heads. I want to be in the know, know what's going on, if you get my drift."

"I certainly do, my lord. If Igor and his men come up with this impertinent being, then we can torture him until he tells us what he's up to."

"My, my, my, what a difference a year makes. I am heartened that you have come so far. Yes...I can see pulling out his teeth, or...or frying his testicles, cauterizing his eyes. Torture would never have entered my mind, had you not put it there in the first place."

"I would never deem to suggest that I could put something into your mind." Trudal inclined forward in an awkward bow.

Cardassin paced nervously. "This party isn't what I expected. I'm here and Igor is there. He's having all the fun."

"Sire?"

"Call Igor back. I want to go with him. I'm tired of ruminating behind the scenes."

"But, sire, your health."

"Fokk my health. I'm ready for some action, raring to go. Did you hear me or not? Never mind. Call Igor."

"Yes, sire." Trudal left the tent.

Cardassin sat and wondered if he had overdone it this time. After all, it was really cold out there.

The mutants didn't seem to mind, but they were more or less bred to put up with it.

Zug! I'll have to put on all my body armor as well as my purple boots.

He was rummaging around trying to find his equipment when Igor re-entered the tent.

"Yaw summoned me, sire."

"Yes, dear Igor. I intend to accompany you on this foray to capture said individual."

"Very good, sire." Igor's eyebrows jumped up and down in a nervous twitch. "The men will be most enthused to have you with them."

"Enthused or not. Do you think it would be inappropriate for me to wear my purple boots?"

"Not at awl, sire. I think I can speak for everyone, we really, really like those boots."

Cardassin smiled. *I love this life. Everyone is so obsequious.* He dragged his boots from under his cot and pulled them on.

"I'm ready."

Igor spun on his heel and leaned toward the entrance.

"Trudal," Cardassin whispered. "Where's my ice razor?"

Trudal rushed over and handed an ice razor to him. "You are now well armed, sire. Fear not."

"Fokking rubbish. I've never felt fear." He hurried to catch up with Igor, who was waiting for him along with two other mutants at the edge of the membrane that encapsulated his world and kept it warm.

"All right. What's the plan, Igor?"

"It's simple, sire. We exit, re...con...noiter, proceed to the target, acquire the target and come back here."

"That seems almost too easy. What if he resists?"

"Sire, with awl due respect to yaw second guessing me, we have the element of surprise and in my es...tim...ation, the subject won't have a clue thot we are on to him."

"Okay, let's get to it."

Igor signaled to one of the mutants who stepped to the membrane and used a small tool to inscribe the area they would step through.

The membrane drew apart neatly, and they all piled out into the cold.

Freezing air stung Cardassin's face. He gasped. He rarely ventured beyond the confines of his warm Kanapoi. This was bloody awful. He could even see his breath. "Are we going to be long?"

"No, sire," Igor said over his shoulder. "Maybe ten minutes, give or take thirty."

I like this Igor. He has a firm grip on reality. Cardassin slapped his hands about his chest and followed the hulking mutant's lead.

Igor hunched down and indicated the others should do the same. "Thar." He pointed.

Across the ice, a dark shape scurried, stopped, then scurried again until it reached the remains of the flyer.

Igor motioned for one mutant to flank out to his left and the other to his left.

"Don't you want them separated?" Cardassin sneered.

"Yes, sire. Sorry. I forgot I got two left hands." He motioned the second mutant back and redirected him to the right. "I suggest yaw and me go frontal, sire."

Cardassin nodded. He couldn't very well speak. His jaw felt like it was frozen shut. With a great effort he forced his mouth open. "I want the bugger alive."

"Indefinitely, sire. How else are way going to torture him?" Igor winked.

Cheeky bastard.

They crept close to the flyer and waited.

Five minutes later, the figure re-emerged and started back toward the plateau.

Igor stepped into the figure's path. "Hold it right thar."

The figure came to an abrupt stop and fumbled for the ice razor at his waist.

"Don't even think about it." Igor fired a burst from his ice razor wide of the figure's feet.

The figure stilled.

Igor walked up to him and flashed a light into his face. "This the guy?" he called, never taking his gaze off the figure.

Cardassin peered. "Nope. Got the wrong one, but we can torture him anyway."

***

Jamil stood. "I go now."

Akilah cast an apprehensive glance to Michael, who shrugged.

"Yes, I understand," Akilah said. "You have your family. You've been with us a long time."

Jamil hesitated as though he had more to say, thought better of it, then turned and slipped through the doorway.

"Will he be all right?" Akilah asked.

Michael smiled. "He's probably safer than we are."

"I suppose he is."

Dayna hefted the nano-assembler.

"Well?" Akilah asked.

Dayna turned away coyly, forcing Akilah to strain to look over her shoulder.

"Don't push. I'm just scanning the stored programs. Some of them are quite interesting."

"I'm not interested in interesting programs," Akilah said. "We've got a lot of work to do."

"No? Look at this one. It's for some sort of warm bath, in a pool." Dayna looked up hopefully. "We've always wanted something like this."

Akilah shook her head. "You're such a romantic but we are getting ahead of ourselves."

Dayna nodded and returned her concentration to the assembler. "Here's an elevator program. It's not perfect, but it's better than anything we might come up with in a short time."

"Go ahead," Michael encouraged. "Implement it."

Dayna pressed a button, waited, then took the pellet the nano-assembler expelled. "Now what?"

"Since the pellet contains millions of nano-assemblers, their effectiveness is usually enhanced if the pellet is ground into a powder and dispersed. The assemblers are all pre-programmed and will organize themselves to work in concert."

"Like this?" Dayna reduced the pellet between finger and thumb, then walked over and tossed the resulting powder into the void of the elevator shaft.

In a matter of seconds the shaft became engulfed in a cloud of activity.

Akilah peered down the shaft. "What's happening?"

"The nano-assemblers are going about their business. Usually the first phase consists of doing an inventory of available material. The rock of the shaft appears to be rich in iron derivatives, so the assemblers shouldn't have too much trouble conforming its atoms to steel and then into the elevator structure."

"What if the rock wasn't rich in iron?"

"It'd take more time, but could still be done. A transmutation of material, a draw down of energy, but in the end the same result."

The cloud cleared and gave way to loud grinding and clanking. Shiny brackets sprouted from the rock walls, then grew long tendrils that became rails. The rails in turn exuded feathery sheets that flapped across the void and joined, then thickened to become a platform. Arched steel closed over the platform to receive a snaking cable that descended from a winch and pulley mechanism anchored to the ceiling above.

"That's incredible," Akilah said. "I didn't even see what was going on overhead."

"No less incredible," Dayna said, "than a lot of other cool things this assembler is capable of doing. I wonder if that winch is powered?"

Akilah tested the platform with her foot, and once assured that it would not give way, walked to its center. "Seems sturdy enough. Looks like controls over there." She crossed to the side of the platform and studied a tight cluster of buttons. After a moment's hesitation she punched one of them.

An alarm bell rang and the platform gave a slight lurch, then glided down smoothly with a distinctive hum.

Dayna peered over the edge of the shaft at the descending Akilah. "Everything okay?"

"Works like a charm." Akilah pressed another button. The platform reversed its motion and came back level to where the others still stood. "Now we can go up and down, but I think we have more pressing matters to attend to in the tunnel."

Michael and Dayna joined her on the platform and they descended.

"I suggest," Michael said after they had arrived at the bottom, "we first secure the perimeter of the tunnel. I don't think Cardassin will try an assault through our front door, but he might try to squeeze a mutant or two through some breach in the collapsed walls of the tunnel's former entrances."

"How are we going to do that?" Akilah asked. "I doubt the nano-assembler has a perimeter sealing program."

"It does have a water sealing program," Dayna said. "That would serve the same purpose. Set the assemblers loose and they will seek out and seal any place water could infiltrate. We could beef up the sealant to something harder than the silicone based stuff I see here. Something like concrete. At least then if a mutant tries to bash his way in we'll hear him."

Akilah clutched her arms around her chest. "Could you get some heat in here? It's freezing. And some more light." She peered into the gray depths of the tunnel outside the limits of their lights. Hoar frost still dusted the far reaches, giving the tunnel a sinister black and white appearance.

"Here's a faux sun program," Dayna said. "It's probably the same one Cardassin uses in Kanapoi. Should I activate it?"

"That would be wonderful."

While Dayna busied herself with the nano-assembler, Michael wandered the floor of the tunnel. "We'll have to devise a way to open the roof so A4-Ni can rise once she is ready to launch."

Dayna did a quick double-take. "You're not serious?"

"Of course I am. We will construct A4-Ni here--" Michael waved his arm to indicate an area at the center of the tunnel, "--and then launch her straight up."

"How are we going to get through solid rock and all the ice?" Akilah asked.

"You underestimate the capabilities of the nano-assembler. I would guess that the roof rock can be transformed quite easily into levered flats that would open, given that we blasted away the overlying ice."

"Probably a piece of cake." Dayna extracted a pellet from the nano-assembler. "Stand back. This should be interesting."

She cast the pellet into the area indicated by Michael and waited.

"Well," Akilah said. "Nothing seems to be happening."

"Patience."

A pinpoint of light caught Akilah's attention after Michael's admonition. It appeared where Dayna had cast the pellet. The light enlarged to melon-size and rose to the ceiling. Light flooded the interior of the tunnel, followed by a perceptible rise in temperature.

"You want palm trees, too?" Dayna asked excitedly.

"You're kidding."

"No. Not at all," Dayna said. "I'm just scrolling here, and this thing has got everything that Cardassin has back in Kanapoi."

Akilah looked to Michael, who shrugged, then to Dayna. "So, what are you doing now?"

"Surprise!" Dayna cast a pellet on the ground near a confining wall and stepped back. She glanced apprehensively at Akilah.

Does this make me a part of whatever she has concocted?

The floor of the tunnel melted, then erupted in a bubbling mass of molten rock, only to settle back in the form of a rimmed depression with a gleaming interior surface. Controls puckered around the top edges. Orifices popped through the side walls. Water began to condense out of the air over the tub and fill it.

"Dayna?" Akilah stared suspiciously.

269

"You said I could do it." Dayna stepped to the tub and pushed one of the control buttons.

The orifices jetted circulating water as a draft of steam rose above the surface.

"I believe it's called a hot tub," Michael said.

"I believe my words were that you were a romantic. I don't think I actually gave you free license to proceed with the construction of this...this pond."

Dayna gaped. "But..."

"No harms done," Michael said.

"Yeah, but...," Akilah mocked. "Get rid of that thing."

"You get rid of it." Dayna tossed the nano-assembler to Akilah, who lunged to grasp it.

Dayna strode to the elevator, and stabbed the button that raised the platform. A moment later she was out of sight.

***

Cardassin slapped his arms across his chest. *Enough of this cold and adventure.* "Best we be getting back." Without waiting to see if the others had heard, he stomped his way rigidly toward the membrane.

Upon reaching it, he realized he had no way to open it and began pounding on its surface. "Help me! I'm fokking freezing out here."

The membrane parted and Cardassin fell through into the arms of Trudal. "Sire, are you all right?"

"No damn it. I'm freezing to death."

270

"I'm sorry to hear that, sire. Come, let me wrap you in my cloak." Trudal grasped the edges of his cloak and held out his arms.

Cardassin gazed at Trudal a moment wondering if the seer had lewd intentions, then concluded that the poor man only wanted to make him warm. He fell into Trudal's embrace.

"We've not been like this before, Trudal."

"No, my lord. Nor have you been so cold."

A mutant barged through the opening, shoving his prisoner ahead of him. "He says his name is Ferral."

Disappointed, Cardassin gazed skyward. *Ferral. The goof who affronted me when we stormed the ruin. But who knows? He might be fun to ride.*

The membrane closed. The temperature in the enclosure cycled up and soon everyone was toasty.

"Ferral. That is your name isn't it?"

The wretched soul glared at him. "What's it to you?"

"Oh, a live one! I love it when they talk dirty."

"Sire, shall we cut off his testicles, now?"

Ferral's eyes went wide.

"Trudal. You're making our subject here apprehensive. I perceive that if we are patient, and do not cut anything just yet, he will prove to be a very informative captive."

"Go to hell!"

"My, my. I have been wrong in the past about these Maraia, and I suppose I've misjudged this one."

Trudal hefted a large knife.

271

"Well?" Cardassin leered at Ferral.

Ferral shot a pained gaze, first to Cardassin then to the knife in Trudal's hand. "I have a proposition for you."

"A proposition," Cardassin leered "I love propositions. Let's hear it."

"I have access to the guardian. I will tell you where it is in exchange for a nano-assembler."

Cardassin threw back his head and guffawed, then grabbed his side in agony. "God, I hate it when people make me laugh like that. What makes you think that I would be willing to give you a nano-assembler for the guardian. You must be pretty convinced about the fairness of the trade to come here and risk being wrong."

Ferral shifted nervously. "I don't think I'm wrong. You want to trade or not?"

Cardassin stroked his goatee in thought. "What would you do with a nano-assembler anyway?"

"I have my reasons."

Trudal stepped forward. "Don't do it, sire. He means to repair the flyer, retreat to Nairob, and rebuild the Maraia population."

Cardassin glanced from Trudal to Ferral. "Is that true? But it must be, Trudal is a seer."

Ferral stood mute.

Igor stepped into the tent and motioned for Trudal to come to him.

After a whispered exchange, Trudal grinned broadly and saddled up to Cardassin. "Igor has found the guardian." Trudal opened his hand surreptitiously and showed Cardassin a small gleaming sphere.

"Well, what do you know?" Cardassin picked up the sphere and tossed it lightly into the air in front of Ferral.

Ferral blanched. "I...I...."

"Precisely," Cardassin said. "Now we get to play for free."

"How did you..." Ferral glared at Igor.

"Yaw can't fool me." Igor grinned.

Trudal ran his thumb across the knife's blade.

Cardassin raised his hands. "Let's just hold on a second. Seeing as how we now have an unprecedented advantage, maybe there's something we can squeeze out of Mister Ferral in exchange for our mercy."

Trudal looked up a bit confused from his knife. "But, sire. I already know--"

"Shut up, Trudal. I know you know. I want to know what Mister Ferral knows."

"Hey." Ferral began to sweat. "I'll tell you everything you want to know about the Maraia. No secrets."

Cardassin yawned. "There's not much I don't already know, my dear Ferral. The Maraia are such a pitiful group. Well beyond saving. What I am truly interested in is the newest member of your tribe...the one who appears to be synthetic, the one from the Shepherd, a being not meant to be, if you get my drift."

"You mean Michael?"

Cardassin let his mouth drop open in mock surprise. This Ferral was denser than he had figured. "Yes, deary. Michael."

"Yeah. Freaky bastard, that one.

"And..."

"And, well, he just showed up one day. I don't know where he came from. At least I can't be one hundred percent sure. He did mention the Shepherd, and he's pretty well got Akilah wrapped around his little finger."

"Ah, yes. I love my fingers to be wrapped. Perhaps not the littlest one, but you get my drift."

Ferral just stared.

"My lord." Trudal spun the knife in his hands. "I do believe this individual is wasting your time. Shall I begin cutting?"

"Trudal. You will begin cutting when I tell you to."

Trudal's shoulders slumped. "Yes, my lord."

Cardassin paced. He grasped his hands behind his back and lowered his head in thought. *What to do? I have a hyperactive dolt on my hands, who seems to know very little. Torture would be of no use aside from the pleasure of it. Return him corrupted? Better.*

"Trudal."

Trudal rolled his shoulders such was his eagerness. "Yes, sire."

"We shall return this Ferral to the Maraia."

"Return...?"

Cardassin glared. "Are you questioning my orders, Trudal?"

"No...no. Of course not, sire."

"It sure seemed to me you were questioning my orders."

"I'm sorry, sire, if I gave that impression." A smile played across Trudal's face. "Shall we return Mister Ferral a whole man?"

Cardassin rubbed his chin in exaggerated thought.

Ferral let go a whimper. A dribble of sweat creased down his temple and dripped onto his shoulder.

"I suspect a Maraia man has little use for his testicles. After all, there are precious few Maraia females left wherein those accoutrements would come in handy. So let's put away the knife for now..."

Ferral blew out a relieving breath.

"...better to gouge out his eyes. Just to teach him a lesson. Slow him down. They do have a nano-assembler after all--thanks to you--so they'll be able to repair his sight, but it will take a bit of time."

"The Maraia already have a nano-assembler?" Ferral stammered.

"Indeed," Cardassin said. "There must be some irony in all of this somewhere."

Trudal moved toward Ferral.

Cardassin put out his hand. "Dear Trudal, I think I want to do this myself."

Chapter Fourteen

"Was that wise?" Michael turned from the elevator shaft where Dayna had just ascended.

Who is he to question my behavior? Akilah gave him a hard look. "She overstepped."

"But you encouraged her."

Akilah squared off in front of him. "Let's cut the crap for a moment. Cardassin made some pointed accusations. I want answers."

Michael looked to the tunnel ceiling for a moment, then down at her. He smiled nervously. "I was afraid you'd ask. I hope you realize Cardassin was just guessing."

"Was he?"

His smile dissipated along with a resigned exhale. "You did a good job of deflecting his questions with fabrications. You were very creative."

"You're being evasive."

"I suppose I am. To be frank, there's some truth to what Cardassin said...to what you said."

"Then the Shepherd *is* here?"

"He was. I'm not sure where he is right now."

"You came from the Shepherd?"

"Yes."

"Are you human?"

"No."

She wasn't surprised. "I'm okay with that."

Michael's smile returned. "I don't think you have a lot of choice."

No, I suppose I don't. Suddenly her father's quest had gotten a lot more complicated. She had long ago become used to the surreal idea that the player Cardassin had arrived in their midst to make their lives miserable. Now she faced getting used to the idea that the Shepherd of myth really existed and had deposited a synthetic man on Earth to help them.

"Choice?" Akilah said. "I always have choice. Not you, nor the Shepherd, that excrement Cardassin or Ferral can take that away from me."

"I understand our situation somewhat differently," Michael said. "From what I know, we are all caught up in a predestination. A4-Ni*'s* creation has everything to do with the existence of the Shepherd. Since the Shepherd exists, then A4-Ni must have been created."

Akilah's first reaction was of walls closing around her but that was quickly replaced by a sense of relief. "Then we have nothing to worry about."

"Unfortunately, it's not that simple. Though the gross fact of the Shepherd's existence is secure, the means to that end can take a number of different paths. But obviously, having a nano-assembler is of paramount importance."

"Then my father must live as well. He's the only one with the plans for A4-Ni."

"There's also the guardian."

"But we don't have the guardian."

Michael stared at her, started to say something, thought better of it, then said. "We don't now. That's one of the unknowns in the path ahead."

Akilah put her palms to the sides of her head. *How much more of this do I have to take?* "Please, I'm going to take a break and go in what you have referred to as the hot tub. Its waters look like they could be soothing."

Michael looked astonished. "You're going in after what you said to Dayna?"

"Dayna didn't do what I told her to do. Be that as it may, I'm not adverse to immersions, warm immersions. In fact, I'd have a hard time remembering the last time I experienced an immersion of any sort." She unbuckled the suspenders that held up her jumpsuit, striped off her sweater, then shoved the suit down her hips and stepped out of it.

Michael stared.

"Never seen a naked woman before?"

"Actually, I haven't."

I suppose that confirms his synthetic-ness. "Care to join me?" Akilah sat on the edge of the tub and swung her legs over into the warm water.

"I don't know if that would be good for me. The Shepherd said I should avoid immersions." Michael took up a sitting position at the end of the tub where it met the wall of the tunnel.

Akilah slid into the water and lounged against the side of the tub opposite Michael. She ran the cauterized end of her forearm back and forth in the warm water, leaving in its wake a faint trace of red. "It's stopped throbbing."

"I could repair it completely if you weren't so stubborn."

Akilah shrugged. "You can call me stubborn. That's your choice. I have to live with my handicap and reconcile it with my beliefs. I admit it's not an easy juxtaposition to maintain." She smiled as she bobbed in the water. "Sure you won't join me?"

"I'm sure."

Akilah glided across the steaming pool and pushed one of the control buttons. A blower began to drive air through the water, increasing the cloud of steam above it and roiling the surface.

"Now that you've admitted being a synthetic and coming from the Shepherd, tell me something else I don't already know."

"Like what?"

"Like, where does the Shepherd come from?"

"As far as I know he's of this universe."

Akilah stopped pushing water. "This universe?"

"Well, obviously, there are others."

"That may be obvious to you but not to me."

She lay back against one of the sides and studied the bubbling water. "This could be a model of our universe," she said thoughtfully.

"You read a lot into bubbling water."

"Not really. You have a medium. You have a driving energy source. You have the creation and destruction of structures. Ephemeral structures."

Michael smiled and shook his head. "Your universe is a lot more complicated than that and not as kindly."

"Really? Complicated I can buy, but kindly? What's to be kindly?"

"I don't think telling you would make you feel any better about your situation."

Akilah frowned. "Really, Mike. After all that has happened, why don't you let me decide how I'm going to react to information?"

"I've often wondered why you call me Mike. My name is, after all, Michael."

"Don't get off the subject."

Michael waved a hand at the steaming cloud.

"Well?" Akilah felt a certain impatience. Mike could be so obtuse at times.

"You remember I made reference to us all being caught up in a predestination?"

"I thought you were just giving some context to the Shepherd's connection with the building of A4-Ni."

"I was. But the context is much bigger than that. The universe, at least what you consider to be the universe, is caught up in this predestination."

Akilah laughed. "A universe without free will?"

"Pretty much. Your universe is a small, closed part of a larger structure. Nothing that is in your universe can ever get out of it. Everything is destined to cycle, beginnings meet ends, ends meet beginnings, forever."

Akilah wove her hands in the water before her, a motion letting her gather her thoughts. "So, we go once around the circle, then we go again. It all repeats?"

"Yes."

"What do you call that?"

"Closed-timelike-curves." Michael looked smug.

Give it a guess. "General relativity."

"General relativity."

Wow. "Closed world lines."

"Very good," Michael said. "I didn't know you knew so much."

"I know a lot of things, Mike. You have to remember that long ago the guardian was with and instructed the Maraia. We have a fairly comprehensive knowledge of the history of humans before the Shepherd created us. I just never extrapolated a mathematical solution to General Relativity into something real."

"I'm sorry. I didn't mean to diminish what you might know. I must admit that unless I draw specifically on data that I can access, I am not always prompted with the information I need."

Akilah gave him a skeptical look. "Okay, you don't know everything. But what about free will? I have options before me, and I make decisions based on what I think is best. I could go one way or the other. That would change everything."

Michael thought for a moment. "You only think you have free will because you see things on a macroscopic scale. The fact that you make a choice at that scale has very little to do with the predestination occurring at far smaller scales."

Akilah shook her head. "It seems to me that there would be far less determinism at smaller scales. Quantum mechanically speaking...if I can say such a thing...the probability curves of sub-atomic particles gives them almost an infinite number of time and place combinations until that same curve collapses when I--at my macroscopic scale--make a choice by observing. I change reality."

"Unfortunately, your universe is still closed. All those potential times and places exist simultaneously, forming a curved probability potential, a surface in a higher order spacetime. You might choose one line on that surface, but all other lines still exist. It's possible to slide laterally across the surface, picking and choosing a different probability line, a different past or future, but still be constrained in a closed universe."

Akilah marveled at Michael's energy. *How to bring it down*? "Ah, the many-worlds interpretation of quantum mechanics."

"Something like that."

"Okay, Mike, I concede you know more about this stuff than I do. Tell me, how does it all impact me in the here and now?"

"I'm afraid it doesn't. You don't have the ability to slide laterally in my analogy, so you're stuck with your closed world line. If we had the guardian, we'd be able to use it to read your line into the future."

"Yes, that would be interesting. Perhaps reading my past would also shed some light on the why and how of us being here. Crashing the flyer was no accident."

"Indeed. I have my theory about that."

"Really?" Akilah blurted a laugh. "Have you suddenly developed perfect hindsight?"

"No. But it seems obvious to me that Ferral cut the control cables. I think he's a player spy."

"Ferral? He's not the easiest Maraia to get along with nor is he a *TrueMen*, but a player spy? I find that hard to believe."

"Are you so gullible to be taken in by his ruse? He brandishes the guardian and exits to bargain with Cardassin. That seems like a cover for simply giving the guardian to Cardassin. Why else do you think he felt so confident heading out? The place is crawling with mutants. He'd be razored sooner than taken into custody."

The elevator hummed.

Akilah hoped it was Dayna returning, but she was disappointed to see that it was only Nicholai.

When the elevator came to a stop, he hesitated for a second, looking from Akilah to Michael, then crossed the intervening space and stood at the edge of the tub.

"I'm sorry to interrupt you," he said condescendingly, "but your father has taken a turn for the worse. I think--if you can manage to leave the comfort of your tub--you'd better go to him. He doesn't have much time left."

Akilah flushed. "You don't have the right to talk to me like that, Nicholai. If I want to soak in a tub, I will. I've paid my dues." She rose and slicked the water from her body before yanking her clothes over her still damp skin.

Nicholai shrugged. "I'll wait for you at the elevator."

Prissy Nicholai. Father taking a turn to the worst. I suppose I've been expecting this. She finished dressing and hurried to the platform with Michael close behind.

Nicholai activated the control, and they rose toward the main level of the ruin.

As they neared the top, she could hear Father's screams.

***

Akilah rushed to her father's side. She stared. "What are you doing?"

"The plans for *Afareni*," Rasmussen muttered, his screaming something past. "I must get them down before I die." He scribbled on a sheaf of papers.

She lifted one of the sheets. The writing was incomprehensible. "Save your strength. There will be time later." She offered the page to Michael to see if he could make sense of it.

He took it, turned it over and then over again, then shrugged.

"What are we to do?" Akilah asked him. Not waiting for his response, she turned to her father. "You need rest."

"I am dying," Rasmussen drew his hand across cracked lips.

"There's the nano-assembler," Michael said.

"Never." Rasmussen coughed fitfully.

"Please, Father, it is your only hope."

"I am resigned to dying. I will not let go my faith. Who is that man? He's not Maraia."

"It's Michael, Father. You remember."

Rasmussen looked bleary-eyed at Michael, then shook his head. "No matter." He motioned to Akilah. "There's something I have to tell you."

284

"Save your strength, Father."

"No...must tell you now." He closed his eyes momentarily as though summoning his last remaining strength. "I was the one who cut the control cables that caused the crash."

Akilah felt a white hot flash of shock. Then her cheeks seemed on fire. "But why? We all could have been killed. Some of us were."

"*Afareni* has to be built. I thought the only way to ensure her construction was to prevent any possibility of turning back. Promise me you'll build *Afareni*."

"You know I can't promise. I can only try."

"Promise me!" Rasmussen rose up gripping Akilah's jumpsuit, then flopped back.

He began to shake uncontrollably. His fingers swelled to the size of grapefruit, then twitched and slimmed out into long tentacles. "What have they done to me?" His voice was raw.

"Oh god." Karin keened into the silence of the ruin. She broke free from Lorry and rushed to Rasmussen's side. "We must force him to use a cure from the nano-assembler."

Akilah held her back. "I wish we could. But forcing a cure on him would surely kill him, too."

"I am hideous," Rasmussen croaked.

The mutant-genes spread to his legs, causing them to tremble, then turn into slithering root-like structures. A background popping sound marked the snapping of his tendons.

Lorry hurried to Karin and pulled her off Akilah. "Come away. You're hysterical."

Rasmussen ceased moving and stared vacantly.

Akilah knelt beside him. It seemed the designer genes had run their course. There were no further visible transformations. He lay still.

"Is he dead?" She turned anxiously to Nicholai.

He stepped over and placed his hand against Rasmussen's throat. "Yes." Nicholai arranged what remained of Rasmussen's hands across his chest. "A great man has passed. Why did he have to be so stubborn?"

"The nano-assembler would have cured him," Karin wailed. "We should have used it whether he agreed to or not."

"Now the plans to build A4-Ni have died with him." Nicholai stood. No signs of grief, just a face contorted with worry. "What are we to do?"

Akilah's eyes suddenly smarted and loosed a tear down her cheek. "You stubborn old fool. You certainly got us into a mess this time. And then you bailed on us."

Nicholai was beside himself. "I asked a valid question. If you aren't prepared to answer it, then consider this. Since you cannot proceed with building A4-Ni, our only recourse is to get the hell out of here, by repairing the flyer."

Akilah scanned the contorted faces of the remaining Maraia. Was Ferral right? Without Father and the guardian they had no way to build A4-Ni.

Michael came up beside her and put an arm around her shoulder. "I'm sorry about your father. Losing two parents in one day is more than you should be called upon to bear."

Akilah remembered her earlier rebuff of Michael and decided to say nothing. He was obviously trying to be caring. "We do have a problem, Mike. No plans. No guardian. No Ferral." She shook her head in dismay.

"I know how to construct A4-Ni," Michael said.

Akilah stopped short. "You do?"

"You forget that I used the guardian."

"I haven't forgotten. I just didn't know you could learn the plans from that brief encounter. You're saying you remember it all?"

"There are aspects to my...construction that facilitate memory."

A low rumbling sound drifted up the elevator shaft.

"That sounded like rocks tumbling." Akilah knew instantly that one of the entrances to the tunnel had been breached.

Dayna ran to the hallway that led to the tunnel overlook. "Mutants!"

"Nicholai," Akilah commanded. "Set up in the corridor. A mutant shows his head, razor him!" She spun on Michael. "Can you build a door to seal the corridor?"

"Doors are easy, but it will still take some time."

"Get started."

Dayna stepped to the opening, then did a double-take. "I don't believe it. Two of them have stripped and are bathing in your tub." A razor shot fractured the rock above her head.

Michael took an exuded pellet from the nano-assembler and dropped it at the end of the tunnel.

More razor beams fractured rock, but the pellet began its work. A steel door formed and hung heavily on its hinges.

"Close it, you fool," Akilah shouted to Nicholai.

He lunged forward and shoved the door closed, then slid a bolt home.

"The elevator platform will keep them from getting up the shaft," Akilah said.

"I hope so." Michael was staring at the elevator platform which had started to glow red, then it cooled, then reddened again. "They're trying to melt the platform away but the nano-assemblers are absorbing the energy of their razors and reconstructing the works."

Akilah peered at the elevator. "How long is that going to last?"

"I don't know."

"We'll flood them." Akilah rushed for the exit with Michael close behind. "We have to get onto the top ice and bore a hole through the rock to the tunnel. Then melt the surrounding ice and let it flow into the tunnel."

Once outside she got her bearings and hurried to a spot directly over the tunnel. She took her ice razor from her belt and bored a hole down to the bedrock.

"Our razors are too slow," Akilah shouted. "Use the nano-assembler."

Michael thumbed through its stored programs until he came to one for boring through rock. "I've found one. Given the simplicity of the task, it will take less than a minute to accomplish once the pellets are cast."

I hope you're right.

Mike cast the pellets down the bore hole and stepped back.

To her amazement, the rock dissolved in a matter of seconds. Light from the faux sun in the tunnel shot up through the open roof.

Michael played his razor on the surrounding ice and watched as the melt sluiced down the bore hole. After five minutes of feverish melting, water welled up and spilled over the rim of the hole. The tunnel below had filled.

"Let's check below," Akilah said.

Inside the ruin, Nicholai brushed himself off and stood. The door to the corridor he had been assigned to guard had held, though water was leaking in around the edges.

The elevator platform had stopped glowing but water welled around its perimeter.

"We've got to dam the water," Akilah directed. But as soon as she spoke, the water began to recede.

"It's draining out the bottom of the tunnel and away under the ice," Michael said.

Dear god, there must be a mess of bodies down there. She led the way down the corridor and threw open the door. A tumble of mutants fell into the corridor followed by a gush of water.

Akilah stepped past the bodies and peered over the edge. "So much for the hot tub. There are two drowned mutants floating in it."

Nicholai came up beside them and held his nose. "They smell. Looks like they loosed their bowels." He glanced around. "I count ten dead. We'll have to remove them before they decompose."

Akilah surveyed the tumble of rocks at the entrance. "How'd they get in?"

"Dayna's sealant program either wasn't effective or didn't have time to take effect." Michael walked back to the elevator and lowered himself to the tunnel floor. He stepped along the western end of the tunnel, examining the rock encrusted entrance. "They got in here. The entrance seems weaker. I don't see any indication that Dayna's sealant took hold."

"That's odd," Akilah called down. "She seemed certain it would work."

"I can try another program," Michael said. "Here's one." He removed the pellet, ground it in his hands and sprinkled it along the expanse of the ancient entrance.

Immediately, the rock seemed to congeal and grow together.

"It's working this time," Michael said. "Nothing will be able to get through this."

"We must attend to my father...and the mutant dead," Akilah said. "Then we'll talk about A4-Ni."

Dayna leaned out the tunnel overlook. "Someone's pounding on the main entrance."

Akilah hurried to the elevator with Michael close behind. "It couldn't be mutants. They're dumb, but not that dumb."

Akilah leapt from the elevator platform before it came to a complete stop and raced across the room.

There was indeed someone pounding on the door, although the blows sounded weaker and weaker.

"Who's there?" Nicholai leaned against the braces.

"It's me." Ferral's weak voice sounded from the other side.

"It could be a trap," Michael said.

Akilah considered for a moment the odds that it was and dismissed them. "Open the door."

Nicholai slid back the braces and pulled the door open.

Ferral stumbled inside, tripped, then fell, bracing himself awkwardly with outstretched hands. He rolled onto his back.

"Good Sedroth," Nicholai exclaimed. His eyes are charred sockets."

"They must have tired of playing with him and let him go," Dayna said. "Possibly a warning to the rest of us."

Nicholai laid Ferral out and began examining him. "I don't see any other damage, at least externally."

Ferral let loose a scream. His hands went to his dead eye sockets.

Nicholai lunged to grasp Ferral's wrists. "He's delirious." After forcing Ferral's hands down, he returned his attention to the dead eye sockets. "They did a horrific job. His sight will be difficult to restore even with the nano-assembler."

"What about the guardian?" Dayna said.

Akilah glared at her. "Not now."

Dayna ignored her. "Ferral, what about the guardian?"

Ferral moaned and waved a hand vaguely.

"He's in no condition to give a coherent answer," Akilah said. "We have to assume the guardian is lost and worse yet with Cardassin. Mike, can you get something out of the assembler to begin the restoration of Ferral's eyes?"

Michael nodded and stepped to Ferral where he plucked a hair from Ferral's head and fed the strand into the assembler. After a moment, he pressed buttons sequentially on its exterior, paused, then continued until he seemed to come to what he was looking for.

"This should do the trick. The assembler sequenced Ferral's DNA, then isolated the structure for his eye and optic nerve. The assembler is preparing a salve that once rubbed on his sockets, should begin to rebuild his eyes. But it will take a while given the complexity of the system."

"How long?" Akilah asked.

"I'd say two or three days."

Two small capsules emerged from the assembler. Michael handed them to Nicholai. "Break these open and smear the contents on his sockets. It would probably be wise to bandage him to keep the salve in place and minimize contamination."

Ferral outstretched his arms as though he would help Nicholai in administering the cure. He made contact with one of Nicholai's hands and gripped it fervently.

While Nicholai attended to Ferral, Akilah motioned to Karin. "Will you help me with my father?"

Karin nodded grimly. "What do you want me to do?"

"We'll clean him up, then place him in a body bag. He should be moved to the outside as soon as possible. He'll freeze but that can't be helped. He can't remain inside. Tomorrow night we'll move him down the plateau and melt the ice to bury him."

"It seems so heartless."

"The dead are dead, Karin. What you and I carry in our hearts is what is important. My father wouldn't have had it any other way."

Karin looked at her skeptically.

I know you're thinking I'm being heartless, but you have not walked in my shoes. It pained her to think that she was supposed to demonstrate some sort of remorse, grief, when all she felt was an overriding, compelling pressure to push ahead, to see her father's dream through. She knew in her heart that the Maraia were doomed. Building A4-Ni was the only way out.

She stood over Nicholai as he put the finishing touches on Ferral's bandage. "How's he doing?"

"He's semi-conscious. Mumbled something about having to lose his sight to see."

"That's very ironic, especially coming from Ferral."

* * *

The others were staring at her. They had been for some time. Waiting. Waiting to be told what to do. The problem was Akilah wasn't sure what to

293

do. The former boundaries that made decisions easy were falling by the wayside, forcing her to be more creative, to plot a course that would get these people who trusted her through this turmoil. But her father was dead. Ferral was out of commission. Dayna seemed distant. Nicholai, Lorry and Karin couldn't be trusted.

And then there was Mike. Mike the unknown. Did he have his own agenda? Probably. And did that agenda coincide with hers? Probably not. Did he know what she was going to do before she did it? He talked a lot about predestination. If he knew so much, then he'd know how all this was all going to play out. But he wasn't saying.

"It's dark enough," Akilah said. "Cardassin can't see us. Let's get this over with."

Outside, Michael and Nicholai each grabbed one end of the bag that held Rasmussen's body. After a sharp tug to free the bag from the frozen ground, they dragged it across the ice on top of the plateau as they followed Akilah and the others to the south. At Nicholai's insistence, Ferral remained in the ruin.

"This is as good a spot as any," Akilah said after they had traveled several meters. Though she stood at the center of the plateau, the lights from Cardassin's encircling encampment cast a glow into the sky. The faint noise of music, shouts of debauchery, and periodic sizzles from loosed ice razors drifted up to her.

Overhead the stars shone starkly--bleak and unblinking in the arctic air.

Dayna took her ice razor and melted a grave into the ice, taking care to funnel the runoff into a fissure where it would freeze before reaching the bottom of the escarpment. When she had gone down the two meters to the bedrock of the plateau, she stepped back. "It's done."

Michael and Nicholai slid the body to the edge of the pit and looked to Akilah.

"Do you want to say anything?" Nicholai asked. "Before we lower?"

Akilah knew if she spoke she'd break down. She shook her head and motioned with her hand that they should proceed.

Not having any ropes to lower the body, Nicholai put his end of the body bag in first. Then the two of them lowered Rasmussen until he stood vertically, frozen stiff.

After a moment of hesitation, they gave him a push and he flopped unceremoniously over onto the bottom of the pit.

"If I may." Michael raised a hand, staying Dayna, who was about to melt in the sides of the pit. "I will say a few words."

Surprised, Akilah nodded.

"We are told of peace and happiness," Michael said. "But all that we have hoped for from Sedroth seems gone. So we close our eyes in despair. Though we wait, only nothingness comes to us. When we open our eyes, we find reason to hope. Sedroth would not leave us unattended. Nor shall our wait be in vain. He will come to us. So we have been taught. So it shall be."

The words clogged with emotion in Akilah's throat. "Michael, that was beautiful. Thank you."

Michael seemed embarrassed. "I didn't make it up. It is what I have learned from ancient verses."

"You have captured the moment and what sustains us. Dayna. Please."

Dayna brushed at her cheeks, then stepped forward and started sealing the pit while the others stood around in silence with their heads bowed.

A flash of light lit the landscape for an instant followed by a thunderous explosion.

In the distance, on the plain below, flames engulfed the remains of the flyer. Dark smoke roiled and spread in an opaque, oily stain across the sky.

Dayna let off sealing the grave. "That's the flyer!"

"The flyer?" Akilah said. "So what. It was never high on my list of possible ways to get out of here."

Dayna gazed at the distant inferno. "Ferral will be devastated."

"I don't want to seem heartless, but Ferral has more personal concerns." Akilah knew she was seen as insensitive, but to her the times seemed to demand that someone held firm to the center ground.

Beyond the flames of the flyer, farther east, bright ice razor flashes crisscrossed in an intricate web.

"That's coming from the direction of Jamil's home." Michael started toward the edge of the escarpment. "He's being attacked."

296

Akilah grabbed Michael's arm. "You can't go that way."

"I have to help him."

"I know you do. But you'd never make it through Cardassin's perimeter. The only way is under the ice."

The others stood transfixed.

"Mike and I," Akilah said, "will try to reach Jamil's home though I fear we are already too late. I want the rest of you to stay in the ruin. Be on your guard. We shouldn't be long."

She led the way back into the ruin. After a quick elevator ride down to the tunnel floor she raced to the sealed eastern entrance. "Damn! How are we to get through this?"

Michael came up beside her. "The sealant hasn't taken here." He rolled a large rock aside and exposed smaller rocks that they could dig through. On the other side, a narrow gap between the rock floor of the plain and the ice above loomed.

"It's about ten meters of this," Akilah said, "on our bellies then it opens up, and we can stand. If we can find a lane, we can push past Cardassin's perimeter." She started to crawl forward. After a few meters she stopped and checked on Michael. He was down on his stomach and following.

"This is gross," he said.

It was gross. Wet, cold, with a dank smell of things long ago rotted.

She flashed her light ahead and located a lane that disappeared into the dark. Its sides were lined with the jagged edges of water-carved ice. "Careful through here. This stuff can cut you to shreds."

Michael stopped and retrieved a strip of cloth from one of the toothy ice blades. "It looks like this is the lane those mutants used when they infiltrated the tunnel."

"Let's hope the rest stayed home. I wouldn't want to meet any of them here."

She crawled forward, trying to judge the distance they had come from the escarpment. "Do you think we are past the siege line?"

Michael directed his light to the ceiling and a hollow that opened upward. "That looks like an upward sloping lane, recently cut. Probably leads to the siege line."

"Then we'll go a ways farther before boring out. We'll make faster progress on the surface."

After another five minutes they were able to stand. They walked and jogged until the lane began to give out.

"I guess this is going to have to be it." Akilah played her ice razor on the frozen ceiling and melted the ice until only a thin layer remained between them and the outside. "We'll push through that. I don't want my razor beam lighting up the sky and giving us away."

"I hope we're not too late." Michael hunched over so Akilah could climb onto his back where she reached up and punched through the ice.

It clattered down around them.

A draft of frigid air washed over them.

"Brrr. Let's get going." Akilah leapt up and out, then she reached back and hauled Michael through. She did a quick survey of the surrounding plain. "Nothing. I don't like it. It's too quiet in the direction of Jamil's home."

A dark shape rose from the ice surface twenty meters away and loomed closer.

"It's Jamil," Michael said in a low voice.

He limped up to them. His parka was in shreds. Heavy burn marks from glancing ice razor shots crisscrossed what was left of the fabric. An angry welt pulsed on the side of his face.

Michael grabbed him as he stumbled forward. "What's happened?"

"Mutants attack home." Jamil's eyes were bloodshot, his pupils dark pools of panic. "Kill Baba and Nina. Take Rafiya and Jamani. I try to defend but they too many." His shoulders heaved uncontrollably.

Akilah looked past Jamil to see if he'd been followed, and seeing nothing helped Michael lead Jamil back to the hole in the ice where he sat down.

"But why?" Akilah said, distressed.

"Want you." Jamil indicated Akilah with a general sweep of his arm. "If no, then kill Rafiya. Make toy of Jamani." He shook his head and buried it in his hands.

Akilah felt helpless. Events were spinning out of control, moving faster than she was able to assimilate and cope. "What can we do?" She asked Michael.

He looked long and hard into the dark, then back at the soft glow of light coming from Cardassin's siege line.

"I'll take care of it," he said.

Chapter Fifteen

After seeing Jamil and Akilah safely to the ruin, Michael made his way down to the plain below. The ice of the escarpment glowed red from the flyer's reflected flames.

For all his bravado, he was still unsure of how Cardassin would react to his entreaties. He also wondered about putting himself in harm's way. Was this wise, given his stated mission? Why was he setting off to negotiate the release of Jamil's family when the bigger task of building A4-Ni loomed? Akilah had certainly made her displeasure clear. She couldn't let him go, if he was the only one with the knowledge of how to build A4-Ni. But in the end, he had appealed to her sense of humanity, her compassion. And she had agreed. They all owed Jamil.

He had just set foot on the ice at the bottom of the escarpment when he was surrounded by four mutants.

Michael peered at their drooping faces. He recognized the hulking brute. "Igor?"

Igor gave him a toothy smile. "Welcome, syn...the...tic. Lord Cardassin will be pleased to see yaw."

The other three mutants converged and tied him hand and foot, toppled him over and dragged him feet first toward Cardassin's encampment.

Michael felt he would shatter into a million pieces, he was so cold, but they finally came to the membrane.

One of the mutants scribed an opening, and they shoved Michael through. Though he was back in Cardassin's clutches he thought he had never felt so relieved to be warm. His pleasure quickly evaporated as two of the mutants dropped to their knees and began to toy with him in places that made him uncomfortable and even hurt. The more he squirmed to try to stay out of their reach the more emboldened they became. He was about to scream, when Cardassin appeared and stood over him.

"Enough." Cardassin kicked one of the mutants in the head when he failed to respond fast enough. "Bring the synthetic into my tent."

The two mutants grabbed Michael under the armpits and dragged him past a hanging curtain into Cardassin's inner chamber. The mutant that had been kicked kept shaking his head. Cardassin's boot had raised a pink welt on his cheek.

With a wave from Cardassin they dumped Michael in the middle of the room and left him alone with the player, except for the ever present Trudal.

"What is it you want?" Cardassin asked. "Give me something in exchange for not having you dismembered."

"You have Jamil's wife and son."

"Who?"

"The primitive human, Jamil. Your mutants kidnapped his wife and son and killed his parents."

301

"Ah yes, the primitives. I was told they had been brought in. They must be here somewhere. Pity about the parents. It seems these days have been hard on those choosing to be mothers and fathers. But that is such an archaic concept anyway that I--"

"I want you to let them go."

Cardassin's jaw dropped and hung there for a while before he clamped it shut. Obviously, he was not used to being interrupted.

"I don't doubt that you do," he said amicably enough, having quickly regained his composure. "But what incentives did you bring to induce me to such a capricious act? I certainly hope you've brought me something, or as they say, you are in deep up to your eyeballs."

"You want the Shepherd. I can give him to you."

"What the fokk. The Shepherd for the peasants? That would be a marvelous trade. But do you think I'm an imbecile? You don't have the Shepherd to trade."

"I know who and what you are, Cardassin. You're no imbecile, though you carry on sometimes as though you were. It's a ruse that you--"

"Oh, shut up. I know you know, and I'm not interested in having it all flung in my face. I have a job to do here. Obviously, you know about that, too. But it does intrigue me that you are so accommodating as regards the Shepherd."

"I think the Shepherd can take care of himself."

"Yes, you would assume that. Of course, the success of his self-care remains to be seen. Now, where is our esteemed organic friend?"

"I don't know."

Cardassin's face turned a shade of purple. His lips quivered. His eyes rolled in his head. He grasped one hand in the other until he steadied. "Don't toy with me, synthetic."

"I'm not toying, Cardassin. He'll contact me." Michael held up his hand and proffered the ring on his finger. "This is a finder. When the Shepherd wants me, he will summon me using this ring. I will go to him. You can follow."

"What a beautiful bauble. Trudal, I dare say that if we remove said bauble from said synthetic's finger, we can short circuit all this bovine excrement and access the return and location of the Shepherd directly."

Trudal started toward Michael. "Very astute of you, my lord."

Michael leaned back from the odious Trudal. "You can have the finder, but it will only work for me."

Cardassin raised a staying hand. "Pity. We'll have to think of something else." He stroked his goatee in thought. "Aha!" He raised his finger into the air. "I'll accept that you will tell me when the Shepherd returns, but as a sort of guarantee, I require that you give me two of your Maraia as…umm…hostages."

"That doesn't strike me as a bargain at all. I give you the Shepherd to give up Jamil's family, but you still retain two Maraia."

"From my point of view, it's perfect," Cardassin said. "My quarrel isn't with the primitive and his family, it's with the Maraia and you and the Shepherd and *Gilomir*. This way, I, who already have the upper hand and needn't offer any concessions whatsoever, gain two steps towards my goal. I'll get the Shepherd, if you honor your betrayal. And I'll still have two Maraia to perhaps release if you trust me to keep my end of the bargain."

"Fat chance."

"What was that? Fat what? Oh, I see, an ancient expression. The Shepherd certainly must have scraped the bottom of the linguistic pit to arm you with that one."

"I'll ask Akilah about the hostages."

"Do ask Akilah about the hostages," Cardassin mimicked. "But one must be the female Dayna."

"Why Dayna?"

"She intrigues me."

"And the other?"

"Oh...any female will do."

"Why women?"

"I prefer females."

***

Akilah sat with her back to the wall in the main space of the ruin. She stared at the others. It seemed obvious that her moodiness was putting them off. Not one of them looked her in the eye, not even Jamil.

He sat on the opposite far side, pawing at his wounds, tugging at his torn parka. She'd have to say something to Nicholai soon, if the good doctor didn't leave Ferral alone. There were others that needed his attention.

Lorry and Karin were occupied with something in one of the storage containers.

Dayna lounged nearby, very feline, eyes half closed but probably taking in the scene and thinking the same things Akilah thought.

Michael had been gone for over an hour. Was he coming back? What if he didn't? Where would that leave the Maraia? No flyer, no plans for A4-Ni. Maybe it was time to become mutants. No. Never that. But they did have a nano-assembler. Easy enough to do.

An urgent rap on the door to the ruin.

Nicholai stepped over to it. "Who's there?"

"Michael," a weak voice sounded.

Nicholai opened the door just enough to let in a draft of cold air and Michael. He let Michael squeeze through, then shoved the door back into place.

Everyone stared.

"Well?" Akilah didn't rise from her position across the room.

Jamil tilted onto his feet, the effort to do so obviously causing him a lot of pain.

"Cardassin has agreed to free Jamil's family," Michael said.

Jamil took this in stoically.

"Why would he do that?" Dayna snapped, coming out of her doze.

"I told him I'd give up the Shepherd."

Akilah felt a rush, a momentary blacking out, then a clear thought. *Blasphemy*. "You can't do that. The Shepherd is sacred."

"The Shepherd can take care of himself. It's more important that we concentrate on building A4-Ni."

"That's all you think about," Lorry yelled, then blushed when everyone looked at her. She quickly turned back to her task.

"We should consider other alternatives," Nicholai said. "Maybe something along what Ferral suggested."

"Are you nuts?" Akilah fumed. "The flyer is history. We have nowhere to go but forward. How much time have we bought?"

"Not much. Probably a day or two," Michael said. "The Shepherd will contact me as soon as A4-Ni is built,."

"Is that enough time to build her?"

"Just barely."

"So that's it." Akilah raised her hands in exacerbation. "Cardassin will just let us proceed on your word?"

Michael's gaze shifted around the room. "Not exactly. He wants...Maraia hostages. Two women."

Lorry and Karin exchanged glances. Dayna smiled knowingly. Nicholai's head snapped up. Ferral simply moaned.

"Hostages!" Akilah knew she shouldn't be shrieking. "Never. He's a lying son-of-a-bitch. After what he's done, I'd be insane to trust him with hostages."

"I agree," Michael said calmly. "But those are his conditions."

"Well, damn those conditions." Akilah felt a moment of release. *Let it all hang out.* She usually never swore, but circumstances were driving her to her personal edge.

Michael shifted, ill at ease. He stepped toward her, then came up short, probably realizing that he risked her temper if he came any closer. "I think we have to keep our primary goal in mind."

"You're saying that the construction of A4-Ni supercedes the life and well-being of Maraia? Of the precious few remaining Maraia?"

"Logically, it does. I don't like Cardassin's terms. But I think he doesn't really care whether A4-Ni is built or not. His main focus is on the Shepherd. And that being the case, he would probably release whatever Maraia he has once I give up the Shepherd."

"You are putting too much trust into a mad player," Akilah said.

"My family." Jamil stood. "I go."

Michael looked at him patiently. "I understand you're upset. Please give us a few more minutes to work this out."

Jamil looked at him with suspicion, then sat.

"Okay," Akilah said. "I like Jamil as much as you do, but you haven't answered my concern. Why are you putting so much trust into a madman."

"We don't have a lot of choices." Michael paced. "If the exchange doesn't suit you, then I'll tell Cardassin as much. It may be that he'll think of something else, given his preoccupation with the Shepherd."

"Was he specific about which Maraia he wanted?"

"Yes. He said the hostages had to be women, and that one of them had to be Dayna."

Akilah glanced at Dayna. "Why her?"

"He said she intrigued him."

"That's not much of a qualification." Akilah eased herself off the wall and marched over to Michael. "This is too much, Mike. I can't ask Dayna, or anyone else for that matter, to be a hostage. I can't expect anyone to go. It's too dangerous."

"Then we are at an impasse. Maybe he'll just tire of Jamil's family and let them go."

Jamil stood.

That the lives of Jamil's wife and son lay in the balance gave Akilah pause. They were innocent bystanders in the quarrel between the Maraia and Cardassin. That they should suffer didn't sit well with her sense of fair play.

She held up a restraining hand to Jamil, then turned to Michael. "Tell Cardassin he'll get only one hostage, me."

Dayna jumped to her feet. "I'll go with you. I'm not afraid of Cardassin."

"If that's true," Michael said, "then either you are insensitive to what he has already done, or you have some special relationship with the beast."

Dayna whirled on Michael. "What the hell do you mean by that?" She spat out the words centimeters from Michael's face.

Michael flinched. "You heard me."

"Are you implying what I think you're implying?"

"I think you and I are...dancing around the same thing." Michael smiled, probably not about the encounter, but about his vocabulary.

Dayna looked as though she was about to hit him.

"Enough arguing!" Akilah wedged herself between the two of them. "If Dayna wants to accompany me, it's her decision."

"No!" Karin stomped to the middle of the room. "You have to lead, Akilah. It doesn't make sense that you should risk your life for ours. I will go with Dayna."

"I don't like this," Akilah said.

"Of course you don't." Dayna walked over and put an arm around Karin's shoulder. "But you know it's the best solution." She looked at Michael. "Where are we supposed to go?"

"Cardassin has mutants waiting at the bottom of the escarpment to receive you."

"Sounds like he knew we'd agree."

"No. If there was a problem, then I was to tell the mutants, and they would tell Cardassin, and he would have...compromised Jamil's family."

***

Cardassin threw a silk pillow at the side of his tented enclosure. "I'm bored stiff! I hate sieges. They take too long."

Trudal shifted from one foot to the other, a clear sign that he, too, was becoming impatient. "I'm sorry about the waiting, sire. Perhaps we should change our strategy and be more forcibly active. You do have the troops to overwhelm these few remaining Maraia."

Cardassin rubbed his scalp with both hands, agitated. "Trudal." He stared at the obsequious seer. "You've never been one for nuanced approaches. Despite the relative boredom generated by what I am doing, it does have a tick in the positive column of proceeding slowly enough so that we don't make any mistakes as we home in on our primary prize."

"But, sire, you have the guardian."

"That is one prize, and not the most important one. If this imbecile of a synthetic keeps his promise and gives up the Shepherd, then we shall have accomplished a lot more."

Trudal frowned.

"Come, come dear Trudal. You aren't having a Maraia moment are you?"

"No, sire. I just find it sad that we are quickly closing in on our objective, and in a little while it will all be over and then what will we have left to do?"

"You, my dear, will have nothing left to do. You will be, as they say, redundant. I, on the other hand, will...actually, I, too, will have nothing left to do. But that is the object of my mission. Once I have accomplished that for which I was heretofore placed, then I shall cease to exist."

"You'll die, my lord?"

"Get real, Trudal. Death awaits us all. The only matter of importance is our focus on what we do between the time we rise from idiocy to the time we become self-conscious beings and have only the darkness of the afterworld to look forward to. Praise *Zug*."

"I have never thought of my life in such stark terms."

"A pity. I find starkness refreshing. It sort of clears away the cobwebs, drives home the point. Sears the nasal passages." Cardassin clapped his hands. "Catch up, Trudal. Catch up."

"I most certainly will try, sire."

"Now, that's enough philosophizing for tonight. Has the synthetic given us any indication whether he has convinced that Maraia bitch to accept my terms?"

"No, sire. We have mutants at the bottom of the escarpment waiting for his response."

"Oh, I do hope that he and the sweet Akilah accept. It will be such a joy to have two of those wenches here to play with. The primitive woman and her son have been nothing short of uninspiring."

"But you haven't even met them, sire."

"I just presupposed that they would be uninspiring, and they certainly have been. We haven't harmed them in any way, have we? I'd hate to give them back damaged and have the whole nine meters fall apart."

"The guards have been given strict orders not to mess with them."

"A lot of good that will do. These guards of mine seem to have memories shorter than my little finger. Please check on our charges before something irreversible happens."

"I will do that, sire."

Trudal was at the entrance to the tent and about to exit when Igor brushed through, nearly toppling the seer, and prostrated himself in front of Cardassin.

"Igor, what is this posturing?" Cardassin demanded. He'd have to re-evaluate the procedures he had implemented regarding the composure of mutants. This Igor seemed to be taking matters to a disturbingly creative level.

"I thought yaw all would be pleased with my sub...ser...vience, sire."

"I don't give a fokk about *yaw* subservience. I want to know about the deal, the agreement, the covenant, if you get my drift?"

"I do, sire. And here they are." Igor twisted awkwardly toward the entrance flaps and pointed with both left hands.

Two Maraia females stood framed in the entrance, looking very cold and frightened.

Chapter Sixteen

Michael did a mental check. It had been over a half hour since Dayna and Karin had been taken into custody at the bottom of the escarpment by the waiting mutants. If Cardassin double crossed him at this point, he was...in a pickle, or was it toast? Akilah would never support him again. His mission of building A4-Ni could be compromised.

"Where family?" Jamil stared in the direction of the siege wall, tense, waiting.

"They'll be here." *I hope.* "Be patient."

"No patient. No trust Cardassin."

"I don't trust him either, but it's the best we could do under the circumstances."

Two dark shadows framed against the glow of light from the siege wall.

Jamil pointed. "There."

"Thank Sedroth," Michael said. "I believe that's Rafiya and Jamani."

Jamil rushed to greet them. They practically crashed into each other with clawing hugs and a rubbing of noses.

Michael approached more cautiously, not quite convinced that Cardassin was on the level. "Are they okay?"

After a hurried exchange that Michael couldn't follow Jamil nodded, still clutching Rafiya close.. "They very frightened, but Cardassin no hurt them."

"We should get back to the ruin as soon as possible. I don't trust Cardassin to keep his word for long."

"We no go to ruin. I no trust people there. Jamil go home, maybe change home, maybe not.."

"You'll be safer with us. There's strength in numbers."

"No like numbers. We go somewhere and hide. Cardassin never find."

Michael realized there was little he could do to dissuade Jamil. Rafiya looked as grim and determined as Jamil. Jamani jumped up and down, exuberantly showing his happiness at being released.

With a turn of his head, Jamil beckoned Rafiya and Jamani to follow him. He moved away from the escarpment and directed his ice razor into the ice on the plain. A few seconds later he had drilled a hole to the caverns that wove beneath the ice between barren ground and the ice above. Then they were gone, having dropped one-by-one silently out of sight.

Not even a farewell. Michael searched in vain for some indication of the way they had traveled under the ice, but realized that Jamil would not have needed a flash to find his way. He probably knew the passageways like the stitching on the back of his gloved hand.

Alone in the dark, cold night with the ever present stars and a half moon above, Michael searched for a sense of purpose. At least he and the Maraia were moving forward, be it by smooth progress or lurching degree. The situation seemed to be stable, at least for now. He would proceed to set up shop and build A4-Ni. After that, the rest was up to the Shepherd.

The cold began to seep through his parka. He took a last look at the siege wall, then turned and climbed the escarpment, aided by a rope he had used to facilitate his descent.

At the top, the warm glow from the entrance to the ruin beckoned.

***

"I'll do it." Akilah said to Michael. "But I don't know how."

Michael picked up the nano-assembler. "I will help you. I'll need some DNA. A hair will do."

Akilah felt a wave of apprehension. "Are you sure you know what you're doing?"

"I think I've shown that I'm adept in the use of this gadget."

She smiled weakly. Her arm had started throbbing again. So much so that she had begun to care less about the ethics of using the nano-assembler and more about ending the pain and getting her hand back.

She reached up, plucked a single hair and gave it to Michael.

He fed the hair into the end of the nano-assembler. "It will only take a minute. The nano-assembler has to sequence your DNA. Once it has your profile, I can request a build for your left hand."

Akilah stared at the nano-assembler. It seemed the machine had swallowed her up and was now dicing through her entire being. And then it would spit out something that was supposed to....

"What's that blinking light?"

Michael glanced from the light to Akilah. "The nano-assembler has your DNA signature. I can now ask it to locate the sequences that give rise to your hand. Even though they have been channeled into a specific form, the nano-assembler will take age into account when it fashions the string of DNA to insert into your system. The DNA will home in on where your hand should be and reconstruct it."

"It's that easy?"

"I wouldn't call it easy, but that's what nano-assemblers can do, plus a lot more."

"Could the nano-assembler have brought my father back to life? I didn't even think of it at the time. He was so opposed. But what if we had used it after he was dead?"

"Given the massive disruption from the mutant genes that infected his body, it would have been difficult if not impossible to reconstitute him. But even if he hadn't been so infected and died naturally, all the nano-assembler could have done was clone him. You would have received a Doctor Gregory Rasmussen that had no past and knew no future. A blank sheet, if you will."

Akilah shivered, not because she was cold, but because she found the prospect abhorrent.

"There's also the problem of age," Michael said.

"The clone wouldn't be the same as my father?"

"The clone could be. But he could also be anywhere from a nursing infant to a ripe old granddad."

316

"Given what you say, I don't think I like the idea of clones. All this talk is also giving me pause regarding my hand."

"Then I suggest we leave the discussion of clones and get right to the matter before us."

A small pellet exited the nano-assembler. Michael held it up. "Well?"

Akilah eyed the pellet suspiciously. "I have my ethical concerns, my beliefs, but after what I saw happen to Father...I'm not stupid. I have to survive, and I have to survive in as strong a form as I can possibly manage."

Michael smiled. "You had me guessing given your earlier speech. But I think somewhere in the back of my mind I always thought that you would come around." He handed the pellet to her.

"What am I supposed to do with it?"

Michael glanced at the nano-assembler's small screen. "This pellet can be taken orally."

Akilah popped the pill into her mouth, swallowed and waited. "How long is this going to take?"

Michael shrugged. "It shouldn't be that long. It's not like it has to combat a lot of negative DNA to fix your hand."

The end of her stump trembled. As she stared down at it the blackened seal flexed. A moment later it separated from her wrist and fluttered to the floor, leaving pink flesh behind.

"I think something is happening," Akilah said, feeling rather embarrassed and foolish with all the others staring at her. "Should I do anything?"

"Just be patient," Michael said.

317

From the stump, slowly, a rod of flesh built outward. It had no particular form, but after a minute it stopped extending, then five small articulations protruded from its end. These quickly resolved themselves into distinct digits. And after a while fingers formed. "I'm almost there, aren't I?"

"How does it feel?"

She wiggled the budding digits. "Strange. Not much feeling, yet."

"Be patient."

Akilah flexed what were quickly becoming fingers again. "They work," she said incredulously.

"What did you expect?"

"I don't know. We've been taught to abhor this device, but now I wonder why. My hand is completely restored." She formed a fist and opened it. The skin was still pink, but the underlying bone structure felt strong. "Thank you, Mike."

"You needn't thank me. You're the one with the courage to proceed with the reconstruction. I only spirited this machine out of Cardassin's lair, and I couldn't have done that without your--."

Ferral stumbled over to them. A white bandage still covered his eyes. He was pale and drawn.

Akilah shuddered. He looked terrible, a shadow of the insane presence he usually projected. A pity in a way, but he had betrayed her and was now paying a price. "What is it?" She kept her voice level, trying not to show her disgust.

"It...it's Karin."

Akilah detected a real anguish in his voice. "What about Karin?"

"She has been returned dead."

318

"What are you talking about?" Akilah's gaze darted nervously around the ruin. "You can't see."

"I was at the door. I heard a noise. I opened the door." Ferral gulped. "I felt around outside. There's a body lying there. I...I know it's Karin."

"Karin and not Dayna?" A cold knot formed in Akilah's gut. If Karin was dead, then almost certainly so was Dayna.

"Dayna was not returned to us."

"I need to see her." Akilah followed Ferral, who felt his way back to the door.

"She's just outside."

Akilah pushed the door open against some resistance. Karin's body lay curled in a fetal position, white, frozen and obviously very dead. "Mike! Get over here and help me drag her in."

"I don't understand." Ferral muttered. "I don't understand."

Akilah stared down at Karin's inert form. How could Cardassin do something like this? They had an agreement.

"There's a note stuck to her chest." Michael plucked the note. "It's from Cardassin. He says that he lost his patience waiting and apologizes for taking it out on Karin."

"Lost his patience?" Akilah couldn't contain her sense of betrayal mixed with a good dose of "I told you so". How could she have been so stupid to let them become hostages? But she had been helpless to prevent it. "What of Dayna?" Akilah checked herself. If she said more, then her anguish at the thought of Dayna being dead would flood out into the ruin and not help matters one bit.

319

"There's nothing about Dayna here." Michael handed the note to her. "I understand that you feel a certain loyalty to Dayna. But under the circumstances, I think you should re-evaluate."

"Shut up, Mike. You know nothing of loyalty. She is like a big sister to me."

Michael stood as though frozen to the spot. To his credit he didn't try to argue with her. Akilah turned to Nicholai. "What have they done to Karin?"

Nicholai had already cut away her clothes in an effort to examine her.

"She is stiff as a board," Nicholai said, "and not from just being frozen. It's like they filled her capillaries with sand."

Michael gestured at Karin. "It is not logical that Cardassin would torture Karin and not do something similar to Dayna unless she was in league with him."

Not bad for a synthetic showing his emotions. "Mike, I told you to shut up. This is a Maraia matter. We've all have been through a lot together, more than a synthetic like you can imagine." Akilah took a modicum of satisfaction seeing Michael blink. "I'm getting tired of your paranoid accusations. You were wrong about who cut the cables, and you're wrong about Dayna. I've known her all my life. She would never turn."

"I admit I was wrong about who cut the cables, but there's been too much else that points to her complicity."

"She's loyal."

"Are you sure?"

"I'd bet my life on it."

***

Cardassin clasped and unclasped his hands, then gazed at them as though he had never seen them before. The drugged Maraia had requested an audience. He didn't like Maraia, much less drugged ones, and one requesting an audience seemed...unseemly. Despite the advantage a drugged Maraia gave him he still didn't like what they did. But he supposed he was putting an exaggerated, moralistic twist onto a trivial matter.

Trudal stood inside the tent entrance. "She's here, my lord."

Trudal held back a heavily embroidered drape. It hung from a bar overhead, caught in his hand and fell vertically to the ground.

I must do something about the colors, Cardassin thought. *Gold and brown, shot through with ochre? It looks like someone puked on it.*

"Excuse me, sire. But she's here."

Cardassin focused his thoughts, but found them uncontrollably drawn back to the garish colors. *Who picked those? I didn't.*

"Sire?"

"Do you know what she wants?" Somehow a part of his mind devoted itself to the matter at hand. It wouldn't do to let on that he was preoccupied with interior decorating.

"Not specifically, my lord. She does seem upset about something."

"Well, show her in." No, wait. What was he thinking? That wouldn't do, druggies being

321

druggies. "I want you and a mutant here, too. If she's drugged, she can't be trusted."

"But you drugged her, sire." Trudal's arm began to quiver from the weight of the entrance curtain.

"Even the more so. You may tie the entrance open, Trudal."

"Thank you, sire. I was about to collapse."

Cardassin smiled, pulled his sheepskin robe tight about him and hoped that he looked accommodating. *Fokk silk.* He couldn't conceive of why he had avoided sheepskin for so long. Probably some subconscious aversion to another animal. It was said that shepherds lay in the olden days with their sheep. Pity. There hadn't been any sheep hereabouts in over a thousand years.

The drugged Maraia female entered.

"My lord," Trudal said with a flourish. "I present Dayna, your last but not least Maraia druggie."

Cardassin waved a hand vaguely in the air, wondering what prompted Trudal to alternate between *sire* and *my lord*. He'd have to keep a tally and see if there was a pattern. *Fokk, I really hate those colors.* "Dayna. How lovely of you to come."

Dayna walked briskly to the center of the room and stopped. "I've been drugged?"

"Tsk, tsk, my dear, you must have heard Trudal talking out of turn. You don't feel drugged do you?"

"Certainly not. What have you done with Karin?"

322

Cardassin stared hard at the female Maraia. Such impertinence. Never could get the right proportions of controlled substances. But the Maraia were never very easy to deal with, at least the ones who stayed away from the nano-assemblers. But she'd asked a question. "Karin. Am I supposed to know a Karin?"

"The other hostage."

"Trudal, do we have a Karin on our guest list?"

"Not any longer, sire. May I remind you that we toyed most recently with a Maraia wench? I believe her name might have been Karin."

"Ah, yes. The *rub* has made my short term memory short." But he did vaguely remember another Maraia female. In fact, he had last seen her lying just about where Dayna stood. He could swear that the stain still soiled his carpet. "Pity. Did we kill her in the end?"

"We did, sire. You were very creative turning the blood in her capillaries to sand."

"Yes, yes. Somehow we got into desert themes. I remember now." Cardassin's face crinkled at the stain on the carpet, then he let the garish colors of the entrance curtain intrude on his thoughts again. *Am I going insane? No, not even remotely. I've always been insane by any definition.* "Did Trudal answer your question sufficiently, dear Dayna?"

"He did. Another Maraia gone. Though, I don't like that she suffered despite her being a fruitcake."

Cardassin stared. "Fruitcake?"

"Forget it," Dayna said. "An ancient Maraia expression."

"Fruit and cake aside, I do believe she enjoyed what we were doing to her...almost right up until the end. Go figure."

Dayna seemed nervous. At least that is the way her behavior had to be interpreted, not that Cardassin had a lot of experience dealing with Maraia. Pure Maraia. "Trudal, don't you think our deary seems a bit put out?"

"Indeed, my lord, she exhibits all the behavioral patterns of a put out Maraia."

That's a one for my lord.

"I presume you have the guardian," Dayna said.

"Oh, most assuredly. That idiot...what's his name...Ferral practically walked in here and gave it to me."

"Have you used it?"

Cardassin sat up straight, mentally clawing at cobwebs that laced his thinking. "No my lord, not even a sire? How am I to keep count?"

"I don't think an appellation would change anything." Dayna appeared bewildered. "I've risked years being with these insufferable *TrueMen* to get you that bauble." Dayna stopped, looked around confused. "What am I saying? What have you done to me?"

Cardassin giggled. "Not much, my dear. Perhaps a little boost to your inhibitions...setting free thoughts you harbor but are loathe to express."

"I've never held back what I think. Have you used the guardian or not?"

Cardassin scratched his crotch nervously. This upstart of a Maraia female was causing him a lot of grief. "I am not used to being talked to in that tone of voice."

Dayna put a hand to one hip. "That's because you've been surrounded by incompetents like this...this excuse for a Maraia--" She stabbed a finger in Trudal's direction. "--while I've been in the field. And now that pusillanimous synthetic thinks I'm a spy." Again the confused look.

"Very good, dear Dayna. You are coming along nicely. The synthetic did seem very perceptive."

Dayna eyed Cardassin curiously.

He stilled his hand and smoothed out his robe.

"He was guessing," Dayna said. "First he thought Ferral was a spy, then he ran out of Maraia. Those remaining three aren't worth their weight in ice. So he accused me. He was wrong about Ferral, so his opinion doesn't carry much weight with Akilah."

"How is my fair lady?"

"You'd better be careful of her. She's driven. Killing her mother and father wasn't the smartest move you could have made."

"But I didn't kill her mother." Cardassin turned down his lower lip. "She did."

"Pouting isn't going to help, either. You and I well know who's responsible. If she catches you, she'll kill you."

"Do you expect me to quake in my boots?"

"The purple ones?"

325

"All right." Cardassin's face hardened. "I've had enough of this sparring. What the hell do you want?"

"You never answered my question. Have you used the guardian?"

"No, if you must know. I haven't. I fear what I might learn."

"But I thought that was the object of your quest."

"Don't be impertinent."

"I'm sorry if I seem impertinent but I thought long and hard about how to get you the guardian only to have Ferral cut me off and hand the damn thing to you."

"Be that as it may, I don't know how to use it."

"Gregory simply wrapped his hand around it, and it worked."

Cardassin fingered his goatee. "Have you tried it?"

"No."

Cardassin motioned to Trudal, who stepped to an ornate stand beside the bed, lifted the lid of a similarly ornate box and withdrew the guardian.

Trudal held the small sphere between index and thumb as though it was something odious.

"Come, come, Trudal. Let's cut the dramatics." Cardassin palmed the sphere and closed his fingers tight around it. At first he felt nothing, then a jolt, like an ice razor turned on and forced up his backside. "Ah...I see. The force of it goes right through you."

"I wouldn't know," Dayna said.

326

Cardassin stiffened. He forced his hand open as control over his bodily functions ceased and he felt a warm splash down his inner thigh, wetting his robe. The guardian dropped to the carpet, bounced once and rolled still.

"That was quite a kick." Cardassin peered at the large stain on his robe, glared at Trudal and Dayna lest they say something untoward, then toed the guardian. When it remained inert, he knelt and picked it up. "Maybe one just has to get used to the surprise." He smiled, trying to project courage, then closed his hand again around the guardian.

"Ah...this is better."

Cardassin opened his eyes.

The others were all staring at him.

"What?" he said. He had lost touch with his surroundings. How long, he couldn't tell.

"It's been over fifty minutes, my lord," Trudal said.

"Fifty minutes? Well, no harm done. I've learned a lot."

"Indeed, my lord."

Cardassin rubbed his eyes. *I should be counting. Oh, fokk it.* "The guardian confirms that this Michael is synthetic and that the Shepherd is here to see that A4-Ni is built."

"I could have told you that," Dayna said.

"But you didn't my dear. And besides you don't command the same authority as this here bauble."

"That there bauble," Dayna harrumphed, mimicking Cardassin, "could be feeding you a line of you know what."

327

"Dear Dayna, such language. I'm inclined to take the bauble's information straight up, but with a grain of salt. Did you know, for example, that the Maraia want to build A4-Ni so they can put their genome on board and escape the universe?"

"That's been our stated purpose all along."

"But--" Cardassin giggled. "--and this is a big but, the genome is destroyed before it can get out of here. The Shepherd is facilitating this enterprise knowing full well that it will fail."

To her credit, Dayna didn't move, but her eyes registered shock. "Then the Maraia are doomed."

"Why, sweet thing, I thought that was obvious."

"We are the last of a race."

"You have been that a long time. Children? Where are the children?"

"But that's so selfish, the Shepherd's actions, I mean."

"Yes, I suppose one could pass judgment on it that way. To my thinking he is just looking out for his own existence."

"I'm not following you."

"This A4-Ni thing, along with guidance from the guardian, is destined to create the Shepherd some eight thousand years ago. If predestination is to be realized, then A4-Ni must be built to ensure the Shepherd's creation despite the cost of terminating the Maraia as a race in the process."

"But that's awful."

"So are a lot of things, my dear, but one mustn't lose sleep over them."

"The Shepherd exists, so A4-Ni must have been realized."

"You know, that's where this bauble fades on me. It has shown me the basic facts but leaves a lot of gaps. I don't even know but fully suspect that it is in the business of manipulating what it shows me."

Trudal glanced at the entrance, then back at Cardassin. "My lord, Igor is signaling me that he has some information."

Cardassin waved a limp hand. "By all means, Trudal, find out what it is."

Trudal stepped out of sight.

"Dayna, dear." Cardassin leaned forward and gave her his best leer. "Tell me, what is it like making love to a Maraia female?"

Dayna gave a start. "I'm...I'm sorry, my lord. Though my feelings for Akilah run deep, I have never had the pleasure of her intimate company."

Cardassin tried to hide his disappointment. He felt a certain vicarious pleasure thinking about the two of them together, and now that was gone...gone, gone with nothing left but an emptiness.

Trudal rushed into the tent and over to Cardassin and put his head very close to Cardassin's ear. "Sire, Igor has the Maraia bitch Akilah captive."

Cardassin couldn't suppress a smile.

"You're sick, Cardassin," Dayna said. "I never would have thought you to get off on--"

"Be still, my dear. I am no longer interested in your sexless life. There has been an interesting turn of events. Your esteemed leader left the confines of the ruin and headed this way in what must have been an attempt to negotiate your release. Pity she didn't know that you have been confounded into whom you are. She could have saved herself the trouble. But since she will be here shortly, I think we should at least humor her before deciding what to do with her. I've asked Trudal to escort her here...as a guest to this interview."

Dayna's mouth dropped open. "Please, sire. I don't want to be a part of this."

Cardassin stared at her blankly. Her distress seemed to be genuine. "Ah yes. I can see your point. I only thought, given your deep attachment to the woman, you might like to see her again. But, you can join us a little later if it pleases you....after Akilah and I renew our acquaintance." Cardassin clapped his hands. "Habibi!"

The misshapen boy showed.

"Show Miss Dayna to a tent where she can await the outcome of my tet-a-tet. And...Ah...Dayna, please leave Habibi alone. He's mine." Cardassin smiled.

"Yes, Sire. Of course. I never--"

"Of course you didn't." *She's begun with the sires, of all things. What a turn around.* "Habibi! Go now!"

Chapter Seventeen

Michael stared at the door where Akilah had just exited. *This is not right.* But he was torn between achieving his mission and keeping things on track here with the Maraia. Akilah was making assumptions about her own invulnerability, the seeds of which he felt responsible for planting. Seeds he had no business planting since he wasn't even sure himself about how A4-Ni would be built.

"I'm going after her," he said to Ferral, Nicholai and Lorry, who had lined up back from the door, almost as though they were a send-off committee.

When they said nothing but simply stared, he stepped to the door.

A motion from Ferral sent Nicholai to intercept Michael.

"We can't let you go," Nicholai said.

Michael came up short. "No? Why not?"

"The nano-assembler. You went to a lot of trouble to get it. We obviously need it. We can't let you go out there with it."

Michael glanced at Lorry, who nodded.

Ferral eased himself from his lounging position against the wall. "We have something else in mind for the nano-assembler." He looked like a mummy with his eyes bandaged white. "It's been put to evil uses. It's also grown limbs. We all thought we might give it a go at reproducing Maraia. Every other plan set forth here seems to have ended with more complications than it set out to give a solution to."

Michael stared at Nicholai and Lorry, who stared back with blank expressions. "You heard the reservations I enumerated about cloning."

"We did," Nicholai said, coming out of what seemed a near trance such was the tension in the air. "None of them seemed to me to be insurmountable."

Michael lunged for the door.

Nicholai wrapped an arm around his neck and pulled him back.

Michael fell awkwardly.

Ferral was on him before he could get up, rummaging through his pockets.

"Here it is," Ferral said holding up the nano-assembler.

Nicholai stepped up and grabbed it.

Michael couldn't believe their audacity. "You'll never be able to use it properly."

"Oh, I don't think so," Nicholai said. "It's not that much different than the DNA sequencer. I suspect a lot of its functions are automatic, and of course if we go too far astray, I trust that you will pipe up and correct us. We wouldn't want any corrupted Maraia running loose in here, would we? Too much like having a mutant among us."

"Let's get started," Ferral said, easing himself off of Michael.

Lorry came over to Nicholai and whispered in his ear.

Nicholai smiled. "Lorry, has made an excellent suggestion. What better place to begin cloning

Maraia than to start with our recently departed esteemed leader."

Ferral snorted a laugh. "That's the last person I'd want to see cloned. I had enough of that arrogant son of a bitch while he was alive."

Lorry frowned. "I don't think that's what we had in mind, Ferral. Nicholai and I have always wanted children and have never been able to conceive. I suggested that we try to clone Doctor Rasmussen, making him about ten years old. If we are successful, he'd be no threat to you and we'd have the child we always have wanted. I don't think having a clone of the master will inconvenience us too much. In fact, it will give us a reason to hope that there will be a future for the Maraia after we are gone."

Ferral muttered something under his breath that Michael could not make out.

"We'll need a source of his DNA." Nicholai looked around.

"Too bad we just buried him," Ferral said.

"There must be a hair or something still on the cot." Lorry began examining the blanket on which Rasmussen had lain.

"I wouldn't use anything from there as a DNA source," Michael said.

"Well, well," Nicholai said. "Do we have an accomplice here after all?"

"No. Not a willing one. But if you are intent on proceeding I see no reason why I should stand by and watch you make a mess of the operation. We are talking about another life."

Ferral spread his arms expansively. "Hurray. I win."

"You've done no such thing," Michael said. "But if you use DNA from that blanket, it would probably be corrupted by whatever Cardassin gave to Doctor Rasmussen. There's no telling what kind of creature you would end up cloning. You need a pure source."

"Use me," Ferral said.

Lorry dropped the blanket she had been holding. "Please, Ferral. That's not funny. I do remember that Akilah kept a small chest with belongings the Doctor had given her in the past. Maybe there's something in there that has his DNA on it." She stepped over to one of the canisters and rummaged its contents. "Here it is."

She retrieved a small chest, set it on the floor and opened it.

Nicholai peered inside. He lifted out a red, checkered cloth. "Looks like a man's bandana." He took out his magnifying glass and examined the weave.

"Here's a hair," he said, using tweezers to extract a hair the size of an eyelash. "We'll try this."

"What's happening," Ferral demanded.

"I've got a hair. A source of pure DNA," Nicholai said.

Ferral stood and thrashed about. He couldn't see, but his frustration was obvious. "How do you know it belongs to Rasmussen?"

"I don't." Nicholai glanced at Michael apprehensively.

"If you feed it into the nano-assembler," Michael said, "and ask to have it compared to a more recent sample, the nano-assembler should be able to tell us the probability that it is Doctor Rasmussen's."

He fed the hair into the end of the nano-assembler and waited while looking at the small screen. After a few minutes, an LCD on the nano-assembler flashed green.

"I do believe we have a sequenced string of DNA," Nicholai said. "Now what?" He looked at Michael.

"You'll need a nutrient rich container in which to grow the clone," Michael said. "You'll have to ad lib. Fortunately, humans are mostly water."

Lorry dragged a container from the supplies. She then poured in water from three, twenty liter containers. She rummaged through the rest of the supplies. "I'm looking for organic materials."

"Don't we have to be careful what we throw in there?" Nicholai asked.

Michael felt an instant of hesitation. *Why am I helping these people? Probably because whatever they do doesn't matter.* "Not really. As long as the elements are present, the genes will seek them out."

Nicholai swished the container around, mixing the contents, then pushed a button on the nano-assembler but nothing happened. "How do we get the pellet out?"

"There's a bit of a trick to that," Michael said. "I could show you."

"Please, do," Nicholai said.

Michael looked to Ferral who sat, obviously alert, but having a hard time following the conversation. "If I expel the pellet for you, you have to promise me that you'll let me go after Akilah."

Ferral stood. "That's not a problem. Do whatever it takes to expel the pellet and we'll let you go."

Nicholai handed the nano-assembler to Michael.

Michael hit a couple of buttons in rapid sequence with Nicholai craning to see what he was doing.

A pellet eased from the end of the cylinder.

Michael caught it and handed it to Nicholai. "This pellet, if placed in a vat of organic material, will generate a clone of Doctor Rasmussen."

Nicholai took the pellet and dropped it into the mix.

They all stood back, arms folded across their chests and waited.

Lorry peered into the mix. "I don't see that anything has happened. In fact, the contents of that container look absolutely disgusting."

"Somewhere in there, a being is forming," Michael said. "You'll have to monitor the progress of the construction. Once Doctor Rasmussen has been cloned, you'll have to pull him clear of the muck."

"Tell me what's happening," Ferral said, moving tentatively closer to the container.

Lorry pointed, barely able to contain her excitement. "I saw a hand!"

"And there's a foot," Nicholai said. "I'm surprised it's proceeding so quickly."

"Building from scratch," Michael said, "is a lot easier for the nano-assembler despite the complexity of the task."

The turmoil in the container subsided.

"It's stopped." Lorry looked anxiously to Michael. "What do we do now?"

Michael gave a resigned sigh. He reached his hand into the muck, felt around, hit on something, then pulled. "Help me. He's heavy."

Nicholai handed the nano-assembler to Lorry and gave Michael a hand. "I have him. Pull."

Together they drew a body out of the container. It was very slender, with pale skin still streaked with dark residual liquid.

"What a stench," Nicholai said.

They stood the clone up, but his knees buckled, so they lay him down. He opened his mouth and exhaled a sputtering breath.

"Clear his eyes," Michael said.

Lorry gently wiped the child's eyes with a cloth. When they were clean, he blinked them open. They were blue eyes just like Doctor Rasmussen's but with no hint of intelligence or cognizance.

"Is he flawed?" Nicholai said, alarmed.

Lorry grabbed Michael by the arm. "Well?"

"From what I know, he is whole. No flaws. But you must accept that his mind is blank. He is ten years old but has all the intellect of a newborn."

"Can't the nano-assembler bring him up to speed? Some program that will fast forward his learning?"

"The Shepherd might have such a program. This nano-assembler doesn't."

Ferral grunted. "Then what are we to do with him?"

Lorry closed ranks with Nicholai. "That will be none of your concern, Ferral. If this clone is indeed whole, then we have succeeded. Nicholai and I will tend to his needs. Though it will take time, in the end, he should quickly evolve into a normal ten year old."

"Gaaaaaa!" the child said.

Lorry brushed back tears of joy. "I...I am at a loss for words. The master has just died, and we buried him. Now I am witness to his rebirth. But he is not the master. He is a child. A child that we can love and nourish."

Aside from the child's blue eyes, Michael had to admit he didn't look the least like Doctor Rasmussen. Still, the child was destined to become the continuation of the Maraia if they ever succeeded in getting out of there alive.

"Gaaaaaa!" the child said again and began to shake uncontrollably.

A sudden panic swept over Lorry. "He's having a seizure."

"I think he's just cold." Nicholai bundled the child in a blanket, lifted and carried him across the ruin to the cot recently vacated by the dying Rasmussen.

The irony of the situation was not lost on Michael. It had only been a few hours since the Doctor had died, and now his clone was reborn like a Phoenix rising from ashes.

"I'll check his vital signs," Nicholai said. "But I suspect that everything is okay. Then he will need to sleep for a while. We will prepare some food for him to eat when he wakes up."

"Gaaaaaa!"

"Lorry?" Nicholai asked. "What do you have to say?"

She fidgeted. "Are we to name him?"

Nicholai stood and put his arm around Lorry. "You know we have the perfect name."

She smiled up at him. "Yes," she murmured. She turned to Michael. "If we had had a son we would have named him Justin, after the founding father, Truman Justis. His name is even more appropriate now as it will symbolize what we shall be."

Convoluted logic, but they seemed sincere. Who but an insensitive oaf wouldn't take heart with a child to care for? "I think the name is most appropriate," Michael said, hoping to mollify them.

"And thanks to you, Michael," Lorry said almost apologetically, "for making all this possible. I already feel that the world is a better place."

"May I go, now," Michael asked.

***

Akilah sat on a padded footstool, her arms wrapped across her chest. The air felt cold, though she knew it wasn't. She was probably nervous. Had

339

she made the right decision coming here to Cardassin's camp to free Dayna?

Michael had argued against it. To no avail. She'd also caught it from the others. Especially Lorry, which wasn't like her at all.

"Dayna's already dead," she had said. "And you know it. You can't leave!"

Then she had burst into tears. Not that Lorry didn't make a lot of sense. But if there was a chance that Dayna was still alive, then it was worth the effort to try to free her. Dayna would have done no less if their positions had been reversed.

After leaving the ruin and sliding down the escarpment, Akilah had almost gotten herself killed. A random mutant spotted her and let loose a shot from his ice razor before she could convince him that she had come on a diplomatic quest and shouldn't be interfered with.

The mutant had become confused and passed her on to someone higher up the mental chain of command. She ended up with Igor.

The odious mutant now stood across from her in the small field tent, gazing at his hands.

How did he get two left hands? It looked like he was trying to decide which had been the original one.

The tent flap was brushed aside and Trudal entered with a flourish. "How nice to see you again, my dear."

"Cut the phony familiarity. I'm not here to see you, Trudal. Cardassin has one of my people, and I intend to get her back."

"So you waltz in here and expect our lord to acquiesce to your demands. As far as I can tell, he now has two of your people."

"I'm not talking to you, Trudal."

"You could have fooled me, but enough of this word play. Lord Cardassin has invited you to his chambers for a chat."

Trudal stepped to one side and indicated the exit. "Igor will lead the way."

Outside the tent the landscape was much like that of Kanapoi, but on a much smaller scale. That the encampment was inside some sort of artificial enclosure was very apparent. The faux sun was missing, replaced by a long line of bright lights that snaked along the top of the overarching tubular enclosure. The ground underfoot was covered by a synthetic turf that seemed a half-hearted effort to duplicate real grass. Upon closer examination, the plants were crude plastic renditions of their real selves.

Cardassin's tent was at one end of a line of other tents. She assumed it was his by the gaudy ornamentation, hastily stitched swirling patterns of red and gold embroidered on gray canvas. A heavy curtain that covered the entrance to his tent was embossed with gold and brown mermaids.

Gold and brown? Akilah wondered at the choice of colors. Probably another one of Cardassin's idiosyncrasies. The repugnant odor of *rub* drifted out the door and filled the confines of the enclosure.

Inside, Cardassin lay sprawled on his bed, surrounded by silk pillows that looked like the ones

341

in Kanapoi. He obviously wasn't about to give up his creature comforts for a siege.

"There's my princess." Cardassin heaved himself to a sitting position. He threw an end of his long sheepskin robe over his shoulder. "You are clutching yourself again. Shall I raise the temperature? Oh my, I see that you have a new hand."

"I've come for Dayna. If you can't see your way to release both of us then take me but let her go."

"Pray tell, how did you know how to use the nano-assembler to repair your hand?"

"Mike knew."

"Ah yes, Michael. Clever man. Does it work to your satisfaction?"

"I'm not here to discuss my hand."

"Indeed. I do admire your loyalty to the wench. She's a regular jack of all trades." Cardassin smiled and picked the space between his front teeth with his fingernail. "But excuse me if I appear dense. Whatever gave you the impression that I would give up Dayna, especially now that I have both of you? It just doesn't compute."

"I have been told that the future is written."

"Very poetic, my dear. I presume the synthetic told you."

"It doesn't matter who told me. What matters is I believe it. As such there are things existing today that depend on actions I will take tomorrow. Since they exist, it means those actions will be taken by me. Since I haven't taken them yet, I feel immune to your threats."

"Riddles, riddles." Cardassin shook his head. "I hate riddles. You're talking, of course, about the existence of the Shepherd and the fact that the universal constructor you intend to build creates this Shepherd eight thousand years ago."

"That's what I think."

Cardassin sighed heavily, almost in resignation. "I can't quibble with your logic. I don't even want to. What interests me more is the whereabouts of said Shepherd. Your Michael was going to give me a nod when next the Shepherd showed, but that hasn't happened. The nod, I mean."

"So you had to kill Karin?"

"My dear, look at me. I sit here in the midst of mutated confusion, of my own making I admit, and I get bored. Stuffing a Maraia like a holiday turkey was a blast. It lifted my gloom for a brief moment."

"And you left Dayna untouched?"

"Back to Dayna, are we? Well, there are things you don't know about this jack."

"Like she's one of your spies? That's what Mike thinks. I don't believe it."

"Tsk, tsk. I guess there is only one way to settle this. Trudal, please ask Miss Dayna to join us."

Oh Sedroth, let this not be happening.

Trudal returned a moment later with a defiant Dayna at his side. She held her head high, her eyes blazing, a tight lipped smile on her face.

"Dayna, I've come for you." But even as Akilah spoke, she knew something was terribly wrong. A knot formed in her stomach. She suppressed a retch.

"You *TrueMen* are insufferable," Dayna said.

Cardassin clapped his hands gleefully.

"Your self-righteousness. Your elitism," Dayna said as though reciting. "I've put up with your overbearing father and his fatuous dreams of Maraia salvation for years. There are truths you *TrueMen* will never grasp with your myopic pursuit of a failed ideology. Lord Cardassin has shown me the wisdom and power of *Zug*. It is only through him that we will be led into the light."

Akilah wheeled on Cardassin. "What have you done to her?"

Cardassin rubbed his nose. "Actually, my dear, very little. The bitch seemed ripe for plucking at the outset. All I did was give her a...little boost, shall we say."

"Is that true, Dayna? All these years? Was Mike right?"

"We shall prevail." Dayna folded her arms across her chest and stared silently at Akilah.

"Poor Akilah," Cardassin said, bouncing off the bed. "You seem disturbed by this turn of events."

"I feel nothing but loathing for you and your methods. You can drug my friend but I can see in her eyes that she is speaking falsely." Akilah took a step toward Dayna, who quickly moved back.

"Falsely?" Dayna mocked. "I killed Jason. One more Maraia down, a handful to go."

Akilah stared, shocked. Could it be true? No. Cardassin was having his way with her.

Cardassin clucked his tongue. "What shall we do about this, dear Akilah? I hate to see you come all this way for nothing."

344

Dayna's gaze seemed to fog out for a moment as it swept from Akilah to Cardassin. "What are you talking about?"

"Why don't we resolve it this way?" Cardassin drew his ice razor and thumbed it on. One flick of his wrist sent the beam vertical, catching Dayna in the crotch and moving with a sinister sizzle through her pelvis, stomach and chest to her neck where it paused briefly as though encountering some resistance before slicing diagonally, leaving her head to fall whole with one of her body halves.

As the halves tipped, he made a short horizontal cut through her waist. The four pieces dropped to the floor.

Akilah's mind numbed with the horror she had just witnessed. A confusion of overlapping emotions cascaded her consciousness. Betrayal. Love. Revenge.

"I've found that quartering removes the victim from the realm of being re-habilitated by a nano-assembler. Trudal, get this cleaned up before it soaks the floor. The carpet is already a mess, and I have to sleep here tonight."

Cardassin peered at Akilah. "I can understand that you are speechless. I would be, too, if someone took an ax to my best friend, but then I don't have any friends that I know of. A moment, Trudal." Cardassin stepped over to a body quarter that held one of Dayna's arms. He lifted it, grabbed her index finger, which was hanging by a thread, and twisted it off her hand. He proffered the severed digit to Akilah. "A souvenir, my dear?"

Akilah's stomach churned. She swallowed hard and turned her head away. Was there no end to the madness?

"No? Well then, I'll keep it and consider it a trophy. Trudal, do you think we could graft this onto someone?"

"Yes, my lord. You know that grafting is the least of our capabilities."

"Capabilities be damned." Cardassin wiped his hand on his robe and frowned at the bloody stain. Then he stared Akilah directly in the eye. "Now, pul...eeze tell me, just how did you expect to get out of here?"

***

Michael headed south across the plateau's top ice, frustrated that he had not been allowed to go after Akilah earlier. The delaying tactics of Ferral and the other two had wasted precious time. By now, Akilah would already be in Cardassin's clutches. No telling what he'd do.

Have you lost sight of your mission? The metabase.

He wondered that he felt any remorse at all for what would transpire. He had, after all, no roots in this theater. He was a passing figure, created, inserted, then what?

He had tried his best to dissuade Akilah from going after Dayna. But she was too headstrong, had brushed his best arguments aside, as well as the arguments of the others.

And now an infantile ten year old was in the mix. The Shepherd had certainly not prepared him for anything like that.

"You should not be asking these questions." Almost seeming annoyed, the metabase persisted. *"The Shepherd has given you a direction. It would behoove you to follow it."*

Michael gave a start. It had been awhile since the metabase had offered any advice or even been needed, much less consulted. *You're saying my programming gives me no say in the direction matters take?*

"Not at all. The Shepherd left you with leeway on how to proceed. He couldn't foresee every circumstance that you would come up against. However, he has programmed me to monitor your progress and advise you when you are going astray."

If you claim to know so much then answer a question that has been bothering me since I was thrust out to accomplish this mission.

"I will if I can."

The Shepherd exists, that is obvious. A4-Ni is his creator. That has been established. But A4-Ni is being built to carry the Maraia genome out into the universe in an effort to escape a crushing annihilation here on Earth by the players...a player right now, Cardassin.

"I thought you had a question?"

What was A4-Ni doing eight thousand years in the past, constructing the Shepherd, when her mission was to disseminate Maraia everywhere else?

"A4-Ni will be built in this present time. She will be primed with Maraia genome and sent into space. She will round a black hole and arrive...by

347

unfortunate circumstance...five million years in the past--"

Five million years?

"If you let me finish my narrative, you might understand. She evolves, uncontrollably as it were, for a million years, at which time she confronts the original Shepherd. After relieving him of the Gilomir genome he carries, she plants it in an ancient hominid and lingers to nurture it. The Shepherd finally catches up to her eight thousand years ago. There's a confrontation. The Shepherd flees, presumably mortally wounded. A4-Ni is then manipulated by the guardian to construct a new Shepherd, our current benefactor."

I know all that. What happened to the Maraia genome she carried?

"You should stick to the mission the Shepherd has handed you."

You are not answering my question.

"You should stick to the mission the Shepherd has handed you."

Do you know the answer or are you simply avoiding the question?

"Yes."

Play your games. I'm done with you for the time being. The metabase could be an irritant at times. Fortunately, he had some control over turning it on and off.

He slowed his pace. *What to do?*

After settling himself, Michael looked up at the stars. Always there. Neat points of unwavering light. Giving a false sense of infinity. Poor Maraia, poor humans. Locked in a universe they were ill

348

equipped to understand. But no matter. It would soon be over for them if everything the guardian foretold came to pass.

The lights of Cardassin's siege wall sparkled before him. A pity he knew the sinister barrier they represented. But at least the carnival colors had a certain appeal. At this point they soothed him more than the regressive output of the metabase.

"Hey, Mike." A whispered call.

Startled, Michael peered into the dark. "Cardassin?"

"Your friends call you Mike, don't they, or do I have it wrong?"

"You're very bold to come here."

Cardassin appeared out of the shadows, hunched over, grasping his cloak about him. "I'm not so bold. Technology. Hologram."

Michael nodded, probably unseen in the dark. "What do you want?"

Cardassin's head rocked, no, bobbled would be a better term, on his shoulders as he gazed out over the landscape. "What a beautiful evening. I detect a touch of spring in the air."

Michael stared out over the plain below. Indeed, the air did have a wet feel to it, as spring, for what it was, had begun to take its hold on the region. Here and there ice slumped after a full day in the sun, collecting puddles of melt at the bottom that quickly froze as the temperature dropped at night.

Jamil had said that during the spring and summer some of the ice on the plain melted all the way to the ground beneath, and grass and lichens grew. It was an odd time of the year. A hint of what once must have been. By late summer the temperatures would begin to plummet again, and the long winter would set in.

"What do you know of springs here?"

"Ah, my dear Mike. That seems an odd challenge coming from you, a synthetic who knows nothing but what the Shepherd has deemed fit to program into you."

"I'm more human than you can imagine."

"I doubt that."

Michael waved him away. "I'm too tired for this play. Is Akilah all right?"

Cardassin squatted down. "I thought we had a deal," he said. "You were going to tell me the next time you met with the Shepherd. I don't like being betrayed."

Michael gave Cardassin a baleful look. "I told you to wait until I gave you a signal. I haven't had reason to do so. I don't know where the Shepherd is."

Cardassin shook his head. "I detect a certain air of depression in your demeanor."

"You have abrogated our agreement by returning one of the hostages dead. Sedroth only knows what you have done with Dayna and now Akilah."

"Hmmm, a bit of a slip up on my part. I should never have left her out of my sight. You know how it is down there. It's a fokkin' jungle."

"Jungle or not, you promised me something, and you didn't keep your word."

Cardassin shoved hands on hips. "I never!"

"You did." Michael stood. "Let's get to the point, Cardassin. I presume you now are seeking to amend our previous agreement."

Cardassin searched his pockets and located a thin pick, which he applied to his teeth. "They never seem clean," he said distractedly.

"Are you going to get to the point or not?"

"This is not like you," Cardassin whined. "And certainly not like the product of our esteemed Shepherd."

"It's my humanness coming out when least expected or appreciated. You bring out the worst in me."

"Tsk tsk...I admit, I'm not known for my patience. Now where shall we go from here?"

"What about Akilah?"

"Akilah. Yes. She's my hole in the ace."

"I suppose she is. And Dayna?"

Cardassin seemed to shift a bit. "Ah...Dayna. She's gone."

"Gone? Gone where?"

"Where she belongs." Cardassin giggled. "You were right, you know, she was one of my spies, though she never knew it. Wonderful thing, drugs. But I decided I no longer needed her services."

"She's dead?"

"Yes." Cardassin waved a hand. "Dead, dead, dead. We'll just have to move on without her." He pocketed the toothpick and rubbed his teeth with his forefinger. "I perceive you have made a decision about building A4-Ni."

"How would you know?"

"You forget that I have the guardian."

351

"So you know the truth. You didn't need the guardian to know that you kill Akilah."

"My, my, Michael, you are jumping to conclusions. I don't think I have it in me to kill Akilah. She will manage to do that on her own."

"How do you know?"

"Ah, ah. The guardian, remember?"

"The guardian told you that? I don't believe you."

"Be that as it may, let's forget for the moment your female interest. I have more pressing concerns. For starters, I don't care if you build the A4-Ni machine or not, but I am still interested in meeting ole Shep. I could see a way to give Akilah back to you, if you honor your original agreement with me."

"You're a bloodsucker."

Cardassin smiled. "I won't deny that. Are you prepared to honor your agreement?"

"For Akilah, I will."

"Splendid. Now. Consider this. The guardian has told me that the genome entrusted to A4-Ni will perish before it can be multiplied. The Shepherd knows this too, but doesn't care, since all he is interested in is getting himself created."

Michael felt an unease like the approach of an impending storm, something he couldn't put his finger on, but something definitely there. The metabase had also been evasive. How to proceed? "You're lying. The Shepherd would never deceive me like that."

"I suppose it boils down to whether you believe the guardian or not. Do you recognize this?" Cardassin held up the guardian.

"Of course. Your must have taken it off that idiot Ferral."

"How I got it is of little importance. What is important, at least to you, is that I'm done with it. It has told me everything I want to know. Obviously, A4-Ni will be built--the Shepherd exists after all--so go build A4-Ni."

To Michael's surprise, Cardassin tossed the sphere to him. "I guess you're not a hologram after all."

"Darn. Have I been caught in another lie?"

Michael glanced at the sphere, then pocketed it. "If all this is so pre-determined, then why don't you let me have Akilah back now?"

Cardassin made a face as though he had just bit into a sour fruit. "My dear Michael, that would spoil all the fun. I'll give you four hours to complete the construction of A4-Ni, signal the Shepherd you have done so, and alert me to the fact that he wants to see you."

"Four hours?"

"Okay, three hours." Cardassin stood and prepared to go.

"You can't be serious."

"Oh, but I am." Cardassin rummaged in his pocket and withdrew a coin-shaped piece of metal. "This is a homing device. To activate it just slide this little thingy to one side. It's not as sophisticated as your finder, but it will serve to alert me when the

Shepherd has asked to meet you. I will monitor your progress and take care of the rest, as they say."

"When do I see Akilah?"

"Dear Michael, if you keep pressing me I'll shorten the time even more. And as you probably have surmised, it won't take me three hours to toy with the bitch and have her stuffed if you fail."

"You didn't answer my question."

"No, I didn't."

Chapter Eighteen

Michael lurched across the escarpment's top ice, splashing through puddles of quickly freezing water, slipping to his knees in the wet, then steadying himself before continuing.

His insides churned. What had been an impending storm of angst moments ago had become full-blown anguish. He had been deceived by the Shepherd. He knew it. His metabase knew it. This was all a charade of going through the motions, thinking the object was to help the Maraia save themselves when in fact they were already doomed and didn't know it.

Somehow he felt unclean, not only from interacting with the reprehensible Cardassin, but also from realizing everything he had done and said with the best intentions in mind, had resulted in nothing more than complicity in the Shepherd's plot to ensure his existence.

Michael came to the door of the ruin. Light filtered out through cracks around its ill-fitting edges. He pounded on the door with both fists.

The light from the inside went out, followed by hushed whispers. "Who's there?" a voice that Michael recognized as Nicholai commanded.

"It's Michael. Open the door."

A cover over a small peephole slid back.

Michael couldn't see Nicholai peering through but presumed he was.

"Hurry up. It's cold out here."

The heavy bolts that reinforced the door locks slid back and the door groaned inward.

Michael stepped inside.

Nicholai and Ferral confronted him.

Lorry stood on the far side near the computers that controlled the lights. The child, Justin, lay on the cot beside her.

Nicholai's face was pinched with anxiety. "Back already? Where's Akilah? Dayna?"

"Dayna is dead." Michael didn't feel like softening his words. He was tired of the stress, tired of dealing with the likes of Ferral, Nicholai and his mate.

"I knew she was dead," Lorry blurted.

"Akilah is still alive," Michael said, "but Cardassin has her. I have made arrangements to have her freed."

"What arrangements?" Ferral demanded.

Michael's patience was non-existent. These people had no part in the scheme of what he had to do. He didn't know where they otherwise figured into the future and didn't care. Then his gaze fell on what looked like a man-sized lump of flesh. "What's that?"

"We...," Nicholai began. "We tried to clone a grown Maraia. But as you can see our results were less than optimal."

"You fools. There are more important issues that need addressing now than trying to clone Maraia."

"I don't think so," Ferral said. "You'll have to help us perfect our methods."

Michael paused and thought for a moment. They had the nano-assembler. He needed it. There was no way to wrest it from them, even with Ferral handicapped.

"Gaaaaaa!"

"You hear that?" Nicholai shouted, letting pent up tension boil over. "It's not that simple, anymore."

"No, it isn't that simple, anymore." Michael walked over and knelt in front of the cot beside Lorry. "How's he doing?"

"As well as can be expected. He has no deformities that I can see.

"That's no small accomplishment as cloned material more often than not picks up aberrant gene sequences that lead to problems down the road."

Justin squirmed under multiple layers of blankets. When his head came clear, Michael could see the boy's eyes. They disappointed. Clear blue, but without a gleam of intelligence. The head disappeared again, followed by intermittent whimpering.

"He hasn't improved since I last saw him," Michael said.

Lorry sat on the cot and played her hand gently over the agitated form under the blankets. "He's distraught. I think he's not able to assimilate the sensory perceptions that are coming in. He's physically ten, yet hasn't developed any of the filtering mechanisms a normal ten year old would have."

Michael shook his head. "You know this was an ill-conceived idea in the first place."

Nicholai stared at Michael. It was as if he were seeing him for the first time and trying to decide who he was and what his motives might be. "The deed is done. We're prepared to cope with what is. It will take some time to bring the child's mental capabilities up to his physical age, but I am confident that with patience it can be done."

"Gaaaaaa!"

Michael winced. "Hasn't he said anything else?"

"That's all so far," Nicholai said. "But it's only been a few hours. I expect his learning will accelerate as he becomes more accustomed to his surroundings."

It's a wonder these Maraia have come as far as they have, Michael thought. His gaze traveled to Ferral. Another casualty of poor decision making. "Look, I'm going to need the nano-assembler for a few hours. After that, I'll show you how to work it to avoid mistakes like this." He gestured to the lump of flesh.

"How do we know you'll keep your side of the bargain?" Ferral asked.

"In a few hours my mission here will have been accomplished. I really have no stake in the Maraia or what becomes of them. I will have no further use for the nano-assembler."

"I suppose you can't go anywhere with it." Ferral extended his hand with the nano-assembler.

Before they could engage him further, Michael snatched the nano-assembler and was on his way down to the tunnel. His first priority was to find a

358

place of solitude. He had to consult the guardian. He had to ask it for the truth.

Before the elevator stopped he hopped off and hurried to the far side of the tunnel. The faux sun shone overhead, casting his shadow long and bathing the interior in a yellow light. The hot tub remained in disrepair. Thankfully the bodies of the mutants had been disposed of, but no one had been able to figure out a way to drain the water. It lay placid and murky.

It was unlikely that Nicholai or Lorry would follow him down. They looked too petrified to take any positive action. He found a place behind some packing crates and hunkered down. He reached into his pocket. The guardian felt cool to his touch.

Just hold it, and it will activate. He squeezed and waited.

Nothing.

A fleeting sense of panic seized him. What if the guardian wouldn't respond? Then what? All this effort for nothing.

He removed the guardian from his palm, wiped it on his pant leg and grasped it again.

This time his mind opened to the guardian. Immediately, he lost awareness of his surroundings. It was as if his consciousness had been taken over by another being and constrained, directed, focused only on what that being wanted him to see.

What if I build A4-Ni? Michael thought. *What happens to Akilah?*

"*Akilah dies.*" The guardian's response formed clearly inside his head. It was as if he were thinking to himself.

Michael slumped his shoulders. Though the answer was what he half expected, the explicitness of the guardian's answer left him feeling helpless.

What happens to Akilah if I don't build A4-Ni?

"She dies."

What the hell is going on? Why am I here? What difference do I make?

"You are here because that is what happened. A4-Ni is built, Akilah dies, the genome is lost, the Maraia are doomed."

But I have a choice?

"You know that you do not."

Then what if I don't do it?

No response came from the guardian.

Michael sat still for a moment. *Think.* Either way Akilah would die, but he did have a choice. If he didn't finish building A4-Ni, the Shepherd would not contact him, Cardassin would never release Akilah and she would surely die. If he didn't finish building A4-Ni, then the Shepherd would cease to exist, or would he? Maybe he would simply shift to another probabilistic world line and continue in another future. Did the Shepherd have the power to make that shift? Michael didn't think so. Then the only reality that he could live with was the one he created, that he was experiencing, and in that one the Shepherd existed, so A4-Ni must have been constructed. If he didn't do it, then who would? Certainly not Nicholai, nor Lorry. Or Ferral, for that matter. Forget about Cardassin.

"Ah, there you are," Ferral said, appearing suddenly.

360

Michael had been so absorbed with the guardian he had not heard the elevator's whine as it rose and then descended.

Ferral stood before him, the bandages removed from his eyes. They stared, round open orbs, that gave only a hint that he could see anything at all.

"Aren't you risking the regeneration of your eyes by removing the bandages?"

"I can see well enough." He took a step forward with a small imbalance that a sighted person would not have made. For all of his bluff and bluster he was obviously faking that he had more sight than he did.

"I wanted to be alone," Michael said.

"You have the guardian."

"I do." Michael eyed the miscreant closely. It wasn't like Ferral to waste idle talk. He'd get to the point directly. All Michael had to do was sit and wait.

"What did it tell you? No...let me guess. You are to build A4-Ni, Akilah will be returned by Cardassin in exchange for some diabolical swap you have arranged, and we shall all live happily ever after, though not on Earth."

"Something like that." Michael's breath went shallow, a hominid characteristic when threatened. Or was it surprise that Ferral could be so perversely prescient?

"What does the little ball have to say about regrouping? This course of action is madness as far as I can see. There is little assurance that A4-Ni will succeed in procreating the Maraia. We all know that she is responsible for building the

361

Shepherd. But why was she in that situation, unless she failed to deliver on her primary mission?"

"You amaze me with your foresight."

"Stop patronizing me! My foresight, for what it now is, tells me that we will flush away what little Maraia life we have left in seeing that A4-Ni is launched. We are all going to die. Of that I am certain, clones or no clones. A4-Ni will fail. Cardassin will triumph. The Shepherd, which I presume you have given up or are about to, will perish. And that will be the end of it."

Michael tossed the guardian to Ferral.

It hit his mid-section and dropped to the ground. Ferral dropped to his knees and felt over the floor until he grasped it.

"If you are so bold," Michael said, "then test your prattling against what the guardian might tell you."

Ferral's mouth gaped open. A fast moving cloud of panic crossed his face. "I...I'm not sure I want to do that."

"Then shut up and get out of here. I have work to do."

Ferral stared blankly at Michael as he curled his fingers around the guardian. He flinched. Then his gaze lost all focus. He let his breath out along with a low moan. "I...." His half-healed eyes rolled white, and he toppled back onto the floor.

Michael shifted nervously. He didn't want Ferral to die, which is what it looked like he was in the process of doing. Give him another minute or two. If he wasn't dead by then, the guardian should be done and release him.

After only a few seconds, Ferral twitched, sucked in a large gulp of air, and sat up. He propped himself on his arms and stared around at the tunnel, finally letting his gaze rest on Michael. "You have put the guardian up to this...this horrific show of the future."

"I have no control over what the guardian projects. Did you see something that disturbed you?"

"You know damn well what I saw. It...it was too much to bear. You and the guardian are trying to make the construction of A4-Ni our only way out. You, the guardian and our esteemed Shepherd care little for the Maraia. Your own goals are paramount."

"You can believe what you want. Now, if you'll excuse me, I have a lot of work to do if I'm to save Akilah."

Ferral looked dumbfounded at the dismissal. "This isn't the last of it."

A resignation pulled over Michael like a heavy blanket. "No, it isn't."

***

Akilah squirmed. She'd been left alone on the embroidered foot stool for hours, and her bottom had become numb.

The hulking Igor lounged on the other side of the room, seemingly asleep.

Cardassin reappeared, happily flourishing his hands as though he were brushing falling rose petals aside. The obsequious Trudal followed close behind. Where had they been?

In their wake floated a scent of heavy perfume, laced with accents of lime and an overabundance of *rub*.

Cardassin grabbed both of her hands and yanked her from the stool. Thumping music suddenly issued from somewhere, and it looked like Cardassin wanted to dance.

Reluctantly, she shuffled forward. Better that than for her to sit rigidly and have him tip her over to sprawl on the carpet.

His thin lips parted in a grin that displayed the majority of his front teeth, top and bottom. He grabbed his robe and hiked it up well above his knees, then did what could only be described as a high kicking fling. Yet the music was definitely more contemporary, sprinkled with instrumental riffs accompanied by heavy percussion in a fast, undulating beat.

When Akilah failed to indulge the beast, he slowed, then stopped and looked despondently at Trudal, who had remained on the sidelines not showing any reaction to the music. At least Igor, who had come to attention at his master re-appearance, had tried ineffectually to clap his two left hands.

"Don't the Maraia dance?" Cardassin said between gulps for breath.

"We do. But it is reserved for special occasions with friends and family."

Cardassin pouted. "But I am practically family."

Akilah decided not to indulge the unctuous son of a bitch. Anything coming from her would only encourage him further, and who knew of what he was capable?

"What's the matter?" Cardassin leaned forward, sneering. "Tongue frozen over?"

This was not going to be easy. All she could hope for was that Michael would come up with a way to rescue her. Her previous confidence that she was safe because of some sort of predestination was quickly evaporating. How could she have been so gullible?

A sinking ache still wended its way through her very core. Dayna dead. Dayna her friend, her beloved, and now dead.

"Hello, hello, hello!" Cardassin waved his hands in front of her face. "Where *are* weeee?"

"You killed my best friend."

Cardassin stopped and stuck his hands on his hips, then crossed his hands to grasp his elbows, then straightened his arms rigidly at his sides, fists clenched. "I did. But best friend? Do you take me for a fool? You are only feeling a passing remorse for someone familiar. Besides, since she had engaged a fleeting intimacy with you, then she certainly was no longer of any use to me. I suspect she would have been compromised anyway, if I had returned her whole. Your Maraia cohorts would have done whatever they do to traitors, drugged ones or not."

Akilah blinked, bewildered.

"Like this?" Cardassin draped his arms out as though hanging from a cross.

"What?"

Cardassin snapped his head back and forth, gazing at his fingers, and pretended to be in deep thought. "Oh. Wrong martyr. But you have to admit that old testicle eyes, wass-his-name...Fural, Foral, Ferral would have sliced and diced her up himself."

"You don't know anything about the Maraia or what Ferral might do."

"Just rationalizing my actions, deary. Just rationalizing..." His voice trailed away in a mutter.

Akilah clapped her hands to get his attention back.

Cardassin blinked. "Whaaa?"

"Yeah, whaaa," she said with the fleeting satisfaction of having turned the tables on him. "What are you going to do to me?"

Cardassin frowned. "You think I'm going to hurt you?" He tried to chuck her under her chin.

"Yeah, I do." Despite her projected bravado, she felt absolutely no strength inside. In fact, her insides were about to be released to cover Cardassin's carpet. "I may survive this encounter, but I don't know what I will have to endure before I reach the end of the tunnel."

Cardassin rubbed his chin. "Yes, yes, I see your point. I approve of your metaphor. It captures the moment quite well. You are correct to be apprehensive about my motives and methods."

A wave of nausea swept over her now that Cardassin's intentions were out in the open. And there was absolutely nothing she could do to dissuade him.

366

"Trudal," Cardassin said, "this dame has totally spaced on us. She's no fun at all."

Trudal clapped his hands idiotically. "Perhaps she needs some encouragement, my lord?"

It was obvious that the seer held no affection for her, despite him being a Maraia. *How does one give up one's own kind?* Akilah supposed that she hated Trudal even more than Cardassin. After all, the latter was only doing what he was supposed to do. Whereas Trudal had made a conscious decision to betray his own people.

Cardassin crossed the small room and rummaged in a drawer beside his bed. After throwing a number of items that looked like silicon-embellished sex toys onto the carpet, he held up a nano-assembler with a flourish.

Akilah's heart accelerated to a rapid thumping.

"Trudal, design me something that will make our lady friend here *jump*. You do know what I mean by *jump*?"

"I do indeed, my lord. The deceased Karin *jumped* quite well before we had to put her out of her ecstasy."

They grinned at each other like silly loons.

A moment later Trudal proffered a pellet from the end of the nano-assembler. "I think this will do just fine, my lord. It is similar to the one we used on the hyperactive Karin, but where that one went awry in a matter of minutes, I do hope that this one will prove to be more long-lived."

"Fokk long-life. I want her to burn brightly, albeit shortly."

Trudal tossed the pellet to one side and revisited the nano-assembler. "I have taken your desires into account, sire." He stopped abruptly. "Igor! Take that out of your mouth!"

Igor spat out the pellet he had snatched from the floor.

"There, that's a good mutant." Trudal smiled and might have patted Igor on the head had Cardassin not been tapping his foot with impatience.

The hulking mutant made a face, retrieved the pellet and crushed it in his hands, then slapped them together awkwardly to rid them of the residue. When it didn't come off, he made to lick his fingers. But a glance at Trudal told him *no*. He laid his two left hands in his lap and looked to the ceiling innocently.

"Now, where was I?" Trudal shook his head, obviously feeling the tension of the moment and trying to shake off the distraction.

"My desires," Cardassin said dryly.

"Yes. This pellet is the perfect compromise." Trudal held up a dark blue pellet.

Cardassin danced with glee, twirled and even leapt to click his heels. He grabbed the pellet and fairly launched himself onto Akilah.

She stepped away, but tripped and fell flat on her back. The air whooshed out of her lungs, and she gasped as the skinny beast, all knobby knees and elbows, pressed her down and pinched her nose closed. She struggled to keep her mouth closed, but to no avail. It was either open it to grab a breath of air or suffocate.

When she opened, the pellet slid in.

Cardassin clamped his hand under her chin to force her mouth closed. "Swallow," he whispered, his lips millimeters from her own. His breath cascaded over her with a warm rancid smell that made her wonder if he'd eaten putrefied flesh for his last meal.

"No," she mumbled through clenched teeth.

Cardassin smiled when she swallowed reflexively. He released her and stood.

"Well done, my lord," Trudal crowed.

Cardassin was ebullient. "Now we just have to wait a few minutes and then our party shall begin in earnest." Cardassin waved his hand. "Music!"

"But we *have* music," Trudal said.

"Then make it louder."

Chapter Nineteen

Michael waited until the elevator reached the main level of the ruin, delivering Ferral back to those above.

First to secure the elevator. He could ill afford to be interrupted in what he was about to do next.

He strode to the shaft and disconnected the wires to the elevator control. He saw no other way to disable the cage, it being a primitive model without any safety features.

Despite the boundaries to his domain being secured, he felt a skittering nervousness. Odd. Must be something hominid. Fulfilling his destiny shouldn't make him nervous. All he had to do now was create an environment in which A4-Ni could be built. That would require computers and sensors built from scratch since the complexity of A4-Ni was far beyond the capabilities of anything that existed upstairs.

He would also need to prepare a space for A4-Ni as she grew, something that would accept the smallest increment of her being and enlarge coincident with her own embodiment.

He paced off the space in the tunnel and decided on a central location. It didn't matter what was overhead. What was overhead was pretty much the same regardless of where he started.

He knew A4-Ni's size from the guardian's plans. Something near ten meters across, circular, about three meters high. She would be artificially intelligent, organic and self-replicating, not unlike how one might describe the Shepherd.

He supposed there was a certain amount of building in one's own image. A memory from the metabase floated up, saying that a similar belief had been held by hominids throughout their history and currently was entertained by the Maraia.

If Michael could have shut the metabase off he would have, such was the distraction of its intrusions.

He sat and began thumbing the nano-assembler. It would take time to design the equipment required. And then probably a lot longer to vet what he had created. Lots of false starts and turns down dead-ends.

"*If I may intrude,*" his metabase kicked in. "*You do have the guardian, and it has an interface that can be attached to the nano-assembler. It will then be possible to download the stored plans of A4-Ni as well as designs for all the support equipment you will need.*"

I thought that I had acquired all the plans. But you are correct, the support structures are missing. Why didn't you tell me this earlier?

"*Do you want me to induce the interface?*"

You knew all along.

"*You have been temporarily misled, and if I had anything to do with that then I apologize. It was not in my programming to mislead you.*"

Odd input from the metabase. Was it a subtle play by the Shepherd, realizing that when Michael came to this crossroads he would need a certain amount of coddling?

I don't have a choice in the matter, do I? All these questions are meant to give me the impression that I can or cannot decide.

"I will proceed, given your momentary state of indecision."

Michael withdrew the guardian from his pocket. Immediately, he felt a tingling in the small sphere. A slender thread protruded from its side.

"Attach the end of the thread to the bottom of the nano-assembler. It will then download the data."

Michael guided the thread into the nano-assembler and waited.

"It is done. The nano-assembler will now produce the required pellets for A4-Ni's construction."

If it was that easy, why didn't the Shepherd see to the construction of A4-Ni directly? Why did he need me? Akilah?

"He needed you, and Akilah, because that is the way it happened."

Michael thought to question the metabase further, but decided it would be futile. Riddles upon riddles.

The nano-assembler vibrated ever so slightly in his hand. He looked down and quickly caught pellets as they plopped from one end.

How am I to know which pellet is for what?

"Have you observed they are of different colors?"

I have.

"Blue is for the computer consoles. Green is for the sensor arrays. Yellow will build the

scaffolding. Brown will alter the tunnel overhead. And red will grow A4-Ni."

I just have to sprinkle them around?

"You have done this before."

I just wanted to make sure I have it right.

"Is there some confusion as to the color coding?"

No, you were quite explicit. Does it matter where I initiate the pellets?

"The broad answer is no. But you could facilitate matters by placing the pellets in their approximate locations. The brown one will probably be the hardest to locate. I suggest you throw it at the overhead rock until it adheres. Once it does, it will know what to do."

Michael paced out the various functions and laid the pellets down. He threw the brown pellet at the ceiling and was rewarded with an immediate stick. Then he retreated to the side of the tunnel and waited. He didn't have to wait long.

With all the pellets activated at once, a fine mist of residue from rock and water of transmuting elements quickly filled the tunnel.

He felt very much a spectator, having to nimbly dodge out of the way of erupting consoles, then rods of support scaffolding. He found a tranquil spot at one end of the tunnel and stood to marvel at the majesty of the transformation.

The support equipment stabilized first.

The tunnel ceiling was slowly being transformed in a grinding way to reveal huge, hinged mechanisms at the extremities of what looked like cross re-enforced doors that could be uplifted by unseen motors to expose the ceiling of the tunnel to the night sky above.

At the center of the tunnel the small red pellet pulsed. It grew in size, slowly at first, then with exponential leaps. After no more than five minutes, a shape meeting the perceived parameters of A4-Ni hovered within the intricate lacing of the scaffolding.

The speed with which A4-Ni had come into being stunned him. Stumbling frantically, he reached for a protruding cable from the computer consoles and pulled it over to A4-Ni. The question of how he knew where to shove it home crossed his mind momentarily, but he then supposed that he was being guided by some pre-emptive programming.

The bank of computers and sensors lit up with a pulsing light as terabits of information were stuffed into A4-Ni's memory cores.

After ten minutes, the pulsing stopped.

A4-Ni rested serenely at her moorings, a small LED here and there the only indications that she was alive and ready.

Michael consulted the monitors and confirmed that his impression of her state of readiness was in fact correct.

The finder on his finger vibrated.

The Shepherd.

How could the Shepherd know simultaneously with the activation of the homing device that A4-Ni was complete?

A message scrolled across the crystal of the finder.

"Meet me at the island that sits in the lake to the north."

Michael searched his memory for some reference to an island and found none. He induced his metabase to enlighten him.

"The island is a geologically young volcanic outcrop about five hundred meters to the north from the near shore of the lake. You will have to proceed with caution as the ice covering the lake is weak and non-existent in places."

Why, with all the places we could meet, does the Shepherd choose this remote location?

"I'm sure he has his reasons."

Michael reached into his pocket and withdrew the homing device Cardassin had given him.

A moment of hesitation. Did he really feel that betraying the Shepherd would secure Akilah's freedom? But what were the odds that Akilah would be released if he didn't do as Cardassin demanded?

Michael slid the activating lever home.

***

Akilah's body tingled from head to toe, from fingertip across her chest, like an electrostatic spark, to opposite fingertip.

The beast Cardassin stood opposite her, clapping his hands in gleeful anticipation.

Trudal lounged against a tent pole, looking bored, but presumably unable to be inattentive lest Cardassin demand something of him.

"How are you feeling, my dear?" Cardassin wiped sweat from his brow and licked his upper lip. Though his eyes were staring directly at her, the pupils were enlarged, and his eyeballs made little jerking motions back and forth. "Getting ready to *jump*?"

"I'm afraid your little pellet isn't working." It was all she could do to suppress the urges that had begun to wash through her body in ever increasing waves. At this rate she'd be writhing on the floor nude in a matter of minutes.

Igor, who had earlier asked to be excused to relieve himself, hit the entrance curtain hard and sprawled into the tent. "Sire, excuse me, sire. We have word."

Cardassin's face clouded. "Word. Word of what?"

"The syn...the...tic has activated his homing device. He is on his way to see the Shepherd."

Cardassin pressed his lips together in a tight thin line. His face grew red. "Damn!"

Trudal lurched to attention. "Damn what, my lord?"

"Quick, an antique dote." Cardassin waved a hand at Trudal. "We're going to have to send her back, and we can't send her back this way. Not this time."

Trudal fumbled with the nano-assembler.

With the lights overhead reeling, Akilah unbuttoned her shirt and cast it onto the floor. "Whoops!"

Her hand went to her bodice, and she was in the process of loosing the laces that pulled it close about her breasts, when Cardassin grabbed her.

"Not now, my dear. Maybe another time." He twisted his head over his shoulder. "Trudal, do please hurry. She's already starting to *jump*."

Trudal fumbled a pellet out the end of the nano-assembler and watched in dismay as it thumped onto the carpet and rolled. Immediately, he was down on hands and knees grabbing for the thing.

Akilah let out a gleeful shout and twisted free of Cardassin. She latched onto the clasps that held her pants up and pulled.

The clasps ripped free. Her pants dropped around her ankles.

Trudal pinched the wayward pellet and held it out to Cardassin.

He snatched it from him. "Fool. It may already be too late." He knocked Akilah to the carpet and straddled her.

Akilah's hips seemed to have an energy of their own as she gyrated beneath him. She giggled and grabbed the edges of his robe in both her hands, pulling her head up, lips puckered.

"Ahhhhhgggg!" he cried, trying to shrug her off, but only managing to swing her from side to side as he evaded her sucking embrace. "Igor, help me!"

Igor lumbered over to them, seized both of Akilah's hands, pulled them over her head and stood on them.

Though she struggled, she couldn't move anything except her pelvis. And with that free she bounced up and down.

Cardassin wedged the pellet into her mouth and clamped it closed. He peered at her expectantly.

The dry pellet snagged on the back of her tongue. "I cun't swa...woo," she said through clenched teeth, trying at the same time to stifle a giggle.

Cardassin looked about wildly. "Water! Water! Hurry!"

"Dun't you want me now?" She felt poised on a precipice, dimly realizing if she slid down she would never be able to get back up.

Trudal rushed up with a cup of water, half of which had sloshed out on his way to them.

Cardassin grabbed the cup, squeezed Akilah's cheeks and poured what was left into her mouth.

She felt the liquid hit the pellet. In her mind's eye, the pellet absorbed the water, released itself from her tongue and slid down her throat. Immediately, she felt a sense of loss, as though the tide were going out quickly and leaving her boat stranded. Another moment and she might as well be in dry dock. Her previous lascivious movements transformed into energetic efforts to rid herself of Cardassin. *Strong stuff*. "Get the hell off me!" Some semblance of her former self returned.

Cardassin glanced at Igor, who remained standing on Akilah's hands, then he nimbly rolled off of her and sprang to his feet. "Pity," he said, shaking his head. "From what we briefly saw, you would have been one fine *jumper*."

"You're a pervert."

Cardassin smiled and nodded. "Such language. But very perceptive, my dear. Igor, you can let the lass go now."

Akilah pulled her hands free and flexed her fingers, reassuring herself that Igor hadn't broken any of them. She vaguely remembered that he had barged in with some news, though she couldn't be certain what it had been. She glared at Cardassin. "Are we done?"

"Oh yes. Definitely done. Done, done, done. Mike has secured your release in the nick of time. A few seconds more and you'd a been *jumping*, and we wouldn't have been able to stop you."

"You're going to let me go?"

"Oh yes. Definitely. I presume if we escort you to the base of the escarpment, you'll be able to find your way home from there?"

"I can do that." She suddenly realized that she was standing with her pants about her ankles and her shirt a couple of meters away.

Cardassin reached for her shirt and handed it to her. "Ahem...your pants are still dropped. You should probably pull them up before you try to leave. You might trip." He started to giggle uncontrollably as his eyes flicked from her breasts to her face, then settled on her breasts.

She grabbed the shirt, bit into it to hold it while she pulled up her pants and reattached the clasps. Then she shoved her arms into the shirt and jerkily buttoned it up. "Where's my parka? I don't want to freeze out there."

Cardassin clapped, and Trudal appeared at his side with her parka. "We didn't have time to get it dry-cleaned," Cardassin said with a regretful frown.

Akilah snatched the parka and dragged it over her shoulders while pushing her arms into the sleeves. She pressed the closing seam tight. "Okay. Get me out of here."

***

The mutants escorted her to the base of the escarpment.

These were low ranking mutants with not much going on upstairs. Igor, dimwitted as he was, would have scored double these wretches on an intelligence test. But when Igor started to accompany her, Cardassin had nodded for him to stay.

She stood rigidly, waiting for the mutants to leave. Of the four of them, three headed back complaining amongst themselves of the cold. But one lingered.

He stumbled back toward Akilah, his arms outstretched.

What's he thinking?

His intentions became quickly obvious.

"If you leave that exposed, it's going to freeze off." Akilah stepped to one side at the last moment of his lunge, and the mutant plowed into the vertical ice of the escarpment.

He recoiled, holding his nose. "Hurt." Blood gushed over his fingers.

"Yeah, you hurt, now pull up your pants and get the hell out of here before I indulge some selective surgery." She fingered the ice razor that Cardassin had been kind enough, or foolish enough, to return to her. She couldn't figure the beast. So many facets to a complex being. But he always seemed in command, in a bumbling way, of what he was doing, and that made him especially dangerous.

380

The departed mutants called to their wayward companion.

"I go now."

"That's a good mutant," Akilah said.

He gazed longingly at her, started licking the blood off his fingers with a grin, then loped in the direction of the call.

After he lumbered out of sight, Akilah turned her attention to climbing the escarpment. She searched for the crease that would enable her to ascend to the top.

After a few minutes of searching in the dim moonlight, she located the crease and levered her way up.

As she pulled herself over the top edge, Michael appeared. "Are you okay?"

He seemed overly concerned. "You cut it close. Another few seconds, and I would have been hot Giselle on the dancing pole."

Michael looked bewildered. "But I was in time?"

"Yes, Mike. In the nick of time. What's the situation?"

Michael blinked. A human characteristic. Could it also be interpreted the same way?

"Ferral has regained some of his sight. He seems more himself, at least the self that I experienced earlier. He's back to calling me names and telling me what to do."

Akilah started toward the ruin.

Michael tugged on her sleeve. "What of Dayna?"

Akilah stopped, refusing to turn, refusing to show the grief that must have slid across her face. "She's dead, Mike." Akilah turned and gave him a defiant look. "I was so afraid that Cardassin would kill me. But he killed Dayna instead. She wasn't a spy. He drugged her. She didn't deserve to die like that."

Michael let go of her arm. His face showed a mix of emotions...confusion, triumph, remorse...it was hard to gauge on a synthetic.

"I am sorry for her passing," he said. "I know you cared for her. Though I cannot in all honesty say I can feel your loss, you do have my understanding."

That's pretty good for a synthetic. "I'll take you at your word. I loved Dayna. I know you can't comprehend what that must mean, but that's okay. Just file it away and maybe your internal server will elaborate on the subject sometime."

"You are...selling me short. I do have feelings. I might be synthetic from your point of view, but I am a hominid at base, and that base is giving off...stimuli that I have no way to comprehend other than to ascribe them to feelings."

"So what do your feelings tell you? That the Maraia as a race are doomed? That we are a bunch of mixed up nobodies that are here to see in their last light the dawning of a player's triumph?"

"You needn't be so cynical."

"Cynical?" She felt a heat rise to her cheeks. "No. Nothing of the sort. Just a bit suspicious. How did you convince Cardassin to release me?"

Michael withdrew a flat, coin-shaped object from his pocket.

"I have labored on your behalf, on behalf of the Shepherd. I have completed A4-Ni. When it was done, I activated this device Cardassin gave me. I agreed to do so to effect your release."

Michael's words hit like a blow to the head. Not his complicity with Cardassin, but a welling sense of destiny. *A4-Ni complete.* "That's incredible. A4-Ni is all that we have strived for. She is complete and ready for launch?" All other thoughts dropped away. There was only one...A4-Ni.

"There are matters that must be attended to before you can launch her."

Akilah's sense of destiny hit a bump in the road. "Matters. What matters?"

"The Shepherd has told me to meet him on the island that stands off the shore of Lake Turk. I must speak to him before we launch A4-Ni."

"This is not what you led me to believe would happen. You were to assist us in her construction and then we would place our genome on board and launch. Why the delay?"

"It's important that you trust me on this. Can you?"

Akilah stared over Michael's shoulder. The door to the ruin let out a sliver of light. It had become home in these few short days. Despite all the tragedy that had befallen them, there was reason to hope. But dare she? Not with Mike cooking up some delaying excuse. Should she stand down and wait?

"I'll give you three hours to meet with the Shepherd. If you are not back, or if you return and somehow have not resolved whatever is bothering you, then I'm going to launch A4-Ni myself."

"Fair enough. Now, there's something you must know."

Akilah felt the tension in the air. *What now?* She clasped her hands in front of her and waited.

"Nicholai, Lorry and Ferral have cloned your father."

Chapter Twenty

Michael trudged across the frozen plain. He had left Akilah, shocked, dismayed, but there was nothing else he could have said to her. She had to confront the others on her own.

In the dim starlight, the plateau loomed, cold and gray. In front of him, to his surprise, Cardassin's siege wall was gone. Where once boisterous laughter shattered the night, and carnival lights circled the plateau and the ruin, nothing but smooth ice remained.

Events were gathering a momentum that disturbed him. All the actors in this drama were now coming on stage. That they didn't like one another was an understatement. How to maneuver amongst them?

He headed in what he thought was the direction to Jamil's home.

When he told Akilah where the Shepherd had requested that they meet, she at first expressed surprise, perhaps a sense of betrayal. He couldn't have told her the real reason for the delay--how superfluous her goal of launching A4-Ni was. After his silence on the matter she had been adamant that he not go. The island was remote, hard to reach, and filled with unknowns. Dangerous lava tubes snaked through its bowels. Jagged rock that would rip a person to shreds covered its exterior.

"Why the middle of the lake?" she asked in desperation. "The Shepherd could meet you anywhere."

He didn't have the answers she wanted to hear. He just knew he had no choice but to go.

Easier said than done. He had only a vague idea of how he was going to get there. He would need Jamil's help. With the lake waters thawing in places, the route would be treacherous if not impossible. Surely the primitive had some sort of boat that they could drag with them and use to cross areas already thawed or too weak to support their weight.

Still, a nagging thought. With the siege lifted, and Akilah returned, was there any compelling reason for him to keep his side of the bargain? Perhaps he could toss the homing device to one side, head in another direction? Cardassin was probably destined to win, anyway, at least as far as the Maraia were concerned. But he felt compelled to honor his agreement to Cardassin. It wasn't an ethical issue. His programming made him a relativist. It was more a curiosity to see just what the Shepherd would do.

Michael came to a gaping hole in the ice that led down and out of sight. He felt a moment's disappointment. Obviously, this was the entrance into Jamil's home. Just as obviously the home looked abandoned, and Jamil had not bothered to close the exit.

Nonetheless, Michael decided to investigate to make sure. Anyway, he was getting cold standing outside.

He eased himself over the edge and dropped to the slippery corridor below. With his flash out in front of him, he walked toward the great hall, where he had first shared a meal with Jamil and his family.

The hall was empty, as were the other rooms that led off from the hall. He found the corridor that Jamil had said led to the lake, where the fish came from.

The corridor was in disrepair. Fissures that must have led to the surface let in ice melt that froze in long jagged daggers. The floor was dimpled and uneven where water had dripped and then refrozen.

A hundred meters on, the steady lapping of water echoed off the walls. Michael came to the end of the tunnel and stood at the lake shore.

Water rose and fell gently against an ice edge. Overhanging ice, forming a crowded ceiling, seemed it would all come tumbling down any moment.

Michael directed his flash across the waters. The beam disappeared in the distance where the overhead ice met the water in a dark gray emptiness.

Discouraged, he turned to retrace his steps to the entrance.

"Michael." Jamil's voice was at his ear.

Michael gave a brief start, simultaneously thinking how odd that his body had taken up hominid reflexes. "You're here."

"In side tunnel that leads to gorge. Cross gorge, then north to Turk edge. Good hiding place. No one know."

Michael surveyed his erstwhile companion, savior, friend. Jamil's outer garments looked worn and tattered. He had let his beard grow. Black and thick, it crowded over the neck of his skins. "I need your help."

"You always need help." Jamil raised what looked like goggles from his eyes and parked them atop his head. "What this time?"

"I have to meet the Shepherd at the volcanic island that lies in Lake Turk."

"No like. Island bad." Jamil shoved the pointed end of his ice axe into the slippery floor. "Melted rock form many tunnels. Island sing death songs when waters come and go."

Michael laid a hand on Jamil's arm. "I didn't know that," he said quietly. "All I do know is that the Shepherd wants me to meet him there."

"Akilah safe?" Jamil stared hard, his face taut with anticipation.

"Yes."

"Cardassin go back to Kanapoi?"

"The siege has been lifted."

"Then why you go?" Jamil's grin spread wide, as if to reinforce the conclusion of his logic.

"I...I have to. There's something that I must ask the Shepherd."

Jamil grabbed Michael's hand. "Use finger."

Michael looked at the finder on his finger. "I could, but it's not the kind of question I'd want to communicate remotely."

"Don't know about remote." Jamil cast Michael's hand loose. "Path to island very dangerous. Ice rotten."

"I know. I was hoping you had a boat."

Jamil peered at Michael for a minute, then nodded and led the way to a side corridor in the direction of the gorge.

At the gorge, Jamil stopped.

The ice ended with an abrupt edge that dropped a meters to rushing water below, all that was left of the gorge as it neared Lake Turk and flooded into the larger body of water.

"How will we get across?" Michael knew that they could tunnel into the overhanging ice and cross over. They had before. But the ice had become rotten near the lake and probably could not be trusted.

Jamil pointed his flash across the water and clicked it on and off. After a moment a diminutive figure appeared out of the gloom. Jamil pointed with some show of pride. "Jamani."

Jamani threw a rope across and tied his end to an embedded ice axe.

Jamil swung his axe into the floor and assured himself that it was secure. He tied the rope on his side.

"But how did you get across coming the other way?" Michael still didn't even see how the rope was going to get them across this way.

"Swim. Change clothes." Jamil indicated a pile of what looked like frozen skins off to one side.

A second rope leapt across the four-meter wide current. Jamil tied this rope off a couple of meters overhead. Jamani clambered up the opposing sloping wall and similarly anchored his end.

Jamil tested the ropes and found them taut to his satisfaction. Then without any hesitation, he toed the bottom rope and grasped the top rope. His weight swung wildly at first, then steadied, and he began a slow sliding step forward.

Michael didn't like what he was seeing, but there was no other way to get across.

Jamil reached the other side and waved Michael over.

After saying a silent prayer to his maker, Michael ventured onto the rope. Almost immediately, his feet slipped off the bottom rope and he dangled with half-frozen hands from the top rope. He struggled to regain his footing.

"No kick," Jamil called.

Easy for you to say. Michael slowly repositioned his feet on the rope. This time he made slow but steady progress across the flowing river.

At the other side he fell into Jamil's arms with a great sense of relief. And this was only a prelude to what probably awaited him if Jamil took him to the island.

"This worst part." Jamil smiled, then tugged on two guide ropes. The knots on the far side came loose, some sort of slip knots, and Jamil with Jamani's help pulled the ropes across the river.

"Jamani good boy." Jamil patted his son on the head.

Jamani beamed. "Hello, Mister Michael." He stuck out his hand.

"An ancient custom," his metabase said. *"Grasp his hand and shake it."*

Michael took Jamani's hand and shook it.

"Thanks for your help," Michael said. "Is your home much farther?"

Jamani looked to Jamil, who nodded. "Not far. Come." Jamani headed off into one of three tunnels that originated at the crossing.

Michael grasped Jamil's arm and pulled him to a stop. "There's something I have to say to you."

Jamil gazed at him, his expression blank.

"I made a bargain with Cardassin...in order to free Akilah...that when the Shepherd contacted me, I would tell Cardassin. He gave me a positioning device to track my movements."

Jamil nodded. "Not good. He follow here."

"Yes. I think you should transfer Rafiya and Jamani to the ruin for their own safety."

Jamil eyed Michael.

It was the first time that Michael felt a sense of hesitation, given what he had been programmed to do. His primal urge was to proceed with his mission, but increasingly, he was being bombarded by thoughts about whether or not he was proceeding in a proper way. Where did this dissonance come from?

"You no tell me first about danger," Jamil said.

"I meant to."

"Rafiya and Jamani go, but not to ruin."

Michael couldn't imagine where they would be safer, but if Jamil had a better place then so be it. Michael had done his best to forewarn his friend.

Jamil called Jamani back and took him aside. After a low conversation, Jamani nodded and ran down an opposite corridor.

"Jamani take Rafiya to another place. We go now." Jamil strode off down the ice tube.

Michael followed, all the time hearing the rising sound of water rushing against a shore.

***

"I am here and they are there, and what the fokk is happening?" Cardassin traced a worn path in the carpet of his tent. It was a relief to be home again. Kanapoi was so much more accommodating than camping out in the wild. Well, it hadn't been really *wild* in the true sense of wild. He had experienced pleasures there. The idiot Ferral, then that Karin person, finally the druggie, Dayna. Pity he had been interrupted with the head Maraia bitch, Akilah. But that's the way the ice melts.

He suddenly realized that he had asked a question and then been in thought for an awfully long time and no one had answered him. "Trudal!"

Silence.

This is absurd. Cardassin stomped to the tent entrance and peered out.

The faux sun shone. The trees, hanging heavily with ripe fruit swayed to the ever-present breeze. The burbling brooks gurgled down to the pond where ducks quacked.

"Trudal!"

Igor lumbered up the path. "Sire, Master Trudal has gone over to the Maraia."

Cardassin started to speak and realized that he was sputtering. He shut his mouth, nodded, then waved Igor away. When the mutant had left, Cardassin re-entered his tent and screamed.

That only brought Igor back. "Is everything all right, sire?"

"No, you fokkin' idiot. Everything is not all right. My seer and most trusted advisor has gone over to the other side!"

"But I thot he was a Maraia?"

"Get out of here!"

Igor backed out of the tent.

Cardassin slumped heavily on his bed and tried to think of consequences, but couldn't. *I really must reduce my intake of* rub. For a moment his senses cleared, as fast moving clouds first obscure the sun, then leave it to shine free.

It didn't matter that Trudal acquiesced to a moment of conscience. The end was near. Cardassin had the synthetic on track to give up the Shepherd and that was all that was important right now.

Cardassin fumbled in the bedside stand's drawer for his nano-assembler and began dialing. It was time to create. He smiled as his nimble fingers flicked through embedded programs and modified others.

Then he leaned back, satisfied. In his hand he held a pellet that should do the trick.

He looked around at his enclosing tent. Such creature comforts. He would miss them. This was the last act, the final chapter, the end. He shuddered with anticipation, all the while hating himself for his earthly weaknesses. *Zug* must have had in mind someone stronger.

But life here had been a blast. And now it was all coming to an end. Trudal had been right to regret life's passing.

With a look to the tent ceiling, as if *Zug* might deign to appear there, Cardassin placed the last nano-assembler in his possession under his foot and smashed it flat.

***

Akilah entered the ruin and waited for her eyes to adjust to the light. Before she could open them, Lorry practically bowled her over.

"You're back and safe!" Lorry's arms went around Akilah and squeezed.

Akilah shoved her away. "You cloned my father?!"

Lorry looked disappointed. "I didn't expect that reaction."

"What the hell did you expect. We're trapped here, the few of us that are left, with Cardassin cutting down our options for survival as we speak. Whatever possessed you to think that cloning anyone, much less my father was in our interest."

Lorry waved a hand in front of her as if batting away flies. She grabbed Akilah's sleeve and pulled. "Don't say another word. Come. Look at him."

Reluctantly, Akilah let herself be dragged to the cot.

Lorry pulled back the blanket.

The child was pulled into a fetal position, probably cold.

Akilah couldn't help but feel an empathy. Though the child looked nothing like what she imagined her father had been, still, his physical presence hit home. "Is he okay?"

Lorry beamed. "He's more than okay. Everything went as it was supposed to. He's ten years old, but still an infant."

"Maw!" the child awakened and was pointing to his mouth.

"Did he say more?" Akilah asked.

"He's learning very quickly," Nicholai said. "We fed him strained foods at first, but since his teeth are all in, we tried solids. It would have taken an infant weeks to learn to chew and swallow, but he had it down after a few tries."

"Where did *maw* come from?" Akilah asked.

"We tried using sign language, since it was obvious that the voice centers of his brain were not yet functioning. He took to that rather quickly."

"What is *more* in sign language?"

Nicholai bunched the fingers of his hands and touched them together. "We said *more* along with the sign. At first we only got the sign back, but lately, he's been accompanying it with verbalization."

"So he's not going to be a complete idiot?"

"I don't think we ever thought that."

Akilah felt herself drawn toward this close cabal of Nicholai, Lorry and their clone. "Have you given him a name?" She hated herself being drawn in.

"We have," Lorry said. "We chose Justin. After the founder."

Akilah smiled inwardly. She liked the name. Very apt. "I approve. One can only wonder if--"

395

Ferral barged forward. "If it only takes a few hours to learn to ask for more food, think what a few days or weeks would do to an army."

Akilah back-stepped unable to hide her revulsion. "Your sight seems to have improved."

"Damn my sight. We have to take action here."

"We aren't going to clone an army, Ferral. We don't have days or weeks. We have a few hours. Our only hope is to launch A4-Ni."

"Your squeeze Michael said he was going to help us with the nano-assembler. Where the hell is he anyway?"

"Mike has gone off to see the Shepherd," Akilah said, hands on hips, chin thrust out. "I gave him three hours to do whatever he has to do. Then we will launch A4-Ni. Michael finished building her."

"Praise Sedroth!" Lorry cried. "Michael practically barricaded himself in the tunnel below. We didn't know if he was successful or not."

"He doesn't care what happens to the Maraia," Ferral yelled.

"I see you have regained your strength," Akilah said. "Mike mentioned that you were as belligerent as before."

"This whole plan is flawed." Ferral rubbed his temples, agitated. "There are precious few of us left. A4-Ni is an untested machine. Are we to entrust our genome to her? We know that she survives, but does our genome? How does she end up eight thousand years ago? What is she doing there?"

"Questions, questions," Akilah said. "It's good that you ask them. But Mike is with the Shepherd, now, and I presume when he returns he will have answers for all of your questions. In the meantime, we need to get A4-Ni ready for launch."

"It would be better to spend our time cloning Maraia." He shifted his blank gaze to Nicholai. "Surely you can get around the complication?

"I...I wish I could. But Michael is the only one who can help us now."

Ferral scrunched down. Pain filled a contraction of his body. "But we could have an army in no time." His voice faded to a whisper.

"An army of mindless beings," Akilah said. "You've seen how Justin turned out. It would take an indeterminable time to bring clones up to where they would be of any use to us."

"I agree." Lorry sat next to the sleeping child. "We are finished." She glanced at Justin. "I don't know what lies in store for him, but the rest of us are all that remain of the Maraia. Better to take our chances with a machine that the Shepherd has helped us build than do nothing at all."

A loud pounding came from the door to the ruin.

Akilah drew her ice razor and motioned to Lorry to dim the lights. Nicholai sought the protection of a packing container. To Akilah's surprise, Ferral had drawn his razor and quietly taken up a position opposite her where he could catch whatever came through the door in a crossfire.

"I come in peace," a weak voice said from the outside.

"Is that who I think it is?" Akilah asked.

"I'll be damned." A smile crossed Ferral's face. "Shall we let him in?"

Akilah stepped closer to the door. "What do you want?"

"Help me. I have nowhere to go."

"Let'm freeze out there," Ferral said. "We'll check him out in the morning."

"I'm inclined to agree with you." Akilah raised her voice. "Why should we trust you? You've probably got ten mutants waiting to come in behind you."

"I assure you I'm alone." Trudal's body thudded against the door, a sign of exhaustion. "It will serve no purpose for you to let me freeze to death out here. On the other hand, I can help you in many ways."

"Why the change of heart, Trudal?" Akilah wasn't so much worried about his change of heart, or even letting him in. She was more worried about what Ferral might do if he got his hands on the seer.

Chapter Twenty-One

"We must get above the ice," Michael yelled, trying to keep up with Jamil. "We can't go very far like this."

Either Jamil didn't hear, or he didn't care. His gait quickened. He lunged into a slide that took him down a steeply inclined ice tube, where he rounded a bend and came out at the bottom on a gravelly shore. The waters of the lake lapped darkly not two meters forward.

"Now what?" Michael only saw the dark waters disappearing ahead of him, the looming ice overhead. No sign of a boat.

Jamil gave him a hard look, one that said, be quiet and follow me.

He dodged around an ice pillar and returned dragging a boat made from skins or some sort of fabric.

"That doesn't look like it's going to get us very far." Michael began to question enlisting Jamil in his attempt to get to the island. The primitive certainly understood Michael's goal, but didn't seem to have the where-with-all to help him. But who was he to question the primitive's expertise. Jamil had never let him down before.

Jamil shoved the boat into the water and clambered aboard. "Come."

Michael hesitated, then decided that he had no choice but to obey. It was either that or reverse course and almost certainly run into Cardassin's pursuing mutants. They probably wouldn't harm him, not having instructions one way or the other, but the resulting confusion would only make Cardassin anxious, and that was the last thing that Michael wanted.

Michael stepped into the boat, fearing that his foot would plunge through what seemed a very thin shell.

"Good boat," Jamil said with a bit of a smile.

"I'm sure it is. How far do you expect the two of us to go in this flimsy craft?"

Jamil pointed.

In the near distance a faint light shone.

"Ice hole. We go there, climb to top. Haul boat."

Michael sat down. Jamil pushed the boat off the shore and with a pole guided it toward the light.

After a few minutes they arrived beneath an opening a meter in diameter that penetrated upward and gave onto the open air and the star studded night.

Jamil steadied the boat and indicated that Michael should stand and use his ice axe to climb up the hole.

On his second attempt at securing the axe, Michael was able to lever himself up. Jamil threw him a rope, and in quick succession both he and the boat were hauled up.

Jamil pointed in the distance to a looming dark shape about half a kilometer away. "Island."

Jamil squatted and gazed at the ice ahead of them. "Best way." He pointed in a direction oblique to the island.

Michael wasn't about to argue. Jamil could probably read the convoluted ice better than most people could follow a path over dry land.

Jamil walked ahead. When Michael tried to catch up and walk alongside him, Jamil stopped with his hand outstretched. "You follow."

"But..."

"Look." Jamil stomped his boot in a spot where Michael had been about to step. A thin veneer of ice caved and fell several meters into the icy waters of the lake below.

Without another word, Michael fell in step behind Jamil.

A minute later Jamil stopped again and dragged the boat up to them.

The ice before them had slumped. Probably, it had melted enough to weaken and had cracked and now floated on the lake waters. A half meter of water covered the top for as far as Michael could see.

Jamil stepped carefully into the boat and gave Michael a helping hand, then Jamil poled them forward. All the time the island grew closer.

Once across the large puddle, Jamil turned toward the island and after taking a torturous zigzag route, came to a sheer rock wall.

"We here," Jamil announced unnecessarily. "Where Shepherd?"

Michael peered left then right and saw nothing but primitive lava rock rising vertically out of the ice. "I don't know." He consulted his finder. "I think he's over that way." Michael indicated their right.

They began circling the island and soon came upon a break in the lava wall that led into a lava tube. At their level, the tube ran almost horizontally with one end diving down to the lake waters and the other sloping gradually upward.

Michael checked his finder. "We should go up."

The climb was steep, but not impossible. The rough edges of the tube gave good traction. After twenty meters, they emerged onto a flat surface. Ahead of them sat the Shepherd, gray and ovoid, with a slight dusting of snow.

If Michael didn't know better, the Shepherd looked dead.

Michael looked back the way they had come.

Bobbing lights in the distance indicated that Cardassin and his mutants were not that far behind.

"Come on," Michael said. "We don't have much time."

"I stay. You go."

Michael thought to object, but understood Jamil's reluctance to approach something that was totally foreign and probably held a good amount of superstition.

Michael hurried over to the Shepherd. At the outer surface, a seam opened, and he was drawn inside. He was home. An odd sensation after what he had been through. He hadn't really been in the Shepherd that long in the first place, but the cloying walls gave him a sense of comfort and safety, not to mention warmth.

***

Cardassin despaired. He was wet and cold. His mutants were of no use. They kept plunging through the ice and disappearing into the dark waters below. At the present rate he would be out of mutants to lead the way well before reaching the island.

"Igor!"

"Sire."

"You did bring a boat, didn't you?"

"No, sire."

"Idiot."

"Yes, sire. But we have many mutants."

"We had many mutants. Look around you. Where are they?"

"Swimming?"

"Precisely." Cardassin eyed the large puddle of water ahead of him. "Now, how are we to get across this rather large body of freezing water?"

"I will carry you, sire." Igor held out his two left arms indicating that Cardassin would be cradled in them.

He had to admire Igor's dedication. A pity the weak Trudal had failed to serve him as well. Cardassin looped an arm around Igor's massive neck and waited until Igor comprehended that it was time to lift him.

Cardassin rolled up into Igor's massive arms and leaned against his chest. A distinctly rancid odor lifted off Igor's clothes and body. "*Zug*! Igor. When is the last time you took a bath?"

Igor grinned, revealing rotted teeth. "I have never taken a bath, sire."

"Well, you're about to."

Igor's grin faded abruptly as he waded into the freezing water, all the time raising Cardassin higher and higher. "It's very cold, sire."

Cardassin pulled his robe up to keep it from getting wet. "I'm sure it is. Don't drop me."

They were close to where solid ice recommenced when Igor stepped into a soft spot and sank up to his neck.

Cardassin let out a yelp. "I'm wet!"

Igor disappeared below the surface of the water, still lifting Cardassin as high as he could under the circumstances.

What a loyal mutant, Cardassin thought. But Igor had plunged out of sight and was probably starting to freeze. Cardassin wrestled free from Igor's groping hands and dog paddled to firmer ice. He hauled himself up, breaking two nails in the clawing and gave a backward glance only to see that Igor was probably done for. His hands reached out of the water, but no longer groped for anything. Not wanting to meet the same fate, Cardassin forged ahead toward the black wall of lava that was the island. What he would do once he got there was still under debate. He did gain some comfort from the fact that he was wearing his sheepskin robe. Its fibers seemed to repel water very well, and where they were wet, they nevertheless provided some warmth. But it was still god awful cold.

A pity Igor was dressed so thinly, but who was Cardassin to suggest what the idiot mutant should wear, much less when to bathe?

At the wall of lava, Cardassin guessed he should make a right turn after the requisite eeny-meeny and began circling. He came upon a broken lava tube and, bless the freezing weather, boot-prints in the soft ice. After a few minutes of scampering through the partially collapsed lava tube, and he came out on a flat plateau. The Shepherd lay before him.

At least he assumed it was the Shepherd. It was about the right size, twenty meters in diameter, and had a dark green or gray tint to an orange-peel textured outer hide. No signs of life, except--

A swift movement off to the left caught his attention.

The primitive Jamil charged, mouth open in a bellowing scream with what looked like his ice razor raised overhead.

The brief moment before being bowled over seemed to expand in time.

Indeed, Cardassin thought, *can the idiot possibly harbor a grudge against me for kidnapping his family?*

***

"Congratulations," the Shepherd intoned. "You have completed your mission. You have built A4-Ni."

Michael had forgotten how intimate communication with the Shepherd could be. His voice seemed to come from everywhere at once, and worse, it entered Michael's brain directly. He forced himself to concentrate. There were questions that had to be asked. That the Shepherd wanted to laud him with success had to be shoved aside. "What about Akilah and the Maraia?"

The Shepherd paused, as though he had received a shock, something he could not compute.

"They no longer matter."

Now it was Michael's turn to be shocked. "How can you be so heartless?"

"I am a machine, remember?"

"And I? What am I?"

"You are also a machine, but one constructed on a hominid base. You have unforeseen attributes. In any case, the Maraia are not going to compromise your mission."

"I have learned that their genome will perish before it can be secured in some safer region of this universe."

"Poetic. There is nothing I can do about the Maraia genome. Everything is locked into a predetermined path."

"My metabase...rather, your metabase, has briefed me on this CTC universe. But you come and go as you please. Aren't your movements willful?"

"There is latitude as to what can happen. Distortions of worldlines by the likes of you and I are temporary. Worldlines conform to their original patterns once the disturbing influence is removed."

"Can we divert some world lines enough to help the Maraia?"

"I don't know how to do what you suggest. The guardian surely distorts world lines. In fact, the guardian can probably drag reality across a spectrum of world lines until it finds a way forward. Obviously, it has foreseen the outcomes of the disturbances we have already initiated and will take corrective action. But I digress. You must return and see that A4-Ni is launched. That is your destiny in this set of world lines."

"Never." Michael wondered that he actually said that, but pressed on. "In your effort to make me near human, you erred on the positive side and gave me a conscience. Having uncovered your duplicity, how else do you expect me to react?"

"I am not duplicitous. You have only been made aware of events and circumstances as the guardian has seen fit. I, too, follow orders. If you have a problem with the path we both follow, take it up with the guardian."

"I already have. I was told that no matter what I do, Akilah will die."

"Is that so surprising? All humans die. You will die. Not as humans do, but your internal energy will run down and out...if other circumstances do not intervene."

"I realize we all die, but isn't what we do here important while we are alive?"

"To some extent. But you have no influence on what you ultimately do."

Michael was at an impasse. The Shepherd probably realized they were there, too. But unlike Michael, the Shepherd would know things that Michael didn't.

"I could force you to obey, but--," the Shepherd cut out. "--excuse me. There's a player outside being assaulted by a primitive."

Michael started. At first his surprise dealt with Cardassin being so close. Then he wondered why the Shepherd was so interested in the outcome of a

Cardassin-Jamil encounter. If Jamil beat Cardassin into a pool of slush ice, then the world would be a better place.

Minor vibrations rattled Michael, followed by silence.

"What's happening?" Michael asked.

"I have extracted the player from outside and brought him inside. You can observe him to your left. He is separated from you by the thinnest of membranes. But fear not, he cannot see nor hear you."

Michael felt that Cardassin had come into his space and plunked down much more intimately than the thinnest of membranes implied. "The thinnest of membranes?"

"Yes. Just look."

Michael did, and he saw Cardassin not a centimeter from his own body. Michael stood stock still feeling that if he moved, Cardassin would react.

But Cardassin seemed oblivious to his circumstances.

Very strange, Michael thought. *If I were in Cardassin's purple boots, I'd react quite differently. Maybe he's just savoring his escape from being pummeled to death by Jamil?*

Cardassin struggled against the cloying walls of the Shepherd's womb, reaching for something in his robes. After a moment he found what he was looking for. He held it up with a triumphant grin on his face, and the vision that the Shepherd was providing Michael went blank.

"What's going on?" Michael shouted.

Silence.

Michael blinked. Then blinked again. "Why is it dark?"

But there was no answer from the Shepherd.

Chapter Twenty-Two

The supple womb of the Shepherd encased Michael. Pitch darkness enveloped him, and Cardassin was still millimeters away. The Shepherd seemed dead, or at least he was not responding.

I have to get out of here.

Michael pawed at slackened flesh, wondering if it had already begun to die. *Where is out?* An overhead orifice let in a pencil-thin stream of light.

He reached a hand upward. Where he pushed, the fleshy wall gave way to pressure. He pressed and probed, then suddenly his hand slid through an opening, and he felt the cold chill of the outside.

Gripping a flaccid edge, he levered himself up, then shoved his arm all the way through, desperately trying to gain purchase on the Shepherd's slick exterior. He popped his head out.

A panic washed over him. Could the Shepherd actually be dead? That wasn't possible. But no responses. If the Shepherd were dead then Cardassin must also be dead as there was no sound or movement coming forth from the membrane separated cell next to him.

"*You have a mission to complete. Do not worry about the Shepherd.*" The metabase said.

He told you to say that?

"*The future is written.*"

Michael lay on top of the Shepherd breathing heavily. *I'm supposed to race back to the ruin to*

make sure A4-Ni is launched, when every cell in my
body tells me I should be doing just the opposite.

"You have a mission. You may think what you
will, but your mission will be completed."

Jamil, still wielding his ice razor, raced up to
Michael. "Where Cardassin?"

"He's inside. You can't reach him."

Jamil peered at the seamless skin of the
Shepherd, seemed to think about the situation, then
lowered his razor. "I go now. Rafiya, Jamani not
safe." He turned and hurried toward the lava tube
that would lead to the edge of the island and the ice
separating it from the mainland.

"Wait!" Michael yelled. "I'm coming with
you."

Jamil never wavered, leading Michael to
believe that if he was to gain Jamil's assistance
getting back to the ruin, then he would have to keep
up on his own.

Jamil plunged down the tube, leapt to his feet at
the bottom and headed across the ice. When he
came to the large puddle of water that required the
boat to get across, he stopped and waited, much to
Michael's relief.

Breathing heavily, Michael ran up beside him.
"Thank you." His gaze drifted away and locked
onto two left hands frozen solid, showing just above
the water line. He shook his head and stepped into
the boat.

"Hurry," Jamil said.

"Shouldn't we help him? At least see if he's
still alive?" Michael figured the odds of Igor being

411

alive were exceedingly small, but he had come to know the inept mutant and felt a tinge of sorrow.

A tinge of sorrow? Now that was new.

"Dead." Jamil readied the boat. "Long time in water."

Michael knew Jamil was right, but still...that tinge of sorrow. Was he becoming human? Michael suppressed a rising excitement as Jamil lost patience and began to guide the boat away from the icy shore. "I'm coming!" Michael leapt and sprawled into the boat, nearly upsetting Jamil, who glared at him.

"Be still," Jamil said with suppressed anger. He jabbed the pole into the icy depths and sped the boat toward the far shore.

Michael barely had time to right himself and peer over the edge of the boat, when they reached shore.

Jamil ran the boat up on the beach, jumped out and headed into the gloom.

"Thanks," Michael shouted at Jamil's fast diminishing back.

Michael climbed out of the boat and trudged toward the plateau. At the escarpment wall, he climbed laboriously, finally flopping onto the top of the escarpment ice. Immediately, he sensed something had gone wrong, or on second thought, something had gone according to some preordained plan.

The door to the ruin stood open.

Shouts and the sizzle of razor cuts burst from inside.

***

Michael staggered up to the door and peered around the jamb.

Three mutants stumbled about randomly. Two of them drifted their razor beams off the overhead concrete, raining a spray of hydrated calcium and gypsum over the floor below. The third staggered to one side of the ruin and relieved himself against the wall.

Trudal staggered out of billowing smoke and destruction, waving his hands above his head. "Stop, you idiots! Lord Cardassin is dead! We are all free men!"

The mutants stared at each other.

If Cardassin was compromised as Trudal seemed certain, did that mean the Shepherd was also...compromised. What the hell did compromise mean in this context.

The mutants gaped.

"No Cardass?" One of the mutants giggled.

"No Cardassin!" Trudal yelped, clapping his hands.

A second mutant swiveled his razor in Trudal's direction and loosed a sizzling beam.

"No..." Trudal shouted before taking the razor's energy in the stomach. He flopped forward onto the floor.

The mutants converged on him like hungry vultures, lifted him overhead and marched out the door, all the while chanting some ancient cadence.

Ferral emerged from the shadows, brushing dust from his clothes.

"Where's Akilah," Michael demanded.

Ferral cast a blank gaze about the dust laden ruin. "As soon as the mutants breeched the door, she headed for the tunnel." He jerked his chin, more times than necessary, in the direction of the elevator.

"And the others?"

"Dead." Ferral waved vaguely at a jumble of containers across the room. "I don't know if they did themselves in or the mutants got them. Either way, they're dead."

The clone Justin staggered into view. "Gawk! Gawk!"

Ferral wheeled on him and drew his razor. "Best we put this one out of his misery and out of our concern."

Michael lunged at him and knocked the razor from his grasp. They squared off.

Ferral sagged, jaw slack, drool seeping from the side of his mouth.

"You look terrible," Michael said.

Ferral backed toward the elevator to the tunnel. "You babysit."

There was something in Ferral's tone that made Michael wonder. Before he could say anything, Ferral was on the elevator and descending out of sight.

Michael's first reaction was to go after him.

"Gawk! Gawk!"

Michael stepped up to the obviously terrified clone, squatted down and drew the boy into his arms. "It's all right. It will be okay."

"Gawk."

The voice was calmer, less afraid. Michael led the clone back to the cot and made him sit down. "Stay here."

"Gawk." The clone tried to rise.

Michael pushed him down and held him firm. "Stay here. There's something I must do."

When the clone blinked but didn't move, Michael eased away, then turned and ran for the elevator.

At the bottom of the elevator, the tunnel loomed dark, the faux-sun extinguished.

Michael played his flash over the computer consoles, the snaking cables and then to A4-Ni. She sat moored to her tethers.

He moved the light methodically around the tunnel and finally illuminated Akilah at the nerve center of electronic circuits that would initiate A4-Ni's launch.

Ferral stood over her, his hand gripping the twisted straps of her jumpsuit.

***

"Akilah!"

Thank Sedroth, it's Michael, Akilah thought. His cry reverberated in the tunnel's vast volume. His dark form drifted behind his bright flash.

Michael lowered the beam and stumbled across the tunnel's rough floor. "What's going on here?"

Akilah struggled to free herself from Ferral's grip. "I transferred the genome. I'm ready to launch."

"You can't." Ferral strained to hold Akilah back.

Akilah wrested herself free and stood defiantly. "Why shouldn't I?"

"A4-Ni's mission is doomed," Michael said. "The genome she carries will perish."

Akilah felt a moment of doubt. An admonition coming from Michael had to carry some weight. "That's news to me."

Michael lay his flash on the rocky floor. "A4-Ni launches well enough, but she runs into problems and the genome she carries is destroyed. There's a long history after that where she becomes involved with the guardian and eventually builds the Shepherd. The one out there on the plain. He is here only to ensure that A4-Ni is launched, because without her launch he will cease to exist."

Akilah gave a half laugh. "You're not making a lot of sense. The Shepherd exists, so obviously A4-Ni is launched and survives. Does she lose the genome? I don't know, but what are our odds of survival if she doesn't launch? Nil."

"You're being used. We're being used."

Akilah looked blankly at the perplexed synthetic. "Give it up, Mike. You can say whatever you want, but I know what has to be done. A4-Ni is all that stands between the Maraia and annihilation." She glanced at the launch button, some two meters from her hand.

"Have you seen the aura?" Ferral blurted.

"What aura?" Akilah said.

"The field." Ferral seemed to be going south by the second.

Akilah peered at A4-Ni. "I don't see anything."

416

"A4-Ni is surrounded by a nano-assembler induced field that will corrupt anyone who ventures into it."

Something shimmered.

Akilah gasped. "Where'd that come from?"

Ferral giggled idiotically. "A gift from Cardassin. A gift from me. He who passes the shimmering shimmer will pick up a disease."

"You're insane," Akilah said.

She tried to remain calm, but an impending heaviness came over her. She was on this side of danger, and what she had to do was on the other side. The heaviness took form and had a definition. *Zug.* She could swear that she was face to face with evil, and all she had to do was barge through the shimmer, slam home the launch button and the world would be righted. She feared her face belied her intention. "*Zug* is here in this room. I feel his presence."

"There's no *Zug* here," Michael said. "Only betrayal."

"No!" She lunged through the shimmer and pressed the launch button.

Immediately, she felt a tingling sensation. She slumped to the floor of the tunnel.

For a moment nothing happened, then the rock ceiling overhead crumbled and giant plates rose, opening to the starry sky above. A4-Ni lit up, sending vibrations throughout the hall. She sat there, silently, as though the systems that controlled the whole operation were taking their time and consolidating. Finally, she rose, lifting steadily. The cables that tethered her to the consoles snapped free. She paused briefly at the tunnel ceiling, then shot straight up and out of sight into the darkness.

Akilah rolled onto her back. The shimmer had disappeared. She raised her arms skyward. "We are saved. Praise Sedroth."

"You don't know what you've done," Ferral said.

"Of course I do," Akilah rolled to her feet and stared up to where A4-Ni had vanished. "I've launched A4-Ni. The Maraia are saved."

"You are so naïve." Ferral fairly bounced with pent-up rage. "You...we are doomed. We are all doomed."

Akilah stared.

Something was wrong with Ferral. Though his speech projected clearly, other mannerisms faded.

To her horror, Ferral began to implode. His extremities retracted until he had no arms and legs. He toppled over and lay quivering on the ground. Still conscious, he obviously knew what was becoming of him.

"Cardassin," he muttered.

"We'll find a cure," Akilah said. "We have the nano-assembler."

Ferral coughed with what was left of his chest. "We had the nano-assembler."

Akilah cast Michael a concerned glance.

"I don't know where it is," Michael said. "Maybe the mutants grabbed it."

"We'll find it." Akilah could only sound hopeful.

"You're smarter than that." Ferral tried to smile. "And you had best be careful of what you have contracted having launched *Afareni*. Cardassin is nothing if not thorough."

***

The cold air, the dark night sky, the stars all seemed to come together and wrap Akilah in a familiar blanket. Michael had been carrying her over the ice fields for what seemed an eternity. They had searched for the nano-assembler, but Akilah had weakened suddenly, and Michael had said their only hope was to get her to the Shepherd.

"Where is Justin?" she asked.

"Gawk."

"He's right here. He's been following us on his own."

"What of Nicholai and Lorry?"

"They're dead. I don't know the circumstances. Neither did Ferral."

Akilah absorbed the information stoically. Nothing to get upset about. They were all going to die, just like Ferral said. "And Trudal?"

"Probably dead or dying. The mutants carried him off after shooting him in the gut."

"How do you know Cardassin is dead?"

"There was a change. Something that neither you nor I could have felt, but Trudal seemed to know. He's the one who made the pronouncement."

"I don't feel too good."

"We have time. Once we get to the Shepherd, he'll make you whole."

"You said the Shepherd was dead."

"I thought he might be when I left him."

419

"Please, Mike. You know this is useless. I have fought my fight. A4-Ni is launched. The rest is up to Sedroth."

"False prophets," Michael muttered under his breath as he crested a low rise in the top ice of the plain.

"What did you say?"

Michael didn't answer.

"I heard false prophets," Akilah said feeling the strain in her voice, unable to conceal her weakness. "Correct me if I'm wrong, but as far as I'm concerned, everything has happened as it should have happened."

"There's still a chance that you can be saved," Michael said.

"It doesn't matter if I survive or not." Akilah smiled up at him as she jostled in his arms.

They came to the edge of the frozen lake.

"I was hoping that Jamil would be here." Michael scanned the gray distance beyond to the island.

"I don't think I have been infected with anything." Akilah sucked in a painful breath.

"You aren't very convincing. I can get you out to the island without a boat. I just have to be careful."

Akilah realized that her eyes were closed. She might even be dreaming. Michael shifted her weight in his arms and took the first tentative steps across the ice leading to the island.

He had only walked for a couple of minutes when he slipped sideways and sank to his knees in slush ice.

Freezing water splashed over her as Michael struggled to right himself. "At this rate," she said, "we will both die."

"I made it back from here without a boat. All I have to do is follow my steps. But that weak spot wasn't there an hour ago."

He edged forward only to lose his balance again and soak them both.

"Give it up, Mike."

"No. Never."

Strong hands gripped Akilah's wet parka and dragged her out of the water.

Jamil.

"Use boat."

That Jamil didn't berate Michael for his foolhardiness probably meant that he understood the seriousness of the situation. Michael had to get her to the Shepherd or she would die.

Jamil bundled her into the boat.

"What about Justin?"

Jamil gave her a blank, uncomprehending look.

"The child, the new one," Akilah said.

Jamil pointed over his shoulder with his chin. "Back with Rafiya, Jamani." He left Akilah and fished Michael out of the water. "Why you no wait for me?"

"I didn't see you."

Jamil frowned. "Get in boat. I pull."

Michael tumbled into the boat alongside Akilah. He shivered.

She wrapped her arms around him. "You tried. I'm grateful for that, but I think it's too late."

"Don't say that. The Shepherd will be able to fix whatever Cardassin has done to you."

They lapsed into silence as the boat slid and bobbed across the ice and through puddles of melt. Jamil seemed to have an uncanny sense of where he should and shouldn't step. All the while the island loomed closer.

"When we get there," Michael said, "we'll have to climb a lava tube to a level area above. That's where the Shepherd is."

"You seem so sure he's still there."

"He has to be."

Jamil gave the boat a final pull that ran it up on a narrow beach of rock. "We are here."

"I don't think I can stand," Akilah said.

With Jamil's help, Michael carried her out of the boat, then ascended the lava tube.

Akilah lay back and tried to rest, but felt strange surges inside her body. Pressures against her skin. Hot liquid seeping into her clothing. She dared not think what her body would look like if exposed.

Michael gasped.

Akilah roused from her stupor. "What is it?"

"The Shepherd is gone."

"Is that so surprising? You have accomplished what he sent you to do."

"I didn't think he would leave me behind."

Akilah tried to laugh and found that her lungs hurt. "Now what do you propose we do?"

"I'll ask the guardian what has happened. Maybe it will give us a solution." Michael pulled the guardian from his pocket. He curled the small sphere into his hand and closed his eyes. Whatever he learned only took a moment.

He opened his hand and stared at the guardian in disbelief.

"What is it?" Akilah felt sorry for Michael seeing his anguish, knowing that these emotions were new to him and not easily assimilated.

"The Shepherd has left with Cardassin."

"Why would he do that?"

"To neutralize him. Players exist in limited time frames. Take them out of their designated frame, and they cease to be players."

"Then the Shepherd will return for you after he has disposed of Cardassin."

"No. The guardian said that the Shepherd's mission here had been accomplished...thanks to me. A4-Ni was built and launched."

"But what about you?"

"The Shepherd has more important things to do. I...I seem to be expendable."

Akilah smiled weakly. "Aren't we all." Akilah winced. Something was definitely not right. She could feel it worming its way under her skin.

She tried to stifle a scream but it slipped out. "Mike, this isn't working." She clutched his arm desperately. Her head fell forward onto his chest. "Please...please put me out of my misery."

Michael stared at her.

He certainly must know that her situation was hopeless. What could be going through his mind? Some sort of ethical debate about mercy killing? She doubted that.

"I can't."

"Yes you can. Use your ice razor."

"No."

Akilah reached for Michael's razor, but was too weak to pull it out of its case. "Please."

Michael put his hand over hers and helped her draw out the tool.

She guided its business end to her chest and stared at him. "Do it."

Michael's eyes teared up. The drops slid part way down his cheeks before freezing in place.

"Hurry." The snakes running across her would not remain contained much longer. "I hurt, Mike."

Michael pulled the activator and sent a razor shot into her chest.

She stiffened with a jolt, her lips parted, relaxed. "Thank you," she sighed.

***

"You do right thing." Jamil grasped Michael by the shoulders and eased him away from Akilah. "Finished here. Come."

Michael turned a tortured face to Jamil. "I can't." He rolled awkwardly to one side. Where his hip rested on the soggy ground, green root-like tendrils protruded through the layers of his pants and dived deep into the lava bedrock of the island. "I think I'm taking root."

Jamil stared.

It was more of Cardassin's doing. *But how?* Maybe the signaling device had been contaminated. No matter, now. Cardassin was gone. So were the Maraia. And soon so would he. So much death.

"I cannot help this time," Jamil said.

"I know. I don't expect you to. Please leave me. Go to Rafiya and Jamani. Take care of Justin." Michael bowed his head and fingered the thickening tendrils. "I wonder if I'll flower?" he said wondrously.

Jamil started back toward the plateau.

Michael reared up and with a grunt, heaved the guardian. It flashed briefly before hitting the ragged edge of the lava tube and disappearing out of sight.

His whole body began to shake. He stiffened, arms outstretched. Dark branches burst from his fingertips, from his head, from the sides of his chest. He felt no pain. They grew geometrically, giving forth dark leaves and finally glowing pink blossoms.

I am flowering.

Jamil's dark hulk silhouetted against the sprinkling of stars as he trudged toward the mainland, never looking back.

EPILOGUE

Rafiya called to Jamil.

He looked up to see her standing on the distant shore, waving her arms in the air and pointing behind him. On one side of her stood Jamani and on the other, the clone, Justin. Soon Jamani was waving and pointing, and then, after some hesitation, Justin waved, too.

Jamil stopped and turned around to stare in wonder.

A tree silhouetted against the dark looming sky. Its branches spread unnaturally. Its blossoms glowed pink.

Jamil gained the shore and trudged up to them. He embraced Rafiya. Jamani clung to his leg. The clone remained detached.

Will he always be of blank mind? Jamil thought. How does one measure the age of a clone that came forth a child and not an infant?

"Akilah lies dead," Jamil motioned back to the way he had come.

"Where Michael?" Rafiya asked.

"He be tree." Jamil pointed to the tree with the pink blossoms. "Cardassin make him."

Rafiya nodded sagely.

"I get Akilah body," Jamil said.

"Not safe."

"All dead."

When he reached Akilah, he was startled by her appearance. He'd seen dead people before, but she

426

was different. Her features were corrupted by whatever Cardassin had sowed inside her. He wondered about the wisdom of even touching her.

In the end, he took out his ice razor, found a thick lens of ice and melted a hole into it, then with his foot he nudged her body into the freezing water.

She sank slowly. The water dulled and refroze.

A yelp from Rafiya startled him.

He raced back to her, his mind processing the looming shape of a man standing next to her.

As he came up to her, Jamil took out his razor and prepared to cut the being in half.

"Wait. Don't hurt me," the being cried out.

Jamil recognized Trudal, the Maraia traitor.

"I think you dead," Jamil said, ice razor pointing at Trudal.

"I almost was." Trudal removed his hand from his mid-section to reveal a hole burned into his thick coat. "The mutants carried me away when they found out that Cardassin was gone. They headed for Kanapoi, and at first I thought they were reveling as was I, but then I realized they wanted to kill me for my association with Cardassin."

"Should have," Jamil grumbled.

"We all had to survive the beast," Trudal pleaded, spreading his hands wide. "Please don't kill me. Not now. I can help."

"How help?"

"I know things that you do not. I can guide you. I can--" He glanced at the immobile Justin. "--Where did he come from?"

"Clone."

Trudal didn't miss a beat. "I can help educate him, and your son as well."

Jamil wasn't so proud as to dismiss the knowledge that Trudal had. And if the odious worm wanted to tend to the clone, then that would be one less person that Jamil had to worry about.

"You can live. But I no want bother."

"I'll be no bother. Definitely, not a bother." Trudal smiled graciously and extended a hand that Jamil ignored. "That's okay...Jamil, is it? Yes, I thought so. Might I suggest that we retire to the ruin and take stock of the remaining supplies. There will be nothing left of Cardassin's compound at Kanapoi after the mutants are finished with it. There won't even be any mutants left after a few days. With the nano-assemblers gone, they'll quickly die off."

"Nano..." Jamil reached into his pocket and withdrew the cylinder he had picked up earlier off the floor of the ruin. "Know this?"

Trudal stared, dumfounded. "That's a nano-assembler. Where did you get it?"

"Ruin."

Trudal reached for it, but Jamil pulled it back.

"It will save our lives," Trudal said. "You know it has great powers."

"Don't know. Just a stick."

"It's hardly that. Here, let me see it."

Jamil was reluctant.

"I'm not going to run away with it," Trudal said. "I just want to see that it is still functional."

Jamil handed the nano-assembler to Trudal, then peered as the latter turned it over and thumbed some flush-set buttons on its surface.

Trudal handed the nano-assembler back to Jamil with a broad smile. "It responds. We are saved."

THE END